The Dark Side
of the Moon

The
DARK
SIDE
of the
MOON

Anju Kanwar

AMIKA PRESS

First Edition   ISBN 13: 978-1-937484-80-4

AMIKA PRESS
466 Central AVE #23 Northfield IL 60093   847 920 8084
info@amikapress.com   Available for purchase on amikapress.com

Edited by John K. Manos & Ann Wambach. Cover photography by ImageDB. Author photography by Anju Kanwar. Book designed by Nathan Matteson. Typesetting by Sarah Koz. Body in Torrent, titles in Begum; both designed by Manushi Parikh, for Indian Type Foundry, in 2015.

▶ ● ◀

For Updesh Kaur and Lachhman Dass,
my foundation stone.

For Sunil, my Once Upon a Time.

THANK YOU

Roshini and Subi George, for bold support
and participation that saw me through.
John K. Manos, for a wonderful editorial
passage. How amazing this second coming.
Bare Papaji, for steadfast love. It remains.

Contents

THE CHADDHAS

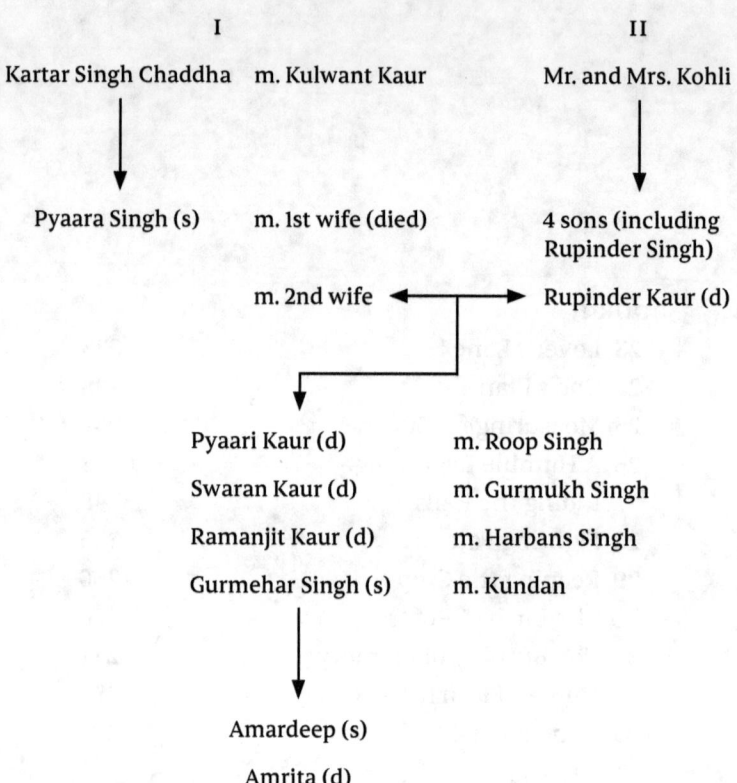

I		II
Kartar Singh Chaddha	m. Kulwant Kaur	Mr. and Mrs. Kohli

Pyaara Singh (s)   m. 1st wife (died)   4 sons (including Rupinder Singh)

m. 2nd wife ← → Rupinder Kaur (d)

Pyaari Kaur (d)   m. Roop Singh
Swaran Kaur (d)   m. Gurmukh Singh
Ramanjit Kaur (d)   m. Harbans Singh
Gurmehar Singh (s)   m. Kundan

Amardeep (s)
Amrita (d)

THE SHARMAS

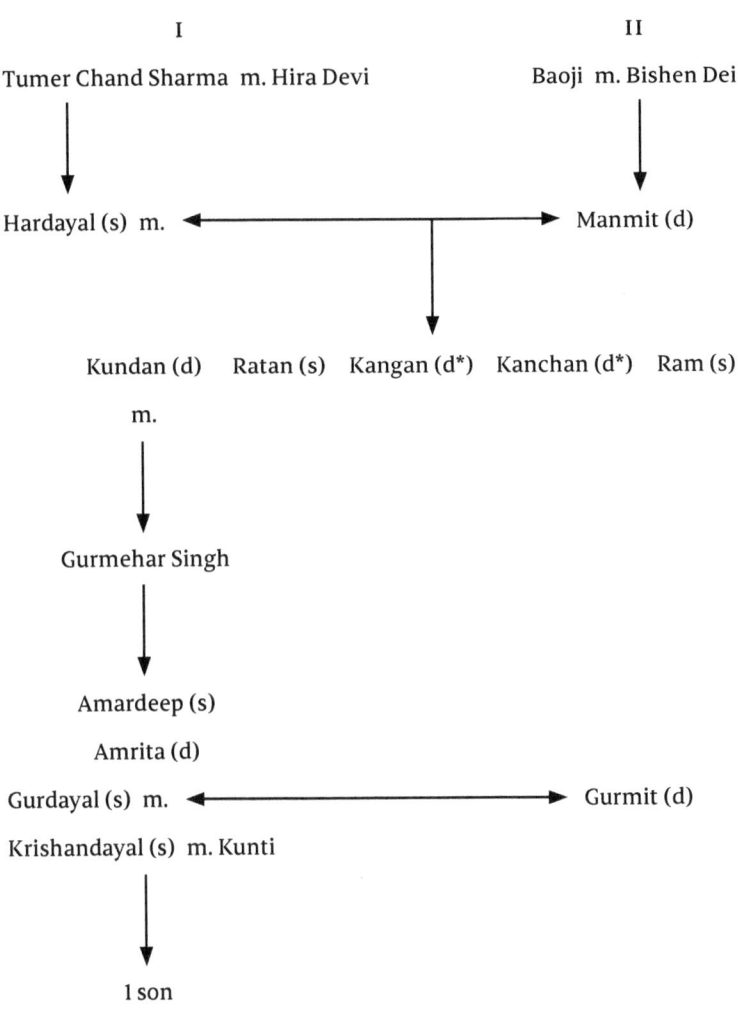

I

Tumer Chand Sharma m. Hira Devi

↓

Hardayal (s) m. ←————————————————→ Manmit (d)

II

Baoji m. Bishen Dei

↓

Kundan (d)   Ratan (s)   Kangan (d*)   Kanchan (d*)   Ram (s)

m.

↓

Gurmehar Singh

↓

Amardeep (s)

Amrita (d)

Gurdayal (s) m. ←————————————————→ Gurmit (d)

Krishandayal (s) m. Kunti

↓

1 son

*= twins

Book I

1   *March 1967: The Guava Tree*

THE GUAVA TREE was short and spare. Its trunk twisted. As though a *dhobi* tired at the end of the day had not had enough energy to give the wash a final vigorous airing after wringing it free of moisture. It also did not bear fruit every year. For some reason, the guava tree bore fruit only every few years. Sometimes years passed by and there was nothing. Till one fine morning—in any given season—you might wake up to see tiny green berries hanging from the branches. Tiny green berries crowned with tiny white flowers. There was really nothing quite like the smell of the guava tree in bloom. After the rains it was even better. Then, the fresh young leaves unfurled their tight spiral. And burst open. Eager to participate in everything.

The neighborhood children had a strange bond with the guava tree. Though there were flowers and vines and grass in the garden, they only noticed the guava tree. Just like the sparrows that jockeyed for position on its delicate branches.

peck peck peck

The children delighted in sneaking into the yard and cutting into the delicately veined, light-green, tiny leaves and the tiny pouch-shaped buds. One by one the children dug deep with their jagged and dirty little nails till they tore through the surface, a satisfying dirty green beneath the nails with remaining fiber and pigment sticking to their hands. Mmm, it was fresh, that smell. It was a miracle of course that any buds survived these attacks at all. In time, however, the surviving buds became bigger, changing color from a soft green to a darker green hardened, nut-like substance till they turned a soft, voluptuous yellow. Then, everyone agreed that, though drooping with weight, the guava tree was a magnificent sight.

That was in the daytime; at night, it was another story. Unlike the pipal tree at the end of the road whose adventitious roots, huge trunk, and dense dark leaves were said to house *djinns* and *bhoots*, there were no such stories attached to the little guava tree. Nonetheless, in the dark, the children swore they could see faces lurking between its branches. The silvery gray moon, on a clear night bright and shiny like a freshly minted coin or behind the shadows of a heavy gray cloud lying dull, seemed to invite interpretation. Just like the clouds at night could terrorize with their floating shapes across the sky, so could this little guava tree. This nature call was even darker and more mysterious during certain times of the year. On a full moon night, the giant ball hung in the sky like a drunken paper moon draping the backdrop of the local *nautan-ki* theater curtain—a dull, red-gold disk a little mysterious, very unreal—and threw an extra penetrating ray of burnished molten copper through the jigsaw of branches and leaves. During *amavas*, the moon disappeared to play hide-and-seek with the children. This was worse. A known enemy is easier to handle than an unknown one. The darkness, relieved only by ill-lit streets, added fresh faces in the tree. At all times, if you looked hard enough you could find the shapes of people you knew in the shapes of the leaves. As the breeze blew, these shapes swayed and spoke. The brisker the breeze, the more the branches leaned forward to whisper and sigh secret messages into the children's ears. The shapes of the dead from afar did not bother the children; it was the shapes of the people they had known that scared them more. They had heard stories of how these spirits—if angered—could inhabit *their* bodies and take over their lives. So they were afraid.

The low front walls of houses as well as the open windows created an imperfect boundary between the houses and the street. So that everywhere there were voices. Tears and laughter. Voices raised in anger or gentled in love. And there were smells. Pungent and sweet. Sour like a sudden burp after eating *chaat* or aromatic like the incense sticks burning at an altar. Every day, the competing sounds and smells of food being cooked in kitchens (of the piercing quality of the pressure cooker's periodic whistle or the first surprised searing of slightly moist vegetables as they were dipped into hot oil) and grown-ups standing around in groups and little girls jumping rope or playing hopscotch and little boys working on their batting averages and balloon sellers and the Kwality ice cream man and the Gaylord ice cream man and the *chaat* wallah and the *paan* wallah and the *dhobi* and the meandering vegetable and fruit sellers and shoe menders and the stray cats and dogs and the (large number of) dogs and (hardly any) cats that were not stray and cows (dropping dung cakes) that had been brought (dragged) in to sanctify a new home and cows that had no business to be there and the occasional squealing pig who had made a rash and foolish bid to escape the butcher's block and bicycles with three wheels and bicycles with two wheels and bicycles that had no wheels at all but were yet dragged around by one end of a handle like a prized trophy and motor vehicles going at a stately pace and over the residential speed limit and birds and jets swooping and swirling (dropping small black cones or splats of thick green with white centers), all melted into a carnival in the street. A little less at times, a little more at others.

And so the grown-ups did not really know of the fears or the separate little sub-life the children seemed to live playing till late under the flickering yellow light of the streetlamp with its inebriated metal hat waving madly in the wind. If they had known, perhaps the fears could have been nipped in the bud. As it was, the secret had survived among the children for a long time and was not likely to be dispersed in any great hurry.

The guava tree grew in the front yard of the Chaddha house. It was the last house on the street; the street, a cul-de-sac. The street turned on itself and led to another row of houses around the right corner. Here, there was a huge public park in front where members of the RSS held their *shakha* every morning at dawn in long khaki shorts to perform light exercises. Their thin, hairy legs and knobby knees peeked cheekily over long socks and uncomfortable shoes.

The park was surrounded by a fence of short, vertical metal spikes that stood firmly in cement broken only in two places. The local government had tried to make fancy, U-shaped cement curves in the gaps to control traffic, but somehow these never stayed intact. There was no formal gate anymore; to new residents, the jagged concrete on the ground over which people stumbled at the entry was a mystery. Situated in the middle of one length of the park was a bald, square face with two lidless eyeballs and a single ear. Two times during the day, at dawn and in the late afternoon, the ear flapped open and the eyeballs rolled forward to thrust glass bottles—branded hollowly by DMS, brimful of milk squeezed into them, and protected only by a fine, silvery-blue foil—toward the noisy lines of people who appeared out of nowhere in the neighborhood only to disappear a few hours later. All around the park, on the inside of the metal fence, was dense shrubbery. On one side, however, from time to time, laborers would dig holes as though preparing the ground for fresh planting. A few weeks later, they replaced the mud. Then the process began all over again.

When the rains filled the holes with muddy water, the excited children rushed out to sail their paper boats. But, more hindered less encouraged by spindly wooden stems, the boats usually sank before reaching the other side. When the rare boat, soaked and sinking, managed to get to the other side, the park rang with the cry of victory.

It was a good location for a house. The school-bus stop could be seen from their front veranda. They would be able to see their children playing games like *langri-taang* before boarding the school bus every morning. It was a nice little neighborhood and reasonably affordable. That had been the extent of their concerns when the Chaddhas agreed to purchase the modest, two-bedroom house in Bengali Market, an up-and-coming quiet neighborhood tucked neatly behind Connaught Place. As for the guava tree, they had inherited it from the previous owner. At first they had considered cutting it down to prevent it from blocking the view from the drawing-room window, but somehow they had never got around to doing that. Soon, it became as much a part of their household as any other member and it became unthinkable to get rid of it.

For the seven-year-old Amardeep, the guava tree became a powerful tool in his frequent battles with his sister, Amrita. Having discovered her susceptibility to suggestion, he learned to use that knowledge wisely and to his advantage. In fact, it was he who introduced her to the people who lived in the tree. First, there was "Witchni," the woman who lived at the other end of their street. She was unfailingly mean to the caroling children every *lohri*. The moment she heard sounds of *Sunder munder i-e ho,* she double-barred her doors, shut her windows, and screamed to the children to stop making a racket and get out. Then, there was "Midwife," who lived two blocks away. She was not really a midwife; she was a housewife who could be seen daily striding (chest out, shoulders straight, hair only slightly askew) to the temple—carrying a covered plate and a tiny, child's basket made of woven strands of plastic and full of roughly plucked marigold petals. But one year a mistake had been made by the local housing association in their printing of the residents' names and occupations in the directory. It could be said that the neighbors did not try very hard to rectify their mistake. In any case, the name had stuck. Everyone knew that she too never let go of an opportunity to scream at and abuse the children. While the grown-ups were not unaware of these anti-social neighbors, there was little they could do to correct them. So the children took the matter in their own hands. One night they made rough effigies of their enemies and carried a procession around the park shouting slogans against them. "Witchni *hai hai,* Midwife *hai hai.*" Though the procession did not last long and almost all of the children got into trouble for their behavior, the children had succeeded where no grown-up had. They had successfully relegated their terror, while still alive, into the tree.

"Look, Amu, did you see that?" Amardeep asked his sister one night as both of them sat on the floor in the drawing room finishing their homework. It was nine thirty at night and, according to custom, their parents were out taking a walk.

"What is it?" Amrita did not look up from her careful task of tracing a human skeleton for a General Science class.

"Look quick-ly or you might missit—like all important things."

This crack got her attention as Amardeep knew it would. "I do NOT miss...," Amrita raised her head and voice to answer her brother and successfully lost her place on paper. Irritated more than ever, she turned on him. "Now look what you've made me do." Her hair, constricted briefly on top of her head within the twists of a red rubber band that had glittering golden thread around it, flowed down in a thick ponytail like the Ganga from the confines of Shiva's twisted locks. Each time she moved her head, her hair moved with her in double emphasis.

"I didn't do anything. You did it yourself. Anyway, it's only a stupid trace, you can do it a-gain." And Amardeep pulled her ponytail. It was Ganga rushing down madly from the mountaintop.

"Don't do *that*." Amrita reached her five-stemmed hand to his leg before he could move away. A red-laned highway immediately linked the ankle to the knee. She continued, "Not before Mummy-Papa get back, I can't." With this she returned to her homework for Mrs. Simons' class.

The time for procrastination was obviously over. Amardeep knew that he had to get his prey with the element of surprise if he wanted to have the right impact. Their parents were expected back home soon. So it had to be now. "There are faces in the tree," he blurted without any finesse.

"Ev-eryone knows that."

"I'm not talking of the pipal tree, youninny."

"Which tree then? Not ours?" Just that afternoon she had been playing under the tree and she did not like the suggestion her brother was making. So her reaction was immediate as he knew it would be. He had to pursue his advantage.

"Of course ours."

"No there aren't. I asked MummyPapa."

"You didn't. Anyway, they don't know ev-erything."

"They do."

"They don't."

"How do you know?"

"I just do. Look, see for yourself. That shape in the right corner. Come, look at it from my seat," he generously offered.

Langoors. Angoors. Like laburnums.

Peering through the green-painted, horizontal, metal grille of the drawing-room window, at first Amrita just saw a dark mass, which she knew to be a cluster of leaves. But egged on by Amardeep, under his direction and by squinting hard and long, sure enough Amrita soon found a shape lurking in the shadows. As she saw something move, right in front of her the dark mass began taking a recognizable shape. She wondered how she hadn't noticed it before.

"It looks a bit like…"

"Yes, I know." There was no need to complete the sentence. They both knew who that shape resembled.

"Can it hear us?" Amrita asked.

Brother and sister talked with the confidence of childhood. Snatching at life to peek into the eye of fear. And giving it a name. For language was their secret friend. It was young like them with round eyes, round mouths, round planes, and edges of words yet in awe of discovering their form and round with the expectation of meaning.

They played along.

History lay splattered like chewed betel-nut leaves. Memory lay close, curled under the guava tree in moonlight. And hard hats hung with cricket hats, up on the hook or on heads not around hearts. For love and hate had not yet differentiated themselves by a garb of blood.

But Amardeep hadn't really thought his plan through beyond scaring his sister a little bit. He should have known that he couldn't really win. Though they were only eleven months apart, he was always expected to be protective of and responsible for his sister. It had something to do with the fact that he was a boy. Mummy-Papa had told him that. And Guptauncle. And, who else…? For a moment he let his mind wander till he realized that almost every grown-up had told him so. Somehow, despite the many lectures, he had never quite grasped the concept; he of course understood that that was something he must never share with any adult. For another fleeting moment he allowed himself to wonder who was supposed to look after him? But no, only sissies worried about that, and he was not a sissy. Now, once again, he would have to pay for not fulfilling his father's expectations. Meanwhile, separate from Amardeep's fears, Amrita continued to look for and find even more faces in the tree. When Amardeep tried to change the subject he found Amrita would not let him. He hadn't bargained for this kind of success. It had backfired of course.

In the days to follow, while he was able to use this fear to get Amrita to do little tasks for him, he, in turn, had to take over the role of Amrita's escort and guardian. Like a shadow. More truly, a shadow double. Formed by the split graphite point of an imperfectly sharpened pencil. At first, only apprehensive alone around the pipal tree, now, she grew to be afraid of all trees. She could not or would not go anywhere alone after dark. (Everyone knew that in the daytime the people dwelling in the trees had no power.)

In any case, the guava tree brought brother and sister close together in partnership.

2 *June 1985: And Justice for All*

WHEN GURMEHAR AND Kundan returned to the house, Gurmehar rushed straight into their bedroom to change his clothes. Kundan rushed after him, stopping only briefly to pick up the day's mail. Getting into a comfortable *kurta pajama,* Gurmehar turned almost listlessly to Kundan.

"Anything important?"

"Just this from the insurance company," and she handed Gurmehar an envelope.

"Hmm."

"What is it?"

"They are processing the information about the accident. They have received all the details, policy numbers, et cetera, et cetera... you know...to check for the third-party insurance and all that, of the buses. It's just that there are so many accidents of this kind that they have to double-check the authenticity of each claim. Recent violence has aggravated the issue. Increasingly, insurance companies are becoming wary of false claims and big payments so they have their own team of lawyers check out everything." Dealing daily with such claims himself, Gurmehar knew well how difficult it could be, and how long, for the aggrieved party to receive reimbursement.

Putting the envelope down, he said, "I think I'll go for a little walk—alone."

"Now?" Kundan moved forward, placing her palm on his shoulder. When he looked at her, she continued, "Don't do this to yourself."

"I can't help it. I just can't." Gurmehar could feel his blood begin to boil. "Maybe a walk will help."

"You can't know everything," Kundan pressed her palm over Gurmehar's shoulder. But feeling him tense, she let him go. "Okay. But don't be too long. I'll wait tea for you."

It was early evening and the streets belonged to the children at this time. Dodging ill-aimed cricket balls, Gurmehar paced up and down the streets of the neighborhood, replaying in his mind the verdict he had just heard: "In the absence of sufficient proof, the court declares the Defense not guilty." Sufficient proof? Hadn't they gone over the details? Weren't they self-evident? The case had been so clear-cut. Something was not right. Vikas Khanna's presentation of the case had been less than strong. He didn't argue for very long and he hardly cross-examined the witnesses. But even before that...something had not seemed right for a while. What was it...? Khanna had been acting furtively, as though not entirely sharing everything. Very suspicious. What about that day when Khanna had called him to his office? He had seemed ill at ease. He kept talking of an out-of-court settlement. What did that have to do with him? Khanna's proposition was ridiculous, but he never doubted his integrity. And what about the fire at the Police Station? Some records were lost, the Inspector said. But nothing important, he insisted. They still had witnesses. And who were those two witnesses who claimed they had seen Amrita laughing and chatting with some men at the bus stop? Saying that she had been focusing on looking and waving at them when she got on the bus and not paying attention to safety. When he left the court-house with Kundan, Amrita was waiting alone in her wheelchair. Looking sideways at the Inspector standing aloof in the shadows. Hand cupped in a tight fist like a funnel, he was inhaling the cig-arette smoke in long drags, exhaling it through his nose in a rush. What will happen to Amrita?

Suddenly, Gurmehar felt a shooting pain in his right leg, just above the knee. He stopped for a moment to see if he had stepped over something. But there was nothing. Rubbing his hand gently over his calf to ease the pain, he continued his walk.

Till now Gurmehar had never had to work with lawyers, and so when he heard Vikas Khanna, the Public Prosecutor, had the right credentials and the right number of years of experience working with criminal cases, he had felt relieved.

Now they had just lost their case. The Metropolitan Magistrate had announced that as they had been unable to establish the burden of responsibility upon the Defense, the Defense was absolved of all charges.

Was Vikas Khanna influenced by the Defense? And the Police Inspector? Neither of them sounded convincing in their reports, Gurmehar mentally flagellated himself for the hundredth time.

Once again he remembered his visit to Khanna's office.

Gurmehar had been waiting outside Vikas Khanna's office for fifteen minutes. Khanna's office was located in one of the older buildings on a side street. It was the standard yellow of government buildings. Though the color was not really discernible where the west corner was covered with huge *jamun* trees that dripped rain water and leaves and bird shit that all ran down the side in a greenish-black slime. Two rusty, iron gutter pipes ran down the side of the building. Where there were tiny holes in the pipes, the unsuspecting passerby was sprayed by a thin coating of dark froth and occasional flakes of rotted iron. The pipes led into a metal-grille-covered trough in the ground. The gap between the gutters and the trough caused the water to splash all around, creating a puddle of still water coated by a floating mass of green scum with its very own population of mosquitoes and flies.

There was no boundary wall and no gate to the building. A few scooters and motorcycles could be seen parked in the back at a little distance from a happy-red Maruti and a pouty-white Ambassador with the Government of India plates. Looking at the Maruti, Gurmehar closed his eyes momentarily as he felt a sudden darkness descend upon him. Like a blackout. At a forced vasectomy. Almost imperceptibly he winced, raising his left leg in front of him in a protective gesture. "Uff, uff, uff," he muttered briefly. Then, as though shaking his head free, he continued to look around. The open plot of burnt grass in the front led to a raised cement veranda with a diamond-patterned, wooden fence that ran around it. A half-hearted attempt had been made to decorate the fence with flowering vines, but the aimlessly hanging, stray bits of jute string showed that the attempt had been abandoned long ago. On a stool, just inside the veranda's entry, sat a sloppy sentry. Behind him, and raised on a rusting, three-legged (upwardly curved at the bottom) metal stand, was a small earthen vessel for storing water. Across its earthen cover lay an aluminum scoop. A small glass stood under the stand; the faint, mud-brown-colored stain at its bottom and the sickly sweet smell that arose from it was a constant reminder that it doubled as a tea container. The gap in the fence led through a main door into a large, high-ceilinged room with several desks placed one behind the other. Tiny windows revealed (or concealed) how the furniture and human beings competed for space in this room. In the back was a smaller door that opened into a narrow passage which in turn opened into various rooms.

Gurmehar found that the waiting area was nothing more than the bit of corridor facing shut doors, in one corner of which a bench had been placed for people to rest or reorganize their anxiety. Once upon a time the bench had been covered by a black Rexine seat, but the random tufts of coir with a scrap of Rexine nailed to one corner of the wood were now the only memory that remained of its former glory. Someone had thoughtfully tried to provide a cushion for comfort. Perhaps bringing in a discard from their home. But the faded and dirty cushion did not invite peace or thought. All around there were brown-colored boxes piled on top of each other. In one corner, there was an ancient fridge, yellowed with age and chipped paint. It had a long, steel handle on one side, the kind that moves forward when you try to open the door making you feel it's going to come apart at any moment. But does not. Like magic. A meager bulb hung naked from a long wire, as though surprised to find itself so exposed. It was the only source of light in this narrow, dark passage.

When Khanna had called Gurmehar for an urgent meeting, Gurmehar had dropped everything to get there. It was just a few days before their court date. On his arrival, however, he was told by the peon that "Khanna sahib is on the phone."

"Sorry to keep you waiting Chaddha *ji*," Khanna spoke in an unnaturally loud tone as he walked into the waiting area.

"What is it?" Gurmehar was a little irritated to have been asked to rush and then kept waiting.

"Can I get you anything? Campa cola, Campa orange?" he tried to appease Gurmehar.

"No, thank you."

As they walked into Khanna's office, Gurmehar couldn't help but grimace at the chaos. Nothing so disorderly as the corridor but still files and boxes lay around every available surface in the room in no particular order. The black telephone sitting snug in its cradle as well as the wooden nameplate with bronze lettering held pride of place on his desk. Of all things, they were the most visible. On a side wall, next to the bookcases and large clock and calendar, hung a black coat. A quick change of dress or identity, or both. In a corner sat a tall, three-tiered, steel, tiffin carrier on top of a brown-paper bag. It was clear that Khanna had just finished a late lunch. Nothing else personal marked the room. Dust and flies just reshuffled themselves from time to time or were reshuffled by someone else. Now Khanna moved some things to make room for Gurmehar on a chair. Gurmehar sat down gingerly.

"A Campa will be refreshingly cool in this heat. Take it, come on, take it. I will. It's been unbearably hot all day." Khanna, sitting obliviously in front of a cooler that chilled then blew his spicy breath around the room, rang the buzzer and when a clerk came in asked for two Campas to be sent up. He exchanged pleasantries till the drinks arrived ignoring the fact that Gurmehar barely answered him.

Khanna was shuffling around in his seat, swiveling it around. Raising his left hand, he slightly loosened his broad, red-colored, paisley-print tie that was held together by an incongruously slim, artificial gold pin (the kind that has to be pried apart and quickly slipped on before it snaps close upon the finger), and he undid the top button of his striped-blue cotton shirt. Then brought his hand down under and around his belt, gesturing as though he would like to loosen something there as well. Then dismissed that thought and began abruptly, "Well, the case does not look strong."

"What?" Gurmehar exploded. He had reluctantly accepted the Campa but now he put it down, unmindful of the flies that homed on to its bottled neck.

"Well, you know how it is. The men, Amrita, your daughter, claims were troubling her are nowhere to be found."

"Are you saying my daughter is a liar?"

"No, no, of course not." Khanna was a medium-sized man. Not large but not too little either. With his round-shaped, thick-rimmed, black glasses, he carried the air of a perpetually surprised raccoon about him. Now, he looked like a hot raccoon. He ran his hand over his jet-black hair, but it was as usual well oiled and slicked back. Almost unconsciously, he pulled his tie further down and opened the second button of his shirt.

"Then what are you saying?"

"I just think we would be in a stronger position if we dropped the charges and tried for an out-of-court settlement. Why put your daughter through this unnecessary stress, I say? I am thinking of her. Yes, I am thinking of her, that's why I say this. She's like a niece to me. She's already been hurt. This will only cause her more pain."

"I thought you said earlier this is an open-and-shut case. A criminal offense has been committed. The focus is on the drivers, in any case."

Just then a peon looked in. "What is it?" snapped Khanna.

"Phone call for you sir," he meekly said.

"Can't you see I'm busy? I said to hold all calls."

"Yes sir. It's urgent. About some fire—"

"Yesyesyes. Take the name of the person and I'll call him back."

"It is—"

"Are you hard of hearing? Get out." As the peon quickly left the room, a slightly flustered Khanna looked at Gurmehar. "Honestly, it is so difficult to work with these people. Now...where were we? Ah, yes, I hadn't had a chance to study the case more thoroughly as I have now. I tell you there is nothing to gain. The owners will win in any case. You know their strategy is to back the drivers. Whether they were right or wrong. So that they do not have to pay anything later. Even with the insurance and all, they will try to watch their backs. They will bring in witnesses to prove that Amrita was at fault. That she was negligent. I just want to avoid that. I am thinking of her."

"Even so," Gurmehar paused, then asked, "have you heard anything from the owners?"

Khanna jumped a little, "Wha-at? Nono, nono." Recovering quickly, he continued, "The police report clearly shows, and Amrita even admits, that she was standing on the footboard—"

"Has anyone else been in touch with you about a settlement?" Gurmehar interrupted. He was agitated and beginning to look a little anxious. He still had to meet a client for an appointment and take Amrita to the hospital for a checkup. "A settlement is not what we are looking for. You can tell that to the owners' lackeys when they call you next." And he got up to leave.

"Chaddha *ji*, Singh sahib," Khanna called after Gurmehar, "I just want you to think about this with a cool mind. You are angry right now... Matters must be discussed, maturely, you see. Man-to-man."

"Why do they want a settlement if they are so sure?" once again Gurmehar interrupted Khanna. Khanna did not answer at once.

"They are trying to be fair. You know, they are not monsters. They will pay whatever is reasonable—"

"Khanna sahib, what do you think is reasonable? What do you think is reasonable?"

"We could draft a proposal..."

"I don't want any proposals drafted. There will be no out-of-court settlement."

Now Gurmehar could not help wondering if he should have discussed Khanna's offer with the family. *Did I make a mistake?*

▶ ● ◀

As Gurmehar and Kundan moved toward their room, Amardeep followed fixedly Amrita's rigid body and the imperceptibly shaking fingers resting on the arm of the wheelchair. No one wanted to discuss their recent ordeal.

"Are you all right? Can I get you anything?" he asked as they entered her room.

"When do you think dinner will be ready?" she countered with her own question.

"I don't know. I could ask Mama. Maybe I can pick up something later from the *dhaba*. Are you hungry?"

"Why did you stop playing with me, Amar?"

"What?"

"You know, when we were growing up. You suddenly did not want me around."

"I don't know. I don't recall any particular reason."

"Just being like the rest of the boys, I suppose. I think I'll just lie down for a while before dinner." It was a dismissal. Amardeep left the room. Amrita couldn't wait to be alone with her friend. But it was a little early yet for her to be here.

Should she work a little more at her anvil? The hard hat must be a perfect fit. She must make sure of that. That is why she was forging it herself.

But as she looked around, the silver mirror on the almirah showed a gaunt, distraught, stranger's face. Eyes sunk, forehead furrowed, nostrils vibrating. Like an engine. Revving. How low she sat from the ground. Impatiently, she wheeled the chair across the floor. Soundlessly. Deafeningly. Then pulled the almirah doors apart. Inside, rows of hangers hung from the rod above. Neat piles of clothes and knickknacks rested quietly on their assigned shelves. Her eyes were drawn to a tiny box that lay almost forgotten in its corner. It was a finely crafted simple box made of cardboard covered with glazed red paper. Zaveri's was scrolled on top in gold lettering. She reached her hand toward it, then pulled it back. No, she would not open it. She turned as though to shut the door. But the box would not be ignored. It seemed to invite her to touch it, to open it. Inside, lay a pair of heart-shaped gold earrings. They twinkled as though sharing a secret.

putuson putuson putuson

Franz seemed to be calling to her. Through the yellow heat of the cold metal. *Oh Amrita, have you forgotten? Let me in, please let me in.* But Amrita quickly shut the box and then the almirah door.

Where was her friend? Anxiously, she looked through the window, then turned slightly—frowningly—to look at the floor. What would she say to her when she got here?

"In the absence of sufficient proof, the court declares the Defense not guilty."

What more proof do you want? Do you not see me? Is my presence not the only proof you should need?

"Mummy, Amar won't playwithme."

"Did you have a fight?"

"Nnno...yes. Hesays my batting is weak. And bowling worse. Not enough arm. A baby over is ALL he's willing to give me. Girlscan't-throwagoogly, hesays. Or at least notverywell. But I can. I'm as good as an-yboy."

"How about starting a girls team?"

"The other girls don't wantto."

"Do you know the local children's theater group is looking for actors? They are putting up *The Merchant of Venice.*"

"Really? I could be Portia. Icouldshowhimthen."

To be a star. A lady. And a Shakespearean lady at that. In school, they had begun reading plays by Shakespeare. One could never begin too young. It was an approach to Shakespeare of course. The abridged and portable version. With much paraphrase and summary and some quotation. Amrita pored over it, impatient each time her glasses slid down her nose. Then, standing in front of the mirror, in shorts and shirt and Kundan's *chunni* trailing behind in a train, she practiced.

"By my troth, Nerissa, my little body is aweary of this great world."

"Bymytroth, Nerissa, my little *body* is *aweary* of this great world."

"Bymytroth, Nerissa, my *little* body is aweary of this *great* world."

But Portia's part was not available. In fact, it was only by chance that Amrita got any part at all. The boy who was to play Shylock had fallen sick and had to be replaced quickly. It took the young actors awhile to learn the lines.

"I don't wanttoplay a bo-y's role," she demurred at first. But Kundan reminded her of her claim that she was as good as any boy. Amrita rallied round. With Kundan helping to put together the costume, Amrita soon got into the spirit of her role.

"Mummy listen tome. Here, follow this," she said placing the book on Kundan's lap. And Mummy took the book and listened and followed.

"Thisis where Salerio asks Shylock, ME, if he will exact his pound-offlesh if Antonio for-feits. After all, what good will it do? I say... waitwaitwait, do you think I should change my voice?"

"Did the teacher ask you to?"

"No, teachersays I can be myself."

"Then do what the teacher says." Amrita continued as though there had been no interruption.

> To bait fish withal. If it will feed nothing else, it will feed my revenge. He hath disgraced me, and hindered me half a million, laughed at my losses, mocked at my gains, scorned my nation, thwarted my bargains, cooled my friends, heated my enemies; and what's his reason? I am a Jew. HATH NOT a Jew eyes? HATH NOT a Jew hands, organs, dimensions, senses, affections, passions? Fed with the same food, hurt with the same weapons, subject to the same diseases, healed by the same means, warmed and cooled by the same winter and summer, as a Christian is? If you prick us, DO WE NOT bleed? If you tickle us, DO WE NOT laugh? If you poison us, DO WE NOT die? And if you wrong us, SHALL WE NOT revenge? If we are like you in the rest, we will resemble you in that. If a Jew wrong a Christian, what is his humility? Revenge. If a Christian wrong a Jew, what should his sufferance be by Christian example? Why, revenge. The villainy you teach me I will execute, and it shall go hard but I will better the instruction.

Amrita's voice rose and fell as she spoke with gusto and great passion. She had large eyes. Warm brown. And she carried her heart in them. Now, they were the eyes of a Jew. Her arms, flung out to the world. Then raised to her heart. In appeal. Shylock was a Jew, but he needed to be on the team before he could throw a googly.

Standing by the window, Amrita could still not see any sign of her friend. Only four weeks had passed since her accident, but from the accounts she had heard in the court it would seem that already people's memories were fading. Let someone else care, it was not their concern.

3 *May 1985: Waking Up*

WHEN AMRITA FIRST regained consciousness, it was only for a few seconds. Automatically, she looked at the wall facing her bed where the big, ugly octagonal clock hung in her bedroom. The clock showed five twenty, but before she could figure out why she could not hear the tuneless Mrs. Joshi practicing her singing from the bathroom window adjoining her bedroom window, she drifted back to sleep again. It seemed like the start of another ordinary day in the Chaddha household. There was nothing unusual about Amrita snuggling in bed for a while after waking.

The next time Amrita woke up, it was the result of a shooting pain in her right leg. Automatically crying out, "Mama," eyes still closed, she waited for the pain to go away. Unlike previous times, the pain did not go away. It increased.

"Amrita, *beta* Amrita, I'm here," a voice seemed to reach her from somewhere, but she could not really tell who it belonged to.

"Amrita, I'm here," the voice seemed to be reassuring her in some way. Or did the person belonging to the voice need reassurance herself?

"Mama?" *I spy you. I spy you.*

"Take it easy, there is no need to rush anything," another voice had joined the symphony now. This voice sounded more authoritative, Amrita thought.

"Is Amrita awake? I heard she's awake. How is she?" A rush of warm air entered the room. Amrita recognized this heat in an instant, evoking laughter and memory and response. Spying concern and grief heading and shouldering their way through as well, she tried to sound them away. But before she could call out, she heard the authoritative voice again telling the other voices to let her sleep for as long as she wanted; it would be best for her to wake up naturally. *How lovely, if only MamaPapa were this considerate every morning,* Amrita thought before drifting back to sleep.

It was not until the third day in the afternoon that Amrita completely regained consciousness. She came to with a giant ball of pain, it seemed to her, in her right leg. Thinking it was another of those giant leg cramps that often doubled her with pain till she got up and massaged the skin vigorously, she automatically reached to do so, chanting, *"Darji Biji, Darji Biji,"* under her breath. The chant was like a secret mantra her mother had taught her when she was a child to combat the pins and needles that had often awakened her in tears in the middle of the night.

"Mummy, Mummy," she would call from her bed.

"Shh, go to sleep. It's nothing. Here, I'll rub your leg and you say *'Darji Biji.'"*

"Why?"

"I told you why."

"I forgot. Tell me a-gain."

Kundan saw through her little daughter's attempt to squeeze a story out of her. Suppressing a smile, she said, "Far, far away, up there in the sky with the other stars, *Darji* and *Biji* are looking down upon you. Whenever you need them, just say their names. But softly, softly."

"How did they get there?"

"Shh."

"How did they become stars?"

"Shh, just say their names."

"Darji Biji, Darji Biji," Amrita spoke loudly, wanting to make sure that she was heard so far away.

"Shh, softly. Amar is sleeping, he'll wake up."

"But how will they hear?" the worried little voice wanted to know.

"They'll hear."

Now, following a long-established pattern, Amrita tried to repeat that chant and reached down to ease her pain. Her confused cry rushed everyone into the room; soon she was sedated and oblivious of her body once again.

A day later when she recovered complete consciousness, the doctors offered the usual advice. They said there was nothing unusual about her lapse. That her body had suffered a rude shock, a trauma, and this was nature's way of healing. She needed the sleep.

"Is Pa-pa home yet?"

"Wha-a-t... She said something? Amrita? What is it Amrita?"

"Leave her alone, she's dreaming."

"Is Pa-pa home yet?" Amrita whispered to her mother as she saw her going to the back door from her bed.

"Wha...you startled me. Go to sleep. You will wake up Amar. And you know you both have to go to school tomorrow."

"Can't sleep," she said in a sleepful lisp far younger than her years.

"Why *beta?*"

"Feeling fri-ghten-ed."

"Of what?"

"Thecat is cry-ing."

Kundan too had heard the cat crying in the distance and been disturbed by it. The loud, piercing wail was uncomfortably human in tone. She knew it was superstitious of her to read it as an ill omen, but she could not help wishing that Gurmehar were home. It was almost eleven at night. They had not yet got a phone. It took forever in Delhi to get a phone connection. And so she was very worried. Since his business partner had stolen from him and skipped, Gurmehar had had to work day and night to meet his insurance development goals and to fulfill his family responsibilities. The nationalization, the change of companies, had increased manifold the burden upon him. Loudly, however, she said, "She's only crying because it's so late and she can't find her kitten. Now go to sleep."

"When will Pa-pa come home? Is he all right?"

"He'll be home soon," Kundan did not want to worry Amrita. "Go to sleep," she repeated gently.

"Okay." But Amrita lay awake, peering through slit eyes at the moonlight shining on the lenses of her glasses sitting on the side table, till her father came home more than one hour later. He was at the mercy of clients who agreed to see him late at night when all their other business was taken care of; they must be humored and cajoled into good sense.

"Where were you so long? You are so wet," was Kundan's first anxious question as Gurmehar stepped through the door on his Vespa.

"I got out awhile ago but I had a flat tire and there were no shops open so it took me some time to fix it…. It's pouring near ITO, you know how that floods the roads there. There was a poor rickshaw wallah stuck in the road further down. He had to get off and shoulder the stuck wheel out of the muck…."

Before the conversation was over, Amrita was asleep.

Two days later, Gurmehar was late again.

"You are very late. I have been so worried about you," Kundan was saying.

"Rathore is being really difficult. He is a lonely man despite his business and family interests. He just sits around drinking for hours at night."

"But he knows that you don't drink."

"Yes, but he also knows I need his business. He doesn't really want a conversation. He just wants someone to hear him talk, spend time with him. It's amazing how many lonely people there are like him. I am so tired."

"Have you eaten?"

"No, where was the time? These people don't care about things like that, for others that is."

"You will spoil your health. Did you remember to eat the lunch I packed you or did you forget again? You should have said something." Kundan was furious.

"Said something? What could I say? After the business premiums have been made, I am worth just ten rupees a day, Kundan. Just ten rupees a day. That is, from Monday to Friday. On Saturday and Sunday I have no value. Unless someone gives me a call."

"Don't say that!"

"I'm afraid I have failed you. Failed you all. You could have married a much better man than I, you—"

But Kundan did not let him complete his sentence. There was silence.

Though Gurmehar and Kundan were talking to each other in low voices, Amrita had heard everything. She had been waiting for her father's return as usual. She knew she would be scolded if they knew she was awake, so she kept quiet. On the cot next to her, Amardeep lay asleep.

"I am worth just ten rupees a day...from Monday to Friday. On Saturday and Sunday I have no value. Unless someone gives me a call." Amrita lay awake all that night. She never told anyone what she had heard.

"Shh."

"Shh? Is she trying to say something?"

"No, no. Just let her sleep. She should wake up naturally."

For days now the Chaddha family and friends had been practically living at the hospital waiting for her to wake up.

"Khoon pi jaon ga tera."

"I'll drink your blood."

All the while Gurmehar paced up and down the hallway talking to himself or anyone who would listen to his frustration, shouting at the ASI who was waiting to complete his report, shouting at the medical, legal, governmental systems that inadequately provided for their citizens, till he was asked to wait in a less public area. Kundan seemed to have retreated into silence. When Amardeep complained to his mother about Gurmehar's behavior, it was hard to reach her.

"Mama, you need to talk to Papa. He is out of control. He has antagonized the staff so much, they've asked him to restrict his presence."

Why do I have to worry about such childish things at this time? she wondered. Loudly, she tried to console her son. "Don't worry about it. It will be all right."

"No it won't. Not as long as he continues to rage around."

"He is hurt Amar," she quietly offered.

"We are all hurt. None of us is behaving like him. Why does he have to be so loud and attract unnecessary attention?"

"I don't know. Perhaps you can ask him yourself." Kundan was growing tired of her son's questions. He seemed to be holding her responsible for her husband's behavior. God knows, for years she had considered herself responsible for her husband's and everybody else's behavior, but lately it was just too much for her to bear. For years she had stood between her husband and her son, protecting them from each other. But now she had Amrita to think about. *What will happen to her?* she wondered, fingering her daughter's hair gently as she used to when she was a baby. Then, "Mummy, doit a-gain," Amrita would chant.

That was a time when Amrita loved to watch the young Kundan get dressed to go to a wedding in her brocade *salwar kameez* or Banarasi sari. The rich colors and textures fascinated the little girl. She constantly ran her little fingers up and down the patterns trying to trace them over and over again as though committing them to memory. "Mummy, you look just like a *dul-han*. Ooo, can I touchit a-gain?" she asked, rubbing her soft cheeks against the rich fabric before she had got an answer. Kundan unconsciously smiled at those memories when her greatest worry had been that Amrita should not hurt her soft little cheek with a rub burn.

"Mama, can I get you anything?" Amardeep asked.

"No *beta,*" was the absent reply. Seeing his mother quiet like this, Amardeep knew that he had lost her attention. He was angry and frustrated. Not with his mother but with his father, with the world, and, yes, even with Amrita. He quickly crushed that last thought. For a moment he looked around at the whitewashed walls of the hospital room, bare except for a basic clock on one side. A fan was whirring desultorily above as a stray fly or two seemed to chase madly after the circulating wings competing with their own buzz.

He thought he saw a streak of dust that created a whirling pattern on the moving wings. He chased after it with his eyes till he realized what he was doing and turned to look at his mother. In a muted, fawn-colored sari she was the only splash of color in the room. But how that faint color jarred and mocked, forcing him to look at the bed and the figure on the bed. Five feet two inches of sadness. *Speak Amu speak, why are you so still?*

Outside, the world seemed to be whirring much faster than this ceiling fan ever would. Through the window screen Amardeep saw the hordes of people that flocked from far and near to visit friends and family. Unable to afford lodgings, many of the poor often ate and rested right there in the grounds, often peopling hallways of public wards. It was like a *mela* outside with balloon sellers and *chaat* wallahs hawking their wares over each other, hoping to make their usual sales. There is a very fine line between a celebration of birth and a mourning of death. Celebrants and mourners sniff their quarry from miles around and arrive in droves. Gulping in a high dose of dissatisfaction with the disinfectant, Amardeep left the room. In the hallway, he tried to look for his father, hoping to prevent him from embarrassing their family any further with his violent anger about the "the incident" or "that day."

It had started as just another day in the Chaddha household. The faintly peeping sun from behind a cloud—that every Delhite knew to be smog created by the many factory chimneys that functioned without filters, or inefficient ones—was already creating a heat that was unbearable. As the day progressed, the sun would reflect off of bright gulmohurs and laburnums, blindingly. May in Delhi. Hot, dusty, dry. Dry, that is, compared to coastal cities like Calcutta or Bombay, but to the seasoned Delhite the heat is as wet as the monsoons that follow in July. Before six in the morning and after eight at night are really the best times to do anything physical. For most, however, that is just a pipe dream. The majority of the people —the vegetable and fruit sellers, the janitors, the daily help, the countless faceless people who make a living conducting business from corner stands—are already out in full force in the early hours of the morning. The umbrella is their prized possession. And then there are the innumerable beggars who make their living off the streets. They have to be out up and early, too. They have a strategy to follow in an area assigned to them by local warlords and mini-kingpins with giant egos and even greater appetites for money. Often kidnapped, abused, and exploited, these children learn to survive the street. Old children. Children with old eyes. For the many beggars and homeless who people the streets in as deter-mined a fashion as any other person on their way to work, May is a good month. In fact, summer is their favorite time of year. It is not as brutal as winter when shelter and homelessness become an inescapable reality. No, May is kind—except during a sudden dust storm or rainstorm or extra scorching temperatures. Mostly, it is a time when they can find shade and shelter under any large tree. If forced to leave that spot, there is always another spot they can find. Though many of the trees, such as the *jamun* trees along the roadsides, are really privately managed and let to some fruit sellers, the beggar children are sometimes lucky enough to steal *jamuns* to eat. And so they survive.

The smell of fresh *jamuns* in the fruit tray beside Amrita's bed per-meated her consciousness till she woke up completely after be-ing on sedatives and painkillers for several days. It happened at around four thirty in the afternoon when everyone was around her. The dreaded moment was finally here, but it was not the emo-tionally fraught moment that everyone had expected it to be.

"Mama?"

"Yes, *beta.*" Kundan's voice was heavy with tears, but they never ran down her face. Unable to look his daughter in the face imme-diately, Gurmehar quickly left the room. Amardeep did not know what to do. "Amu," he began but then decided to finish his thought in silence staring out of the window. *God, the noise. It's deafening. Those hordes of people never let up. Where do they come from? Where are they going to stay tonight?* he wondered. His heart wanted to say one thing, but his mouth just would not cooperate. His legs were shaking in dread of the next few moments. But no one need have feared. Amrita somehow had woken up with a sense about all that had happened. Amrita knew. There were no tears.

The hospital authorities had informed the Police Station and, though it was a Sunday, the ASI was soon there to take Amrita's account of the accident. "You need to give her time. Where is the SHO? I've been trying to reach him," Gurmehar tried to reason with the police.

"Just doing my duty, Chaddha sahib," Golakh Ram said, ignoring the reference to the SHO. Grateful to the SHO for his newly salaried position, Golakh Ram was happy for the chance to cover for him. Also, it was heady to be in charge.

"And where were you when my daughter needed you to do your duty?" Gurmehar's voice began to rise and a crowd began to collect. Everyone had an opinion.

"Andher nagari hai."

"Kalyug aa gya hai."

"One can't let one's mother or daughter out of sight these days. No *ji*, one can't. God knows what may befall them."

These are dark times indeed, but do we have to deliberate that in the corridor? Amardeep was more concerned about not antagonizing the ASI. About just getting the task over.

"Papa, I think Mama needs a rest. She hasn't rested in a week. You should take her home and I can take care of things here."

"She is all right. And I need to be with Amrita right now."

"You would be more helpful if you could only take Mama home. I can take care of things here," Amardeep repeated. Gurmehar must have been really tired to accept his son's suggestion without criticism. Also, perhaps he had heard something different in Amardeep's voice. But he was too tired to question what.

4   *Circling*
the Wreck

SINCE AMRITA WAS going to be released the next day, she insisted she did not need anyone to stay with her that night. As Amardeep too left, Amrita switched off the lights, lying in her hospital bed looking straight up at the whirring fan. After the first few moments of blindness, her eyes adjusted to the darkness. Round and round the fan whirred. Seemingly tirelessly. Carrying its smudges of dust and flies on its wings.

A chance onlooker peeping in upon her still form covered in a white sheet could be forgiven for mistaking it for a corpse. As the lamps around the hospital campus came on, however, a faint stream of light coming in through her window fell at an angle on her face so that the left part of it was exposed. Her hair lay dull and unprotestingly confined in one thick braid for comfort during sleep. A few loose strands fell over her face. A face that had begun to lose some of its roundness and taper down to a firm point with each passing year (so that Amardeep could no longer say that God must have used a compass to draw a perfect circle for her face). The rich honey color upon it presented the usual picture of health. On her upper left cheek, in the shadow of her straight nose, sat a tiny black mole, God's mark of protection, to ward off the evil eye—that is what Kundan had told Amrita when she was a child. Below, her generous lips lay at rest like a bow that had lost its arch. Neither upwardly nor downwardly curved. Only her one deep-brown, visible eye showed any mark of feeling. It was sunk in a dull shadow that fell like a half-moon under it. The more sinister for being the single one exposed like a pirate with his patch hinting at stories untold.

On the table by her bed lay her glasses. She automatically wore these now.

The buses as usual had been coming packed to the Income Tax Office bus stop. Strategically located next to all the major newspaper offices and several other office complexes, this bus stop is crowded at all times of the day. The crowds of passengers are not the only crowds to be found here. Like all bus stops in Delhi, this stop too is well serviced by all kinds of food stalls. A row of these stand behind the public booths, reducing the pavement space for pedestrians. The public toilets leaking their secrets into the streets stand shoulder to shoulder with *chhole bhature* wallahs. Because of the tremendous crowds, these toilets are often occupied or too unclean to use. In those circumstances, and sometimes just because they can, many men turn their backs to the crowds and lean toward the boundary wall separating the offices from the bus stops to relieve themselves. The walls, here, when dry, show mountains and valleys of light and dark stone.

"*Jamun kaale kaale raa,*" hawked a jamun seller.

"*Tarboooj. Tarr-booooj,*" the watermelon man raised his voice.

"*O jamun mithe mithe raa,*" the jamun seller continued.

"*Tarr-booj,*" the watermelon man raised his voice even further.

"*Chanai garrum. Chanai garrum,*" a meandering gram seller insinuated himself into the crowd.

"*Chana jor garrum, chana jor garrum.* Fifty *paise,* just fifty *paise,*" another more enterprising young man burst into people's faces.

"Get away from me, you oaf," an old woman muttered waving her umbrella in his direction.

"Hee, hee," the boy giggled, neatly jumping out of her way.

"Hey," shouted a thin man from his booth. "Yes, you. Why are you pretending to look away? Don't bother the lady. Get away from here."

"Why? Your father's territory, is it?" the boy cheekily asked.

"Come here, you. I'll tell you whose territory this is," shouted the booth owner, and got up slightly as though to make good his threat. Seeing him raise his behind, the boy disappeared into the crowd for a little while.

"Shoo, shoo," a man tried to drive a dog and cow away from under one bus shelter. The rabid dog slunk away while the cow looked in innocent sport at the man, swished its tail over its ample behind, and then turned away.

"There are so many numbers listed on our shelter. Can we take them all?" The little boy was restless.

"No, stay here. But we can take some others that come to those other shelters," the woman automatically replied to her son. She was holding a sleeping child and juggling a heavy shoulder bag as well. There was a plastic basket full of baby needs at her feet.

"Look at that beggar."

"Come away."

"She is naked."

"What are you looking there for? I told you to come here."

"Can I have a slice of *tarbooj?*"

"I'll get you one at home. Look at the flies on this one."

"Can't we get a scooter?"

"A bus will be coming soon."

"But it will be vomity."

"We do not know that it will be vomity," the woman repeated her son's sentence structure. His observation was not entirely unreasonable. Harassed, she looked around. Meeting Amrita's eyes, she shrugged imperceptibly. The last is almost a natural byproduct of traveling in little space and less air.

"The last one was vomity," the child seemed to have grasped hold of that image. "It was hanging in spittle and food, little pieces, over the horizontal metal bars of the bus windows. And there was a thick puddle in front of the seat. See," and he displayed his caked shoe.

Amrita looked away. The woman was looking for something to distract her son with. "Mummy, Mummy, is that our bus?"

"Which one? Quick, read the number," the woman asked.

"It says 425."

"Quick, it doesn't come to this stop. Pick up the basket. I have your sister. Let's run."

"It's full," the little boy hesitated.

"Don't be a baby. Now don't drop that bottle. It cost money."

"Can't we take a scooter?" the boy tried again.

"And who'll pay? Now pick up the basket," the mother scolded.

Waiting for her own bus, Amrita couldn't get the boy's remarks out of her head. The bus she had traveled in from the university to ITO had been strewn with litter, splats of *paan*, and suspiciously caked material on the window bars. It was baked a dark brown. She looked away. The desire for freedom had once united the nation briefly; today, the film industry had taken over that role for a large segment of the population. Small and large movie posters were glued to every available surface. Pictures of Dimple Kapadia, Madhuri Dixit, and Sri Devi in wet saris—Bollywood's red flag to the establishment—vied for attention with pictures of Shiva, Durga, and Guru Nanak. It was not clear to whom the little piece of incense stuck to the side of the blaring radio offered respect and worship, the mortal or immortal gods.

Opening her purse, Amrita checked the time. It was around three thirty in the afternoon; the bus service was slow. Watching buses go by on school routes, distracted briefly by a Muslim call for prayers, Amrita walked back and forth impatiently. So when a private shuttle came along, against her better judgment, she climbed in—just about. She got just enough space to stand at the back of the bus, inside its open back entrance. *Franz would be back soon from his trip. Had he missed her as much as she him?* she wondered. It wasn't a surprise when the minibus coming from behind screeched to a halt, impatient to move on. This happened twenty times a day, but usually after the drivers, conductors, and even many passengers—who took sides against each other in the heroic tradition of the Indian mob against the visiting English, West Indies, or Australian cricket teams—had exchanged a few choice abuses and many refusals to budge from their positions.

Only then did either one or the other driver succumb to the grumblings of the waiting public and give in.

That day, as each driver jolted his bus an inch forward at a time, seeing his chance the private bus driver, a Sikh, revved up his engine suddenly to rashly move into the stream of traffic on the road... *Raj Karega Khalsa*...then...the bus jolted...again...and came to a screeching halt at the red light before the turn into Sikandra Road. Before any person standing by her could react, Amrita had slithered down the footboard on to the road—the sound of *"Mere sapnon ki rani kab aye gi tu"* still ringing in her ears.

Not to be slighted, the minibus driver, a Hindu, raced forward. *Har Har Mahadeva.*

How distant the steps of her bus seemed from the ground and how menacingly close the bumper of the light blue minibus and how merciful the oblivion.

Abruptly, the bulb in the lamp outside flickered and died, leaving an uncanny darkness behind. Breaking Amrita's reverie. In the darkness, the sounds outside seemed louder than usual. Distantly, a dog howled. Another returned its call. She heard a truck start and stop several times. The air had turned vaguely pungent. She wondered who it was and how far had he to go. The police themselves had pridefully informed her that the bus drivers had been arrested and a case for rash and negligent driving had been registered with the local Police Station. Now everyone said they had suddenly been released on bail. They should not be held accountable, they claimed; they had been driving safely and Amrita fell because of her own negligence while standing on the footboard.

"Not accountable?"

As Amrita watched, the tired arms of the fan mechanically chased one thought after the other. Whirring them forward to bring them back again to the same still point.

Raj Karega Khalsa.

Har Har Mahadeva.

5   A Prosthetic Life

FOR A MONTH after the accident Amrita was on painkillers. Painkillers that saw her through the brief court proceedings and all else. Dr. Chitranjan Thomas from All India Institute of Medical Sciences had also been consulted but the diagnosis remained grim.

"We have to amputate."

"Is there no alternative? Surgery?" Kundan was anxious.

Dr. Thomas shook his head. "If we do this right now, we can at least save it partially."

"How partially?" Gurmehar's voice was hoarse. Anger, worry, and guilt had corroded his palate.

"Above the knee."

"Prosthetics?"

Again Dr. Thomas shook his head, "It's too soon to discuss this. There are complications with the injury as these X-rays show. But in time, yes."

The visits to the hospital for periodic checkups and bandages... took an emotional toll on the whole family. Each time they got back home, they felt they had been through the accident all over again. Only once did Amardeep insist on accompanying her to the room where they changed her bandages.

"What's the matter?" The nurse had seen him change color.

"Nothing, absolutely nothing," he said as he slid to the floor. Amrita looked at him, then looked at her leg. The nurse was cleaning the mishmash of scarred tissue, angry red and unhealed; it looked like a secret at the end of a cul de sac. As someone assisted Amardeep out of the room, Amrita gazed blankly down at her leg as though it belonged to another body, not hers.

"Amu, about this morning," Amardeep was eager to talk.

"What about it?"

"I just wanted to say—"

"There's nothing to say. Forget it."

"But—"

"Just forget it. It was nothing."

"I tell you, I must—"

"And I tell you, I don't."

Not talking about the things that were uppermost on all their minds, tempers and emotions were becoming increasingly frayed as everyone moved closer toward the edge. The June heat just magnified the situation.

) ● (

"Amrita, guess what was happening at the canteen? It was a meeting." Amardeep began talking to his sister cheerfully as usual.

"I really don't care about your stupid meeting."

"Well, there was this guy—" Amardeep was becoming used to Amrita's sulky tones.

"I thought I told you I don't care, or doesn't it matter anymore what I care about?"

"Dressed in *khadi* clothes. Very fiery. About the need for action. I came in late but it seems he was talking of some terribly ugly experience...," Amardeep continued as though no one had interrupted him.

"I don't give a damn about this guy, girl, whomever; leave me alone and get out of my room." Amrita was suddenly hysterical.

"Okay, grr, grr," Amardeep grinned and growled away.

Perhaps the fact that they were so close in age had something to do with Amardeep's unemotional reaction to her outburst. In any case, fighting had been such a major part of their growing up that they had it down to a routine. It always ended with Amardeep doing goofy impressions that dissolved Amrita into uncontrollable laughter.

Since Amrita's return from the hospital, things had been different, however; her reactions were no longer predictable. Amardeep, along with everyone else, knew this of course, but unlike the others he had come up with a plan. It was really quite simple: he meant to coin the jukebox and push the button for yesterday. Playing Court Jester to her wounded Queen.

Kundan and Gurmehar had heard the exchange from the next room where they were sitting drinking tea. "Makhan Singh and Mahinder Gupta came to see me again," Gurmehar lifted his cup.

"The bus owners? So what did you do?" Kundan had one ear trained to Amrita's room.

"Nothing, as usual."

"She's awfully quiet," Kundan whispered.

"Hmm."

"The doctor did warn us about sudden mood swings, anger, depression, for a while, but still... I wish there was something..." Kundan left her thought incomplete.

Gurmehar immediately got up. "Amritya," he had barely begun when Kundan pressed his arm to quiet him.

"Amardeep...are you all right?" Kundan gently asked. He nodded slightly and kept walking toward the veranda, not really wanting to talk.

"Why did you press my hand? I think we shouldn't leave her alone."

"You know what the doctor said. We have to give her time."

"It's four weeks."

"Yes, only four weeks."

For a moment Gurmehar tried to follow Kundan's advice. He knew she was right. In his heart, however, he felt a fire that had begun to rage a month ago. He tried not to dwell on it, but he knew it would only die if and when he could ease Amrita's grief in some way. "I can't bear it. I'm going to see if she needs anything." With these words Gurmehar approached his daughter's room.

"Amritya," he spoke gently, "What's up? Do you need anything?"

"Yes. To be left alone." Short, brusque, not to be challenged.

Gurmehar turned away immediately, hurt. His eyes colliding with the black leather seat of the wheelchair. Unable to bear his own helplessness, Gurmehar decided to go out for a stroll. Maybe he'd meet one of his buddies and he would have the chance to settle somebody else's problems. Kundan, too, turned into the kitchen. Peering into shelves, she surveyed the row of glass jars full of colorful pulses.

"Tora man darpan keh laye, tora man darpan keh laye
Bhale bure saare karmon ko, dekhe aur dikhaye
Tora man darpan keh laye."

"Mama, I think I'll go out for a little while as well," Amardeep gently interrupted his mother from the door.

Kundan paused in her cherished song from the film *Kaajal*. "Anywhere special or just around the block?"

"Just around the block."

"Okay, be home in time for dinner."

"What's for dinner?" Amardeep lingered at the door.

"Well, I haven't thought about it as yet. I was just trying to make up my mind. Did you want anything special?"

"No, Mama." Amardeep returned briefly to give his mother a quick hug. "You are always doing this you know, you must stop."

"I just want the best for you children," Kundan's voice was a little shaky.

"I know, I know. But don't forget yourself. We can look after ourselves."

"Yes, I see how you can do that. How you both can do that." Kundan's voice was sad rather than angry or even reproachful. Amardeep was silent. He knew his mother was thinking of Amrita's accident and how neither her love nor her prayers could spare her daughter any pain. He hugged his mother again briefly and left without a word.

6   *Shifting Perspectives*

AMARDEEP KNEW HE was a disappointment to his father in many ways. When he finished his Bachelor's in Commerce and quickly followed his friend Titu into a junior Accounts Executive position with Duggal's, father and son had enjoyed a season of amity. Working hard, he had quickly risen to greater responsibilities. There was even talk of a promotion. In four short years that was a remarkable achievement. And it seemed that Gurmehar, who had not been eager for Amardeep to either pursue this discipline or career, seemed finally appeased.

It was only a brief respite, however. Amardeep, meanwhile, had been growing dissatisfied by the monotony of his job. He especially did not enjoy the accountancy aspect of his work anymore. He wanted to shift to something more than spreadsheet analysis. For a while he floundered, till he finally decided to combine his Accounts degree with a degree in Business. He therefore resigned his job and joined the Institute of Management at the University of Delhi.

Amardeep's resentment of his father went way back. His earliest memories of his father were of being carried by him. Being carried on his father's shoulders had been one of his favorite pastimes. He had felt so protected then. As though nothing could touch him. But it had all ended far too suddenly and quickly. Removed from his vantage position one day where he could survey all below and around him, he suddenly found himself observing the world from between his father's legs or his mother's side. The view was not the same and there was nothing to hold on to or break his fall if he fell.

Seven was a tough year.

That night, he had just been about to enter his parents' bedroom where Gurmehar was talking with his sister Pyaari. It was the night before *Rakhi*. Amrita was in the kitchen resisting learning the song Kundan wanted her to sing to Amardeep the next day when she tied the *rakhi*. "It will please *Bhua ji*," she coaxed.

"It's funny, Mummy," Amrita giggled.

"It's not funny at all," Kundan glared at the grinning Amardeep. "Go see if Papa and *Bhua ji* are ready for dinner," she told him. He went.

"Amar is growing up," Pyaari was saying to Gurmehar.

"Umm," Gurmehar replied, satiated it seemed both by the thought of his lineage and the delicious glass of *kanji* he was drinking. Really, no one cooked quite like Kundan did. And her *kanji*...deep purple, tangy just to the right degree, with pieces of crunchy purple carrot and the right amount of herbs and spices. Gurmehar felt a man could ask for little more.

"He must have grown a couple of inches at least these last few months," Pyaari added. There was no reply from Gurmehar this time. He expected this kind of exchange twice a year when he met his sister on *Rakhi* and *Tika*. Pyaari was the only one of his three sisters who had tried to reestablish contact a few months ago. And, even though the gap between them was the widest, she was family, and it was comforting to be with family—especially during such holidays.

"Don't you think it's time to stop babying him so much?" ventured Pyaari after a while. She had finally got Gurmehar's attention. Recognizing a hint of criticism in his sister's tone, he decided to answer her.

"He is *my* son. And it is several years yet till his *dastaarbandi*. He is still in handkerchiefs."

"Yes, your *son.*" Pyaari conveniently addressed the first part of Gurmehar's statement. Seemingly placing an odd emphasis on that last word as though that word were significant in itself and ought to give Gurmehar a clue as to *his* behavior without her having to explain herself further. Still, after moments of silence, recognizing her defeat, she said, "You know, sons are different from daughters. I mean...when it comes to upbringing. Too much babying can lead to emasculating them. Makes it difficult for them to be men."

Gurmehar did not know that, but he had already spoken out. After all, she of all people should understand. She, who had been thrust into womanhood before her time. Moreover, he respected his older sister. So he kept silent. There was no further discussion about Amardeep; the talk shifted to family politics as Pyaari described in great detail the latest attempts of Swaran's sons to take hold of their mother's house before her death.

"Dinner is ready," Kundan announced from the next room. She had got tired of waiting for Amardeep. Seeing his mother approach, he quickly moved away from the door.

The next day it seemed to Amardeep that his father was different. When he begged his father to carry him on his shoulders so that he could see a passing procession, his father refused. In time, Amardeep forgot Pyaari's part in the conversation. But he never forgot his father's refusal.

Over the years, a stiffness entered into his posture. It was to keep things from falling out, that is, to keep things in their rightful place, like in the mouth or heart or eyes. One day, he tried seriousness on for size, and, finding it comfortable, he made it part of his daily wardrobe. Increasingly, when he laughed, he did not open his mouth very wide. There were times, of course, when he forgot these self-imposed rules, like sometimes with Amrita, but those were rare times. In any case, the moment he realized what he was doing, he stopped abruptly.

Now, as Amardeep stepped outside in the dusk, he noticed some children still playing in the little park between their block of houses. *Ayas* sat around supervising the play. The Raghunathans' *aya* was among them. Some were huddled together in a group, taking their chance to smoke a quick *biri* before going in. The Munjals' *aya*, Madhumati, was standing by the railing a little distance from the rest. There was a thin young man dressed in jeans on a bicycle on the other side. They had been spotted together a few times; some parents had complained, not wanting their children to be contaminated by such sights. But the Munjals had not been able to stop her behavior.

The moment after the initial sighting in the park, Mr. and Mrs. Munjal had asked Madhumati to explain herself.

"What you have heard is true." Madhumati was quiet but not meek.

"Oh...! You leave us no choice. We must ask you to stop meeting this young man."

"I cannot do that."

"What? But...you must." Mrs. Munjal was uncomfortable but strangely insistent.

"I cannot do that. I see him in my own time."

"Times have changed. Time was...in any case you work for us."

"Not all the time. And it is not wrong...."

"No, no, it is not wrong. But so long as you work for us you are our responsibility," Mr. Munjal quickly intervened.

"He works in a factory. And he can do what he likes in his free time. He comes and goes as he pleases," Madhumati obliquely referred to the cause of her problems.

"We have tried to take care of you I am sure. You are not short of money or clothes or anything," Mrs. Munjal answered the silent criticism.

"Not money or clothes or anything else, but...," Madhumati agreed.

"But?" Mrs. Munjal prompted.

"There is more." When the Munjals kept looking at her, she just shrugged.

"You haven't joined any union, have you?" Mr. Munjal allowed himself a mild joke.

For a while, Madhumati lowered her eyes and scuffed her toe against the ground, then said, "No. But with all due respect I am not always on the clock."

"That is true. But…to be an example for the children—"

"This has nothing to do with the children. And anyway, I cannot do that all the time. To do that, I would have to…"

"What?" prompted Mrs. Munjal.

"I would have to become like my mother, my father."

No, Madhumati had determined not to repeat her parents' life. Her parents had been lucky in some manner for they had met at their common employers' house. Being a generous couple, the employers had even paid for their wedding and then given them housing in the servant quarters behind their house. But for Madhumati, having a better life had meant growing up in the shadow of the employers' children. Bent by the many kindnesses of their employers, her parents had learned to put their own lives second.

"You must learn to be more grateful," they scolded Madhumati.

"But I want to play," she tearfully objected.

"Do you want to go back and live in the *jhhuggi?*" threatened her mother.

"How will you do that? You live here," she asked curiously.

"Don't be insolent. Have you forgotten your aunt still lives there. I can send you to her. A few days in that tiny space with no running water or electricity will teach you to appreciate what you have."

Madhumati had forgotten. *Why must life teach me things and these other children nothing?* she wondered, but remained silent.

"Loyalty above all else," now her father said wisely. Then turning to his wife, he asked, "What else is there?"

His wife shook her head, as though to say, "Nothing else."

Hiding her resentment, Madhumati quietly got up to clean the children's room. It had been especially difficult when her education had been discontinued at the local government school after the free primary level. At sixteen, when she heard of the job with the Munjals, she was excited. It was a live-in position like that of her parents, but it did not require her to do any housework. The Munjals had at first tried to make that part of her job description. But she had been adamant.

"I am an *aya,* not a household servant."

"We can give you more..."

"No."

That was two years ago. And neither the Munjals nor Madhumati had regretted the decision. The system worked perfectly for all. Until now.

"I mean, we don't care about Mohan Krishen. Not personally, no."

"Then?"

"We believe attitudes need to change about all this stuff. Don't we?" Mr. Munjal consulted his wife. She nodded.

"Then?"

"Well, our daughter...it's a matter of safety."

"From what?"

"Kidnapping, abuse." Mr. Munjal was clearly uncomfortable.

"Are you doubting me?" Madhumati began growing red in the face. She got up, gathering her sari with her dignity, "After two years of service...this is what I get?"

"No, no, it is not you." Mrs. Munjal was flustered. "But we do not know this man."

"Then you should meet him before you say anything. He comes from a similar background to me. But he has finished school," she added proudly. "He is currently working at the Khanna garment factory in Okhla where he works under the assistant to the Floor Manager in charge of the daily production of long skirts made of cheesecloth and exported to the United States. It is quite a prestigious job." Madhumati smiled remembering he had a plastic designation tag that read his name, Mohan Krishan, on one line, and his title, "Administrative Staff, Production," beneath it.

Old Mr. Khanna, as he was fondly remembered, had recognized the value of plastic tags. He had understood well designations and the role they played in keeping order in the system. This was one legacy that did not belong to the British; the Indians had it well entrenched in their own feudal system for centuries. His sons continued that same tradition faithfully.

Mohan Krishan responded well to the authority invested in him, and, in turn, the men, women, and children working at the machines sewed more skirts per hour than they might have for a man whose tag had simply read "Mohan Krishan."

Madhumati had often been regaled by his tales of victory over the other staff. Carrying his little Rexine bag that contained samples of material that he did not really need, he held every semblance of a Babu in her eyes. A Babu who worked in an office (that it was an office in a factory was just a minor technicality) with a street address.

"Okay, let's meet him," said Mrs. Munjal.

Madhumati knew this was a victory. She knew how easily they could have refused to listen to her and told her to pack her bags. But they were reasonable people. Moreover, they knew good help was hard to come by. It had taken them months to find Madhumati.

◗ ● ◖

Madhumati and Mohan Krishen were leaning against the metal fence of the park on either side and talking. "Are these new?" Madhumati was asking.

"What...these?" Mohan Krishen pointed to his jeans. When Madhumati nodded, he continued, "I bought them recently."

"Karol Bagh?"

"Chandni Chowk. Pooran Singh...owner found connections in Singapore. Hurt his own tailor of course. But can't be helped. This is business," Mohan Krishen said almost smugly.

"Oh, so they are real." Madhumati moved her hand forward as though to touch the material, then pulled it back.

"Perfect fit. Just like Mithun *Da's* in...I can't remember the movie. Anyway, can you get away on Sunday for a movie?"

"I suppose so...they'll be watching TV or if the movie is not good they always get a tape from the video store."

"They won't want to go out to a movie themselves?"

"They hardly do...not since Munjal sahib got the video from Hong Kong."

"Well, that's settled then. I'll get two box seats."

"Box seats of course. The noise in the stalls... *baap-re-baap.*"

"Those rikshaw wallahs, what do they know? They are so common. They whistle and sound every emotion." Mohan Krishen spoke with the superiority of a worker with a designation tag.

As Amardeep passed by, Madhumati exclaimed, "Oh, that reminds me, I heard the strangest thing a few days ago. I'm not sure how true it is, but—"

"What? Weren't you visiting your cousins?"

"Yes. In Chandni Chowk. Well, Prasad told me—"

"Who's Prasad? The older or younger one?"

"The older one. Well, actually I happened to mention Amrita and the bus accident and the court case. *Baap-re-baap,* what a case. He wanted to know if I was talking of Balwinder Singh and Gopal Das. 'Who?' I asked. I didn't know any names. He said that two bus drivers had celebrated their victory grandly."

"Oh, so they are friends?"

"I don't know about that. The entire colony was decorated with gold and silver streamers. Baskets of garlands of marigolds were brought in by tempo. An all-night *jagran* was arranged for that night. The twenty-third annual *jagran* by the local temple committee. Very pious committee it is. Keeps busy. Time for poetry, this is it, they said. Music was blaring from loudspeakers into every home. There was much drink and loud talk. But the pride of place was given to a water stall."

"A water stall? That's big."

"Yes, you know the kind they set up at religious functions in temples and *gurdwaras.* A huge, aluminum tub was set on top of a wooden table. It was filled with water and slabs of ice."

"Ah, chilled water. Heaven on a hot day."

"And free. Not ten *paise* per glass as you can get from the water vans. The children and the grownups couldn't have enough of it. Prasad saw some children sucking on little chips of ice and blowing their cold breath on each other, while others cooled themselves by rubbing chips on their chests and cheeks. I didn't know whether to laugh or cry when he told me about a child who dropped his chip to the ground and wept inconsolably as it melted away."

Mohan Krishen nodded in understanding. Madhumati continued, "It was a festival and everyone was invited. A crowd was carrying around two men on their shoulders; they were covered with garlands."

"The drivers?"

"Two other men."

"Who?"

"He didn't know."

"And someone talked?"

"And someone talked."

"What did they say?"

"Power to the people!"

"Power to the people?"

"Why? I mean how?"

"Strike!"

"Ahh...so what happened?"

"Apparently, they—the drivers, I mean—live quite close together in a group of shanties. Drawing water from a common tap. It's fixed near Balwinder Singh's shanty, however. There are always long lines outside and the water runs all over the place. Creating quite a mess in the mud around."

"Yes, I can imagine."

"About a month ago, Balwinder Singh was back home from an early shift and watching TV. Like a few other privileged neighbors, he had paid the local electrician to draw an electric connection from the main electricity pole to his hut and then paid the local policeman to keep his mouth shut. That day, while he was trying to watch regional *Chitrahaar* or something, the commotion of the crowd at the tap was getting louder. Angry, he got up to see what it was about. Since it was particularly hot that day, the people were anxious to store as much water as possible. In some cases, they had brought along not just multiple containers but also more than one member of family to stand in line. This maddened the others who had come alone and with single containers. Neither did they have someone to send home to get more containers nor could they do so themselves, for fear of losing their place in the line. Unable to persuade the crowd to control itself, Balwinder Singh loudly announced that since they could not draw water peacefully from now on only Sikhs could draw water from that particular tap...."

"Wha-a-a-t, just like that?"

"Just like that. The Hindus protested immediately. After all, they had been used to drawing water from there from the beginning. The other tap would be much farther off for them. The argument got much worse when Gopal Das arrived."

"Why?"

"It seems he was looking for his wife who had gone to get water a long time ago. Their children told him that when he returned home tired after a long shift and a visit to his bus owner's house in Greater Kailash II."

"That's a long commute. But sounds he was more than tired."

"That's what Prasad says. For some time, the owner has been trying to get him to move with his family into the servant quarters. There would be a job for everyone. Gopal Das was attracted by the idea of getting his children out of the shanties, and yet he was concerned about losing any amount of independence. Also, he did not want his wife and children to be at anyone's beck and call...you understand."

Mohan Krishen nodded his understanding.

"He was trying to negotiate moving into the slum colony in Gobindpuri and so upgrade a bit and cut the commute, but the owner was adamant that it was all or nothing," Madhumati continued.

"Hmm, so then...what did he do?"

"Protested loudly the unfairness of Balwinder Singh's statement. But Balwinder Singh said he did not care."

"Did the tap belong to Balwinder Singh?"

"No. It was installed by the Municipal Corporation. So they all had equal rights to it. In any case, one thing led to another. Balwinder Singh and his friends sat in a protective ring around the tap. Gopal Das and his friends stood around them. Soon there was a fight. Everyone jumped on to everyone else."

"So who got the tap?"

"No one. Apparently, some people fell on it. And others fell on top of them, so that the tap was bent out of shape. Then there was another fight to determine the responsibility for breaking the tap. Meanwhile, only a trickle of water chokes through it till someone comes to fix it."

Madhumati and Mohan Krishen looked at each other. They both knew how long that could take.

"But are you sure these drivers are the same? I mean, there are many accidents at ITO. And people tend to exaggerate."

"Not totally, I don't. But the description seems to fit."

"How come no one from their colony has come forward with this story?"

"I don't know. The case is over, isn't it? In any case, no one wants to get involved, I suppose. They have enough headaches of their own."

"Hmm."

"I was wondering if I should mention what I heard?"

"I don't know. After all, it could be a celebration of something else. Did Prasad see these people and talk to them?"

"No, he heard about them from someone else...so I guess not then. What do you think of this nose pin? I just bought it...."

❭●❬

Amardeep passed by Madhumati and Mohan, aware of, but not acknowledging, their stares. The whole neighborhood had been aghast and sympathetic after the accident at first. In a rush of emotion they had all descended upon the Chaddhas, offering condolences for a fate they figured was much worse than death—for a girl, especially. But they had soon changed their tune when they heard of Amrita's fits of rage and silence. *So unnatural. Especially when there are daily much worse crimes and consequences in the city.* Amardeep saw his father a little ahead of him standing talking to Mr. Munjal. Mohit Munjal was in his late thirties, closer in age to

Amardeep than his father, yet he and his wife were friendlier with Gurmehar and Kundan. Amardeep, who had seen Mohit Munjal waving to him, used the falling darkness as an excuse to not join his father and him. He abruptly turned around.

At home, Kundan announced that dinner was ready and they could all eat when Papa got back home.

Why must we always wait for him? Amardeep momentarily gave in to his irritation. But it was only for a moment, and only in his head. He knew it would have hurt his mother too much if he said anything to her. "There are such things as family loyalty, such things as respect and tradition that must always be followed," she insisted. He turned into Amrita's room, looking for his companion in irritation.

"Papa is really inconsiderate. The least he could do is be home in time for dinner. We wouldn't have to starve that way."

"You just got in yourself."

"Yes, but he did not. And it's dinnertime."

Amrita turned down the radio. "Something in the way she moves." The compère that night had picked all Beatles numbers for *In the Groove.* "He still has ten minutes. It's eight twenty and we don't eat till eight thirty." That was when the news in English began. Everyone ate in front of the blaring television that peppered their meal with news of disaster from all around the world while they tried to digest their fried brinjals and cucumber *raita* or whatever else their mother may have cooked. That was another source of irritation for all members of the family except Gurmehar. No one had been able to convert him to turning off the television, and so while the other three talked about their day, Gurmehar caught up with the rest of the world.

He now came in, rushing into the bathroom to wash himself prior to settling down to his meal. Gurmehar's hot water was ready for him in a nickel dish covered by a steel plate. Mixing a little cold water, loudly he rubbed and splashed his face and the mirror on the wall. Till both dribbled with fat beads of water. Then, towel in hand, still rubbing his face vigorously, he placed himself in front of the TV that had now been moved into Amrita's bedroom. The news was just about to begin. The two rotating crescents that faced each other around a circle—eyelids around an eyeball—the insignia of the Delhi Doordarshan Kendra, were rotating and moving in and out, backward and forward, to the beat of music. Like a kaleidoscope view of open-heart surgery. Underneath flashed the Doordarshan motto *satyam shivam sundaram*. The theme music was keenly penetrating and for a moment lulled everyone into complacence and drew them in.

"Kundan, did Savitri not come this morning?" Gurmehar asked.

"Yes, why?"

"Just that there is dust here in this corner. See," and he blew over the surface of some papers and ran his finger across the top of the side table to lift it to Kundan's face. Kundan saw, calmly wiped the surface with a cloth, and continued to lay the food.

"Amritya, are you comfortable?" Gurmehar now began.

"Yes, let's eat."

"Kundan, what have you made today?"

"Fried ladyfingers and *raita*."

"Did you put potatoes in the curd today?"

"No, *boondi*."

"Why not potatoes? You know I like potatoes in my curd."

"We had that a few days ago, Papa." Amardeep quickly regretted butting in. He had determined that he would not get irritated, and yet here he was. Even before they had got into the meal he was fed up with being there.

"I'll make the potato *raita* tomorrow," placated Kundan, gesturing to Amardeep to eat his food.

"It won't be the same tomorrow. It goes perfectly with the fried ladyfingers." While Amardeep fumed at what seemed to him further callousness, Gurmehar had already turned to the TV. The news had begun, and for the next half hour he was unavailable to his family.

While Amardeep talked to his mother, praising her cooking, Amrita remained quiet; she would have preferred to be alone. Remembering established limits of behavior now and watching her brother talking to their mother, she wondered at his anger. He always seemed so tense around their father. Why? And he seemed increasingly lost in his thoughts. She wondered what he was thinking.

"Mandakini just phoned," she now told Amardeep in an effort to change his brooding expression.

"What did she say? How come you are still not on the phone with her?" he grinned and asked.

Amrita pulled a funny face. "I talked to her earlier as well."

"Well, when did that stop you from talking again?" Amardeep ribbed.

"Papa was trying to reach home...as usual," Amrita grinned back reluctantly.

"Of course... So did he tell you that or the operator...as usual?"

"This is not funny."

"It really is. So what did she say this time?"

"The usual."

"Your father is waiting to get through."

"Yeah yeah yeah."

"So Mama were you there when Papa came home?"

"Don't involve me in this." Kundan kept on eating.

"So is this cold war?" Amardeep turned back to Amrita.

"I don't know what you are talking about."

"What? No make-up trip to the ice cream man and a tiff on the way back?"

When Amrita remained silent, Amardeep bit his tongue.

Even Gurmehar strained to hear her answer. He had been listening as usual while pretending to focus on the television. *Let's go for an ice cream, Amritya.* Phew, there he had said it. But a surreptitious glance around revealed that he had only spoken in his head.

Amrita was also straining to listen to her father. But he seemed to be engrossed in the troubles around the world. Why couldn't she just say it? *Let's go for an ice cream Papa. Oh, and a stroll afterward. You know what Mama says, after lunch rest a while, after dinner walk a while.* Shaking her head, Amrita wondered, "What will we do now?"

"What are you thinking about Amritu?" Kundan asked, using her pet name for her daughter.

"Just that these ladyfingers are delicious, Mama. They are my favorite."

"I know. I've kept some for you to have tomorrow for breakfast with *paraunthas.*"

"Oh, so that's why I got less vegetables. So that Amu could get more," Amardeep teased. "So you never said why Mandakini called."

"She wanted to know if she could come for lunch tomorrow. Her teaching finishes by eleven and then she has to go to the univ. She is going to stop by Hindu College to bring me my mail."

7 *Old Bridges*

THE NEXT DAY, Mandakini arrived around one o'clock. *"Namaste, Aunty,"* Amrita heard from her bedroom. After that the voices mysteriously disappeared; Amrita tightened her lips as she realized her mother must be saying something about her in confidence to Mandakini.

Later, as the two young women exchanged pleasantries, Kundan joined them in the bedroom with two glasses of *nimbu pani*.

"Thanks, Aunty. It's terrible outside. I really think they should cover the roads or something, to protect us from the sun you know."

"With what?"

"Oh, I don't know. Let the architects figure that out. Architects, engineers, whomever."

"And what would happen in the winter? Are they supposed to remove those covers then? Because we need our sun then, don't you think?"

"We do, but for how long? Maybe they could cut holes in strategic places or something. In any case, sometimes I'm amazed I've survived yet another summer. How is anyone expected to do any work? I envy the stray dogs or the beggars for that matter. How wonderful just to find a shady tree and curl up. No sun and dust storms to navigate to go and teach kids who would just as soon be curled up under another tree. Well, actually, I don't think the summer has anything to do with their attitude," she added thoughtfully.

"And why must we wear saris in this heat?" she asked no one in particular, combing her fingers through her shoulder-length, blunt-cut hair. Amrita wisely did not reply as Mandakini continued as though she had just been taking a breather, not to be mistaken with the end of her turn. Mandakini Bhatia spoke in her fast-paced, Bengali-accented speech. She was originally from Calcutta where her father had accepted a job with Tata Textiles after taking early retirement from the Air Force.

"They look beautiful, elegant, feminine," Kundan offered.

"You don't agree?" This time Amrita joined the conversation looking at her friend who was as usual stylishly draped in a low-slung sari.

"Who said anything about not agreeing?" Mandakini practically turned on Amrita. "They look wonderful, but mostly when we can travel in a car or sit in air-conditioned comfort. But forget it if you are going to take a bus and actually navigate through the crowd." Mandakini could have bitten her tongue. She tried to change the subject with talk about her frustration with supervising rehearsals of the upcoming college play and the continuing breakdown in talks for updating the ancient department syllabus.

But Amrita remembered the day she had worn a sari to meet Franz because he had asked her. Walking around in it had required a little negotiation but it had been worth the look in his eyes. He had extolled its romance; she had pointed out how it wound between the legs in the heat. Only some kids troubling a stray dog had averted their attention.

"The dogs look kind of angry here."

"Damn straight, they do."

"Damn straight, hunh?" Franz looked in amused puzzlement at Amrita's enthusiasm over angry Indian dogs.

"It's the sun; it irritates the dogs just as much as it does the humans. Cats too, but I don't know anything about cats," she replied with the confidence of an animal researcher. But the conversation suddenly shifted as Franz had remembered his mother's lost cat.

"Stonehenge?" Amrita had laughed, unbelieving. Seeing his serious face, she had tried to match it, but he wouldn't tell her anymore. She would try again later, she had thought then.

Now, as Amrita looked at her mother and her friend, she felt faintly puzzled, even afraid, by how this thought had escaped through the barriers she had been building.

"Did something happen today?" she asked. Mandakini did look a bit ruffled.

Glancing quickly at Kundan, Mandakini caught herself from blurting out her true feelings. "Nothing more than usual," Mandakini shrugged. Amrita waited for her to continue, but when she didn't, Amrita nodded, not pushing her friend further.

"So do you have any mail for me?" Amrita now asked, changing the subject. Kundan slipped out of the room, comforted somewhat by the normal-sounding conversation.

"About Franz...," Mandakini quickly began.

"What about him?" Amrita was almost belligerent.

"Don't be like this. This is not like you. You should reconsider...," Mandakini pressed Amrita's arm appealingly. But Amrita determinedly ignored the gesture. There was no knowing what else she might have to acknowledge otherwise.

"There is nothing to reconsider. Did you get any mail for me?"

"He is hurting too," Mandakini persisted.

"How would you know?"

For a split second Amrita's eyes clouded. Ever since the accident, she had set herself modest goals. If she could just get through a single day. Mimic the motions of others. But...waking up was the most difficult. If she could do that, then each second could tick its mechanical tick and roll her along to the end. And what an end it was. Already, and inevitably, nightfall nudged memory awake to contemplate the "ifs," "ands," and "buts" of her existence. Spreading loneliness like eternity ahead of her. Shaking her head, however, she told Mandakini, "It was just an interlude. Now it's over."

"Just like that? Don't you care?"

Care? thought Amrita. *Do you also question if I remember how to breathe? To speak? To walk? Does life consume, then dissipate with-*

out a trace? Without even an aftertaste? Does its memory atrophy? How do you forget something that inhabits every cell of your body? Something, that no matter how deeply you embed in your heart... Loudly, she half laughed to herself and said, "Care..."

"Then...?" Mandakini persisted.

"There's something so diminishing about pity, like leftovers," she mocked.

"Leftovers! How do you know?" But Amrita refused to answer, so Mandakini backed off for the time being. "There's just the usual junk. I've got it here for you to look through. Oh yes, there is this official-looking letter for you. I think it's from the Vice Chancellor. Were you expecting anything?"

"Yes."

When Amrita did not elaborate, Mandakini decided to probe in her usual style. After all, that's what friends are for.

"So...are you going to open it or not? I'm dying to know what it is about."

"Maybe later."

"Forget it. I got it for you. The least you can do is open it in front of me."

Since by now, having overheard the reference to the letter, Kundan had reentered the room, Amrita decided to comply to her friend's demand. She opened the letter, taking her time by first pulling straight the slightly curling edges of the envelope. Next, taking a paper cutter, she tried unsuccessfully to wedge it in place under the top flap. It was a dagger-shaped, delicate paper cutter, more ornamental than practical. Made of sandalwood, it had tiny elephants carved all around it on one side. The feet of the elephants formed a lattice-like chain that led to the top that was shaped like a pillar supporting one more triumphant elephant on top. For a few moments Amrita just looked at the paper cutter, fingering its smooth surface lovingly as its natural fragrance teased her senses. Her mother had bought it for her in Connaught Place, in the Tibetan market. Kundan had reminded her at the time of the significance of the elephant. As Ganesha, he was revered as the god of new beginnings. As Amrita was going to begin her new job, this symbol seemed appropriate. "Doesn't the elephant's trunk have to be turned upward for it to bring good luck?" she had asked her mother later. But Kundan, as usual, had discouraged Amrita from giving in to superstition.

Now, shaking those memories, not for the first time Amrita cursed the way in which the clerks seemed to paste the flap all along the sides just like society guarded the virginity of its women. Determinedly, she found a millimetre of space that she slowly widened with a hairpin and then her fingernail. Running her paper cutter between the inside of the envelope and the backside of the letter to which it was stuck by the overzealous working of someone's tongue or water pad, she carefully slid the single sheet of paper out of the envelope. Momentarily, she held the folded letter in her hand, then opened it.

"What does it say?" burst forth from both Kundan and Mandakini.

"Good wishes for recovery, et cetera, et cetera. But, no."

"No?"

"Yes, I have to return to work in July if I want to keep my job. Even though these are special circumstances, because it's the beginning of my probationary year for the permanent position, the Vice Chancellor has turned down my request for an extension of my leave. His committee is confident that I can discharge my duties despite the accident. They also offer to make any special arrangements I may need."

Even before she had finished relating the news, Kundan rushed out of the room to call Gurmehar. In the room, a now-somber Mandakini gazed at her friend reflectively. After graduating with a Masters in English, she had gone through a frustrating time finding a job; department politics seemed to be involved. How long it may have continued however is moot because, fortuitously, her father was asked to move to New Delhi to become the Northern Region Marketing Manager of his company. In no time at all, she had found a job against a temporary leave vacancy at Jesus and Mary College. She still remembered the day six months later when she and Amrita had met.

It was January of 1981, six o'clock in the evening. Late for their first class in conversational German at Max Mueller Bhawan on Curzon Road—or Kasturba Gandhi Marg as it was now called under the new wave of Indianization (complete erasure or a fresh perspective?)—they had literally run into each other. It was not until the break that they had a chance to exchange a few words.

They decided to rendezvous next time in Connaught Place before class. Drinking cold coffee at DePaul's, having a burger at Nirula's, they soon knew the minutest details of each other's lives.

"How was your day? Anything exciting?"

Mandakini made a face. "Same old, same old, with the students, that is.... Oh yeah, there was a big crowd outside the Prime Minister's house this morning. Some Sikh delegation had come early to her morning garden meeting. There was a lot of police."

"Must have made you late."

"Nope. They let our Special through."

"Anyone you recognized?"

"Nope."

8 *New Bridges*

IN JANUARY OF 1985, Mandakini and Amrita had joined the Max Mueller Bhawan again. The first time around their successful social experiment had necessitated their dropping out of the class.

A scholar of German descent, Franz Frederick Gorani, was visiting from England at this time. They met him as they were trying to quickly exit the classroom one evening about a month after they had joined, having decided to skip the class after all. Running straight into the man who was walking in, Amrita grinned impishly and in broken words quickly explained, *"Entschuldigen sie, mich, bitte. Wir…umm, wi…schwanze? Schwanzen? Vorlesung."* Little did they know he was the special speaker for that day. They did not find out till the next class when he came to answer some questions raised by his talk the previous day.

A little sheepish, but insisting on seeing the funny side, Amrita went up to him during the break to apologize for their behavior. Mandakini had told her there was no need, but Amrita was adamant. She said that it was absolutely necessary.

"Not at all," Franz faintly smiled at Amrita, accepting her apology gracefully.

"Will you be our regular teacher now?"

"No, as I explained to everyone yesterday, your teacher invited me to speak to your class. I have some special interest in the modern period. I spoke a little on the emigration and refugee experience of the German Jews in the wake of the Nuremberg laws. You will not now need to run away," he ended jokingly.

Amrita smiled and continued to talk. Later, during the break, Mandakini was curious. "What were the two of you talking about for so long?" she asked.

"I was just apologizing for *both* of us."

"Well, you needn't have bothered for me." Then, "So what's his story?"

"He doesn't have one," Amrita was a little short.

"I mean..."

"I know what you mean. Anyway, I don't know yet." Then, "Looks good, hunh?"

Mandakini gave Amrita a strange look, then looked at the staid-looking German in front.

"But he's German?" She must have said that out loud because Amrita was looking at her angrily.

"Actually, he's not."

"No?"

"No. His mother was German Jew, but his father was Ethnic Albanian."

"Oh, so he's Albanian?"

"No, he's British by nationality. He was born and raised in England."

"This is all too confusing. In any case, he's a foreigner."

"So?"

"Why are you so angry? Since when have you been interested in any foreigners, for that matter?"

"Since I met Franz."

"Who's Franz?"

"That's his name."

"I thought it was Mr..." Mandakini stopped to avoid further making a fool of herself. "Yes, I suppose he's good-looking. If you like that type, that is," she added.

"And what is his type?" Amrita was getting angry.

"I don't mean to be insulting..."

"Well, you are," Amrita was quick to remind her.

"Well, I don't mean to be," Mandakini was equally insistent. "You mustn't misunderstand me. You just took me by surprise, that's all. I wasn't expecting this."

"I wasn't expecting this either," Amrita returned shortly.

Luckily, the end of the break prevented the two from having a more serious argument. By the end of the class they had forgotten what they had been arguing about in the first place. As they strolled toward the bus stop, this time Mandakini brought up Franz.

"He looks good." She did not have to say who she was talking about. Amrita knew. After that, Amrita saw Franz several more times at the Bhawan. She did not realize it immediately, but, though he did not work there, she subconsciously looked out for him when she came into the building. Her heart beating fast and erratically, she wondered if they would talk that day. She always went to the library a little before class, and it seemed to her that he was always there. In the beginning, she had worried that they would not be able to communicate because she had just started learning German and so could not really express herself freely in that language. But Franz spoke English fluently. He also had been studying Hindi for some time in preparation for his field visit to India.

As a Cultural Anthropologist, Franz studied society as a system of communication to define the notions of structure and to analyze the way in which human beings organize and classify their own experiences. In England, having graduated from the London School of Economics and Political Science, Cambridge University Press's publication of his retooled dissertation, "The Colonial Mental Atom: Role of Religious Myth in the Freedom Struggle of India," had created a mild flutter in academic circles. This had catapulted him at the age of twenty-seven to the position of latest in the line of academic demigods, and from there to a position at King's College.

Since the increasing democratic and technological revolutions, data from different parts of the world was more easily available and had opened up immensely this field of inquiry. Franz spent his time mainly focused on research and lab work.

But in England, as well, he was caught up between the endless battles between the Functionalists and the Structuralists. In fact, Franz had begun his formal training in the school of the Function- alists and, over the years, had moved from field-based cultural rel- ativism toward a more Structuralist approach.

At King's College, Franz did some preliminary work combin- ing linguistic theory and mythology to understand the behavior of the post-colonial mind to study and develop for local govern- ments an effective plan for economic and political growth. His focus was on India.

But the journey was not planned; it just happened.

) ● (

"Da-da choo choo."

"Yes, my lad, choo choo."

"Tracks."

"Yes, tracks."

"Tunn-el."

"Hmm, tunnel."

"Ta-tion."

"Shh, station," the man leaned over the child and whispered soft- ly in the child's ear as the woman beside him looked up from her desultory survey of the scenery to smile. "We talked about it. Do you remember? You must hold my hand when we get there. C'mon, let's go," he encouraged his son.

"Mumm-see sad?"

"No, not sad. Mumm-see doesn't like train rides like we do. But next time, next time."

"Next time," the child repeated a little sadly, then squealed loud- ly as his father hoisted him on top of his shoulders.

"And where are we going today?" the father continued to talk on the way out.

"Circus," the child replied confidently.

"And what will we see there?"

"Elephants..."

"Yes, and Bengal tigers."

"Whee, whee."

"Ticket please, sir, ticket please." Franz felt a gentle hand on his shoulder and looked up with a start to see the ticket inspector looking at him a little impatiently.

"Was just thinking there for a while, mate," Franz groped in his pocket for his ticket. "Got on from Southampton Row. Tough day, hunh?"

"Unhn," the inspector grunted unsmilingly, as though to include Franz in the people who made the day tougher for him.

"Oh yes, yes, here," Franz smiled his apology. But the inspector had already turned away to the next passenger.

Unable to return to his thoughts, Franz picked up the newspaper next to him. But the conversation going on next to him soon made him put it down.

"What do you think of them strikes?" one man was asking another. Franz strained to listen.

"Fat lot them'll serve. And you?"

"Like so, like so."

"Were you there?"

"Missus wouldn't let me. Four children to feed, no small feat."

"Unhn."

"And you? No missus to stop you."

"Nah."

"So?"

"So what?"

"So what happened?"

"As them papers said."

"Them papers!"

"Never reached the lines."

"Not them police?"

"Them so."

"And them leaders?"

"Traitors."

"Give a man power enough, will sell you out."

"True enough, true enough..."

"What now?"

"Monkey suit, necktee and all. Not easy with them foreigners. Ah, that's my station. Till tomorrow then."

"Till tomorrow."

Franz leaned forward to tap the sitting man on his shoulder. "I couldn't help hearing your conversation, sir..."

"Hunh, what? What?"

"Just now, just now you were talking to your friend..."

"What friend? Who are you?" the man looked suspiciously at Franz.

"Just a fellow traveler..."

"Are you a spy? From them police? I know nothing." The man looked agitated and got up to leave.

"No, no, sir, you misunderstand me," Franz tried to speak calmly. Just then a Sikh man in a turban passed by. A little child whispered loudly, "Birdie numnum," before his mother quickly hushed him. The man just kept on going.

"Leave me alone. Father of four children with missus no less. Want no trouble."

"There is no trouble sir, just wanted to know—"

"I know nothing, I tell you I know nothing...them foreigners," the man muttered under his breath.

"I am not a foreigner, sir. A Brit like you..."

"If you say so, if you say so."

"I do say so."

"No offense mister...I know nothing am sure," the man hastily gathered his things to move on to another compartment.

Sighing, Franz sat down, trying to ignore the woman next to him who was glaring at him as though he should have been the one to move away. Unable to lose himself in his papers, he turned to look outside at the passing scenery. But the scenery kept leaping backward, out of his grasp.

"What is left?"

"Excuse me, sir? Did you say something to me?" It was the woman next to Franz, and she was looking at him peculiarly. He now looked at her.

"What? What?"

"I thought you said something to me." She sounded a little irritated.

"No, no, not at all. I was just thinking aloud for a moment," Franz explained politely. The woman pursed her lips and looked away. For a moment Franz focused blindly on the woman. She was dressed in a knee-length, thick, tweed skirt and a neatly tucked, long-sleeved blouse with a ruffle in the front that was held by a circular brooch; the brooch was made of some kind of Prussian-blue-colored paste, and she fingered it constantly. Thick stockings tapered into sensible shoes. Under neatly brushed, shoulder-length blonde hair, her eyes constantly changed color, turning blue, gray, or green with every flick of the light. When the sunlight got trapped in them momentarily, they turned an uncanny silver. By her side was a sweater with a store badge, a romance novel, and a lunch box. She looked like so many young professional women who daily traveled long distances to work in small department stores in the city. Catching Franz's eye, the woman smiled coyly. But when Franz did not smile back, she turned away pointedly with a sniff, letting him know that she was all right.

"I think my approach has been all wrong, too academic," Franz blurted out suddenly. This time the woman looked up only to exchange a knowing glance with someone else. Conscious of other eyes on him, Franz pursued his thoughts a little more quietly. How far he had traveled from his Functionalist background. He now felt that a Structuralist model is valid only when its operation can account for all observed facts; it is good for the study of social relations but not other fields. He felt the urgent need to develop some special kind of instrument, like a particle accelerator—linear and cyclic—that would provide anthropologists with a means to study the structure and properties of the atomic nucleus and subatomic particles of society.

Distracted by sounds of people getting off, Franz realized he had arrived at his station. Quickly gathering his things, he began weaving through the crowds, when someone pushed past him in a hurry. He stumbled. Turning to see who it was, he found himself face-to-face with a poster advertising the circus: elephants in dopey hats trailing a thick tassel stood in a ring on their hind legs with their trunks curled around colored batons and a tiger jumped through a fiery hoop while a pretty girl in a short dress of some sequined material, ankle-length boots, and a perky majorette's hat sporting a feather cracked her whip. The clown, wearing an exaggerated smile upon his face, seemed to be winking especially at him. Franz shook his head, then carried on.

Later that day, Franz was taken out of his reverie by the repeated ringing of the telephone at his desk. It was James Avery, an old and respected colleague. Any other time and Franz would have been thrilled to receive this call, but now he was just irritated. It had taken him a long time to get down to work. Ever since he had gotten in this morning, taken off his coat, and sat on his chair to survey the rows upon rows of scholarly books and journals with the usual almost smug satisfaction, he had the uncanny feeling of being surrounded by rows upon rows of eyes of all shapes and sizes and colors. They sat glued on the spine of books from which vantage position they seemed to mock him. Shaking off that fancy now, Franz cleared an imaginary space on his desk and turned to answer the phone.

"My boy, for a moment there I thought you had disappeared," lightly laughed the old professor.

"Only in my books at present," Franz mocked himself.

"Ah yes, quite, quite. Have you given some thought to that paper I had proposed on the post-colonial Indian approach to social re-construction? What would you call it—chaotic? Apathetic?"

"Not yet. I have been a little preoccupied. And I am not so sure I want to approach the issue from the same standpoint...."

"Whatever do you mean?"

"I mean, is 'apathy' the right word? Look at us. Law and order, welfare, education, all are in disarray. And what does the person on the street have to say? Or do we even care? So does it mean we are apathetic?" As Franz spoke, his eyes collided with the coatrack, really no more than three hooks on the wall behind the door. He hung his all-weather coat on one of them. Another hook held his umbrella. The third hook was free, in case someone dropped by. Underneath were his shoes, his travel shoes.

"My good chap, of course, it doesn't."

"Well, then, my point is, we have not really studied these people...." Franz couldn't stop looking at his shoes by the door. *By God, they need a good clean,* he thought.

"Why certainly we have, my boy. We do have access to the latest data from—"

"But what do we know of the people? I haven't met them..." Franz reached to twirl the heavy paperweight on his desk, somewhat fascinated and dizzied by the trapped rotating underwater scenery inside it.

"You have no idea how undependable that can be. And tedious. It could mean...," he paused. Then, "You can't be everywhere, you know." Avery sounded a little curt, as though explaining himself to a little child.

"No, I can't. But still, to write about them as though they are statistics. I need more time to think about this."

"Yes, I think you do. I won't expect you for dinner tonight then. I shall advise Mrs. Avery of that."

Franz saw that he was being punished, but still he persisted, "Yes, not tonight. Please thank your wife for inviting me."

"Of course, my boy," Avery was impatient. This was not the way he had meant the conversation to end. He gave it one last shot, "But should you change your mind..." Old Avery was ready to forgive if his young disciple was ready to be forgiven.

"I won't."

"All right then."

"All right." Franz put the phone down with the feeling that he had burnt a bridge. *Where to now?* he wondered. Looking around at his books, this time he fancied mouths had joined the eyes on the paper spines and they were all openly laughing. At him. Really, it was clear he was not going to get any work done that day; he needed a good night's sleep. He hurried out. At the railway station, he passed by another poster advertising the circus. Suddenly he stopped and smiled. He knew he must get away.

The new revolution of rising expectations magnifies with each struggle what has not yet been won. Individuals and institutions rush to fill this gap. Franz too was hired to fill holes.

"Isn't it difficult working in this advisory capacity for a foreign people?" Amrita asked. Then, without waiting for an answer, she continued, "Look at how Rajiv Sehgal has been trying to undermine you."

Rajiv Sehgal, a senior scholar at the Office of Economic Growth and a fellow member of the government advisory team with Franz, had indeed been setting up as many roadblocks as he could with his constant questions and surveys. Safeguards, he called them. So far, the roadblocks had only made Franz more determined to prove himself. But writing to his old friend and colleague from King's College for advice had been disappointing. James Avery's letter had merely clinically listed his current research projects, then mentioned in a footnote the fruitfulness of such endeavors. Franz understood well that the downside of his assignment was not only having to deal with suspicion from some of his Indian colleagues, but, at home, he was regarded as a mere technician. More than that, he understood that despite the clear moral appeal to the social consciousness of the anthropologist, within himself as well he had to resolve daily the fact that his personality, decision-making, beliefs, and value systems could impact his recommendations. So now he said, "Challenging certainly."

"I can't imagine why you would want to put yourself in a position where people look at you with suspicion?"

"It sort of comes with the territory."

"Well, then, why choose that territory? Sounds a bit masochistic to me."

"We all have to put up with something or other, I would think. As a natural by-product of the choices we make. You live in New Delhi and put up with—"

"Yes, yes, I do," Amrita interrupted softly, smilingly.

"There you go again," Franz leaned forward in a frown.

"Whatever do you mean?" Amrita mildly laughed.

"Don't."

"Don't what?"

"You know what... Don't pretend." There was an undertone of impatience in Franz's voice.

Amrita nodded but remained silent. Franz continued, "Why won't you tell me what happened?"

"I will...."

"When?"

"One day...soon."

This time Franz was silent. "Where would I go?" Amrita now asked, carrying on the previous conversation as though there had been no detour.

This was not the first time Amrita had evaded this particular question. But for the moment, Franz knew he had to wait. "Some-place else," he now said.

"This is India. Quite a different society with a different set of choices, especially for women—"

"Could you go abroad to study?" this time Franz interrupted Amrita.

Amrita laughed, "Yes, isn't it funny? It would be easier for me to go abroad than to move to another city while unmarried." She paused for a moment, then continued almost defensively, "Things are changing of course."

"Of course," Franz agreed.

Franz was also curious about Amrita.

"So you are interested in Constituional law and politics?" Franz asked her.

"Yes. With an emphasis on history. I mean Political Science is not all objective. People forget that it is intrinsically related to culture. That's why I chose History as my Subsidiary subject in college and then tried to combine it with more interdisciplinary course work in MPhil. Now, I am trying to formulate a dissertation proposal for my advisor."

"Do you have any concrete ideas?"

"Not a clue," she grinned. "But that's part of the journey I just know that it is the idea of beauty that strikes me whenever I think about it."

"Beauty? How so?"

"I can't really explain it...not like the flowers are beautiful...or maybe so, but more than that...what I mean is there is something beautiful about the concept of democracy, maybe the principle of accountability, that seems to have been lost in its translation into reality."

"So it is more a metaphysical idea of beauty?"

"Yes...no...I don't know. Just that...it must not be taken for granted. As I said, I have yet to work it all out."

"Hmm, I would like to see how you connect it with something so practical and down to earth as the Constitution?"

"Me too," Amrita grinned, not put down by Franz's response. Each class that she taught included fiery discussions on the fragility of democracy. Beauty seemed elusive. Ugliness was more understandable. To the students, ugliness was a mask that perpetrators put on and set aside as and when it suited their agenda. Potential law students, IAS officers, Political Science scholars, and even housewives, all had a stake in the promise that had been made by the founding fathers to the people. Like a promise by a parent to a child. The students wanted to know and understand the value of words. How should they value them? How could they value them?

Over the next few months, questions about politics and poetics, turned into more personal questions.

"Amar seems really distracted these days. In fact, he has been like this for some time now. I thought he would be happier in the MBA program, but he seems to be drifting," Amrita expressed her concern. She was strolling around the inner circle in CP with Franz before her German class.

"He sounds the way I felt about ten years ago..." Franz did not complete his thought.

"Why, what happened at that time?"

"I'll tell you another time."

"Why not now? We've still got some time before class."

"No, another time," his reply was firm. For a while, they walked quietly. Amrita knew it must be something important if he needed to be prepared to talk about it.

Waiting for the light at the road before the Emporia, Amrita asked Franz, "Where to from here?"

"Anywhere will do."

"Let's go to Janpath. That way we'll be closer to the Bhawan."

"Okay, let's go through Palika Bazaar then."

"Are you ready for that?" Amrita impishly looked at Franz.

"What do you mean?"

"Remember, it's your decision," she said not explaining herself.

"I'll remember."

"Now don't blame me later."

"I won't."

"Okay then, let's go." Both Amrita and Franz turned to take the flight of steps into the underground market. Franz held Amrita's arm as the jostling crowds going in both directions threatened to cut between them. As they hurried past tiny stores and conflicting sounds and smells, following the arrows directing them toward Janpath, some passersby turned to look at the contrast they made. Then knowingly looked at each other.

"Sur, Sur, jeans faar sale. Skults faar the lady. Aal-trations away-lbul." Amrita and Franz carried on. A young boy, an apprentice at his trade and seeking to impress his employers with his entrepreneurial abilities, moved forward toward them boldly. Waving several boxes of bangles and other brickabracks in front of Amrita, he trained his eyes on Franz.

"Bangles faar yaar beautiful lady, Sur. Espaeshally faar her. In aal colors. And bows faar her hair. Take one. At least one, Sur. Only twelve rupees. Spaeshal price. Vairy cheap. Just faar you."

As Franz momentarily paused, turning to look at Amrita with a question, she shook her head. "No thanks," she told the boy and kept walking.

"Ten rupees then," the boy persisted.

Amrita shook her head.

"Eight, five. Whaat will you give? Take at least one. It will make my sale. Please Madum. PleaseMadumPlease." By now the shopkeepers around were staring at the strange tableau and jeering the young boy on. The sale had become a matter of pride for him.

Now he squeezed a tear from his eyes, "Have naat eaten in two days Madum, Sur. Take one. Whaat will you give?"

Wanting to shake off the boy, Franz dug in his pocket and gave him five rupees. The boy wasted no more time. He quickly pocketed the money, handed over a plastic clip, and disappeared in the crowd with a grin.

"Did you want the clip?"

"Doesn't matter. That's what I got." Then, "Hold your breath."

"Why?"

Before Amrita could say anything, Franz got his answer. The smell of the public toilets announced their location. Holding their breath, the two hurried up the stairs this time to emerge at the corner of Janpath.

"Phew," Franz released his breath in a rush. Amrita just laughed; she did not say anything.

As they strolled along, they saw a small group of people collected around the corner from DePaul's in the narrrow passage that connected the backside of the covered veranda to the front.

"I wonder what's going on?"

As the crowd reshuffled, they saw a palmist had established his corner and was hastily doing business before he was discovered and chased away.

"Let's get our palms read," Amrita suggested.

"I don't believe in it," Franz protested.

"You don't have to. We'll just do it for fun. Come on."

"Look at that crowd. We'll never get there in time for you to make it to your class by six."

"Most of the people are just listening. Come on, let's try." Amrita dragged Franz forward. She thrust her hand in front of the palmist and asked him to do a reading.

"Twenty rupees," he said. His price was according to his surroundings. "Wait your turn please. It will be a few minutes." They waited. In a few minutes, it was her turn.

"What is it?" Amrita asked when he just kept twisting and turning her hand and did not say anything.

"I see a tall man...from far away."

"Yes, that's because he is standing next to me," Amrita was a little impatient at hearing the obvious. The palmist did not rise to her remark.

"You must be careful."

"Careful?"

"Come on," Franz was pulling at her shoulder. Something about the whole situation was making him uneasy.

"No, wait Franz. Careful about what?" she asked.

"Oy Shyam Lal, hurry, pick up your things. The police *kameti* is doing an inspection," someone shouted.

"Hey, what are you doing?" asked Amrita as the palmist hastily started gathering his things.

"Roads," he mumbled briefly in reply without breaking from his task.

"Roads? What about roads?"

"Be careful."

"How can I be careful about roads? There are roads everywhere."

"You asked me to read your hand. This is what I see. That will be twenty rupees." The palmist was already packed and tapping his foot impatiently to be paid. It was obvious he had much practice in this sort of exit.

"Is that all?"

"Yes, twenty rupees. And hurry." He thrust his hand out.

Franz paid him the money and pulled Amrita away.

"What did he mean by being careful about roads?" she asked Franz.

"Just that we need to cross one right now. Come on, let's go." Amrita walked alongside Franz focusing on his face. As Franz made to cross the road, a three-wheeler came out of nowhere and stopped right next to Amrita so that she stopped in startlement. Moving back a step automatically, the heel of her foot made contact with one of the raised pieces of concrete that lined the road separating it from the pavement. As she cried out and bent to check her foot, Franz turned back swiftly.

"What happened? What happened?" He was on one knee examining her foot and passersby were openly gawking at them.

Placing her hand on Franz's shoulder, Amrita tried to make him rise. "I'm fine. It was just the surprise. Get up. People are staring at us."

"I don't care." He had taken off her sandal and was rubbing the bruised skin. He seemed oblivious of the muffled sniggers from some people around the water van nearby. But Amrita was all too conscious of how they must look to the people.

"This is what the palmist must have meant," she tried to diffuse the situation. But Franz was too upset to answer. By that time another three-wheeler wallah, who had watched the preceding from across the road outside Zaveri's, had come to the main road and, making a dangerous U-turn, crept up to them. Franz asked if he would take them to Max Mueller Bhawan. He said he would.

The next time they met, Amrita had still not forgotten about the palmist. But the spot on which he had spread his wares was now taken by another vendor.

"Do you think he really knew what was going to happen?"

Amrita had not said who she was talking about, but Franz understood. "No," he said shortly. Then, "I think you just tripped."

"Do you think some people can see things?"

"See? As in the future?" When she nodded, he continued, "I don't know. I've heard...but I don't know for sure."

"What about when you know a person?"

"What about it?"

"I mean when you know a person, can you then tell...sense... things about them?"

"Know somebody. What does that really mean?"

"It's obvious."

"It's not. Do we ever really know anybody?"

"That's very cynical." Amrita was silent for a while. Then, "Do you believe men and women can ever really know each other?" she wondered aloud.

"As much as is humanly possible, I suppose."

"And how much is that?"

"I don't think it is quantifiable."

"Still," Amrita insisted.

"Why must we analyze everything?" He was just as stubborn.

"How else do we create meaning?" Amrita asked, a little peeved.

"Do we have to make meaning all the time?" He was a little sardonic.

"Now you are just arguing for its sake."

"I guess...but still, why must women always be wanting to unravel everything?... Knit, knit, knit, unravel, unravel, unravel."

"Women? And I suppose men don't do that?"

"No, men don't. I feel you want to know everything. As though you would have my soul and study it inside out."

"How else would I get to know you?"

"Does it have to be so thorough? With you it is all or nothing."

Amrita could hear the tension in Franz's voice. She looked at him for a minute. He looked like a stranger. She wanted all or nothing, he said. She had never thought of herself that way, but now she did. Ever since she could remember she always wanted to know things, people, thoroughly. *Really* understand them. There were no half measures. "What's wrong with that?" she now asked.

"There's nothing wrong..."

"No, you implied there is something wrong."

"People have to have their space, you know."

"And what will you do when you have got all this space?"

"Do? It's not a question of doing. It's a question of having. It belongs to you."

"What?"

"Space."

"Okay."

"Okay?"

"Yes, have it then." And she walked apart a little bit.

"Amrita." She stopped. "I don't mean physical space."

"What kind do you mean then?"

"Mental space."

"A bit convenient, isn't it? You want mental space when knowing a person mentally truly brings people closer but physical space you don't want when physical knowledge brings people together only to a limited extent."

"You are twisting my words. The way you say it, it sounds superficial."

"That's because it is superficial."

"No, it is not. Physical closeness is important. It leads to mental closeness."

"And I am saying mental closeness is where it begins. It is what gives meaning to the physical. And you are wrong, men feel this way too." When Franz just looked at her, she continued, "What do you call it...what you do for a living?"

"Theoretical reasoning into...but that's different. That's for work..."

"And is it effective?"

"Mostly...ah, I see. But in personal matters women do it more."

"Then perhaps, since you yourself admit to its effectiveness at work, you men should try it in your personal lives. You just might learn something useful." Amrita spoke a little sarcastically and walked away a bit.

For a moment Franz left her alone. He too was a little miffed. *Why must she always have her own way?* he thought resentfully. This time he wouldn't give in. Let her make her own way back. He wandered idly to the next store. But five minutes later, she was still standing at the same shop looking at the brassware as though studying it for future identification. When he turned to look at her, she was looking at him surreptitiously. She was not much of an actress and that endeared her to him and made him laugh. From the beginning, he had noticed there was an intensity about her. A kind of heat, an invisible wire that pulled him to her. And others too, from the sidelong glances she was getting from the men passing by. But to all she was oblivious. Almost without volition, he moved back toward her.

Amrita had indeed been watching him from between her eyelashes. Why had she been so stuck up with all her talk of physical and mental space? She mentally kicked herself. Heart beating furiously, she wondered if he was going to let her walk away. So she willed him to come to her.

"Why must we argue? Now, what is it you wanted to know?" he bent over her.

"I don't remember," Amrita looked up with a laugh. Giddy with victory and something else.

But later that night, Amrita went over their conversation. Franz was becoming important to her. What would her parents think? And say? Franz had told her about his fascination with India and Hinduism. The relation of the history of the German language and culture with that of India was something he had always wanted to explore. Since he was scheduled to visit several cities, Amrita was jealous of their time together. *Does he think of me as just an exotic experience or, worse, an academic one?*

Increasingly, Amrita thought less about the history of Indo-Germanic languages, the inflections of tenses and verbs, and more about his deep, gray-blue eyes and lean strength. Eyes that hinted at stories untold. A body that defiantly declared its purpose and spat his quiet determination to get there. A body that dared touch, at the other's peril. What might it unfold? What would that be like? To know him, and have him know her too. But she kept her thoughts to herself and satisfied herself with just looking. Quick glances at first. Then longer and longer.

Till one day he looked at her. They were outside the Nirula's ice cream parlor.

"A couple of my friends are going to Ghungroo tonight," she told Franz. When he didn't answer, she continued, "I can't believe you don't dance."

"I never have."

"The movies from the West would have us believe that that is all people do over there for entertainment. Drink and dance."

"Yes, well, I skipped the dancing stage."

"Not the drinking one?"

"Not exactly."

"And is that over?"

"It has been for a long time."

"What you needed was a good, strong parental hand, young man," Amrita waved her finger playfully in Franz's face.

"I think we all do." Franz's response was curiously quiet.

Amrita bit her tongue. "I know you have spoken to the class about refugee life and your parents, but...what about you? It couldn't have been easy. That, and then to lose them both...so abruptly, I mean. Almost at once. You were so young." When Franz merely kept silent, she prodded, "Tell me."

Franz shrugged somewhat distantly, his eyes gray. "It was a long time ago," he said.

"But..."

"It's a beautiful evening."

"Franz..."

"There's quite a crowd today."

Amrita was quiet for a moment, wondering what to do next. Then, suddenly she began to sway in rhythm to the beat of the music filtering through the parlor walls.

"What are you doing?"

"Dancing."

"Here?"

"Why not?"

"People are looking."

"Let them. They probably want to do the same." And Amrita continued to sway. Lightly, gently, moving her shoulders and her feet. Fluidly, like the making of meaning.

"Come on Franz. It's a wonderful feeling."

But Franz just looked at her. Amrita fancied she saw a hint of envy, but it might just have been the angle of the light.

Franz was looking at her, lost in thought. This blue-jeaned and T-shirt-clad figure was moving uninhibitedly among other blue-jeaned and T-shirt-clad figures. Absently he looked down at his formal pants and shirt; he had come straight from work as usual. Every time Amrita spoke, he watched the expressions on her face. She had such an animated face. If he missed anything she said, he was sure to find it in her face. Momentarily he wondered what she was doing here with him. Then deliberately shrugging off his thoughts, he asked what flavor she wanted.

"Pistachio."

"I think I'll skip it."

"If you are not having, then I'm not going to either," she said.

"Don't be silly. You don't need to watch your waistline."

"This waistline thing…it affects women before it does men, you know. Quite unfair, but there you have it," she finished in mock irritation.

"Okay, so let's both not bother. I'm going to get a nutty buddy."

Amrita laughed, "I swear you like saying that name more than the ice cream itself."

"Don't you be mistaken," he rolled his eyes in exaggeration, "anything chocolate is what I go for. Not vanilla, not strawberry, it has to be chocolate."

Amrita rolled her eyes as well in her best immitation of chocolate salvation and leaned forward in laughter. He leaned laughingly into her.

In that moment she understood how overrated speech can be, how open to misinterpretation. But the body, that is another matter. The body does not lie. Amrita felt something from him reaching out and wrapping itself around her. She felt herself reaching back. Across physical space.

9   *Hide and Seek*

"AMRITA, PHONE." AMRITA was shaken out of her reverie by her mother calling out to her. It was a few days after Mandakini's visit.

"I'm sleeping."

"Okay. Franz, is that it? I'm afraid that Amrita is asleep right now."

Amrita had not known that it was Franz until her mother spoke his name. *But still,* she thought to herself, *this is better. Things are different now.* She turned her face to the wall. But unable to settle, she picked up the letter she had received the day before from the Delhi University Teachers Association president, a Mrs. Rita Chandrawarkar. After offering the usual apologies about her accident, the letter went on to say that the summer holidays made it difficult for DUTA to organize anything to mark their response. The available members of the Executive Committee however had offered to take the matter up with the full Committee at the end of the holidays. They also had a few suggestions. Perhaps they could hold a token protest outside the Vice Chancellor's office at the university or a small rally at the Boat Club. What did she think, the letter invited.

Too tired to think, Amrita put the letter aside and picked up the *Bhagavad Gita* lying by her bed. She had asked Amardeep to pick up a copy of it from Galgotia's. It was one of the English translations. Now she opened it to the section where Arjuna hesitated to open fire against the enemy because they were his brothers. His charioteer, Lord Krishna, then began explaining to him the nature of life and death and duty.

Franz's voice on the other side of the phone had disturbed her. Still she tried repeatedly to return her mind to the *Gita Updesh. Karmanye vadhikaraste ma phaleshu kada chan.* Human beings must focus on committing action and leave the results to God. She had read about it once before. Long ago, when the cold moon had been ready to be raided by humans, but on earth it was hot. Hot and sweaty. The summer afternoon swollen with children's whispers that were determined to drown the droning of the Hindi teacher's moral science lesson, their desire (especially of those in new glasses) to escape outside palpable.

"Mama, Mama," she now called loudly.

Kundan entered. "So you are awake now? That was Franz. This is the third time he has called. Didn't you know him at Max Mueller?"

"What did he want?" Amrita ignored the questions.

"He didn't say. I suppose just to talk. You know he was not here when…"

Seeing her mother bite her tongue, Amrita hastened to complete her sentence for her. "When my accident happened. Yes, Mama, you can say that. You don't have to pussyfoot around me all the time, you know." Amrita was in a truculent mood and looking for an argument.

Kundan wisely turned to leave, but something in Amrita's face stopped her. "So why don't you call him?"

"Oh, I will, sometime."

"Why not now?"

"Why, Mama, you have never been so eager to have me talking to a guy," Amrita spoke a little wryly. Needling her mother.

Kundan blushed a little but pursued her point, "You have to work a little too. You mustn't expect one person to do all the running."

"And how would you know?" When Kundan did not answer, Amrita kept egging her on. Never before had she felt this desire to make her mother admit her secret of how she had met and married her father. "So how do you know, Mama?" she asked again.

For a moment, it seemed as though Kundan might leave the

room, but then she calmly replied, "I know. Take it from me, I know. And one day maybe you'll understand."

For a few moments Amrita let her mind wander to all the stray sentences of information she had gathered over the years about her parents' courtship. She couldn't understand this shroud of secrecy. When she returned her attention, Kundan was saying, "And you should talk to him. He sounds very nice."

Without her mother's participation, Amrita could not advance her argument, so she gave in. "You haven't even met him. How can you say that?"

"So let's meet. You can have him come over one of these evenings." Kundan, too, could skirt questions.

"I don't think so. In fact, I don't think I will ever see him again." The words were out of her mouth before Amrita realized that she had said them out loud. She wanted to take them back, but she didn't. She couldn't. Fear that they were really true held her back.

"What? Only a month ago you could not stop talking about him."

"A month ago things were different."

"What things?"

"Things, Mama, things."

"They'll be fine again."

"But they'll never be the same."

Kundan was quiet. She knew that things did not always remain the same. Stealing a quick look at the wheelchair that sat mockingly on the side, she said, "Things will be better."

"Yes, better, fine." As Amrita picked up the *Bhagavad Gita* again, Kundan left the room.

Immediately after the accident, every night, Kundan and Gurmehar had held each other and cried. Softly, gently, cradling their pain, rocking it to rest if not release. But each passing night, even as they lay side by side, had led them into quiet journeys of their own. When Gurmehar first slipped quietly from their bed to begin his pacing, a puzzled Kundan had followed him after a few minutes. Seeing him pace up and down the back courtyard, muttering to himself under the starry night sky, she remained standing in the shadows. Then she returned to bed. Since then, though she felt him periodically leave and return, she always pretended to be asleep. But that night, Kundan spoke to Gurmehar about the phone call. Normally, Gurmehar did not want to know anything about his daughter's personal life. She was his child, his daughter. And he did not think it right for a father to even visualize *that* aspect of his daughter. Kundan knew it and usually respected his feelings, even finding them mildly amusing. But this was different.

Already, since the accident, there was talk that the Chaddhas had spoiled their daughter with too much independence. All those parties she went to and all that traveling in buses at all times of day with all kinds of people. Always was a willful child. Attacking life with imagination rather than conforming to established norms. What else could one expect? Something was bound to happen, sooner or later. And so, in the end, behind closed doors and mealymouthed whispers, it was her willfulness that some held against her. Afterall, no one *made* her do anything.

But when Kundan overheard Binder Nangia and Rati Malhotra's conversation, she wanted to leap out at them and tear their eyes out.

Ten days ago, Kundan had just been about to ring the bell on Binder Nangia's flat, when she was distracted by something written on the wall. In the instant it took her to find out that it was nothing more than the scribblings of a child, it was too late. A conversation had begun inside and the women's voices were loud enough to penetrate the thin DDA walls. For a moment she felt an unreasonable anger against the Delhi Development Authority and all those involved under whom these increasingly unaffordable, mass-produced, multistory flats with thin walls were mushrooming all over the city. Then, she focused on what was being said.

"And Amrita, what's going to happen to her?" Rati was asking.

"What do you mean? You have heard that she's still got her job, haven't you?" Binder replied.

"Yes, but can she...you know...manage?" Rati continued.

"Poorthing, time will tell. And she had such a promising future. God's *leela* is amazing. He works in mysterious ways. You can't escape His plan, you can't rewrite your destiny," Binder said piously.

"Yes, and your past life must be paid for in full. But...what about marriage? Do you think...," Rati paused, unable to immediately complete her question. Then continued, "Who will want to marry her now? It's a good thing, she's a teacher. She can at least achieve some fulfillment by mothering her students."

"*Bechaari*. Poor thing."

"*Bechaari*. Poor thing."

"Poor Kundan, she's going to have her hands full for the rest of her life," Rati commiserated.

"And Gurmehar. The bills are going to be huge too. These things take money," Binder agreed.

Sympathy of sorts. Clumsy, bungling, even well meant. And very, very cruel.

A few years after her marriage, Kundan had been able to fill a junior teacher's vacancy at a local convent school. There she had met Binder and Rati, and they had been friends since then. But at this moment, Kundan could no longer bear listening to them; she rang the doorbell to put an end to their gossip.

"Oh, it's you," Rati said as she opened the door.

"Yes, it's me. You were expecting me, weren't you? I mean I can't stay for the kitty but I wanted to come by and give you my month's contribution," Kundan replied with suppressed anger.

"You needn't have bothered. At this time, I mean. Did Gurme-har *Bhai* sahib drop you? Did you just get here? I didn't hear your car outside. I hope I didn't keep you waiting by the door. We were talking about how hot it is and got a little carried away—just like the weather. You weren't outside for long were you?" Rati tried to probe but to no avail. Kundan handed her her contribution and left.

Outside, she raised her hand to stop a passing three-wheeler. It was brand-new, and from its rear bumper hung an old piece of black *parandi*—the kind old women wear to add volume to their thinning hair. The accompanying sticker, warding off the evil eye, read: *Buri Nazar Waale Tera Munh Kala*. This is what made Gurme-har pace, volcanically, outside the hospital room after Amrita's accident, Kundan thought. And since then, night after night in the back courtyard. She knew now that she would need to be very careful in dealing with this situation.

Life is short. A single moment can undo the work of eons of other moments. Kundan rubbed her stomach carressingly as she remembered how carefully she had carried both her children. But especially Amrita. That pregnancy had been difficult—so soon after the first one. She had been advised by the doctor to take as much rest as possible. And she had done everything she was told. When she remembered the sensitive child that Amrita always had been, she felt her heart squeeze. She still had in her jewelry box a letter that Amrita had written to God when she was six. Then, she had quickly made a few important calls to take care of the situation. Now Kundan thought angrily, "What do these women know? What can they possibly understand? After all, their wombs have not been lit by fire, their hearts have never been wrenched by the raging silence of their child." Kundan could dismiss the women, but it was harder to dismiss her fear for Amrita. "Is this how short her road is to be? Will she ever know the look, gesture, expression of love? Will she know that love lies in the quivering of a lover's lash? That every line and groove on the lover's face is a line and groove on your own? That anxiety, concern, rage, and despair, all are labors of love? Or, will she turn her back to all this, churned by bitterness? Who is this wan stranger who lies in my child's bed? Where is my Amritu with her arms folded, legs set apart, and ponytail bobbing up and down?"

"We need to talk," Kundan said to Gurmehar that evening. Gurmehar looked up. "Do you remember Nadi Singh and Swaran?"

"Of course. Why, have you heard from either?"

"No, I was just thinking of them." When Gurmehar did not say anything, she continued. "Do you remember we all met at the same time? They both wanted to get married. But Swaran's parents were opposed to it. After all, Nadi Singh was a Ravidasi and they were Amritdharis. They waited for a while, till Swaran gave in to family pressure and married the man of their choosing. Nadi Singh left Delhi."

"Hmm." Gurmehar already knew all this.

"Nadi Singh never married. And Swaran wrote from Bombay that she was learning to be happy. That was almost twenty years ago. We never heard from her again. She did not want to remember."

Gurmehar was willing to do anything.

A few days passed in quiet. All Kundan's attempts to guilefully introduce Franz into the conversation went unremarked by Amrita. He had called again, twice, but she had refused to take his call each time. The third time she heard her mother at the phone for a little while longer. Though a little curious, even a little jealous, she remained quiet. Kundan too did not return to her daughter's room to recount the conversation. Amrita smiled lethargically. Two can play the game.

"There was another strike in the univ today." Amrita heard her brother talking to Kundan in the next room.

"That *thaila* looks really bad," she smilingly mocked him as he entered her room with his satchel on his shoulder.

"Why, what's wrong? It's functional," he protested.

"That thick, cotton material with threads hanging loose. What does Minnie have to say?"

"Minnie doesn't focus on such superficial things." Amardeep sounded a little irritated.

"And I do, I suppose."

Amardeep did not answer. Amrita was mad at herself. She hadn't meant to say that. It just came out of her mouth. She changed the subject.

Later that evening, playing chess together, both of them forgot their earlier shortness. "You need to make a move, Amu."

"I'm thinking."

Amardeep rolled his eyes and hooted with laughter. Speaking in a high, artificial voice, he repeated, "I'm thinking." Turning to their parents who were sitting in the veranda nearby talking to each other, he said, "Thinking. You mean cheating. How long will your break be this time? You always did need ten to fifteen minutes in the loo to think your next move. Twice, thrice, four times." Before he had finished his last sentence, Amrita had toppled over the chessboard and scattered the pieces. Black and White. The unsteady knight leaned drunkenly over the king. The pawns lay helplessly around not knowing what to do now that their leaders had fallen. Though Amrita had murmured it, Amardeep had heard her words. "I won't be running to the loo quite so often now."

"I didn't mean it like that." Amardeep, too, was upset. "I didn't mean it like that, Amu, you know that, you know that," he repeated with emphasis and even a little anger. Gurmehar and Kundan had heard the exchange. They tried to intervene. But it was all too much. All Amrita could think of was that she was stuck with Ramesh to do odd jobs for her. Life is cruel, she had not known that Franz too could be so cruel. He had not even cared enough to call again. "Aren't I worth even a call now?" She could see the annoyance in his fixed gaze as though he had heard her question. That gaze that could turn from summer blue to monsoon gray. Not the seasonal monsoon of Delhi but the perpetual monsoon of London. Thoughts of a home far away made her feel sleepy. For the last few days, she kept slipping into memories that she had thought were as cold as the ashes that float briefly before sinking into the waters of the Yamuna next to the cremation grounds of Nigambodh ghat.

She felt a strange sort of power as everyone emptied her room. They were out, she was in. Now she would try to catch that fisherman on the shore and see if he would take her across on his boat of sorrow to where she could see a floating garland. Even without looking at it, she knew it would be marigold. Limp, downcast petals that seemed to be carrying the weight of the world or of at least one soul. Before they sank to the bottom.

◗ ● ◖

Amrita was fascinated by the chess pieces spread out at the foot of their parents' bed.

"I have togo to the loo."

"Cheat."

"You cheat."

"Chea-ter-cock."

"You chea-ter-cock. I re-a-lly havetogo to the loo," Amrita begged, pressing one leg against the other.

"Go then, but I'll be standing outside. If I don't hear you, I'll know."

"Mummy, Amar is standing outside the loo...."

"Stop it Amar."

"Yes Amar stopitstopit."

"I don't want to have to come there," Kundan raised her voice from the next room.

"Stopitstopit."

>●◁

"Stopitstopit," Amrita whispered to her pillow, to the white distempered walls, to the horizontal metal bars across her window, to the sliver of the moon that seemed to be in prison garb, even to the wind that night after night came like a persistent lover stealing through her window at odd hours when all else had stopped knocking. But there was no answer. It seemed she had successfully driven away all those who would love her, who could love her. And the psychedelic UNITRA poster on the wall above merely grinned back at her, mocking her victory as loss. Its geometric maze inviting her in only to lose her again.

>●◁

Six and all alone in the house. It was the new *aya's* day off. And Kundan had gone to the market for a little while in the afternoon. She had not wanted to go, fearing they would get into mischief, but the little angels had convinced her they'd be "very, very good."

"What are you doing Amar?"

"What does it look like? It's a fi-re ofcourse."

"But it's not inastove."

"That's only for ninnies."

"Mummy doesit inthestove." Amardeep could not argue with that so he kept quiet.

"You know we are not allowed to play with fi-re. Mummy said so," Amrita continued.

"Mummy's poonchh, Mummy's poonchh."

"I'm NOT a poonchh." Amrita was teary-eyed.

"Poonchhal, poonchhal," Amardeep continued till Amrita started up a wail. "Okay, okay, you are not but you must stop crying first."

"Will you let me help you then?" Amrita managed to negotiate between hiccups.

"No, MummyPapa will KILL me." But seeing Amrita getting ready to let out an even bigger wail, he thought it better to change his mind. He did not want to bring out the neighbors. So Amrita leaned unsteadily over Amardeep as he tried to focus the sunlight through his tiny magnifying lens over a bunch of scrunched-up papers placed between two broken bricks in the corner of the courtyard.

"Are you sure you know howto do this? It hasn't burnt yet."

"You havetokeep re-al quiet and con-cen-trate. Also pray re-al hard."

"And what does the sun do? You told me the sun burns it, the sun burns it."

"Just keep quiet and do what I say." So Amrita kept quiet and did what he said. "God, please burn our papers," she prayed. When God did not listen, she tried again. "God, please, please, burn our papers. And do it before Mummy gets home," she added, just for good measure.

Soon, however, growing tired from sitting awkwardly on her haunches, she started rocking over the magnifying glass. For a moment she was distracted by the trace of a thin line of sweat that was winding its way down her left leg. She watched it make its way down the fine, dark hairs on her leg, like a little *nali* of water overflowing from a larger reservoir during the monsoons. Bringing her short, stubby fingers up from where they curved like a snug cricket cap over the rounded head of her left knee, she jabbed her index finger to the end of the flowing stream of her secret body-water. As though determined to trace the dirty little secret to its source, she now traced her finger backward till the wetness led her in a winding path to its very source in the concave behind her knee. There, she allowed herself to open her entire hand. Back and forth she rubbed. First with one hand, then with the other, then with the hem of her frock that she could twist around and below, till she had rubbed the secret out of her very skin. For the time being she was satisfied.

Amardeep himself was tired by now. But he was not about to show his defeat in front of Amrita. She would never let him forget it. So next time she rocked closer to him, he allowed himself to lose his balance. "Look what you made me do," he said. Amrita looked up, ready to see what she had done. "I just can't do anything around you." Both of them, tired and irritated with their futile efforts, wandered off to play by themselves.

Amardeep went to hang himself upside down on a precariously thin branch of the guava tree in the front garden. Like a langoor, his bottom thrust outward and head reached the ground in danger of being bust open should he fall. *Langoor, Angoor. Langoor,* monkey. *Angoor,* grape. Both hung upside down by their tails with their bottoms thrust outward. Like the lushly plump, velvet yellow laburnums that hung in bunches from branches of trees that lined their neighborhood. *Langoor. Angoor.* Like laburnum.

Amrita amused herself by hopping around the courtyard in tune with a nonsense rhyme she had learned from someone. It was not exactly clear where she learned these things. It was just that she was very friendly and had an air of confidence about her, so that people found themselves talking to her and confiding in her almost in spite of themselves. Now she was singing,

> *Ai ras-gull-ea*
> *tu ke-ri gall-on phhul-ea*
> *dil kar-da hai tenu kha ja-wan*
> *te go-gar wich pa ja-wan.*

She had a martial approach to the sweetmeat that lay forgotten in her song. With each syllable muttered loudly with an air of announcement, her foot came down with precision and exactitude within each longitudinally laid, cement-bound brick that formed the border of the courtyard. She was a little soldier on a mission. A little soldier with no hard hat around her heart.

A few minutes later both children came together again looking for trouble. It was hot and they were thirsty, so they decided to make *nimbu pani*. They had seen their mother make it countless times. There was nothing to it.

"Just fill a pitcher with water and put sugar and stir and stir and then squeeze some lemons into it," Amrita rattled off the recipe. Amardeep knew better than to drag the glass pitcher from the top of the rack. The steel pitcher was in the sink, so he decided to take a small steel bucket. He filled it with water from the tap under the sink. Now the bucket was too heavy for him to carry. But he was wary of complaining in front of Amrita. He had already cut it close with the fire excuse. He did not want to risk losing face anymore with her. So he balanced the bucket over the kitchen step and put it down as quickly as possible over the thin drain separating the courtyard from the veranda. Amrita's hawk eyes saw the huge splashes on the yard bricks, but she was anxious to play mother. She had already got a ladle, the jar of sugar, and the lemons. Now she emptied the entire jar into the bucket and "stir, stir, stir," she went.

"That's too much," Amardeep tried to stop her.

"It is just right," she sniffed, copying Kundan. "Now just squeeze the lemons into the pitcher."

"Taste it first."

"It's just... YECHH, it's horr-i-ble." Her face was screwed up like a freshly squeezed lemon; Amardeep could not help laughing at her. Enjoying being the center of Amardeep's attention, Amrita exaggerated her expression even more. She now stretched out her tongue as far as she could trying to mime her desire to pull it out. It kept slipping through her fingers back into her mouth, but she would put her hand back in to bring the naughty puppy out again.

"You ninny, you'll catch it from Mummy. I told you—" Amardeep was still in the middle of his sentence when they both heard a key turning in the lock. Before they could destroy the evidence, Kundan had walked in. The smile on her face never completed itself as she saw her two children standing over the steel bucket with the remains of a chemistry project gone bad nearby.

In no time at all, Kundan had the situation under control. They were punished for both counts. The second was unprotestable. So they both protested against the first. After all, the fire never took place. "The papers did not burn," Amrita tested a small wail. But Kundan was not to be appeased. "A rule is a rule," she said shaking her finger. Amrita's round eyes followed the up and down motion of this shaking magic wand that always brought with it news of disaster for them. She was not disappointed. "You, Amardeeeeeep, you cannot ride your bike this evening. And you, Amrita, you have become very naughty. I had bought you some new slippers. You will have to wait to get them now." The wand had spoken. The wand could not, would not, be denied.

Amardeep was sulking in the corner. More than his resentment at not being able to ride the bike, he did not like it when his mother called him Amardeeeeeep. It meant she was really angry with him. He was the older one, and he had been left in charge. He had failed her. *Why must Amu always spoil things for him?* he thought. Meanwhile, Amrita had already forgotten her tears. She had even forgotten the wand and homed in on the present. "Whichones-MummyWhichones? The pointy ones with the V-strap?"

"Yes."

"Are they pink?"

"Yes." Kundan was short. She was angry at being disobeyed. More than that she was worried sick at what might have happened in case of a real fire. She also felt guilty about having left them alone. She had really thought they were beginning to grow up and be responsible. And she was only gone for an hour. "Now keep quiet and take a nap. Papa will hear of this."

Neither Amrita nor Amardeep wanted Papa to hear of this. They wondered how they could get out of that. Especially Amardeep. But more immediately, they wondered how they could get out of taking a nap. This was a daily battle. Every day Kundan tried to get them to take a nap with her in the afternoon. Every day they protested they were not tired and then fell asleep in exhaustion minutes after their heads touched their pillows. In the summer, she made them both lie next to her in the drawing room on the dhurrie. In a line they lay. Legs and knees tucked and stacked behind each other. The cool, stone floor and the whirring fan of the cooler made the summer afternoon heat bearable.

Now, as Amrita lay spooned behind Kundan, she felt her eyes drawn to the guava tree; swaying slightly, it seemed to beckon her to come outside and play. Closing her eyes to temptation, she slowly inched closer to Kundan and placed the fingertips of her right hand on her mother's neck. She did this, she thought, secretly, running her little fingers between and around the small wispy curls that lay at her mother's nape. She felt the heaviness of her mother's braid. Kundan always braided her hair when she lay down. At other times, she wore it in a thick bun low at the base of her neck. Kind of like a giant ball, thought Amrita. So big, so round. So big and round. With coils, heavy with meaning, draped in secret pathways that disappeared somewhere into the center. She wondered if it hurt her neck. Big, heavy head collapsed inside the neck so that the mouth was in line with the heart. And had courage. Like the hunchback of Notre Dame they had read about together. Her own hair was nothing like Kundan's.

Kundan felt the little fingers move in circular motion on her neck but did not say anything. It soothed both daughter and mother, that curling sensation.

"CanI wear my pink frock in the evening with the slippers, Mummy?" she mouthed her question on her mother's back with her lips.

"Go to sleep."

"CanI Mummy, canI, canI?"

"We'll see."

"We'llsee? We'llsee?" No good, that we'llsee. Amrita was old enough to understand that we'llsee. But before she could pursue that thought, sleep came and sat on top of her lashes and gently shut them down, carrying her in its boat to the other side. To look at beautiful garlands of marigold floating on the shiny water.

"Just fill a pitcher with water and put sugar and stir and stir and then squeeze some lemons into it."

"I have-togo to the loo."

"Chea-ter-cock."

"Stir and stir and stir."

"I re-a-lly have togo to the loo."

$$\blacktriangleright \bullet \blacktriangleleft$$

Amrita woke up with a desire to go to the loo. She automatically looked at the clock on the wall. It was two fifteen in the night. She had fallen asleep in her day clothes after the chess game. The one she had ruined, she grimaced guiltily. For a moment her mind wandered to her dreams, vague memories now on waking. She also remembered she had to go to the loo. The bathroom was the room next door. There was no connecting door. She could reach it only by leaving her room. And the others might hear her moving around. There was a bedpan under her bed of course. She had been totally dependent on it in the beginning. After a few weeks, she had begun using the bathroom with the help of Ramesh, who had been hired to take care of her physical needs. Kundan would have been happy to take care of all of Amrita's needs, but Amrita had lashed out at that idea. *May you never rest in peace,* now burst out from her in a scream of agony in her head. And it made her feel something more. Something awful, something secret.

She wanted to go out and catch those Romeos and bus drivers by the throat and squeeze them and squeeze them and squeeze them, till each lay at her feet crumbling in his own messy body fluids and whimpering for mercy. All their secrets traced to their source, squeezed out of them like the juice of a squeezed lemon.

Not willing to be distracted tonight, Amita allowed herself to feel all the rage that little Amu would have felt. Little Amu with her tongue slipping in and out of her mouth as she tried to hold on to the naughty puppy. Little Amu who just had togo to the loo. Little Amu who was NOT a chea-ter-cock.

Amrita really had to go to the loo. She wondered if she could hold herself till morning. But the desire once felt would not go away. And there were more hauntings.

"Amrita, I can hold it for tenminutes. Bet you can't."

"I can hold it for twen-ty," she had bragged.

"Okaythen, I'll lock the loo for twen-tyminutes, and we'll see."

Amrita knew she had been tricked. "I re-a-lly have togo to the loo."

Drifting out of sleep again, Amrita looked at the moonlight that lay in a slant on her bedroom floor like a faded cotton sheet. Soft and comfortable after years of use. A valued friend. A confidante. Someone to tell her secrets to. Her body secrets. As a child, Amrita had clearly seen that that ray of moonlight carried within it an image of infinity. Today, alas, that ray of moonlight illumined merely the finiteness of her universe. And the pettiness of her life to come. Unbidden, ugliness had crept out from under the shadows and into the forefront.

The rest of the room lay in darkness. But the sliver of light made it possible for Amrita to see all the objects in her room. In bewilderment. How strange everything looked. The same and yet not the same.

Above, a very old fan whirred at full speed on slender, faded ivory wings. As though determined to prove there was yet life in it. Her eyes skipped over the uncomfortable-looking TV set on its black, painted metal trolley that clearly didn't belong in the room. Draped on both sides of the window were two curtains in dull gold made of some jacquard material with huge flowers woven into it in a darker shade of gold. During the day, when the two curtains were drawn together, they still did not meet all the way in the center.

Next to the window and facing the bed sat a teak study table with a cane-backed chair tucked in. From the gap between the back of the chair and its seat peeped a simple, blue-colored cushion. The table was covered with a dusty-pink cloth of casement that was trimmed in intricate cutwork in white satin stitch. The trim fell a few inches below the top on all sides. Kundan had spent long hours making this tablecloth. On the top left-hand side of the table, a green lamp with chipped-off paint and a shade that was too narrow leaned over an open book. Underneath the lamp stood a square-shaped, gray-and-maroon marble paperweight and tall pencil stand filled with pens and pencils and paper cutters. A few books lay piled on the right-hand side with a small-sized calendar of glossy Indian prints on top. The kind that sits steady like a mini mountain in an inverted *V* with rings on top to flip over the pages of each month. Each page had a picture of gods and monsters in combat with each other. The artists had rendered with great imagination pictures that were very detailed and colorful and brushed in with fine strokes. In each, the characters looked frighteningly human, and it was not altogether impossible to see the shadow of a neighbor's face lurking within. The facing page was still turned to the month of May with a tiny picture of Durga in combat with Mahishasura against the backdrop of a lonely hill and a few barren trees with a city in the distance. It was a miniature painting representing Mughal influence on traditional Hindu culture from the Rajput state of Bikaner. The picture showed a crowned Durga on a lion with four arms carrying a dagger, a sword, and a snakelike lance. Her fourth arm gestured in a sacred manner. Mahishasura was depicted as a fanged, eight-armed demon on a steed. All characters were resplendantly dressed. There was a decapitated warrior on the ground, and there was gore all around.

Next to the table, on the right side, was a small sitting chair. Beautifully molded arms and legs led down to the left foot that was a little chipped. Testimony to the day Amardeep and Amrita had played king and queen. Amrita had sat in the chair while Amardeep dragged her around the courtyard in it. Mercifully, Kundan had heard the squeals and stepped in, and the chair had been saved. It had an elaborately carved back in tiny spindles and shapely open and closed curves that looked like a stately row of pieces ready to make their move when called. On its seat and miniature, window-shaped back there was a fancy pattern of open canework. Five decades had merely added a patina of memory on its rich brown color. The chair had once belonged to Gurmehar as a child

(*Darji,* in his excitement at finally having a son, had had it made for Gurmehar when he was just born) and, together with the fan in her room, was one of the few things he had been able to recover from his inheritance a few years after his marriage.

Peeping below the chair was a faint ring of rust on the floor where Amrita had experimented in gardening by bringing in a giant money plant winding its way around a thick moss stick. Lacking enough light, however, it had begun to wilt and had to be carried out to be resuscitated.

Above the bed, on the side wall, was a giant poster over which hung an octagonal-shaped clock with a black dial. Ugly. Amrita had deliberately hung it here so that she would not always be looking at the time from her study table. The only other ornaments on the other walls were fancy light shades shaped like inverted tulips in frosted white glass.

Next to the bed was a low-level, oval-shaped table on three legs. Books and newspapers and random knickknacks lay scattered on its tray and around it on the ground. Together with the pile of chess pieces and pawns on the folded cardboard. Gurmehar had come home with the chess game the day after he had punished Amardeep for playing with fire. Patiently, he had taught the two children how to play. Amrita still remembered being fascinated by the different moves of each piece. The pawns moved forward in peaks and valleys to try to capture the other side in sudden lateral moves; each time a pawn successfully reached the other side, a lost piece could be reclaimed. The rook, the bishop, the knight, even the queen, all moved forward and backward to protect the king. The poor king, who could move in any direction but only one square at a time. Why isn't the queen more powerful? Amrita had wanted to know. She could move in all directions across the entire length of the board, after all. That's why she is so important to the king, Gurmehar had explained. For his protection. But who protects the queen? Now, as then, Amrita wondered, *Who protects the queen?* There was no answer. The original box of the game had been lost long ago and the pieces now rested in a plastic bag twisted in place at the top by a plain rubber band.

Beside the side table, on a door of the built-in almirah, was a fancy mirror. Full-length. Amrita had insisted on having it installed when Gurmehar had had the house remodeled a few years ago. Lying in bed, she did not have to look at it unless she turned her head awkwardly behind. She quickly turned away from it now.

Only to stop short by the wheelchair. By the wheels of the chair. A mesh of spokes that seemed to rush madly into a hub. All held together by a rigid circular steel ring clothed in sturdy rubber. Ready to pivot on command. And spinning silently, night after night, burning tracks on her soul.

Leaning against the wall was a new pair of crutches.

Everything looked different in the moonlight. With rounder planes and edges. Softer and more comfortable. Inviting her to dare to do anything. She leaned forward toward the crutches.

❘ ● ❙

Everyone had heard Amrita move the night before. Amardeep, sleeping on a cot just outside Amrita's room, in the drawing room, was the first to hear the sound of her padded crutches. But no one mentioned it the next morning. It was one of those no-fun secrets that everyone knows and yet cannot talk about.

10   *Duped*

"HAVE YOU EVER sinned?"

Amardeep was a little taken aback by the question; he chose to take it lightly. "Oh, all the time. In fact, I'm just about to do it right now. I plan on having a huge breakfast. What about you?"

"Have I ever sinned?"

"No, do you want to pig with me?" Amardeep looked at Amrita strangely.

"No."

Amardeep turned to leave the room but then changed his mind and said, "I hope not."

"Would you recognize it if you had?"

Once again he thought. "I hope so."

"Do you believe sinners find any salvation?"

"Amu..."

"I sinned last night," she revealed.

Amardeep was beginning to feel out of his depth. "What did you do?"

"I cursed the drivers...I wished them ill."

"That is not—"

"It is."

"They did you ill." Amardeep's forehead was glistening with the sweat of anger. No matter how much he coined the jukebox, it spurted out only a distant, dusty version of what had been. Yesterday was gone, and the task of Amrita's guardian that he had so reluctantly assumed as a child weighed in all its burden at that moment. For the first time in a long while, however, he did not feel resentful. Since the accident, he had lain night after night on his cot outside her door wondering what was going through her mind. These days there was an inscrutability about her face. As though she had one face for herself and another for the rest of the world.

"Do you believe everyone possesses a conscience?" Amrita asked Amardeep.

"I should think so."

"Hmm. An inactive one perhaps." *Or, are they just morally eviscerated?* Lost in thought, she paused. Then, "I think we must not long so much for things, for people...to be one way," she now said to Amardeep.

"Why is that?"

"It only makes living more difficult."

"Difficult? In what way?"

"You know, when we are disappointed."

"It is not certain that you will be disappointed."

"It is equally not certain that you will not be." When Amardeep just looked at her, Amrita continued, "I have expected too much from people. I mustn't do that again."

"Expectation is natural. Within bounds, of course, but it is natural. It is what makes life worth living."

"And painful. Very painful. When it is not fulfilled."

"You cannot live without expectation. It is a contradiction. It is just not possible."

"You cannot live with it either. Or at least...," Amrita paused, once again lost in her own thoughts.

"Why must you make more of your suffering than of others?"

"Do I do that?"

"Do you suppose you are the only one to suffer? To have suffered?"

"No, of course I don't."

"I too have suffered. And struggled with it every day," Amardeep spoke almost despite himself.

For a moment, Amrita looked at her brother. She knew he spoke nothing but the truth. He too had suffered. Then, she murmured quietly, "Yes. Do you blame me for not being as strong? I would like to be strong. Really, I would like to be. I have prayed for it."

"You go to such extremes. Either you are negating yourself or you are completely self-indulgent."

"Self-indulgent? Have I been thoughtless of others? I don't wish to be. With all my heart." Amrita looked stricken at this new charge against her. It was true that for a while she had fasted. She told herself that she did this to reorder her thoughts, her desires. To bring them in some sort of alignment. Doing penance for crimes that may have been committed long before she was ever conceived. But here was Amardeep telling her that that, too, was selfish.

"Amu..."

Entering the room, Kundan was greeted by two very solemn faces. "What are you children having this morning?"

"Nothing," said Amrita.

"Can we have French toast?" asked Amardeep, glad to lighten the subject.

"Only if you can get me some bread and eggs. I'm all out."

"All right. Anything else?"

"No, unless you want to get some biscuits or something."

"I'll want an extra piece of toast for my effort."

"I'll have to think about that," Kundan smiled. "What about you Amrita? I know you don't like French toast, but I have some of last night's vegetables...."

"Favoritism...as usual," grinned Amardeep.

"And what about you with your orders for French toast?" retaliated Amrita. "This is not a restaurant, in case you didn't notice."

"Oh, I'm not so sure. With two cooks. Two *women* cooks...," he prodded wickedly, sure of a rise. He was not disappointed.

"Where do you get off with all this talk of women cooks? Mama, don't cook him any breakfast." But Kundan was just laughing and so was Amardeep.

"What's going on?" Gurmehar mumbled, walking into the room. He had a late appointment in the area so he was still walking around with his face held up like an egg in a basket by the cloth around his beard.

"Amrita is just about to give us a talk on how women are more than cooks," Amardeep informed him.

By now Amrita had realized that she had fallen into Amardeep's trap. As usual. "Make sure you get Standard bread," she now said changing the subject.

"Brittania is better for French toast. It holds up better," Amardeep replied.

Kundan stepped in. "Yes. Amardeep is right. For sandwiches Standard is good, but Brittania is bettter for French toast. Just make sure it's fresh."

"I hate doing that. Prodding and pressing."

"You just have to touch it a little. Don't dig into the wrapper. And get a dozen eggs. Brown ones, if you can get them."

"Yeah, I like their color," Amrita joined the conversation.

"What does it matter to you what color they are? You don't even like them."

"But I like to look at them."

Amardeep just rolled his eyes and looked at Kundan.

"Get whatever is available," she said.

"What if both are?" Amardeep persisted as though it was a matter of significance.

"Then get whatever suits your fancy since it is your favorite." Having settled the matter, Kundan left the room with Gurmehar.

Amardeep too turned to go. Before leaving, however, he began, "About last night—"

"It doesn't matter," interrupted Amrita. "I was just being silly. Let's play chess later."

"Okay." If Amrita was ready to play chess again, she must be all right; Amardeep was relieved.

Alone in her room, Amrita went over last night. She now remembered a part of it that had been in danger of being forgotten. She was familiar with this nightmare; she had had it for a while now. It came to her from time to time in different scenarios. Like a puppet master pulling strings according to fancy. Never knowing when it might resurface, kept Amrita anxious.

Last night, once again, she had seen that strange shape. It was

vaguely human in form. And white. So very white. Wherever it
fell it left behind a trail of blood. And it was always running. Last
night, too, it ran ahead. As Amrita ran after it, the white shape ran
to a huge mountain, but the mountain turned into glass over a
pool of blood and would not hide it. Then the white shape ran to
the water, but at its approach the water turned to a pool of blood
reflecting a deadly image. Once again, the white shape turned—

"Amrita... what's wrong? Can't you breathe?"

"Wha...?" Startled, Amrita looked up.

"What were you looking at?" asked Kundan.

"Nothing. You just startled me. What do you want?"

"Just to see what you want for breakfast."

"I said I don't feel like it. I'll have something...I'll have some fruit
later."

"There are grapes...otherwise, the fruit seller should be coming
around soon. You could have fruit *chaat.*"

"Grapes are fine."

"Okay." Kundan left the room but she was not entirely convinced
by Amrita's answer. She was sure she had seen Amrita looking
very peculiarly at the morning light falling on the floor through
the gap in the curtains across the window. She had been breathing heavily, as though she had been running. And she seemed to
have been muttering something under her breath. Something that
had sounded like, "I'll catch you yet."

Amrita was worried. She had not heard from Mandakini for some
time, and her calls had not been returned. They were both used
to talking to each other daily, sometimes several times a day. Amrita thought they knew each other completely. And yet several
days had passed in silence and now here Mandakini was telling
Amrita that something had happened that she needed to really
think about.

"And you didn't want me to know?"

"It's not that. This is...strange."

"You know you can—"

"I know. It concerns my dad."

"Oh?"

"And me and Aslam."

"Oh?"

"I'll tell you when I meet you later this evening."

Mandakini hung up. All afternoon Amrita wondered what it could be. She knew that Mandakini had recently met Aslam Khan and they were already quite serious about each other. He was a couple of years older than Mandakini (who was four years older than Amrita), an Automotive Engineer with a degree from IIT-D. He had a good job with Bajaj Auto Limited, had just bought his own DDA flat in Punjabi Bagh, and had no major responsibilites. He was saving to buy a car. The Khans, his parents, were alive and had an independent income. Noor, his mother, was especially a non-interfering lady. But none of this mattered because he was a Muslim. In Mandakini's family, this fact was an issue only for her father. He did not know that his daughter had been seeing Aslam for some time now behind his back.

That evening Mandakini filled her in. "I want you to understand that my father is supportive of me in all other ways."

"I understand," Amrita assured her.

"But marriage, to him, is a family matter. And so is religion important," Mandakini paused to look at Amrita. Seeing her quietly looking at her, Mandakini continued, "I know he got a little carried away but he did not mean it badly...I mean I am his daughter. Seeing that I am a lecturer and all, he thought...well, he thought he could get me a good match. So he looked further than he might have otherwise looked."

"You have had so many proposals."

Mandakini shrugged in acknowledgement, "Yeah, but he found one party from Poona especially promising. The 'boy' was in the garment business. There was plenty of money. The parents were independently wealthy and the older brother was married and settled in the U.S. There would be no interference and I would rule the household."

Again Amrita nodded.

"I agreed to marry him," Mandakini said.

Blankly, Amrita looked at her friend. "You can't do that. You mustn't do that," she pleaded. "Do you care for this guy?"

"NO," Mandakini shouted.

"Then? I'll have my parents call on your parents. Maybe your father will listen to them."

"There's no need. I don't have to marry him anymore."

"Because you are going to marry Aslam, right?"

"I don't know. I hope so."

"What happened with the other guy? How did you get out of it?"

"They asked me to marry the older brother."

"His brother? I thought he was already married?" By now Amrita was thoroughly confused.

"Well, he was. But he had made a contract marriage with some American woman to get his green card. And now he is getting a divorce."

"What does that have to do with you? You are...were...supposed to be becoming his sister-in-law."

"The parents decided that since he is the older brother, he should be married first...."

"He was married first, he had his chance, he blew it," Amrita almost shouted. "What's wrong with your father? How can he do this to you? After all, he's the one who was pushing you into the arms of the younger brother." Amrita was speaking as though the marriage was still on.

"I think when the parents said that, it changed my father's eyes."

"Thank God. So now have you told him about Aslam?"

"He already knows about that," returned Mandakini. This was all getting to be too much for Amrita, but following her face Mandakini explained. "He chanced to pick up the phone extension and overheard me talking to Aslam," Mandakini continued. "After that I told him everything."

"So now?"

"Well, we have a long way to go, but at least I don't need to hide."

Amrita nodded, marveling at the near-miss life could be.

11 *Flight of a Bird*

AFTER MANDAKINI LEFT, Amrita lay thinking about her. Distracted by a sound at her window, she looked up just in time to see a sparrow bang against it as though startled to find it closed. For a moment it perched precariously on the bar outside knocking persistently with its beak against the glass. Amrita felt it look in bafflement at her and then around, before it flew away.

Seemingly backward.

◗●◖

"Class, is everything clear?" asked Miss Peters.

"Please, Miss, could you give the definition of 'centrifugal' and 'centripetal' again?" Amrita requested. Quiet groans went up as some students looked daggers at Amrita for unnecessarily prolonging their agony. Amrita looked back contritely and fiddled with her new glasses. But the question had already been asked.

"Class, who can define 'centrifugal' and 'centripetal'?" Miss Peters turned the question back to the almost-nine-year-olds. When no one's hand went up, she gave everybody a brief lecture on paying attention and the need to ask questions. "How else will you learn?" she reminded. "Now, one more time. Centrifugal is a force that moves outward from the center. Centripetal is its opposite. It moves toward the center. Understood?"

"Yes, Miss," Amrita echoed with the rest of the class.

At home, balancing Kundan's cup of tea in one hand and biscuits in the other, she wondered, *Can a force be both centrifugal and centripetal?*

"Shall we have some *chaishai Bhai* sahib, *Bhabhi ji?*"

"Come Kundan, is that any type of question? No formality here. Chai, of course. *Nahin,* Nitin *yaar?*"

Nitin Gupta nodded, "No formality, *Bhabhi ji.*"

"Yes, no formality."

"No formality *ji,* no formality," Kundan got up. "It will take but a minute. Come children. You Amardeep, get some cups and saucers, and you Amrita, put some biscuits on a plate." When the children lingered over their toys, she repeated herself more briskly, "You can play later." Hearing the firmness in Kundan's voice, the children scrambled up to do as they were told. Amrita went to the low, metal *jaali* standing unsteadily on the side of the kitchen to get the red, plastic biscuit box. After a few tries, the black lid came off with an *umphh* making the biscuits torpedo up at her.

"Got them? Good. Take any, take both," Kundan directed. Amrita dug her hands inside to peel away the wrappers. One by one, she took them out.

Nice buscuits are rectangular in shape and have tiny crystals of sugar baked into them on top. They make a crunchy sound when you bite and hold up quite well in hot tea. Marie Gold biscuits are round. They have a ring of dots around their circumference and hole-like marks in the middle. Like a leaky round bath toy, they sink quickly—poor, sad garlands—to the bottom of a cup of tea, if dipped for a shade too long. The mush at the bottom of the teacup tastes like a paste of sawdust. Horr-i-ble.

▶ ● ◀

The Nehru *Bal Mela* in the India Gate lawns, next to Children's Park, was bursting with people. There was no parking for miles around. They had had to park their car several streets away and walk to the tented area. Makeshift wire fences kept out the intruders who tried to get in without a ticket. Since Amrita and Amardeep were visiting with Amardeep's friend Titu and his much older brother Neeraj and sister-in-law Meena, they were on their best behavior.

The three children walked ahead, while the young couple followed close behind. It was the first excuse for the couple to be alone in some little way since they had got married. So they had almost jumped at the opportunity to take out the six- and seven-year-olds. At the fair, the wide-eyed children flocked around simple machines spinning old women's hair. Soon, their noses buried in the white candy floss on sticks, they were snickering over the antics of the *kathputli* at a puppet show stall and crowing with triumph every time their darts burst the colored air balloons on a game wall. In the colored lights and deliciously playful breeze, the sparkling stream of visitors—mostly families out for fun and laughter—were almost as fascinating to Amrita. She heard snatches of conversation and tried to figure out the rest in her mind.

"Is P.C. Sarkar going to be here?"

"I thought it was Gogia Pasha. Wasn't he Sarkar's student? He is supposed to be better than him."

Amrita had seen P.C. Sarkar's show on television many times. Cutting beautiful girls into pieces and restoring them to wholeness again. His hallmark, however, was the ornate goblet that remained sitting on a small table throughout the show. Each time, between acts, he paused and, with a flourish, raised the goblet and tipped it, pouring out a stream of water. "And this is the water of India." After each time he said this, he turned the goblet upside down and shook it. To show that it was empty. But the water of India was a never-ending stream that continued to flow.

Arriving at the pavillion that held five talking human heads on top of silver platters, Amrita gazed in open-mouth fascination. Along with the others, she, too, lifted the cloth skirt of the table to search for the rest of their bodies. But along with the others, she, too, could not find them.

"It looks like...," Amrita began.

"Never mind what it looks like. Things can often appear one way, but...," and Neeraj mentioned the concept of illusion.

"HowHow?" Amrita wanted to know. "Who appears it?"

Both Titu and Amardeep echoed Neeraj, but when Amrita asked them for further clarification, neither could explain how exactly it worked.

Rather than lose face, they tried to distract her by pointing to the giant wheel. Amrita loved the giant wheel. It was a completely different experience from the tame ride on the wooden animals on the slow turning merry-go-rounds that toured the neighborhoods or even the brief and bumpy ride around the block on the occasional real elephant or camel. "Ai-lae-faint r-i-i-de." "Kaa-mul r-i-i-de." Neeraj arranged the giant wheel ride. It was decided that the three children would ride in one seat and the grown-ups would watch from the ground. Amrita sat in the middle. The man helping the people into the seats told everyone to sit back and then locked the safety bar in place with a latch.

Round and round they went. Amrita liked the sensation when they went up—a little closer to the stars—but felt her heart fall inside her body as they swooped low toward the ground.

After the second turn, the wheel came to a rest to drop off old passengers and pick up new ones. They were positioned right on top. Amrita was a little scared. Sensitive to the wind, their seat swayed gently to its rhythm. Amrita looked down. This did not help; it only made her nauseated. Titu teased her. Ignoring Amardeep, he pretended to remove the latch on the bar of their seat. Amrita's heart beat even faster but she was determined not to say anything. Without turning her neck much, from between her lashes, she tried to focus on the view. She could see over the tops of trees and buildings. The city looked different from on top. The entire Rajpath looked magnificent in the cold winter night.

"There's Collin's Uncle. CollinsUncle, CollinsUncle," Amrita leaned forward dangerously.

Then the wheel began to move and they were down again. On the ground. Collin's Uncle was nowhere to be seen. Titu looked at Amrita. She looked back. He did not get a scolding from his brother.

Back from the fair, Amrita rushed to do her homework. "Think, thunk...," chanted little Amrita learning her English lesson for Miss Gibson's class.

"Not 'thunk,' 'thought,'" Kundan interrupted her daughter's lesson.

"But 'thunk' sou-nds better," Amrita insisted.

Privately, Kundan agreed. "Thunk" did sound better. There was a fullness to its sound that the word "thought" did not have. But English language has its rules that like its people demand to be followed. Loudly Kundan explained present and past tense to her daughter, "Learning a language is like making a new friend. You have to learn to speak their way and think their way. And the only way you can do that is by tracing the language to its roots."

At school, lessons were even more difficult to avoid. And Amrita worried about the future of the tense.

Courage is...?

All the children followed the two, thick, hairy, waving wands of Mr. Bowles as he conducted the class like a new song. Amrita looked at Miss Gibson's substitute, then looked at her classmates making faces for this ordeal to be over. They were already cadets in training for their hard hats.

"What is the exactmeaning of...?"

Before Amrita could complete her sentence, Amardeep said, "I don't know, lookitup."

"Papa..."

"You must look it up yourself. There's the dictionary."

Now, Amrita got up to drag open the correct volume of the *Oxford English Dictionary.* Her father had got the set secondhand from Nai Sarak in Chandni Chowk. And it was one of his prized possessions.

Amrita was especially fascinated by etymologies. The dictionary traced the history of the words from one language to another as far back in time as possible.

Amrita wondered, *Does courage mean to have a large heart? And how large is large enough?*

But just then a popular song from *Johny Mera Naam* blaring from a passing bicyclist's transistor reached Amrita's ear. Distracted immediately, she covered her mouth with a steel glass and began to joyfully croon the catchy duet.

Oo oo mere Raja, oo oo mere Raja
Oo oo my King, oo oo my King
khafa na hona
don't be angry
der se aayi, door se aayi
came late, came from far
...something, something...
vaada to nibhaya
kept my promise.

Amrita repeated the lyrics, singing them enthusiastically first in Hindi and then in English, enunciating the words clearly and with expression. And laughed hilariously at the funniness of the literal translation that didn't allow the association of gender with verb and so left the singer singing genderlessly.

"Silly goon," Amardeep grinned at first. But when that only encouraged Amrita, he protested, "Mummy, Amu is making a noise."

"Keep it down." Kundan raised her voice from inside.

"Oo oo mere Raja," Amrita continued to whisper the lyrics.

Later that night, tired from arguing, brother and sister lay on either side of their mother on a cot in the back courtyard waiting for Gurmehar to come home.

"Once upon a time—"

"WhenMummyWhen?" interrupted Amrita.

"A long time ago," Kundan said wisely, "a ve-ry long time ago. There were two little...people."

"Were they boy or girl?" Amrita interrupted again. She liked things to be precise. But Amardeep was getting tired of Amrita's interruptions. Now Amardeep leaned over his mother and pinched Amrita, telling her to keep quiet or they would never hear the end of the story. Amrita contorted her face ready to retaliate yet wondered how far she could go without jeopardizing hearing the end of the story. Kundan put an end to this struggle by silently squeezing them both to her side. They stopped at once.

"One was called Fear and the other was called Happiness," she continued.

Both children thought they were funny names for people but stuffed their exaggerated smirks and giggles under their pressed fingers on their mouths.

"Now, you must be careful with Fear because it often masquerades as Anger," Kundan warned.

"Mas-kur-ades?" This, from Amrita.

"Yes, like wearing a disguise. So that you look different on the outside from what you are on the inside."

"Where did they live?" Amrita wondered aloud.

Kundan pointed up at the sky, "They lived on the moon."

"Do they still live there?" This time the question came from Amardeep despite himself.

"Yes," Kundan replied quietly. "Fear rules the dark side. It is a tiny little monster that can creep into your life unseen. A monster with two legs. Hatred and Hurt. And on these it crawls to fester and grow. But on the bright side lives Happiness. It has three legs. Love and Faith and Hope.

"Hatred rests on a lonely, parched land. Hurt slouches in a deep well. Love, Faith, and Hope flow in mountains, streams, and valleys of flowers."

"But Mummy I have onlytwolegs," Amrita started in almost a wail. Then, "Canyou escape frommthe dark side? Canyou? Canyou? HowMummyHow?"

"You jollywell know it's a story, you stu-pid, like a fab-le," Amardeep rolled out a laugh and once again leaned over to pinch Amrita.

English is a strange language. Containing tunnels down which you can slip into the ground. And wells that are name-plated happy. They rollick with laughter. But are actually sad. Amrita was worried about being lost in the desert or falling into the well by mistake and not knowing how to get out. She wanted answers.

Meaning must be made. Morals must be stated. And therefore the story must be complete. With a beginning, a middle, and an end. It was frightening to be left with a question mark. And un-thinkable, that, sometimes, there are no immediate endings. Nor, when they do occur, are they necessarily clear or satisfying.

Amardeep, however, would not be ignored, and so Amrita retaliated in kind, and the two chased each other round the courtyard till they both forgot about the moon and its inhabitants.

12   *Down Memory Lane*

SINCE THE ACCIDENT, Gurmehar and Kundan had not left Amrita's side for longer than was absolutely necessary. Every night, Amrita heard her father pace up and down the back courtyard, when he thought everyone was asleep. She wondered if Kundan and Amardeep lay in their beds and wore down the soles of their mental shoes as well. In any case, it was almost six weeks after her accident, and Amrita needed to shed the burden of their presence as she skipped between the past and present.

"Mama, you haven't been out in so long," she began.

"We haven't missed anything."

"Still, it will be a change."

"Amar is also not at home...."

"Really, Mama, it's okay. You both should go. You could get me a patty from that small store on Janpath. Make sure it's vegetarian. No, get me two. One veggie and one mutton."

This was the first time in a long while Amrita had expressed an interest in anything, so Kundan and Gurmehar got up to go. Gurmehar in a starched white *kurta pajama* and black *jalsa jooti* and Kundan in a chiffon sari of pale pink with painted mauve flowers that had a very slender, pale green stem running through them. After one last expression of concern for Amrita, they stepped out of the house. Outside, Mrs. Mahindra was taking a stroll with her older daughter and young grandson.

"Who is that little child Neera is holding?" Gurmehar whispered to Kundan.

"Tony, her son."

"They have...cut his hair." Then, "Even Mahindra."

"Yes, look at the times."

"Hello *ji,*" Mrs. Mahindra called out to them.

"Hello, how are you?" asked Kundan.

"Mahindra *ji* is well, I trust?" asked Gurmehar.

"He just finished his evening meal and is now taking a brief rest." It was a well-known fact that Mr. and Mrs. Mahindra, though married for almost three decades, led independent lives. Completely unsuited in temperament, Mr. Mahindra was a religiously conservative man while Mrs. Mahindra was a woman with deep desires that had never been expressed. Still, they had lived together under one roof all this time without anyone ever having heard a raised voice. Only in private did Mrs. Mahindra sometimes speak of her dissatisfaction. That, and the way she looked at Kundan and Gurmehar gave her away.

"*Namaste* Aunty, Uncle," Neera greeted them cheerily.

"*Namaste beta.* How are you?"

"Where are you off to?" asked Mrs. Mahindra.

"Just to CP. We want to get back soon. Amar is also not home, but Amrita insisted," Kundan replied.

"Don't worry, I'll keep an eye out."

"Thank you. We must get together soon, have a cup of tea," Kundan promised Mrs. Mahindra and then walked on down the street with Gurmehar via Super Bazaar to the inner circle. As they approached the crossing at Nirula's, they looked at the crowds of people, especially the younger age group, gathered outside just waiting their turn to go in. Everyone seemed to be laughing loudly and without inhibition. They looked at each other—*Would Amrita be there again?*

From Nirula's they moved forward toward Janpath. There were a lot of Afghanis in the area. Some of them, walking along in the opposite direction, keenly watched the crowds. Kundan stepped aside to allow a lurching group of men to pass by. In a corner, a very fair, bald, blue-eyed, young *sadhu* sat on his bit of ochre cloth. A short, fat piece of incense hung a cloud of sickly sweet smell over him. Worry beads in hand, this Hare Krishna novice was surrounded by a group of laughing people who were more interested in him than in buying copies of the *Mahabharata* on sale. Along the corridors, there were makeshift stalls of knickknacks like hairpins and rubber bands. All types of foreign goods were on display. Sleek Ray-Bans sitting side by side with local brands of sunglasses. "Goggils, goggils, forin goggils," the vendors waved their wares in people's faces.

"Remember that time we went for a picnic and boating at night? Remember that couple in the other boat—the woman was wearing goggles at night because she did not want to be recognized by anyone under any circumstances," Kundan couldn't help smiling.

Gurmehar laughed. There had been so many times, but he knew exactly which time Kundan was talking about. Amrita had just got her glasses then.

"And then Amrita wanted to wear goggles too because she thought it was something you just did on the water," Kundan continued. They had bought the children cheap, plastic-rimmed goggles from the vendor who had gravitated toward them having smelled a sale. Pretty, neon-colored shades of green and yellow; however, they had turned the world dark in the surrounding darkness.

They had been much more fun the next day. When Kundan heard the squeals of delight coming from the back courtyard, she had rushed out just in time to save the little, antique chair in which Amrita sat regally wearing her yellow goggles in her hair like a two-humped crown while Amardeep pulled her around. ("Ai-lae-faint r-i-i-de." "Kaa-mul r-i-i-de.") She was the Queen, she had said.

"And what about when Pyaari *pehnji* came for the first time?" Gurmehar laughed lightly.

"I remember. 'I am the moon,' she said." Kundan remembered that day vividly. Amrita's innocent remark had broken the ice. Gurmehar had been introducing the children one by one. Bringing

Amardeep forward, he had proudly announced, "This is my son, Amardeep." Seeing no reason why she too shouldn't be part of the solar system, Amrita had piped up, "I am the moon." When the grownups had burst into laughter, Amrita had looked at Amardeep for company. But seeing him laughing as well, she had become confused and ran to her father. Gurmehar had tenderly gathered her into his side and said, "Yes, that's right. This is the moon, my moon."

Both Kundan and Gurmehar's smiles carried a hint of joy and pain.

"Another time we must stop by Bangla Sahib."

"Yes. Is that...?" suddenly Kundan's fingers stiffened their hold on Gurmehar's arm.

"Where? Where?" When Gurmehar looked up, she nodded slightly toward the couple who had caught her attention. Standing behind a pillar was Makhan Singh with his family. While the mother was buying a balloon for her son, the father was leaning down indulgently toward a young girl—his daughter presumably. Watching the scene, Gurmehar's body turned rigid, and he began muttering to himself. Kundan hurried him away.

As a young girl carrying on her head a wicker basket that seemed bigger than her body approached them, Kundan turned to Gurmehar. He asked her, "Do you want one?"

"I'm too old for it now," she demurred slightly.

"Nonsense. Child," he called to the young girl. She came and lowered the basket on to the ground. It contained *gajras,* hand-strung *motia* flowers in a thick strand.

"Which one will you have?"

"Any. They are all beautiful."

Gurmehar picked one, inhaled from it deeply, and paid for it. "Can you tie it around your *joora* or do you need a mirror?"

"No, no, I'm too old. I'll feel silly. I'll hold it." Seeing Gurmehar's face fall, she said, "Remember when it did not feel silly?"

Gurmehar nodded.

"There were so many sellers there then. At the Boat Club."

Gurmehar nodded again.

"You always bought me these flowers and..."

"...And you always wore them."

▶ ● ◀

Amrita was glad that her parents had gone out for a while. Now she could follow them at her own pace, continue her task of heating and hammering in the hearth. Molding metal, tracing patterns.

Like a tourist guide.

Connaught Place. Delhites affectionately call it CP.

The nerve center of Delhi. Its heart. With roads like arteries carrying blood and life to the economic and cultural structure of the city. Amrita felt dizzy just thinking of those similar-height, white-painted buildings in concentric circles. The inner circle has a corridor or covered veranda running in front held up by imperious pillars. All circles are connected by veins of miscellaneous stores and shops. Stunning printed, painted, embroidered zari and zardozi work saris, *lehngas* and *salwar kameez* in bright hues and materials; two- and three-piece men's suits and suiting materials in subdued tones; shirting in the finest cotton, polyester, and silk; beaded sandals and leather shoes with narrow, rounded, and open toes; mini, midi, and maxi skirts with fancy tops and scarves; jewelry in brass, silver, and gold studded with glass or precious stones; sporting goods; high-end kitchen appliances; dried fruit and fresh fruit; rare books and best sellers; practical and not-so-practical home decor; and pretty much anything needed to enhance living can be bought here. Above these stores there are apartments, but who lives in them is a mystery. With the spurt of economic growth in the country, however, more and more businesses are taking over the upper levels of space, thus dissipating the mystery.

Neatly tucked away or facing each other on both sides of the streets are various cinema houses. Many have developed a reputation for the various kinds of films they carry—foreign or domestic-traditional or domestic-artsy or domestic-A-rated.

Posters posters everywhere. New ones are just pasted over old ones. Images of jutting breasts, perkily tantalizing in low-cut *cholis,* pasted over a woman cacooned in a sari bent over an infant. Images of male and female contorted limbs pasted over images of two hopelessly entangled bicycles or two flowers leaning into each other. Images of Silky Smita and Thunder Thighs pasted over images of the latest performance by Bhimsen Joshi or Hariprasad Chaurasia at the Kamani Auditorium.

Side by side with posters of domestic films are posters for foreign films. These days it is difficult to make out the difference. In front of a cinema showing an A-rated film, just before the beginning of a show, you can see people (mostly men) standing outside in a line with their back to the street. They seem not to want anyone to recognize them. At other times you may see clusters of the new wave of young actors gathered outside the small cinema houses coaxing audiences into a viewing.

And for local flavor you come to the outer ring of *khokas* and *dhabas.* These roadside restaurants, formerly favored by truckers and taxi drivers and laborers, witnessed a spurt of growth in the late 1970s when they suddenly began to symbolize national culture.

Meenu always came with Girish. And she of course with Amardeep. They parked here on their motorbikes. All of them nouveau nationalists, a quick and easy way to embrace "Indian culture" while wearing foreign jeans, speaking Hindi with an English accent, and refusing the same cuisine in their own homes. The older generation, not quite able to go this far and yet feeling the impact of the neo-nationalists, tried to do the same by visiting the new or newly named (with Indian names) restaurants that were opening up in fancy five-star hotels. Some others did lose their reticence enough to actually make the trip to these *dhabas* that were known for their excellent-quality, clay-oven food. But they never made it inside. They waited outside to pick up the food and thus started a new trend of car dining. This only increased the traffic on the already busy road.

"Gosh Amrita, this is so good. It doesn't taste like a vegetable at all. More like mutton."

"They probably used the same cooking spoon for both."

A bazaar sits at the center like a giant mass of lonely pollen in the heart of a flower with rings of petals spreading outward. Once a proud tabletop of entertainment, today you must descend here. Dingy and claustrophobic, despite neon lighting and bright shop fronts, exaggerated smells of cold, stale urine emanate from bathrooms. Paan lovers curl their tongues around their teeth to flick and collect the remains of their betel leaves into a wet ball before spitting it out with full force. Often, the spitoons that the municipal government had so thoughtfully provided remain, on the inside, as clean as the day on which they were installed. Outside, they are marked by streaks of maroon-and-purple-colored, misaimed fibrous spittle.

In contrast, the twin towers reach upward. Neither the three-dimensional technology nor the heat-reflective glass balance the assymmetry of this structure in relation to the other buildings. Phallic monuments reminiscent of other asymmetries about how many children one may have and who may have them.

On the streets and all around the corridors is the press and jostle of vendors and other bodies as everyone weaves their way in and out.

"Let's get our palms read."
"I don't believe in it."

The different state emporiums offer some measure of controlled comfort.
"It's hard to resist the stuff here."
"Tell me about it..."
"I don't really have a settled place."

When it comes to dining, there are many options. In the days following independence, the flavor of British times was still reflected in some of their decor and entertainment. Nightly cabaret shows with brown sahibs along with their "Mrs." or "girlfriends" (smiling to show their participation in their independence) watched scantily clad, nubile young girls gyrate to pulsating alien rhythms. *Langoors. Angoors.* Like laburnums.

The new morality of the neo-nationalists has moved the people toward a decor and entertainment more in keeping with their indigeneous (or perception of) post-independence self-image. The decor often harks back to ancient India or is vaguely futuristic; similarly, entertainment, which is usually musical, may be piped through cleverly hidden microphones or it may be served up with an aura of aplomb by B-grade artists who perform to the new crop of Indians as they try to teach their children a quick and easy history lesson.

The heart of Delhi. With roads and streets running inward and outward, receiving blood and pumping it back.

Amrita traveled each and every road of Connaught Place. Like a botanist studying the anatomy and morphology of a leaf on a vascular plant stem. If only brick and mortar could talk, what stories would it tell? And would it berate her for taking it all for granted? Or even for wanting to clog the pores?

Weaving in and out of memory, she traveled with a heavy heart toward the Boat Club.

Here the breeze blew more openly. Invitingly. She could see the wide expanse of lawns flanking Rajpath and cut in the middle by two shallow, man-made streams. There were a few boats tied to the landing. They were bobbing up and down. Others were bobbing at a distance. From *karamchari* unions to Environmental Protection Agencies protesting the dangers of deforestation, all meet here, with each maintaining the superiority of its own ideal and place in the giant wheel of national welfare. Several bus stops form little nodules of crowds. Around them sit poor blind people brailling their reality and poor lepers begging for their livelihood and their place in the scheme of things. Little shops selling juice and snacks provide everyone with (guilty) sustenance as they wait in long lines for their buses. Over the years, the more athletic people have managed to get permission to play volleyball in one of the grounds adjacent to the streams. Now, in addition to the crowds waiting to catch a bus, there are huge crowds of watchers of these daily games.

And then there are national games. And international ones. Sometimes lost, sometimes won. To beat the retreat. As the bugle blows its last call when the dusk is falling at the close of day, troops march up and down and sideways, arranging and rearranging themselves in formations that seem to furl and unfurl like buds becoming blooms.

13 *A Cool Evening and a Hot Afternoon*

"MY ASSIGNMENT IS for a year." Franz's words fell like stones into the water, sinking quickly.

"A year?" Amrita's voice shook a little as though touched by a falling stone.

"There are no fixed dates, you know how these government plans go, but more or less."

"Will that give you time to do everything?"

"That's the plan."

"Plans can change."

"Rarely. There's money at stake."

"And then what will you do?"

"It's too far off. I haven't thought about it."

"You are too easy."

"Are you miffed about something?"

"No, it's a beautiful night, isn't it?"

"Yes it is."

Amrita blushed. He was looking at her.

Amrita and Franz were boating at the Boat Club. It was after her German class, so it was getting late. About eight thirty or so. The surrounding trees threw their own cover of darkness over the boaters. Their vague, distorted reflection in the water made it look more murky than usual. But as Franz and Amrita moved into the stream, the vendors' lights receded palely, and the night sky became more visible; the stars sat in their assigned seats twinkling occasionally as though in a secret wink.

"I mustn't be too late. I don't want to get into trouble with my parents," Amrita broke the silence.

"But you are with me. They know that."

"Don't be offended. It has nothing to do with you. That's just the way it is. I'm lucky to be out with you at all. Many of my friends would not be able to do so."

For a while both were quiet. Then, "How imposing it looks," Franz observed. Amrita needed no explanation. She, too, was looking at the sprawling structure in pink.

"Hmm, but you really need to stand in front of the National Stadium and look straight in through the arch of India Gate to appreciate it totally."

For a while, they were quiet again. Satisfied by an inexplicable fullness in the night air and the pleasantness of their own thoughts.

"So why did you want to go boating at night?" Amrita broke the silence.

"For starters, because you have spoken so much about it. You seem to love it...."

"That's true," Amrita grinned irrepressibly. As Franz tried to lean forward, the boat began to tilt and move against the bank so he immediately moved back. Amrita could not help laughing gently at the chagrin on his face. They had rowed the boat a little distance from the starting point and then let it drift. Though there were other boaters close by and crowds of walkers and sellers all around, they had been pretending they were all alone in the open sea.

"I am the Queen of the Nile and you, sir, are but Mark Antony."

Franz bowed slightly and carefully and with a flourish. "Cleopatra—"

"My Queen," she interrupted.

"My Queen, Mark Antony at your service. Where would your pleasure take you tonight?"

"My pleasure would have me...," Amrita stopped herself.

"Yes, my Queen?" Franz prodded.

"Oh but this is such a narrow stream. A few laps and you hit against a side."

"I will have my men widen the stream.... And what else would you have them do?" asked Franz continuing the charade. Amrita was laughing so hard she couldn't reply.

"And what else would you have them do? Make it more than a few feet deep?"

By now Amrita had given up all pretense of playing. She was doubled with laughter.

"Don't laugh at me," Franz suddenly said.

"I'm not laughing at you," Amrita sputtered.

"Don't laugh at me," he repeated seriously.

"I'm not laughing at you," Amrita looked at him wonderingly. "I'm just...laughing. You are very serious tonight. You said you wanted to tell me something. But I think you just said that to see me." There was a teasing gleam in Amrita's eyes, but she kept it carefully banked.

Franz took a slender, red box from his pocket, careful not to rock the boat. He extended it to Amrita.

"What is it?" she asked even as she opened it. "Oh my!"

"Happy Birthday to you. Happy Birthday to you," Franz whispered under his breath.

"But it's not my birthday. I told you my birthday is in November," she protested.

"Happy New Year to you, Happy New Year to you," this time Franz whispered a slightly different song.

"Really Franz, in April? Though technically there is the Indian New—"

"Does there have to be a reason?" Franz interrupted. "I just saw these and thought of you."

"But I can't take them. They must be so ex—"

"Don't you like them?"

"Of course I do. Who wouldn't?" There in front of her lay two, perfect, heart-shaped gold earrings.

"Then take them."

"Okay, thanks. But I don't dare to move from my seat. The boat may just tip over." Even Franz was beginning to feel frustrated by the limitations of being in the boat.

"Let's go back," he now said. And he began to row the boat back to the landing stage.

Walking up and down the classroom the next day, Amrita was busy talking about the separation between the different branches of the government. "Any questions, observations ?" she ended as usual.

"Yes," Sanjay raised his hand.

"Go ahead," Amrita nodded.

"Technically, the principle is understandable, but don't you think sometimes it hinders more than it helps?"

"In what way?" Amrita turned the question back to him.

"Well, the system is so slow—"

"Slow or thorough?" Nita interrupted Sanjay impatiently.

"Slow."

"Thorough, I think. That's what checks and balances are meant to be."

"There is a gap between what's meant to be and what is...."

"Let one person finish before another begins," Amrita calmly intervened. "Let Sanjay explain himself...then I'd like to hear your response, Nita. Yes, Sanjay, you were saying..."

"It is not the purpose behind the division that I doubt. It is..."

"Yes...?" Amrita encouragingly prodded him.

"It is the fact that ordinary people get lost in the mechanism of the system. I mean, the common person is shunted from one branch to the next and from office to office, trying to seek justice."

"What does this have to do with the separation between the different branches of government?" Nita could not keep quiet anymore. As Amrita turned toward her, she stopped but Amrita indicated she should go on. "The separation between the branches is meant to safeguard the interests of the individuals...."

"Precisely, it is *meant* to, but does it?" Sanjay was belligerent.

"Well, not all the time...," Monica joined the debate.

"Fifty percent of the time? Eighty percent? Are you willing to be part of the fifty, twenty, or any percentage that does not fall into this category?"

"You are taking this too personally," Prakash smiled. Then, turning to Nita and Monica, he repeated himself, "He's taking this too personally."

"And you are not taking this personally enough," Maninder took Sanjay's side.

Sanjay nodded, "The point of being responsible citizens is to measure to what degree the system works for us. Once again, I repeat, it is not the fact of the division that I disagree with, it is the way in which the actual system operates."

"And how does it operate?" This time Amrita intervened.

"It operates often with blindness. It disregards the individual, tossing him from side to side, from door to door, dragging out the process of government."

"Doesn't the individual deserve the attention, the thoroughness, that this system implies—so as to safeguard against injustice?" This time Nita's question was swift. Like a shaft, it found its victim.

"Yes, the individual deserves attention, but dragging issues over long periods of time when the individual has insufficient or no funds serves no purpose."

"And is that the responsibility of the government?"

"Of course, it is...."

"If the government started taking into account the individual circumstances of people, the business of government would never get done."

"What is it there for then?"

"Who?"

"The government."

"To govern."

"Yes, but *for whom?*"

"The people, of course."

"Ah ha, precisely, the people, and yet it is these very people who are lost in the long and overcrowded halls of justice. No, let me correct myself, these are not halls of justice, these are halls of individual egos." Sanjay's eyes were lit by some deep emotion. Amrita wondered what personal demons had fired his response. Before she could intervene, Nita began.

"So what would you have—no separation between the branches? And do you not think that will lead to other forms of corruption?"

"No, I do not doubt the ills that would most certainly result from that, but I would propose a swifter, more efficient form of dispensation of issues. There is more to life than that, you know, there is more to life than that."

Just that moment Amrita felt as though she was being observed. Sure enough, looking up she saw that Franz was lounging against the stone balustrade wrapping around the corridor outside the classrooms. She wondered how long he had been standing there without her knowledge. As she glanced toward him, he sketched her a swift salute. Amrita turned away, not wanting the gesture to be noticed by the students. Even when the class got over and the last student hurried out of the room, she remained at her desk looking over her files.

"May I come in Ms. Chaddha?"

"You are already in," Amrita suppressed a smile, trying her best schoolmarm impression.

"Will you not look up?"

"No."

"Never?"

"No."

"No never, or no you will sometime?"

"Sneaky."

"What me?"

When Amrita still didn't look up, Franz raised his voice to a squeak, "What me?"

Amrita couldn't help it. She looked up with laughter in her voice, "You shouldn't be here you know."

"I wanted to see you."

"You just saw me last night at the Boat Club."

"Was it last night? It seems so long ago."

"It was last night."

"I wanted to see you in the classroom. You didn't look up."

"I was afraid I would be nervous with you watching me."

"But you weren't."

"Wasn't I?" Then, "What are you doing here at this time anyway? Didn't you have a meeting with Rajiv Sehgal?"

Franz pursed his lips, "Another wild goose chase."

"Oh no, not another trip. You just got back."

"I'm afraid so."

"What is it this time?"

"More data. I swear the man loves numbers."

"The meeting ended very quickly."

"That's because we never had it."

"Never had it—how?" Amrita was puzzled.

"Well, it was like this... I arrived at his office to find he wasn't there—can we go somewhere for a coffee?"

"I'm done, so let me get my things together here and we can go to CP. Is that fine or do you have to wait to meet Sehgal again?"

"No, let's go. I'm done waiting for today. So where were we?" And Amrita and Franz strolled out of the classroom.

Driving through the midday traffic, they reached CP in no time. Parking the car in a side street, they decided to walk toward Janpath.

"So where to next?" asked Amrita.

"I thought we'd just take a stroll...," began Franz.

"No," laughed Amrita, "I meant...with Rajiv Sehgal. Seems like he's doing everything he can to stump you."

"He's not going to succeed," Franz was adamant.

For a moment, Amrita looked at him. Franz's face was frozen in determination. Skin flushed. Lines etched. Nostrils slightly flared in deep breath. Eyes narrowed in flinty focus. Their cold lenses like barriers between him and the world. Who was this man after all? What did she really know of him? So it was to her surprise when she actually heard herself say, "Who are you?"

Franz looked at her, "Who am I?"

"Yes, who are you?" Having set herself a course, Amrita decided to stay on it.

"Are you serious?"

"Of course I am. I have never seen you like this before."

Franz shrugged, "Sehgal is testing me. He left a lengthy document for me, ostensibly suggestions, and oh a sketchy 'sorry but had to run.' I know I can do this and he needs to understand that."

"What suggestions?"

"He wants me to go to Kanpur."

"Kanpur?"

"Actually, a village nearby."

"What for?" There was dismay in Amrita's voice.

"He wants me to do a survey among the villagers there."

"Do you have to?"

"Have to."

"How long?"

"I don't know exactly, but hopefully not too long."

"So what are you going to do next?"

"Nothing."

"Nothing?"

"That's it. Nothing."

"Isn't that what he wants?"

"Yes, if it were for real. But it will not be."

"What do you mean?"

"I will give him what he wants for a while, and then…" Franz left his sentence unfinished and just smiled at Amrita.

"And then you'll reappear. That's devious."

"Isn't it?" said Franz, and grinned. "How about a cold coffee?"

14 *And This is the Water of India*

THERE IS NO Lost and Found for lost souls. Souls, once lost, can be lost forever, cast adrift by the undertow of their own emotions to rattle and wheeze in an abyss of despair.

Of all afflictions, forgetfulness is the worst. It is like cutting off one's own legs. For when one does not remember where one came from, one is truly lost; there is no way of going home.

Memory has a long reach. It can reach far and deep into the caverns of the body down to the very soles of the feet, turning human flesh inside out. The skeleton, now, a series of horizontal and vertical bars holding its slumping form. Exposing veins and arteries that run like a maze of streets carrying secrets to and from the heart. Pink. Plump. Palpitating. Throbbing with meaning. Imprints of direction.

Two hours after Gurmehar and Kundan left for CP, the phone rang. It was Amardeep.

"I'll be another hour."

"Where are you?"

"At Minnie's. I'm just starting back."

"Okay."

"Go ahead and have dinner."

"Actually, MamaPapa are still not back...."

"You are alone?"

"Yeah."

"I'll be there soon."

"Don't rush." She put down the phone. And looked around.

The night air was cool. Blowing the curtain mildly. Outside Mrs. Munjal called Madhumati's name. She called back. A motorcycle revved then raced then receded. In the ensuing silence, Amrita leaned forward and picked up the radio. Fiddling around stations and garbled incomplete sounds till she hit upon a relay of a *mushaira*.

Na kisi ki aankh ka noor hoon, na kisi ke dil ka karaar hoon;
jo kisi ke kaam na aa sake, ik musht wo gubaar hoon.
Neither the light of anyone's life, nor the solace of anyone's heart;
I am but a useless handful of dust.

Bahadur Shah Zafar's lamentation rang in her heart.

Delhi. A gigantic landscape that ingests and assimilates all who pass through its caverns. Over and over again, Delhi has been the seat of the Empire. The river Yamuna provides a vital source for drinking water and commerce. Delhi's strategic location between the hills and the desert in the south and the mountain ranges in the north, created a corridor between Old Punjab and India. It therefore holds a pivotal position. With each reign, architecture and urban morphology were affected. The ruins of almost all previous cities of Delhi are still visible. These stones speak of a history of power and glory as the city was reborn each time of its own ashes.

Over the ages, the city has been referred to by different names, but mostly the name Delhi has retained and carried this mystique. The ancient history and urban settlements in and around Delhi are limited neither in space nor time.

"Amm-ri-taa. Amm-ri-taa."

"Franz, I'm here."

"What took you so long?"

"Mandakini was delayed...."

"I've been waiting for a while."

"I know, but I couldn't help it. There was no way of letting you know." Amrita placed her hand gently on Franz's shoulder.

"I was about to give up."

"Good, you didn't. There was some confusion over which entrance we were supposed to meet," Amrita smiled.

"Why do we have to do this anyway?"

Amrita withdrew her hand. "I have already explained to you. The Ides of March, her birthday last weekend, so I wanted us to do something. Come on, it will be fun."

"I had something else planned for us."

"We'll do that next time."

By now Mandakini had paid the scooter wallah and come forward. "It's all my fault, Franz," she grinned.

"Yes, it is," Amrita grinned back. "I have already said so."

Mandakini kept grinning unrepentantly.

"So where to? Is there an exhibition going on?"

"Aren't we going to Appu Ghar?"

"Let's do that. Game, Franz?" Amrita pulled Franz toward the game park.

"Sure, why not," he replied, pulling Amrita to his side.

"Don't mind me," Mandakini spoke from the side.

"We won't," Amrita and Franz returned together. Watching them hold hands, just grinning, Mandakini had to smile. They did not notice.

"So do you know which ride you want to go on?" Amrita asked.

"Let's start with this one right here." Right in front was a giant wheel suspended several feet above the ground by a thick pole. At the base, a tiny man stooped over some controls. He was oblivious of the crowds surrounding him. Long spokes issued like arrows from the center to end in cozy two-seaters. The entire contraption was positioned at what looked like an impossible, not-quite-horizontal-or-vertical angle.

"Amrita, listen," Mandakini leaned conspiratorily into Amrita as Franz moved ahead to buy tickets.

"What is it?"

"Will you sit with me? I don't want to sit alone."

"Okay."

"Will Franz mind?"

"Why should he? It's not a big deal."

"I mean..."

"It's just a ride." When Franz returned with the tickets, Amrita told him, "I will sit with Mandakini."

Franz looked up, nodded, then got into the seat next to them.

"Do you think we can topple?" Mandakini was worried.

"I'm sure that's possible," Amrita grinned.

"How is Aslam?" Franz asked Mandakini, distracting her.

"At work, he couldn't get away."

"It's beginning to move," Amrita raised her voice a little. "Oh my God, this is weird."

"Give me your hand Amrita," Franz stretched out his hand. He was sitting sprawled across his seat. No one had taken the seat next to him. Now he was turned sideways, leaning back.

"I'm scared to let go of the side," Amrita laughed with exhiliration and a little nervousness.

"Just reach."

"I can't."

"Just do it, Amrita," Franz insisted.

Amrita opened her eyes. She did not realize she had had them shut. Ahead of her, some men were also turned backward, mimicking Franz's accent, "Jusst dooh itt Aamritaa." She stretched her hand. Franz laced his fingers through hers, a lazy smile lingering in his gaze. The wheel was not spinning at any great speed. As Amrita looked around, she spotted a big-built man standing quietly on the side. Slightly bent, as though weighed down by a permanent weight. *"Arre o Samba,"* one of the men ahead had also spotted him. *"Tera kya hoga kaliya,"* said his companion. Both men burst into laughter. Gray hair wrapped in thick curls of salt and pepper around his head and face, the burly figure was looking in Amrita's direction. When she raised her hand in a brief wave, he nodded imperceptibly before folding his inscrutable eyes into his dark shadow.

"Who is that?" Franz too had seen the darker-hued man and heard the mockery. "Anglo Indian? South Indian?"

"That's Edward Collins. He's from America originally, but he came here...oh, I don't know, he seems to have been here forever."

"America?"

"Some small town near Chicago."

"Is he the Collins Uncle you told me about?" Mandakini asked.

"That's the one," Amrita nodded, then turned to Franz. "He's a very private man. He lives in the house on the corner of our street, the one with the red gate. On rent. He never bought a house. He lives very meagerly, with hardly any possessions. As though ready to leave at a moment's notice. Never married. My mother did say that once, long ago, she had stopped by his house for something and saw in his drawing room a photograph of a young woman and two children standing in front of a modest building. There was a male figure in that picture as well, perhaps him. But without the beard and with a smile, she couldn't be absolutely certain. The look on his face when he entered the room stopped her from asking him anything about it. No one ever saw that picture again. He often has a wistful look on his face, as though he's not quite there. I wonder what he is doing here."

"How tall those new buildings are." Distracted by Mandakini's remark, Amrita looked around.

The concept of suburban living is alien to the Delhi mind and so Delhi continues to grow—inward and outward and upward. Today, Delhi spreads out in all directions in concentric circles. The far-seeing planners had created the road that runs in a ring around the city. It was supposed to function as a barometer of the city's growth, of its reach. As the city continued to grow, they expanded its limits by adding another ring. But this too could not contain or carry the bursting population of the city. Further demand for housing led to the addition of broken rings farther outside.

There are short roads and there are long roads, wide roads and narrow roads, roads that run in straight lines and roads that mean-der waywardly, roads that stretch unendingly as far as the eye can see from along the outer arms into the inner fold of a backwardly reclining *V* like a prostitute beckoning pursuit, and roads that halt abruptly like a question mark or a mark of exclamation. There are even rich and poor roads like the people in front of whose houses they run, somehow reflecting the character of the people they mostly serve. Bumpy as though racked by a persistent cough, or smooth like quenched soil, or ravaged by life to be split, torn, pot-holed, and—sometimes mercifully—taped over with hot, sticky, liquid tar.

Humans must compete for space with buses, cars, two- and three-wheelers, bicycles, stray cows, dogs, pigs, and, sometimes, escaped monkees on these roads. The white painted lanes on the black face of the road remain disregarded. And the red light remains a challenge that is constantly ignored.

Like lush lashes that frame and protect the dark beauty of the brightest gaze, the roads in Delhi are tree-lined. Lush laburnums with their velvety blooms, gorgeous gulmohurs with their yellowy-orange stamens open to the sun in wanton invitation, and many more nameless trees with thick trunks and abundant foliage. Columns of beauty for the rich, shelter for the poor, and often at the same time. For though sometimes separated by an abrupt boundary wall, it is not uncommon for huge colonies of shanties to sit adjacent to wealthier homes offering the individual a daily dose of someone else's reality.

And over all this hangs the thick smog like a dirty white dome. But even the smog's thickness cannot hide the ferocious glare of the sun. The sun does not allow itself to be looked at directly. It will scorch the eyeballs if anyone disregards its decree.

The day with its unbearable, inescapable heat, makes the people irritable and stifles their potential. The heat is cruel. Relentless. A merciless killer. With a voracious appetite. Especially for the poor and the homeless. Though it will not discriminate when it sees a victim.

It devours them all and spits out the remains by the wayside. Like a trophy.

15 *The Eye of Shiva*

THE MOON IS another matter. This more gentle, luminous astronomical body often lies dulled behind clouds and smog. At other times, it does not. These are the times that Delhites look forward to. During blackouts, which are frequent, the moon hangs as a giant lamp to which the human moths are naturally attracted.

There is something special about nighttime. Nighttime offers recompense. The cooling rays of the moon, its shades and shadows, like doubts and possibilities, are somehow more human. The moon allows us to question and think and dream. To wonder and create.

And when the breeze blows, it whispers tales of possibilities in the light of the moon.

"The moon is an average of 384,400 kilometers from the earth. The moon is an average of 384,400 kilometers from the earth," Amrita repeated to memorize the facts. Every so often she took a break to peer up at the object of her knowledge.

"Its mass is...what keeps it in place? Hmm... Sir Isaac Newton..."

When Kundan came out to collect the clothes that hung on the line, she found Amrita sitting under the back-wall light squinting at the sky.

"What are you looking at Amritu?" she asked, thinking it might be one of her daughter's games.

"The sky."

"And what do you see?"

"Clouds. Will they stop the American astronauts from landing? Chandok Sir says we must focus on the task not the result."

Kundan looked up from folding the washing. She saw that Amrita was serious.

"There are no clouds in the sky." Kundan's tone was gentle.

But Amrita remained adamant. "There are," she claimed. "See, they have covered the moon."

Now Kundan was really concerned. It was a particularly clear and beautiful night, and the moon sat regally among its attendant stars. "I think you should take the day off from school tomorrow. We should get your eyes checked."

"I don't want to wear glasses," Amrita was quick to answer. "Everyone will tease me."

"No one will tease you. Anyway, we haven't been to the doctor yet."

"They'll tease me. I tell you, they'llteaseme." Amrita was getting hysterical.

"No sensible person..."

"They'llteaseme. I tell you, they'llteaseme," Amrita insisted.

"I'll talk to the teacher..."

"You can't do that. Then they'll tease me even more."

"Go and wash your hands. Papa should be home soon. Then we'll talk about it." Knowing she was defeated, Amrita got up sulkily. But when Gurmehar came home, she cornered him before he could fully enter the house.

"PapaPapa, there's nothing wrong. I don't want to go to the doctor."

Unable to comprehend her breathless and teary account, Gurmehar walked into the kitchen, "What is this visit to the doctor Amrita is talking about?" he asked.

"I think she may need glasses." And Kundan explained what had happened earlier that evening.

"I thought you wanted to wear glasses. Have I not seen you trying on my sunglasses?" Gurmehar tried to humor Amrita.

"But that's different...," she wailed.

"How is that different? We will find some really nice ones..."

"Colored?" her interest was piqued.

"The prettiest color. Now what will it be? Come here so we can discuss that."

Amrita was distracted. That was till Amardeep came in from playing cricket. "You'll look like a donkey," he hooted.

"A donkey?"

"All eyes."

"Good. Then we'll match."

"Why?" Amardeep was suspicious.

"Because you look like a monkey. Dawnkeemawnkee, munkee-dunkee," and Amrita dissolved into a fit of giggles. Her giggles ended suddenly when she came back home the next day with her prescription glasses. The thick lenses did seem to make her eyes stand out as though permanently glued to a window looking in. Like two moonpies shadowing a tiny earth. Contrary to her fears, however, Amardeep did not make fun of her. School was a different story. There were the usual kid jokes about four eyes.

"The children should attend religion school at the *gurdwara*," Kundan suggested to Gurmehar as a means to distract the children.

"Is it necessary?" Gurmehar was not quite sure that was the answer.

"It will take their mind off mischief. Anyway, they should learn Gurmukhi, some history."

Once again Gurmehar repeated, "Is it really necessary? I mean if *Darji Biji* were alive it would be another matter, but now..."

"Even so...they should know. It's only for an hour, twice a week."

Twice a week, Amrita went with Amardeep to the *gurdwara*, but every night, looking up at the sky and the giant silvery ball, she felt reassured in a different way.

Ikk oan kaar

sat nam

"Clearasil, the answer to patchy skin," Amrita announced one evening suddenly, breaking her upward gaze.

"What is it now?"

"There are markings on the moon?" she asked Amardeep

"Silly." Not put off, Amrita next asked Kundan.

"What does it look like to you?" asked Kundan.

"It looks like an animal, but ofcourse I know it isn't."

"Of course you do," said Kundan containing a smile. "Some people think it's a hare."

"Isit? I mean...ofcourse it couldn't be."

"Some people even think it could be an old man or old woman, a child or moon girl."

"Moon girl?" she asked excitedly. Then more quietly, she said, "Ofcourse I know it couldn't be."

"Of course," said Kundan.

Rocking gently, Amrita hummed softly to herself the song that just a few years ago Kundan used to sing to her and Amar when they were fractious. Pointing to the image in the moon to distract them, Kundan had sung: *Chanda mama door ke.*

"Which god lives there?" Amrita had wanted to know.

"Not lives, but many people think of Shiva when they think of the moon."

"Doesn't he live on Kailash?"

"Yes, but there are all kinds of stories about him...."

"Stories of demons and restless wandering spirits. He even haunts cemeteries and cremation grounds and wears a crown of serpents and a necklace of skulls. Be careful not to anger Nataraja Amu or he'll haunt you," Amardeep gleefully interrupted.

"Where did you read that?" Kundan tried to distract her son.

"*Amar Chitra Katha.* He can even change his appearance," he continued.

"Yes, yes," Kundan interrupted her son. "But that is nothing to be afraid of. He is sometimes depicted with four arms and five heads... that is so he can watch over the universe. In his four hands he holds a tiger's skin, a deer, the demon's club, and a drum."

"And he has a third eye," once again Amardeep interrupted, slowly opening and closing his cupped hand on his forehead.

"Third eye?" Amrita was not quite sure she liked this description.

"On the forehead. And it flares up and has terrible power when he is angry." Amardeep's cupped fingers, now rigid, stood out like claws irradiating divine wrath. And they were aimed at her.

Seeing Amrita pale, Kundan decided to change the conversation. "Do you remember the story of the churning of the ocean?" she asked.

"Yes," Amardeep replied.

"Tellit again," Amrita coaxed.

"All right. When the world was created, the creatures who would inhabit it, were thrown out of the churning ocean of milk. The first gift was the divine cow Surabhi, whose son Nandi, the white bull, bacame Shiva's companion. The second gift was a crescent moon which he snatched from the waves and placed on his forehead to decorate his hair. The crescent moon keeps Kama, the god of love, alive, and through the waxing and waning—"

"Waxandwane?"

"Increase and decrease in size...of the moon, he creates different seasons and rejuvenates life. The third gift was a deadly poison which he drank to save the world. He didn't swallow it, he held it in his neck which made his neck turn blue. So you see, he's not just scary."

"Hmm," Amrita was intrigued.

"Through his song Shiva begged Ganga to come down from heaven, but he trapped her in the coils of his hair so that she would not overflow heaven and earth. She weaves in and out of his hair till she descends to earth split into seven streams."

All the time Amrita listened to Kundan's story, she gazed up at the moon. The moon that hung in the sky like the ever-open eye of God watching its children. No matter how one tries one cannot escape this eye. Even during the day, when the strong rays of the sun appear to make the moon disappear, the moon is actually there—watching.

16   *A Baby Over*

AS DUSK LED into night and Amrita still waited for everyone to come home, she did not switch on the light. In the dark she could see better the shadow of the moon as it began to lengthen angularly across her bedroom floor. A few square feet of triangular space. Of moonlight. But the way in which it fell upon the gray cemented floor illiberally pock-marked by maroon chips made it appear dull. Like a shadow. The shadow had always been there, but she had never studied it so closely as she had since the long nights after her accident. It fascinated her. The shadow of the *motia* vine draped over her window ledge seemed trapped under the shadow of the horizontal bars of the window. As the breeze blew, the shadows shook and shivered on the floor. They invited her to listen.

The moon also encourages confidence. During the day one must wear a face, hiding one's vulnerabilities from a world that often appears harsh and unyielding. But at night, in the soft light of the moon, the guard can be let down.

◗ ● ◖

"Categories. Will you please. Name some. Names of. Boys. Three times."

"Rohit, Girish, Amardeep. Pass on."

All the time, the girls giggled and swayed forward and backward to the rhythm of their singsong, clapping twice and twice snapping their fingers in the air.

▶ ● ◀

"The Ahujas called again," Kundan opened the conversation.

"Oh Mama, not again," Amrita groaned.

"Well, they want an answer. There's no harm in that," Kundan was calm.

"Not interested. Tell them we are not interested," Gurmehar was impatient.

"Well, not like that, but basically, yes," Amrita spoke mildly.

"It was nice of the Munjals to introduce them," Kundan continued.

"Very nice, I'm sure," Amrita cut in sharply.

"No need to speak like that," Kundan's retort was just as sharp.

"So is it this Frank? What? What? What did I say? Why are you glaring at me?" Amardeep grinned.

"You know it is Franz," Amrita spoke sharply.

"Yes, yes, that's what I meant," Amardeep was unrepentant.

"The one at Max Mueller?" Kundan was curious.

"Yes," Amrita mumbled with her mouth full.

"The one you went to the Boat Club with last night?"

"Yes, Mama, I said so."

"What? Amrita went to the Boat Club last night? Who...? I thought you were at... Why wasn't I told?" Gurmehar looked up from the TV.

"You were told, very much so Papa."

"I don't like being told when I'm doing something else."

"Yes Amrita, when did you tell him?" Amardeep spoke pseudo-seriously.

Amrita pointed daggers at Amardeep with her eyes promising later retribution. Then turned patiently to Gurmehar, "You were not doing anything else. Now can we talk of something else.... Will you keep some *methi* for me for the morning Mama?"

"I like to know what's going on in the house," Gurmehar was saying to Kundan.

"Yes, yes," Kundan nodded. "I am putting this aside *beta* for the morning." She showed Amrita the *methi* she had separated in a small bowl.

"Why don't you give this Ahuja guy a chance. It's an opportunity," Amardeep was still not through teasing Amrita.

"Opportunityshoppertunity. My foot."

"Nalini rang," Kundan changed the subject.

"What did she want?" Gurmehar looked up.

"They were thinking of dropping by tomorrow evening."

"Hmm, good, good."

"Are Girish and Meenu coming?" Amrita asked.

"She didn't say."

The next evening Nitin and Nalini Gupta sat having tea with Kundan and Gurmehar. Everyone was sitting in a ring on the front lawn, close by the guava tree.

"Those were the days," Nitin was saying.

"You've forgotten the struggles," his wife gently ribbed him.

"Golden days," Gurmehar answered his friend. Kundan looked at Nalini; the two women suppressed a smile.

"We should have bottled them," Nitin turned to Gurmehar.

"We need a foolproof formula," Gurmehar came back.

"I have one," Nitin sounded excited.

"What?"

"What?"

"What?"

Startled by three sets of eyes trained on him, Nitin laughed, "It's right here, the solution. Wouldn't it be nice if our Girish and your Amrita...?"

Before Nitin could finish his sentence, Nalini broke in, "Yes, we have talked about it. It would be so nice. *Bhabhi ji* just say yes. You just have to say yes. She is already like a daughter to us."

"It's a nice idea but, well, children like to make up their own minds these days. If they want it....," Gurmehar turned to Kundan.

"If they want it, it would be very nice," Kundan repeated after Gurmehar.

"There is that slight incident with Geeta, of course...but...just a mistake," Nitin looked at his wife.

Nalini nodded her head, "Kundan will understand. Children make mistakes, *nahin* Kundan?"

"*Bilkul ji, bilkul,*" Kundan agreed, her head down.

"What's stopping us? Let's call them and just ask," Nitin was eager to realize his idea.

"No, let us not do that *Bhai* sahib," Kundan intervened. When Nalini looked at her, she explained, "We don't want them to think it is our idea. It should come from them."

"Yes, Kundan is right," Nalini held her husband back.

"Gurmehar *yaar,* how about a walk?"

"Isn't it getting a little late?" Nalini was peering at her watch.

"This won't take a moment. Just some business stuff. We'll just go around the block once."

"How about another cup of tea?" Kundan tried to distract Nalini.

"It's getting late, I really shouldn't. Oh well, don't be long. Come sit here Kundan. Stop rushing around."

"Come on then," Gurmehar put on his *jootis* and the two men slipped outside.

"Mangru, Mangru, now where has that little boy gone?" The sound of Mrs. Nanda shouting in the street made Amrita turn to the clock. Only half an hour had passed since Amardeep had called. The house was still silent.

Suddenly, after the accident, the Guptas had grown very busy, though the parents did visit from time to time.

"How is Girish, Aunty? Haven't seen him in a while," Amrita asked.

"Oh sobusy, sobusy."

"Busy? With what? He hasn't even called recently," Amrita was laughing.

"I don't know. You children do things these days that we old fogies know nothing about." The usually vain Nalini Gupta was willing to be senile to help cover up her son's absence. But secretly, she published her jokes in national dailies for a low fee.

Matrimonial for Brides
Wanted: young, lissome, 20–23-year-old girl for boy, 28 years old. Boy, innocent divorcé, of decent Punjabi family, with father a retired government officer and mother a pious lady. Girl must be well versed in household affairs. Must be very beautiful and fair. Parents of girls who wear glasses need not respond.

"Yes, yes, young people are so busy these days," both Kundan and Gurmehar agreed. Amardeep was too angry to remain in the room. They had all seen the matrimonial ad.

"I wonder why Girish has not been coming over?" Amrita later asked Amardeep.

"Because he's an idiot?"

"An idiot?" It took Amrita a while to understand that though nothing was expected of Girish, he was afraid. She thought, *Poor Girish.*

17 *The Way of the World*

"KUNDAN, HALLO, KUNDAN." It was Mrs. Kiki Nanda peeping from the other side of the front wall. Unlike the back wall, which was about ten feet high with shards of glass embedded on top to discourage intruders, the front wall was just five feet high and was broken in the middle with white-painted, perforated, recessed clay windows. Fine workmanship made the windows look like delicate and complicated lacework. From behind the fancily shaped apertures, parts of Mrs. Nanda now appeared to reach out to Kundan.

Man hi devta, man hi ishwar
hmm hmm hmm hmm hmm...
hmm ujale darpan hmm hmm
dhool na hmm hmm
Oo tora, man darpan keh laye

Kundan, who had been lost in song as she was bent over a plant beneath the window, looked up in surprise.

"Hallo...what are you doing?" Kiki Nanda asked.

"Just a little gardening. This plant here has heavy blooms and a very delicate stem. It needs more support, something to twine around, so I am fixing it to a stake."

Mrs. Nanda lived in the neighborhood. She had shortened her own name from Kokila to Kiki. She said she felt like a Kiki not a

Kokila. Not a day younger than sixty (she claimed to be fifty-three), with shikakai-scented, meticulously dyed jet-black hair draping fair and loveliness squeezed from a slim, plastic tube and a girlishly high-pitched laugh, poking her nose in everybody's business was her official business on the block. She had taken over from the "Midwife" and "Witchni" after *their* demise.

It was a few days after Gurmehar's and Kundan's excursion to CP. As Amrita's bedroom window was partially open, she could hear the conversation from outside. Amrita preferred it shut during the day, even during the power cuts, but Ramesh must not have shut the window completely before leaving.

"Di-i-i-di, good maar-ning," Ramesh said cheerfully as she entered the room. She knew a few words of English and loved to practice them on Amrita.

"Good morning Ramesh."

"Shall I come back later if you are not ready to wake up now?" she asked.

"No, I'm awake. What are you doing with a broom?"

"Savitri is not coming today. So your mother asked me if I could help out."

"Oh."

"How are you feeling today?" asked Ramesh, breaking from humming a tune under her breath. She had a little wild flower in her hair.

"Fine. What are you so cheerful about? Did something good happen?"

"Not particularly."

"Then?"

Ramesh just shrugged and continued to dust for a few minutes.

"Who gave you that flower?"

"No one. I plucked it from the sidewalk."

"It looks nice."

"Here, you take it," Ramesh said, releasing it from her hair.

"Oh no, no. It looks nice in your hair."

"No, you take it *didi.*"

"Okay, thanks." Amrita did not really want the flower, but she did not want to hurt Ramesh's feelings, so she took the flower and put it in a half-full glass of water on her side table. There it hung over the side, its yellow face spread wide open as though in astonishment at this sudden source of sustenance. Like she felt—*used* to feel—in Franz's presence, she thought in sudden fancy.

"Do you like your job?" Amrita asked.

"Yes. What's not to like?" Ramesh gave an extra swipe to the seat of the wheelchair.

"I mean, do you enjoy what you do?"

"What else would I do?" rubbing as though to erase even the memory of any imprint.

"I don't know. Have you ever thought about it?"

"There's nothing to think about. I have three young children at home. Their father, thank God, works, but still I must do what I can." For a moment she dusted silently at the window then continued, "You just do what you have to do."

"You don't *have* to...," Amrita began when Kundan called Ramesh from outside cutting short their conversation.

"Hello, hello," now Kundan stood up to talk to Mrs. Nanda and returned Amrita to the present.

"Howareyou?Andyoursolovelydaughter?Poorgirl.Chchch. Whatatragedy. Haven't seenher outside," she blurted out almost without pausing for breath. Then she looked toward the curtained window.

Kundan just said, "Yes."

"What is she doing? Poorgirl. All alone in her room. Maybe I can come and talk with her sometime. You know me, just a homebody."

"Thank you, I'll tell her."

"What about now?" Mrs. Nanda persisted. *What about it?* Kundan wanted to ask, but did not. "She's reading...er, resting."

"Again? Well, strictly between you and me, too much reading and thinking is not good. Not good at all. All this imagination just leads to trouble. Look at my Rina now. When she finished her BA, I told her, flatly told her, you know I take no nonsense, I told her it was time she got married. Must get that out of the way in time you know. Otherwise it just gets more difficult to compete with younger girls every day, you know. By Amrita's age Rina was already a mother and had another child on the way. Responsibility is what Amrita needs. It will take her mind off unnecessary things." Kiki Nanda was in an expansive mode. Pausing just long enough to fuel her lungs, she continued with emphasis, "Take it from me, all this thinking will just cause you trouble."

Kiki Nanda had cautioned of competition with younger girls, but Kundan's heart had heard of competition with *two-legged*, younger girls. She seemed to hint at two strikes, not one, against Amrita. Before she could stop herself, Kundan said, "Haven't seen Rina in a while. What is it, four months, five months, now since she visited?" Then feeling ashamed of her dig, "I almost forgot, I have something on the fire," Kundan said through pursed lips. Keeping her head bent to avoid showing her anger, she turned away.

As Amrita strained to hear Mrs. Nanda's answer, Amardeep walked into her room.

"Amu, you have not said anything about the accident," Amardeep began tentatively. He had been planning this conversation for a while.

"There's nothing to say. You know everything already. It's all there in the FIRs and the witnesses' testimonies." And then she added, "Isn't it?"

"No, it's not. You know it's not. That's just the report. Of someone else."

"But that's all the authorities needed to make up their mind."

"You are not talking to authorities here," Amardeep was insistent.

"But they are the ones who matter. They make the judgements."

"Only in the legal sense."

"The legal sense! Innocent till proven guilty is a myth. Anyone can go and say anything, and the accused must prove himself innocent."

"Not all people are like that. Most are more responsible."

"But enough *are* like that."

"Yes." Looking at the wheelchair, Amardeep couldn't dispute that. "But those people are not important."

"They are the ones we live with."

"They are still not important. If they misjudge you. To measure life—"

"Poetry is dead. There is no poetry anymore," Amrita quietly but emphatically interrupted.

When Amardeep remained quiet, she continued in the same tone, "How do you measure life? How do *they* measure life? In the salary they make? The number of bedrooms they claim? The car payments they cannot upkeep? The elitism of their children's school? Or the trust that they have betrayed? The trust that each human being owes another for no other reason than the fact that we are human. No, they are not important. None of this stuff is. Just leave me alone. I don't want to think about it." Spent, Amrita turned away.

But though Amardeep left the room, Amrita could not now forget the thoughts she had been running away from for so long. Thoughts that had occupied her mind for the last several years and that she kept forcefully down. With the accident, those thoughts had crowded back in like poor laborers herded like cattle into trucks for government rallies at the Boat Club and Ramlila Grounds. There they lay in her mind, gasping for air. Clamoring to be let out. Amrita was afraid of what they would do if she set them free.

18 *The Two-Faced Child*

A WEEK LATER, Amrita lay reading *The Times of India*. Reading and thinking. Reading the news of what was happening around the city and had been happening for so long. And thinking about her conversation with Amardeep. We have two kinds of thoughts, she had discovered. Two very different kinds of thoughts. Day thoughts and night thoughts. Day thoughts are light. Like birds, with wings. They can soar high above the fluffy white clouds in the blue, blue sky. Night thoughts are heavy. Like stones, big and small. They can start a ripple or an avalanche before sinking down to the depths of the ocean. Also, both can come at any time. These days, Amrita found herself having night thoughts at all times.

The territory of the brain is uncharted territory even when one travels over familiar terrain. Since the accident, Amrita's thoughts, like the pieces of colored glass at the end of a kaleidoscope, arranged and rearranged themselves into a new pattern with every turn of her memory.

Though she had been able to push Amardeep away, it was harder to push away her thoughts. Seeing her resistence weaken, they rushed in like bold headlines of newspaper clippings. Immediately leaping to the wave of violence in the city. Balkanizing culture and state. Would it balkanize the human heart? Had it already? *Will it ever end?* she wondered.

"Hartal!"

For three weeks Amrita enjoyed the unscheduled holiday. Then, anxiety began to set in.

"How can they do this to us Mama? If this goes on, surely the government will declare this academic year void. Students will fail," Amrita complained loudly to her mother.

"They can't fail, silly," Amardeep interrupted. "You can't fail when there's a strike."

"But this is not some lame university in some backward state and time. This doesn't happen here, and in 1984." Amrita was shocked, and she let everyone know it. "I think we teachers should be more responsible."

"Relax. Wait and see what happens," Amardeep suggested. Amrita hated it when Amardeep told her to relax, but she decided to let it go this time.

Sure enough, in another three days Amrita couldn't stop smiling. "I have never seen such perfect attendance." Many lecturers in Mandakini's college as well were holding unofficial classes on the lawn.

"Where did you sit?" Kundan was concerned. "Aren't the classrooms locked?"

"We sat under trees and under the overhanging ledge of a building corner. Ironically, though no formal attendance was taken, just about everyone was there." Amrita spoke quickly and excitedly.

"Are the buses running?" Kundan's concern was practical.

"Right now."

"What about tomorrow?"

"I'll think about tomorrow tomorrow."

"What do you mean? What will you do if the Special doesn't come?"

"I'll get a ride..."

"From whom? Papa has to be told ahead of time, you know...."

"He doesn't have to bother. I'll catch a ride with someone...."

"This is not an adventure, Amrita...."

The Delhi topsoil, mud-colored like its people, now raised itself in the wind to reveal a fiery red. Underneath. Like *gulaal.* But there was no *holi.*

The Constitution of India set forth lofty ideals, but the Sikhs felt they had not been cut a fair deal. The constitution does not even formally recognize their religion though it recognizes Hinduism, Islam, and even Christianity. It was impossible to get away from the topic at college.

"Sikhism, the youngest of world religions, began about five hundred years ago in the Punjab region. Early in their history, the Sikhs were forced by religious persecution and the execution of two of their gurus by Muslim rulers to arm themselves for protection. In 1699, Guru Gobind Singh had organized an elite fighting force, the *Khalsa* or 'Pure Ones.' Their hair, *Kesh,* is one of the five symbols he gave them. They were to remain uncut to provide a distinct identity."

Amrita paused for a breath, then continued, "The Sikhs have a long and proud history of military warfare and bravery. In fact, they remained undefeated until the mid-1800s, when India came under the British Empire. During this time, there was relative calm and many Sikhs prospered. They fought as part of the British army during World War I till disputes over religion ensued. But then came the Jallianwalla Bagh massacre; 1919 was an infamous year. There was a brief reprieve in 1925 when they got management over their own shrines. In World War II, the Sikhs once again fought for the British.

"When Muhammad Ali Jinnah couldn't guarantee them religious freedom, the Sikhs turned to Jawaharlal Nehru who offered them virtual autonomy. As early as 1945, the Shiromani Akali Dal (the Sikh political party), had put forward a scheme for a separate Sikh state within the Union that was to be divided along linguistic lines." Amrita looked around, deciding to change her style.

She couldn't help thinking that the Sikhs and their history was also one half of her family history. Then shaking off personal thoughts, she asked, "Can anyone elaborate on how the Sikh reform efforts have pitched many of their own community against themselves?"

When there was silence, she introduced the Nirankaris, the Namdharis, the Singh Sabha Movement, and the *Rahit Maryada.*

Rounding off her account with the concerns of the Ravidasis and Valmikis, Amrita asked, "So what happened with the independence of India and the creation of Pakistan?"

"Tragedy." Maninder's answer was swift and to the point. When Amrita raised her eyebrows in his direction, he continued with a shrug, "Pakistan was carved out of Punjab. And so millions of Sikhs found themselves in a Muslim country that did not want them. The move was inevitable but led to discontent."

"And then what happened? Let's move forward a few years now."

"Well," Nita began as though joining a fray, "the grant of the kind of state they had wanted, the Punjabi Suba, in 1966, did not satisfy them. This discontent grew with government repression and led to the formation of a militant right wing faction of Sikhs for whom the only goal was a separate Sikh state, Khalistan."

"So what's the problem?" prodded Amrita.

"Punjab's importance to India. That's the problem," Sanjay's answer was droll.

"What do you mean?"

"It's obvious," Ritu jumped in. "I mean, look at the figures. Not only does almost 80 percent of India's agricultural produce come from here, but also, defensively, both Russia and China lie near its northern border."

"There have been some good times," Bindu tried to be fair.

"That's true. The revolution has also been green. Pun intended," Nita tried to lighten the moment. No one laughed.

"Gosh, don't forget those flats we see everywhere. Our mushrooming middle class," Sanjay couldn't resist the dig.

"Aah...and yet...the tension between the government and Sikh separatists grew to violence." Amrita was very aware that she was discussing a very volatile topic. Sentiments were high, especially as Delhi contains a Hindu majority. Sikhs form approximately 2 percent of the Indian population. The only majority they hold is in Punjab. From 1980 things escalated to a head. Since 1966, the

Sikhs had held their own government in Punjab, but the Center suspended elections there after 1980 and in 1983 broke down the state government, overseeing the affairs of Punjab from New Delhi. Thousands of Sikhs were imprisoned on suspicion."

"What about the responsibility of the 'Akali trinity' and their allies?" Ramanathan was generally a quiet student, peppering on-going discussions with his occasional, penetrating remarks.

"What about it?" Ritu turned the question back to him.

"Well, the Akalis protested that it was the police that were killing the innocent Sikhs and presenting it as a consequence of armed confrontations. Negotiations between the Akali leaders and the government never did really work. And so the violence increased."

"Were not 25,000 Akali prisoners released, umm...when was this—summer of '82?" Amrita threw out to the class.

"But this did not work," Sanjay jumped in impatiently.

"Why?"

"Because this did not appease the Akalis," Sanjay continued.

"So what did they do?"

"Yes, do. Do as in respond."

"Well, one thing they did was to try to obstruct the building of a canal which was to settle the water dispute between Punjab and the neighboring states. But, in fact, their violent demonstrations outside the Parliament House that October led to considerable bloodshed."

"Are you sure?" Harjit interjected.

"Of course, I'm sure. It was all in the newspapers. They were protesting against more deaths of their comrades, calling them murder. They now threatened, under their 'dictator' to stage demonstrations during the Asian Games. The government, in answer, increased the ring of security around the city."

"Tell me about it." Mridula's statement was soft but Amrita heard her.

"What was that Mridula?" she asked.

"Nothing, just...nothing." Mridula wanted no part of this discussion. She just wanted things to return to normal.

"Come on Mridula, you must have something to say." But when

Mridula refused to be drawn into conversation, Amrita turned to the class again. "How did increased security for the city translate itself into reality?"

"Haryana." Once again, it was Maninder with his succinct answer.

"This is what I meant," suddenly Mridula burst in. Amrita let her speak. She just prompted, "Yes?"

"My grandparents live in Haryana. And lots of aunts and uncles. We know, they know, what it was like." The entire class was silent as Mridula took the floor with great emotion. "You know that all roads from Punjab come through Haryana, so the Haryana police took extreme measures to ensure the Center's plan. Many Sikhs... from all walks of life and of all affiliations...suffered humiliation. And then several people used this as an opportunity to rouse hatred against the government and the Hindus and sympathy for the extremists."

No one dared to break the silence following Mridula's speech. After a few seconds, Amrita began, "And so President's rule is imposed in Punjab in October '83, and we come to the Golden Temple."

"Oh, we come to the Golden Temple, all right, but do we leave there?" Sanjay had asked a very pertinent question.

"That still does not give anyone the right to attack the holy shrine. With artillery, tanks, for God's sake. 1919." Harjit was adamantly opposed to Operation Blue Star, like many.

"I agree," Ritu too was decisive. Four months after the incident, wounds were still raw and memory fresh.

"I don't know...was there any other way?" Nita wanted to know.

"One thousand, many thousand, people killed. They should have found another way." Harjit looked directly at Ritu and Nita.

"But was Chandigarh the answer?" Sanjay had his own question. "Didn't the demand for a theocratic state still remain?"

"Yeah, don't forget the threat to stop the shipment of grain from Punjab and to cut electric transmission lines."

"And meanwhile Hindus and Sikhs continue to attack each other. Don't they realize they are the same—"

But Harjit interrupted Ritu, "Don't even start that. That's like calling the Sikhs *keshdhari* Hindus. They are not Hindus with hair."

"I did not say that. You did not let me finish," Ritu was equally adamant. "I was only talking about belonging to the same country. Khalistan, for God's sake? The land of the *Khalsas,* the sprritiually pure and clean. Sound familiar?"

"Oh...," Harjit was quiet.

"It's got so that...," Nita didn't complete her sentence.

"...And it's so random," Maninder sounded despondent.

"Is this what life is all about?" Sanjay was dead serious.

"Don't shed blood—shed hatred. That was the appeal at the eleventh hour. But we must remember that blood and hatred have become a part of the daily lives of people," Mridula spoke incisively.

"It's the times we live in," Ritu announced.

"I think it's the people," Harjit offered.

"Times? People?" Maninder sounded puzzled.

"Well...," Ritu began explaining herself.

"Excuses, that's what these are." Maninder was emphatic. When others remained silent, he continued, "And so has it been worth it?"

"It's not our fault. It's not as though *we* did anything...." Ritu was equally spirited.

"Precisely."

"Precisely?"

"Precisely. What have we *done?* What have *you* done?"

"Me?" Ritu looked self-consciously around the class.

"Not you personally, Ritu, but...," Amrita intervened.

"Excuse me, Ms. Chaddha. For a moment, let's say...personally."

"Well...what do you expect me to do?" Then, "What have *you* done?" Ritu asked almost triumphantly.

"Nothing," Maninder's answer rang clearly.

Immediately pandemonium broke out in the classroom. "Then what do you mean by asking these kinds of questions?"

"I am not exempt from my own remarks. I merely want to point out that apart from talking about these things and, of course, reading about them, none of us have done anything about it."

"But this won't happen to us. Will it?" Anil sounded unconvinced by himself.

In the moment of quiet that followed, Maninder's question rang loud and clear, "So what happens next?"

19   *In the Maze*

DREAMS, TOO, CAN die. They can decay or simply die. The question is not why but how.

It was life in the happening. History in the making. Walking the streets and into people's homes. Speaking with its many mouths. Before sitting itself down in spots of ink, chained and silent between paper leaves.

Amardeep began October 31, 1984, as a carefree man, but by dusk he would become anxious and afraid for his life as Delhi began to burn in its own rage. He had spent the day in his college library preparing for an upcoming assignment on the diversity practices of successful businesses, while the entire city had started winding down like the wheels of a fast-moving train trying to come to an unscheduled halt. Once outside, he was only mildly surprised to see hardly anyone at the bus stop across from Hindu College. It was also not so strange that no bus appeared for a while. This was common. He wondered if the student union was striking again. And he waited. But an hour later, with hardly a soul around him, he grew concerned. A hurrying passerby told him the spreading news of the assassination. Amardeep knew he must get home. Fast. If the past were any indication, the entire city would be coming to a halt pretty soon. Walking briskly till Mall Road, he was lucky enough to get a lift on someone's motorbike till Kashmiri Gate.

Here, he was stuck for some time till he gave up and began walking. All the while praying to get another lift. Fatigue and hunger hit him suddenly, but he tried to remain focused. Home was a long way and the roads no longer looked safe. Already the roads seemed to have changed ownership. The regular crowd of businessmen, professionals, idlers, and the merely curious had given way to anonymous groups of people driving around in tempos and taxis. Some strong emotion seemed to have begun creeping into this narrow, busy road that was difficult to negotiate at any given time of day. It was not yet fully dark, and yet the mysterious quietness of darkness seemed to be overtaking the atmosphere. Ahead of him, one taxi rammed into a stray dump and hit it and hit it and hit it. *What is it hitting? Is there something in the dump? Around it? Something not visible to me?* Another group of people emerged from a side street. They were talking loudly and gesturing wildly with their hands. *Are they angry? Drunk?* Amardeep decided he did not want to know. He was afraid.

I'll be twenty-five in December, the random thought crossed his mind. But before he could pursue it, he was distracted by the sound of a passing gang of clean-shaven males in a taxi. At first he thought they would just drive by him. They did not. They neither slowed nor swerved, just drove right up to him brandishing their short sabers, kitchen knives, and big barber's scissors in his face through the rolled-down windows.

"*Sir ki khaal utaro saale ki.*"

"Scalp the damn guy."

A brusque reminder from one of them about the order to meet an official to "hunt big" in Trilokpuri miraculously saved his life.

"*Harami kutte, apne aap ko kya samajhta hai? Apni jaan chahta hai to bhag ja, dum chhupa ke bhag ja.*"

"Bastard dog, who do you think you are? If you want your life, run away; run away with your tail between your legs."

Amardeep had no time to react. Nostrils pinched, his breath coming out in short rasps that rose and fell like an untuned *sarangi,* he jumped backward and fell on his back just in time to see their vicious, laughing eyes and spitting foul mouths. Some of that spit landed on him making him cower as might a sinner from the presence of *Yama;* the stench of death was unbearably close. He knew he had to find cover.

Never had he felt so self-conscious. Of his turban, the royal blue starched material usually wrapped around his head in a point that had become dislodged when he fell. Of his black facial hair combed back and upward along his cheeks. Like the new wave of Sikh boys, he did not hold back his facial hair in glue. It was now sticky with spit and fear. Above average height for an Indian at almost six feet and with his mother's black eyes and his father's royal nose, his well-built body had always attracted attention. Now he wished he could somehow merge with his surroundings.

Where is everyone? Where are the police? he wondered. *Help! Help! Help! Someone please help me,* he called till he realized that his cries for help could not be heard because they had never been uttered. Looking around he suddenly realized the danger he was really in. The normally active business area was quiet. On any given day one could not find one's way through the bazaar, it was so busy. The sheer number of bodies created a wall that was difficult to penetrate. Rubbing shoulders with the increasing mass of human flesh that this narrow road continued to devour year after year, one could never anticipate or imagine it empty as it was in the evening hours of that autumn day. While that density was formidable to get through, this emptiness was worse. In the slanting rays of the dying sun the innumerable side streets opening onto this road looked strangely mysterious and shadowy, as though carrying a secret. He did not want to know.

They were bipeds. Human beings with two legs. One and two.

Left, left, left right left. Left, left, left right left.

The unexpected arrival of an almost empty DTC bus returning to its home depot in Jantar Mantar saved him. He didn't know a time when he had been more glad to see one. Before he knew it, he was back home. He never told his parents about his run in with destiny; he did tell Amrita but swore her to secrecy.

Minnie Chakraborty was the other person who knew Amardeep's story. They had met a year ago at the library. Seeing her reading at another table, he had approached her. They began talking. Moving around in the same group, hanging out in CP with friends, they had shared many a laugh together.

Now, they shared a different level of reality, a reality of ethnic cleansing with scalpings in bloody streets. He told her of his attack on the street. She told him of what had happened to her and her family.

◗ ● ◖

Minnie Chakraborty had a doctor's appointment that afternoon, so she had decided to stay home. She was not thrilled to be living in makeshift accommodations while her family waited to move into their DDA housing. A last-minute hitch had slowed their plans, and now they found themselves living in a hastily cleared, two-room space in the printing plant of her mother's Punjabi friend in a side street behind South Extension Part I. It was not the most efficient of solutions to their housing problem, and socially it was completely undesirable. Minnie was embarrassed to give out her new address to any of her friends. How could she possibly explain to them why they were living here? And how were they supposed to fit in all their worldly goods and themselves into these cramped quarters?

Without a working radio or television, she had not heard any news. Also, there was no one at home. Gaurav, her older brother, was at the university, and her parents were away in Punjabi Bagh. While her father had some work to do, her mother had decided to tag along and visit some relatives. They were not expected back home till late evening.

At one thirty, Minnie decided to get dressed and go to the hospital. Her appointment was not until two forty, but she always liked to arrive early. In any case one had to leave margin for the buses. Minnie leisurely arrived at the bus stop to wait for her bus. The bus stop on the main road was very crowded, more than usual for this time of day. Enjoying the mild sunshine on her bare arms, she carefully sat on the broken-concrete half-wall that formed the front side of the enclosure of the bus stop shelter, gingerly rearranging herself as a *paan*-chewing older man slithered in next to her. "Looking very student today," he complimented Minnie in his best imitation of Bollywood. He pronounced "student" with great emphasis. His lips seemed to enjoy the fullness of the *u* sound as they took a life of their own and in full-blown plumpness eject-ed the word "stoooo-dent" with a side helping of spittle. Minnie knew better than to answer him. The mouth continued to chew unrelentingly. Then it spat neatly on the ground—aiming for some goal best known to itself and the fly that landed on it seconds lat-er and running its tongue over its stained teeth to clear them of stray leaf fibers, as though readying itself for its next move. It be-gan to hum, *"Hum tum, ik kamre mein band honh or chabi kho jai,"* and inch toward her unobtrusively. Minnie had had enough. She had no interest in being locked alone with this man or his lips. She looked around to see and hear the sniggers of some people. On any other day she might have said something, but she was anxious about keeping her appointment.

She had been waiting for twenty minutes and there was no bus. The crowd was also growing restless. But as Minnie got up to walk a little away and think of her next plan, a bus arrived. It was already quite full. Even before it could stop, hordes of passengers leaped on to the footboard of both exits. This created a huge gridlock as the passengers who wanted to get off at that stop struggled to get through at the same time. Minnie stood on the side. She could take any bus down the road. But she needed to get one fast if she was to make her appointment on time.

As she looked around, wondering what to do, she saw the eyes of her street Romeo following her. Holding her tongue, she decided to walk to the hospital. *It can't take me that long. It's only two stops away.* It was three stops away, and it took her a good twenty min-utes. And another ten minutes to get to the gates. Getting closer to the hospital, the increasing crowds of people warned her that things were not all right. As the crowd grew to thousands out-side the gates of the hospital, she wondered what was wrong and how she would keep the appointment. "What's up?" she asked a stranger.

"They are saying the Prime Minister has died," he told her.

"What? Is it confirmed?"

"No, but the world press is here. See those big cameras in the middle."

"I have an appointment with the doctor," she informed him absently, not noticing the strange look he threw her. "Oh well, I'd better go." So saying, she struggled to the front of a side gate and managed to attract the attention of a *chowkidar.* The security guard did not open the gates for her. "But I have a two-forty appointment with the doctor," she repeated.

"There will be no appointment today, baby. Go home," he advised. "Go home before things get dangerous."

"What do you mean, dangerous? Is it true that the Prime Minister has died?"

"You, you people, all of you are responsible," a woman in the crowd screamed hysterically.

"Go home, baby," the security guard merely repeated and turned away to answer some other insistent person at the gate.

Minnie turned away. The bus stop was right across the road. Despite her recent experience with buses, mindlessly she got ready to wait for another bus to go back home. While waiting, she paid attention to the jostling crowd for the first time. Politicians, patients, press, passersby, and police, all were here. All around, people were perched on the roofs of vehicles and surrounding buildings. Some were hanging on to poles and ledges. Large numbers were trying to press forward at the hospital gates. Suddenly, a group of men began shouting for revenge. A number of women close by started beating their breasts and weeping uncontrollably. Another group raised their voices to chant and pray loudly for their national mother's life. The horde here seemed to flow from the hospital. From time to time, Minnie heard the people erupt in strange, loud cries. When she felt them sway toward her, she knew that the crowd was hungry for blood. *I must get out of here.* Scared, she hopped on to a bus to return safely to an empty house.

At home, Minnie began to think. Her brain had finally caught on with the reality of what was happening outside. There was no phone and no way for her to contact anyone in her family. She could only pray that they had heard the news and would be home soon. She checked on the groceries. Then, with the little money she had, she went to the store around the corner to stock vegetables for the next few days. She went home to find her parents had returned. They were badly shaken by what they had seen. "Two Sikh men fighting back an angry mob who were forcing them to wear rubber tires around their necks." The Chakrabortys were traumatized by thoughts of what the rampaging rabble meant to do to those men. They would hear later of people being set on fire. Underlying their panic was the fact that Gaurav was not yet back home. They poured numerous cups of tea down their throats and waited on tenterhooks for their son's return. At six thirty, when Gaurav walked in tired but safe after walking several miles from the last point at which he had been dropped by the bus, everyone was far too relieved to make the usual snide remarks about the temperamental bus system.

True enough, just as soon as the news of the Prime Minister's assassination was announced, things began to turn wild in the city. Political theater played out on the national stage as loyalty to party lines was tested. Casting the dissenters as "the other" and "the enemy" unleashed the dogs of war. Shops and businesses closed and streets were taken over by rioters caught up in mindless hate and retaliatory violence. In the bloodbath in Delhi, the Sikhs were the main targets. Thousands of men, women, and children were butchered. Without a telephone and cut off from their friends, when the Chakrabortys heard of rampant atrocities against the Hindus, they wondered if these rumors could be true.

For three days the Chakrabortys remained holed up in their tiny tenement able to get by on the goods with which Minnie had stocked the fridge. On the third night Maina Chakraborty was worried. The stock of fresh vegetables was almost gone, and there was no fresh milk to make tea. There was no question of sending Bipan or Gaurav outside. That was a risk too big for her to live with if anything went wrong, she thought. On the other hand, through the cracks of the back door she had seen some women slip out in the early hours of the morning heading toward the local temple. Their bulging bags with the curved stem of a squash sticking its neck out like a culprit told her that she and Minnie could do the same. Much against the wishes of father and son, the next day mother and daughter slipped out into the cold foggy dawn with their bags clutched firmly under their arms. Minnie was very nervous. Her public school education followed by her college years had not provided her with any experience for this adventure. She wished she was back at college studying for her tests. Even that would be better than this gnawing fear that was making her heart thud so loudly that she was amazed it didn't attract the killers to her. They arrived at the temple in less than a few minutes. There were a lot of women around the single vegetable seller. Prices were nonnegotiable.

"Are bhaiya, kya baat karte ho. Ye to bahut zaada hai," one woman ventured to protest at the high prices.

"Mata ji, maaf karo. Ek bhao hai. Laina ho lo, nahin laina ho, nahin lo." He could afford to set his own price that day.

Mrs. Chakraborty did not waste her time in trying to reason with him. With Minnie's help she quickly bought as much as filled their two bags and disappeared back into the recesses of their makeshift home.

The Chakrabortys were now set to face another few days of curfew. Since the area around their temporary residence was one of those hardest hit by the terrorist attacks, the Chakrabortys were frantic to plug in their television. After, they sat glued to its snowy and static vision. *Blood for blood.* The pograms continued. The match was lit by ranking leaders. Riled by their incendiary language, armed with electoral lists and canisters of kerosene, the lynch mobs—arriving daily in the capital in tempos and buses—set out to assault democracy. Fire and arson gutted big stores on the front row of the main roads. Other big stores were looted. All reduced to empty, black rubble. All to be burdened forever by suffering and memory. Charred remains of a life that once was. Thick black soot coated the surviving surrounding buildings. Like a sheet of shame. That night, however, the Chakrabortys went to bed knowing that the police were finally trying to control the situation, and it was only a matter of time before things returned to normal.

But that was the night they were wakened by loud raps of wooden *lathis* on their back door. Automatically, Bipan Chakraborty looked at the clock by his side. It was two thirty in the morning. No one made a sound. In truth, Bipan had feared just such an occurrence but had not voiced his fears because he did not know how he would allay them. Now, gathering his son Gaurav by his side with the women in the back room, Bipan picked up a hockey stick. Gaurav, unable to find any weapon, picked up a metal bucket that was lying just inside the door. Assuming as normal a tone as possible, Bipan asked, "Who is it?" There was no reply. "What do you want? You must have the wrong house," he continued. Meanwhile, he tried to keep Maina and Minnie back as they insisted on being there in this time of need. While the Chakrabortys waited with baited breath in fear of the worst, an army tank on patrol entered the area. The people outside their door fled the scene.

They were bipeds. Human beings with two legs. One and two.

Left, left, left right left. Left, left, left right left.

The Chakrabortys did not go back to bed. They spent the entire night talking of what might have happened. They had heard gruesome tales of women being violently raped and pushed naked into the street and of murders for hire. If the police had not arrived just in time they could all have been dead by now. "Did you see how ridiculous I looked with a *balti* in my hand? What did I imagine I would be able to do with it, hold off bullets?" Gaurav was laughing a little hysterically at himself and his father. "And you Dad, you with your hockey stick were equally ridiculous. Oh, well, it is over." But it was not over for Minnie. Though she did not want to think about what might have been, she was not sure she would ever be able to live with the kind of fear she had faced that night.

Suddenly Minnie was reminded of the betel-chewing man at the bus stop a few days ago. "I hate this Maa, I hate this," she whispered softly and intensely. Mr. and Mrs. Chakraborty looked at her quietly. They felt the same way, but they were not sure that admitting their feelings was the best way to deal with her feelings. After all, how do you escape your destiny?

"It will be better soon." They tried to speak as though they believed it themselves. But Minnie had heard the uncertainty in their voices and was in turn protective of them. She understood that it was not under their control, this unspeakable horror in the streets. And the fact that they could not even provide a safe place for their children made them feel inadequate, old, in an unattractive kind of way. Not wanting them to feel that way, she turned away. To friends like Amardeep.

) ● (

Gurmehar and Kundan had been in Chandni Chowk that day. The previous night when Gurmehar had told Kundan of his appointment in that area, Kundan had asked him if she could tag along. She had been meaning to visit Sis Ganj for some time, and this seemed like the perfect opportunity. She would window shop for a while and then meet Gurmehar at the *gurdwara*. Gurmehar thought nothing of it. Even after twenty-five years of marriage, he and Kundan often rendezvoused like this.

They sat in the *gurdwara* till late afternoon. Some ragis were visiting from Amritsar, so they stayed to listen to the soothing tones of their *shabad-kirtan*.

"*Mere Rama Rai, tu santon ka, sant tere.*"

"My Lord, you belong to the saints, the saints belong to you."

Lost in the melodic sounds of song, when they got up to leave it was quite late. It was around four in the afternoon. As they hurried outside to collect their shoes from the *jooti sewa* section, they noticed the unnatural quiet. The man serving at the door told them of rumors spreading about the assassination and advised them to hurry home. Anything could happen.

As Gurmehar and Kundan hurried toward their parked car, their hearts beating fast, they noticed the roads were practically empty of the normal crowds of shoppers. A very different kind of element had overtaken the street. Kundan had a sudden urge to go to the bathroom. She turned to Gurmehar. He automatically put his arm around her. There was no place to go. As they passed a side street in a primarily Hindu and Muslim neighborhood, someone spat at them from a window on top, screaming abuse. *"Gaddaar."* "Traitor."

Kundan's hand began to shake. She suddenly remembered the journey from Pakistan to India when she was a very little girl.

For a moment they took shelter under the awning of a door at a street entrance. As they leaned their backs against the door in relief, they were rudely shaken by the sound of a voice through the other side of the door, "If you value your life, move on." They quickly moved on.

As they turned into the next street, they realized that they were moving away from their car. How much farther were they moving away from life, they wondered. They did not know. They hoped Amrita and Amardeep were safely at home.

In the next *mohalla,* however, someone opened the door to them and gave them shelter for a while. Instead of thanks, the first words Kundan uttered were, "May I use your bathroom?" Later, heaving a sigh of relief, Kundan moved to join Gurmehar on the couch where he was talking with the couple. As she sat down, the cushion covering the broken cane work slid through the gap and settled perilously over the baseboards. Though startled, Kundan did not show by more than a slight widening of her eyes that anything out of the ordinary had happened. Adjusting carefully to make sure that she did not slide through the seat, she looked around to get her bearings. The room they were in was quite tiny. No more than ten feet by ten feet. It was painted a light apple green, and the walls carried streaks of the brush as though they had been painted by a novice. To one side, there was a shallow, rectangular groove in the wall. The bottom of the groove served as a shelf on one corner of which sat a picture of the couple in a heart-shaped frame. In the other corner sat a round clock with a bow-shaped copper ring on top. A small calendar held pride of place in the middle. Above these knickknacks, and placed in the center of the groove, was a picture of a very blue Shiva. Ganga, a beautiful goddess, rose like a spring to flow downward from the coils of his locks. A few random and unclear tiny marks at the bottom denoted the overjoyed earthlings. The plaster-of-paris frame had gentle undulations in it as though its maker had tried to remain consistent with the theme. Separated by a coffee table, their hosts sat across in two mismatched chairs that also sagged under their weight. Stray strands of cane peeped suspiciously from underneath.

"Is there a telephone we could…?" Kundan tentatively began.

"We don't have one. At another time, I could just run around the corner…," Rama apologized.

"No, no, it's all right," Kundan hastened to put her at her ease.

"I was just telling Uncle here that I can make a quick cup of tea. We don't know how long it will take to clear up outside," Rama explained to Kundan.

"Please don't bother on our account. We want to be ready to leave the moment the opportunity presents itself," Kundan was polite.

"Still a cup…while you wait," Jitendra offered.

"No, no, thank you, you have already been so kind. We don't know what we would have done without—"

But both Jitendra and Rama interrupted Kundan, "Please no, Aunty *ji*. Don't think of it. Anyone would have done the same." Then remembering what Kundan and Gurmehar had told them, they paused, "Well…."

"Yes, thank you," Gurmehar smoothly agreed with Kundan.

After a while, Gurmehar got up to peep outside the window. "I think we should be leaving," he proposed to Kundan.

"Are you sure?" Jitendra stood by Gurmehar's side. "You must stay here as long as you need."

"Yes, certainly," Rama seconded her husband. "There's no shortage of food…"

"This is very kind of you but I think if we are to get away tonight, we should leave. Or else we may be stuck here for a long time. The children don't know where we are…"

"Yes, yes…perhaps I should go a distance with you. The neighbors know me…," Jitendra offered.

Looking at Rama who stood by his side wide-eyed, Kundan politely declined the offer, "No, I think we should be able to make it."

"Come on Kundan, things will only get worse as the news spreads in the city. Chandni Chowk contains a high concentration of Hindus and Muslims in their *mohallas,*" Gurmehar cut short any pleasantries. Trembling inwardly, Kundan turned to thank Rama and Jitendra, then covering her head, she stepped into the street.

"Run Kundan run," Gurmehar whispered.

Gurmehar had visited the area before so he knew the streets well. Reaching the street, Gurmehar was relieved to find his car still there. He had wondered about it but had not mentioned it to Kundan, not wanting to worry her even more. Now, he started the car and started moving forward a little bit to more easily back out of the street. Just at that moment, a large stone thrown from somewhere came hurtling toward the car on the passenger side. Only the fact that the car was in motion saved Kundan from serious injury. The stone hit the back window, splintering right through it and on to the back seat. Pieces of glass flew all over the car, but with no police around Gurmehar knew not to stop the car to inspect the damage. He drove on.

The drive back followed a tortuous route as Gurmehar encountered pockets of looters prowling the city. Groups in taxis and tempos were cruising. Their target was anyone they could get. Seeing a group of clean-shaven men torturing a man with a flowing beard, pulling at it as though they would pull it out of his skin, Gurmehar felt the pain in his own face. He turned into a different street. Here, there was a bunch of young boys huddled over a Sikh. One of them was kicking him in the stomach. Over and over again. While the others stood around and jeered. Like a bit of carnival.

They were bipeds. Human beings with two legs. One and two.

Left, left, left right left. Left, left, left right left.

Three hours later, taking ghostly side streets and lanes, past several cars and a bus on fire, Gurmehar and Kundan finally arrived home. Night had fallen.

⟩●⟨

Mandakini was in the main university library. Reading and taking notes in a corner, oblivious to the outside world. Around four fifteen in the afternoon, when she decided to return home, she walked to the bus stop. It was extremely quiet. Unnaturally so. Unlike other days, except for the occasional private vehicle, there was hardly anyone around. When a vehicle did pass her, it seemed to whizz past at well over legal speed. Something was wrong. Shifting her weight from one foot to another, she anxiously waited for a bus. Even though the bus that came next was only going till the Inter State Bus Terminus, she got in.

At ISBT she got out and hurried toward the information booth. Hearing about the assassination rumors, she knew she needed to get in touch with her parents. From a phone booth, she quickly called home and was able to let her mother know she was safe. Her mother urged her to take a scooter or taxi or anything to get home. At all times, there was a line of scooters and taxis outside the depot, but that day Mandakini couldn't get either. Rather than waste time waiting for a bus that would take her straight to Defence Colony, she got on to a bus that was going parallel in the same general direction. She would get off midway and catch a scooter or something from there. If worse came to worst she could even cut across the neighborhood to the other side. Perhaps five miles.

Worse came to worst. As she began to walk through a local bazaar and Bhogal colony containing a Sikh majority, many shops were already shut. Others were quickly downing their shutters. The vendors who usually sat on the pavements were conspicuously absent. Even the windows of the flats on top of the shops were all shut with curtains or sheets pulled across. All normal, everyday sounds of the street were absent. Instead, the streets had an uncanny character to them, a sense of dread and simmering violence that was alive.

Suddenly, a group of Sikh men carrying swords rushed in from a side street. Mandakini almost burst out laughing. It was like being on a period movie set. *Where did they get these swords?* she wondered as, heart pounding, she quickly slipped into a different side street. It was the street of silversmiths. There was nothing open here. She ran till she intersected with the street of lumber sellers. From there she made her way farther to the next street before the railway station where she knew there was a bus stop.

Seeing a group of people gathered at the stop, she faltered. It did not look like a regular group of waiting passengers. She chose not to take the chance. Returning to her original plan to make it to the road on the other side, she once again rushed into the neighborhood through a side street. The sword-brandishing, patrolling youths seemed to guess her mind; they were coming through this street as well.

Are they preparing for something? Against whom? Where's the police? Uncertain of the enemy, she ran to escape them and found herself in front of a women's hosiery store. "Gupta Store." Unimaginative, but at least customers would remember its name. The owner, looking incongruous with all kinds of wisps of lace in hand, was downing his shutter. Seeing her head peeking under the shutter, her shaky voice requesting shelter, he let her in for a moment, advising her to rush home away from "dangerous elements." She had no intention of disregarding his advice. Within a few minutes, the young men jogged away with their swords, and she rushed through the streets again.

They were bipeds. Human beings with two legs. One and two.

Left, left, left right left. Left, left, left right left.

Fortunate enough to find a scooter that was just dropping off its passenger and was headed home in the same direction as her. So she got a ride.

> ● ◄

Amrita heard Amardeep's account of the horrific events in the lonely street as well as Minnie's, Mandakini's, and her parents' with more understanding than they realized. Her experience had been a little different that day. She was one of those who had waited.

Amrita and Rinku had just got out of the furniture and home goods section of the Cottage Emporium to begin strolling on Janpath, just window shopping. Rinku had recently got married and was looking for ideas for home decoration.

"Are you going to the univ tomorrow?"

"Of course, same as usual. Why?" Amrita was surprised.

"Nothing...just the strikes. I mean, isn't it safer to take a scootie?"

"They strike too. Or haven't you heard?"

"No need to be snide. Of course I have. But you could ask Uncle to drop you or Amar."

Amrita laughed, "I'll pretend you never mentioned Amar's name."

"Why are you laughing? It's not funny."

"No, it's not. Tell me, why couldn't you meet me last week? You canceled twice."

"Harminder was not free one time and the other time he did not feel like—"

Before Rinku could finish her sentence, Amrita shrugged as though to rest her case. Then, "What do you think, DePaul's or Nirula's for a snack?" she asked.

But Rinku was staring at the multistory building rising far above the skyline coming up in front of them. "Now here is a case for sterilization. Ugly, just plain ugly," she screwed up her nose at it.

Amrita laughed, despite herself. She had a strong, vibrant, infectious laugh, and others were attracted by it. "So let's get out of here. It won't be so close at Nirula's."

"Isn't it odd that these shops are closing so early?" Rinku wondered aloud. "Look at all these shutters coming down and those people there, rushing. I wonder what— Hey, hey, hey, watch where you are going."

As Rinku was jostled by a small group from behind, Amrita asked loudly, "Is there something wrong? What's going on?"

No one answered. Not getting an answer was scary. More and more people were exiting buildings and making for bus stops and car parks. A flower seller with his plastic bucket of roses tucked under his arm blurted news of some *gadbad* going on with the Prime Minister and that "before long blood will be spilled," disappearing into a side street.

"What? What blood? Whose blood? And *gadbad*? Oh my God, oh my God, oh my God, I must get to Harminder. Nothing must happen to him, Amrita, nothing." Amrita nodded in a daze. Flagging down a passing scooter, Rinku at once jumped in to go meet her husband at the Hong Kong Bank where he worked. Looking on, Amrita felt lost for a moment, not really understanding what was going on. She did not know what was truth and what was rumor, but one thing was clear, she must get back home. Immediately.

"Saali kya cheez hai. Chuski le gi?" Someone randomly brushed up close, muttering under his breath and making deep sucking sounds. Propelled, Amrita began to run.

At home, Amrita frantically checked for food in the pantry. Should she rush out and get some fruit? Some vegetables? By four thirty in the afternoon even that was done.

The radio, the best source for news, was curiously silent about events taking place around the city. Only when she tuned into BBC news did she hear about the magnitude of what was beginning to unfold in the city. It sent her into a panic. *I hope MamaPapa are okay. I hope Amar is safe. Why did they all have to go out today?* From time to time, she checked the telephone to see if it was working. From time to time, she walked up to the gate to see if she could see them coming down the street. But the streets were getting curiously empty, as though overset by some unknown darkness in the midst of day. As time passed, second by second, she remembered some facts about blackouts.

Blackouts can happen at any time.

When two strange men visited their house, Amrita was in her room. Unknown to Kundan, who had sent the youngsters out to play, when the neighborhood kids needed only one more person in their play, Amrita had returned home. The grown-ups had been too busy to notice her come in. At first she just stood sulking with her face pressed to the window. Thinking of Amardeep playing in the park. Soon, the loud voices from the drawing room penetrated her consciousness.

"Six years. Thank God, it's over," someone was saying.

"You did not need to come home. I was going to deliver it as usual," Gurmehar interjected impatiently.

"You have said that before."

"But you always got the money. And your exorbitant interest."

"What are we to think? In the past—"

"That was not my fault. Raza was—"

"Your partner. And his responsibility was yours."

"I have two little children in school, class one and—"

"We, too, have responsibilities. Do you think we are in this for charity?"

"No, of course not, but...it doesn't matter any more."

Alerted by a sound when Kundan came into the room, she saw her little daughter sitting crouched on the floor under the window. She shooed her out to play in the fresh air.

Blackouts do not have to affect your play.

When the planes flew overhead at night, there were strict instructions for a blackout in the city so that the enemy planes could not identify any targets. The stray animals and birds, confused by the early onset of darkness in the city, scuttled away into their corners. The night watchman hurried out and began blowing his whistle wheezily and striking his bamboo stick on the ground. Hollowly. Till he was reprimanded by the residents for attracting more attention than anyone else. Even the moon was not welcome. Everyone prayed for cloud cover.

The grown-ups, especially the men, walked around with a solemn air. Gurmehar insisted on going out after dark alone. Kundan protested, but he was adamant. The local deli store was a popular meeting place for the men. Here, over the din of the regulars and the stragglers, Gurmehar had bent over lists of potential clients and spent countless hours on the public telephone to coax them into giving him a chance. Now, a group of men gathered around a big radio to discuss the news. The old politics of Gandhi and Nehru. Why were borders not better settled at the time of independence? Would there be a cease-fire? And would it be soon?

Kundan went through the routine motions of daily life as much as was possible, but during the night, she threw heavy woven sheets, almost like dhurries, over all the window drapes. She had already got Amrita and Amardeep to cut pieces of black cardboard to paste onto the windowpanes.

Only once did Amrita sidle up to Kundan and ask, "Mummy, willwe d-i-e?"

Kundan looked down at her for a long time, holding her to her leg and brushing her hair. Amardeep's birthday was coming up soon. "No," she said loudly. Amrita quickly bent to land a wet, toothy kiss on Kundan's handle of love where her blouse separated from her sari and then wriggled away from under her mother's fingers. Her question already forgotten.

Mostly, to the children it had seemed like a game. A good time to play hide-and-seek. Rushing from room to room or across the courtyard and into the kitchen through barely a sliver of space had caused an adrenalin rush that had nothing to do with fear.

"I spy you Amar, I spy you," giggled Amrita.

"Shhshh, keep it down," from Kundan.

"I spy you Amar, I spy you," Amrita repeated in a stage whisper.

Amardeep was the den and he must now look for her. He turned his head to the wall and began to count, "One, two...ready or not? I'm coming."

Muffled giggles, the shuffle of a dress against a wall, and...

"You peep-ed."

"I did not."

"Chea-ter-cock."

"You chea-ter-cock."

Amrita was den. Again.

That day, however, was not a game. So Amrita found evening took a long time to come.

Ten days later, when the city tried to make a limping return to life, Amrita ran into some protesters who were leading a procession without a permit at the Boat Club. As usual there were violent elements in the group with their own private agendas. The procession had started from the government offices and was slowly proceeding toward Connaught Place. The protesters knew that the police would have to sit up and take notice at the disturbance caused by the traffic and the crowds in the busy business center of the city.

The police were prepared for this eventuality. There had been many such eruptions in the city following the Prime Minister's assassination. Now they were quick to respond. The crowd had barely reached Parliament Street when police vans arrived and the protesters were huddled into them. They were still shouting, *"Inquilab Zindabad. Hamari maangein puri karo."*

The public was used to such invitations to revolution for meeting the needs of the common people. What the public was not used to or prepared to deal with was the fanatical fervor that propelled such protesting groups. Innocent bystanders were inevitably caught in the crossfire between the various militant groups.

That day of the procession Amrita had to go to the university. Though she knew of the procession beforehand, she had thought that she would not have to deal with it as she was going in a different direction. What she had not counted on was the fact that the police would round up the protesters and drive them to a jail in the area near the university.

At a red light intersection, as the bus she was traveling in came to a halt, Amrita felt uneasy. She wanted to get up and get off. Something bad was going to happen. She could feel it. But she was also afraid to get up. There were very few people in the bus, unlike other days. Now, as her bus stood waiting for the light to change, another huge van came to a stop by its side. It was the police van full of the protesters. It was an open style van, with long, vertical metal bars on the side. Through these, many of the protesters stretched out their arms and made obscene and violent gestures. Their faces, rising and falling in plumpness against the bars, seemed grotesque with the fire of anger and hatred.

After a quick look, Amrita kept her eyes down. Her heart was beating so fast that she was sure they could hear her. Her eyes were darkened and her nose pinched with the effort to breathe. She did not want to attract anybody's attention. For a moment she wondered what would happen if those animals got loose. Would they attack? Kill? Rape? Is there anything else? For a hysterical moment her mind wandered to the task that she was supposed to be accomplishing at the university right this minute. But the next minute, the terror of her present situation warned her of the necessity to escape.

The protesters in the van were getting restless. The police had been so intent on getting them into the van that they had not really bothered to conduct any searches. The protesters had therefore been able to smuggle stones and sticks into their pockets. Now they took these out and started throwing them in the direction of the bus. Just for the fun of it and because they could. All the while they jeered. The stones hit the glass windowpanes. At once, the people on that side of the bus got up and rushed to the other side. Where Amrita was sitting. Many of them fell on her. Luckily, they quickly righted themselves and exited the bus. Or else, she would have been crushed.

They were bipeds. Human beings with two legs. One and two.

Left, left, left right left. Left, left, left right left.

All the time, the shopkeepers, who had come out to watch the spectacle, stood by their quickly shuttered stores. Quietly. They did not do anything.

The attack on the Khanna family in Semkunt Colony was among the most violent. Old Mr. Parminder Singh and Mrs. Taran Kaur Khanna were well known in the community for their generous spirit and godliness. It was the same spirit that, thirty years earlier, had made Parminder Singh such a financial success.

In a last, thoughtless hurrah, the British had built a railway that was to run through the city, cutting through it east to west and isolating some parts of it. With the main passenger area located in the center of the old city, there was a major traffic concentration. Prominent offices and warehouses replaced the wall in the center and also created a major constriction in the center. Into these sur-rounds, Parminder Singh arrived with his family. The streets were narrow, the air was dense, and the sky looked awfully far away. The small business settlement was meager, but the sound of the train whistle was a constant call to duty. Tailoring clothes could be profitable if they could land some big contracts. So when Mu-hammad Hussain, a smoking companion, mentioned his uncle's desire to sell his own business, Parminder Singh paid attention.

Sitting on velvet smoothed by years of use, drinking tea from faded, yellow china cups, Parminder Singh hesitated to mention anything as banal as money to the old man facing him. Dressed in white *churidar pajama* and *kameez* and cap edged with tiny embroidered holes in fine chicken work around the periphery, Nawab Farid-ud-din Hussain sat ensconced in his armchair inhaling deeply from the long, fine tip of his hookah. The sturdy metal pipe sat incongruously in the middle of his thinning gray beard. The Nawab came straight to the point. These were not times to tarry. The transaction was made.

Years later, when the city began spreading southward, Parminder Singh decided to relocate entirely. With more and cheaper space, he hired more people. Taking business to the national level. Later, his sons took it overseas. Now, Parminder Singh was fond of regaling the grandchildren of how he had, almost single-handedly, built the business at the Okhla factory from the ground up. The children let the father tell his stories. They knew them to be nothing more than the truth.

"Hire more of the migrant workers from Rajasthan," he instructed.

"But they are seasonal?" the sons blandly pointed out.

"Don't forget, they have been driven from home, same as us."

"Yes," the sons agreed. Drought and poverty had brought them to live in shanties lining the main road near Okhla, airing their laundry and their lives in full public view.

Humbled by their parents' example, the sons too tried to follow in their footsteps. "How about Mohan Krishen?" the older son once asked his siblings.

"Who?" the middle son was curious.

"A job applicant. Was rejected. But not for—"

"Does he have experience?" the middle son interrupted his older brother.

"No, but he asked us for an interview even after he was turned down at the lower level," the youngest pointed out.

"Certainly gutsy," the eldest nodded his head.

"Let's call him in," the middle son suggested in agreement.

The Khanna family's welcoming spirit was always especially evident during Diwali. That day, in preparation for a special belated factory celebration for the festival, the three sons were visiting their aging parents. Mercifully, the two daughters and their families had not come. As usual, the parents would be making an appearance at the celebration. But this time, warm blankets and cash gifts were to accompany the sweets and party. Having concluded their official business, the family sat around at home enjoying a mildly pleasant afternoon.

"Why don't you stay for dinner?" suggested Taran Kaur to her sons. They had to go back to their homes, they demurred.

But the mother persisted. "It's a while since we have all sat down together for a meal. What with all your busy schedules." When they were quiet, she pressed her advantage, "Why don't you call home and invite everyone over?" All the sons agreed.

Turning around, Taran Kaur asked, "So Ramakant *ji*, is it possible to have the family for dinner tonight?" Ramakant was an old retainer, and the family treated him with respect and consideration.

"*Ji Bibiji.* No problem at all."

"Fine then, tell the driver to take you to the market to buy all you need. Here." And she handed him some money. "Now let's see, what shall we have?"

Soon after the old retainer and driver left for the market, someone rang the doorbell. As Taran Kaur was closest to the door, she opened it. In front of her stood a group of clean-shaven, armed men. Pushing against her chest, they forced their way in. The intruders' mouths were covered with dirty handkerchiefs; still they reeked of alcohol. Only their cold eyes were visible. Expressionless.

"Who are you? I ask you, who are you?"

"Taran Kaur *ji,* what is the matter? What is taking you so long?" Parminder Singh called out to his wife. When there was no answer, the youngest son got up to see what was keeping her.

"Come on *Biji...Beejee?*" he screamed, seeing his mother lying on the floor with a knife in her stomach. Hearing him scream, everyone rushed out.

"Spare my sons, spare my husband, take me, take me. Spare them, please." But it was all over very soon. Except for the old mother, whom the killers kept conscious long enough to witness their beating and slaughter. Thirteen times they stabbed her.

"O *janam jale,* even dogs will not eat you. Oh God, take me, take me. What have I left to live for. *Wahe guru. Wahe guru.*" Ignoring her tortured cries, the intruders, who had been directed to the house by an identification mark on the outside wall, quickly ransacked the house and then torched it.

They were bipeds. Human beings with two legs. One and two.

Left, left, left right left. Left, left, left right left.

The obituary and funeral notice in *The Times of India* caught Gurmehar's attention. The old wounds of Raghubirpur that had scabbed over time were now itching for attention. Though Gurmehar had not retained many of his old ties, he now attended the Khanna funerals with his entire family.

The line of cars outside the cremation ground stretched for miles. Around them, a group of beggar children darted with dirty rags in hand, ready to polish cars, boots, anything, for a fee. Others appeared by the side almost out of nowhere, palms outstretched. "Ten paise, just ten paise." Though they saw a queue of mourners for a separate funeral beginning to form behind, they decided to stay their ground; it looked more lucrative here. It was difficult to get inside.

"He was a good man..."

"A saint. Both."

"Lucky in their sons, too."

"Not so lucky."

"Ah yes, ah yes. Irony. We call that irony."

"You can't be careful enough..."

"Quiteright. Quiteright."

"And whatever happens, don't look anyone in the eye."

"What do you mean?"

"I do my best not to be noticed."

"I don't smile."

"Yes *ji,* who knows who may be watching."

"And watch who you welcome..."

At the gate, three numb-faced, middle-aged women stood in white, starched saris, thanking people for all their kindness. By their side stood their dead husbands' sisters. Also numb. The sisters' husbands and a broken Ramakant made the rounds, taking care no detail was overlooked. Five beloved bodies lay side by side on raised concrete platforms, dressed in holy wood. At the appropriate auspicious moment, the service began.

Terrorists spilled their rage all across the city. No one was spared. Not the old and not the young. Not the rich and not the poor. Not the healthy and not the sick. Violence observes complete democracy. It does not discriminate on the basis of gender, caste, class, or creed. Spawn of an ignorance that is afraid of itself, even when carried out singly, it enacts the mentality of the mob. Blind. Red hot. Self-serving. It attacks by stealth, like a thief. Stealing emotions, the heart and soul, not mere things. To violate the structure, it attacks the foundation, the dream. Repeatedly. And, most of all, it aims to geld the spirit.

On the hills of Nainital, as one tree after another was felled in the name of modernization, the whole of India felt the tremors of the falling trunks. The moon now shone on barren slopes of stumps, revealing the secrets they had carried for centuries. It was the death of tomorrow. Nearby, Lake Naini, the eye of Shiva's love, was rising in readiness to burst its banks.

20   *Lamed*

NOW AMRITA LAY looking forward to Mandakini's visit. She was finally bringing Aslam over to introduce him to everyone.

Till now, every time Amrita had asked, "So, when do we get to meet Aslam?" Mandakini had shrugged and said, "Soon."

"How soon is soon?" Amrita laughed.

"Soon."

"Are you sure he is real?" Amrita ribbed.

"Very sure, very real." Mandakini sounded a little irritated.

"Hey, don't be bugged, just get him here."

"Soon."

Amrita rolled her eyes. It seemed that she would not be able to get anything more definite than the word "soon" out of her friend. She knew Mandakini would not do anything until she was good and ready.

When Mandakini had called earlier that day, she had sounded excited on the phone. "Aslam was able to get the afternoon off," Mandakini answered Amrita before the question was fully asked. "I was calling to find out if we could come over."

"Of course, you didn't have to call."

"Still, Aunty..."

"Aunty...I mean Mama doesn't have a problem with it. I think she's even more eager than I am to meet him."

In no time at all, Mandakini and Aslam were at the house. Filling

Amrita's bedroom with their presence and laughter. Watching the two together, Amrita had no doubt that they were right for each other. While Aslam kept stealing glances at Mandakini whenever he could, Mandakini's smile too was wider, her eyes brighter, each time she looked at Aslam. So when Kundan got up to see who was at the door and Mandakini looked questioningly at Amrita, Amrita unhesitatingly winked back.

"Aunty *ji*, we got out early from the office. So we thought we'd drop by and chat with Amrita. But if she's got friends over, we—"

But Amrita had heard Suchitra at the door. Now she quickly raised her voice, "Come on in, Suchitra. Is Ganesh with you as well? It's Mandakini. You've met her before. Come on in."

Suchitra peeked round the door, "We can come by later."

"Don't be silly. Now is fine. This is Aslam. Aslam, meet Suchitra and Ganesh."

"Let me get some tea, or will it be lemonade?" Kundan announced to no one in particular, ignoring everyone's protestations.

Suchitra jumped up to help her, "Then let me help you."

"Me too," said Mandakini, and she too left the room.

Ganesh and Aslam looked at each other. "Traffic was bad today," Ganesh announced.

"As opposed to which other day?" Aslam couldn't let that pass.

Ganesh grinned in acknowledgement. "There's a rally. That's why I told Suchitra to make sure to come home a little early. If you get stuck, there's no telling how long it may take you to get home."

"That's why I left early too," Aslam nodded.

"Where's the rally?" Amrita asked.

"Boat Club."

"What about?"

"Who knows? Some cause or other."

"It's bad enough for the young people, but terrible for the older folks. My parents feel completely lost," Aslam was irritated. "They've just moved from Srinagar. They thought they were getting away from this sort of thing, but..." He left his sentence incomplete.

Ganesha and Amrita merely nodded their heads. Then, as

though despite himself, Ganesh said, "My parents have moved too. From Hyderabad and its politics."

"You mean *Bharat Desam?*"

Ganesh nodded his head, "Does it fool anyone?"

"There are plenty who are willing to be fooled. He has played God, after all. No small thing, that, for the people."

Ganesh sighed. He knew the statement to be a fact. A frustrating fact. Using the name *Bharat,* a name for ancient India, was a deliberate attempt to raise the national pride and consciousness of the people. "Certainly makes you wary of being in the wrong place at the wrong time."

"You mean wary of being a poor and an illegal immigrant in Assam," Aslam asserted sarcastically.

"Vote banks, I mean." Ganesh was fired.

"Pawns, pawns."

"I thought the Partition was over."

"Not if the '83 elections are any measure. What was it—six villages razed, five thousand dead?"

"Meanwhile, we are daily reminded of the Tamils in Sri Lanka and the interference of foreign military power in this region," Amrita intervened.

"Diversion tactics, won't work, won't work," Ganesh asserted forcefully, restlessly gripping the back of the abandoned wheelchair.

"Who knows? Who knows?" Aslam sounded sick of it all. As though what he was really saying was, "Who *wants* to know?" And the answer was clear—no one.

Kundan, Mandakini, and Suchitra's entry into the room with tea, lemonade, and snacks changed the tenor of the conversation once again. Everyone was silent as they enjoyed fresh *shakar paras* and *mathis.* When Gurmehar entered with samosas, there was even more hilarity as there weren't enough for everyone. Kundan however solved the problem by swiftly dividing them into pieces.

Later that night, after everyone was gone, Amrita lay reading the newspaper. Months after the October doomsday, the newspapers continued to be fascinated by it. As Amardeep entered the room, Amrita said, "Newspapers report that the Prime Minister had anticipated this violent end to her life. She had suspected the same foreign forces that acted in Chile to want to eliminate her. What do you think of that?"

"And *they* are...?"

"...Big Brother in the West. Pakistan was supposedly their conduit. A divided India would be so much less of an international threat."

"Hmm..."

"What do you think of these rumors about there being a foreign hand in India's disasters?"

"Well, that is moot. You have to remember our political relations with them have not been cordial for a long time, especially during the Emergency. And then there are accounts that there has indeed been interference in Indian politics, but it has been to help the Congress party. On the other hand, the Prime Minister herself vehemently denied those claims."

Amrita went back to her thoughts and reading the newspaper. The image of India and the Prime Minister that her party tried to make synonymous, especially during the grueling years of the Emergency, floated into her mind. It had been a sheer marketing of the notion and the image of a single nationhood under a protective Mother India. Amrita wondered if in the game of international chess, innocent Indians had become the pawns.

Despite all the efforts and tactics of the Center, the Sikh crisis remained supreme.

"Hindu, Muslim, Sikh, Isai.

Hum sub hain bhai bhai."

This was the cry for brotherhood during the independence movement that had brought all communities together to display the might on which they rested their dream—to create the largest democracy in the world. A few short decades after independence it seemed to have been forgotten by many. Furthermore, the leaders who had incited the mobs to inflict carnage had not been convicted. Leaving the victims without justice or closure.

And India now lay lamed by factionalism.

It was a national, political, religious, personal disaster.

One by one, the lamps were going out all over India, and a total eclipse seemed almost inevitable.

Amrita set the newspaper aside and twisted her body to look in the mirror. It was a long time since she had done that. Two images jumped back at her. One close and showing every line. The other distant and contorted by the beveled edge.

Just as Amrita turned her wheelchair toward the exit of the court-house after the trial, the Public Prosecutor called out to Gurmehar. Kundan stayed back as well, thinking Amrita was with Amardeep, but Amardeep had just excused himself for a moment. Amrita pushed forward. Outside the door, there were random groups of people who were waiting for their own cases to be heard. Together with the usually busy food stalls and balloon sellers. Nearby, a young child blew on a thin roll of cardboard, startled himself by the piercing quality of the sound, and began to cry. On the left, a group of supporters of the drivers and conductors were dancing in joy. They had already begun their celebration.

On the right, almost hidden behind a pillar, stood the Inspec-tor in semi-profile. He was looking up at the blue sky. His neatly tied khaki turban with the *patka* peeping through melted into a tight-fitting khaki uniform that hugged him like a second skin. The shirt seemed forced together in the front over a generously curved belly. The pant worn low-slung just under the belly, and held up by a broad belt, stretched across his crotch in multiple creases. In the back, it sloped down quickly only to ride up in the middle so that the inside seam lifted higher than the outside one. A strip of khaki socks made the transition into thick-soled, rubber-backed, black shoes—the firm platform he stood on. Plant-ed two feet apart from each other, they looked like the base of an inverted *V*. His left hand was cupped in a fist like a funnel, at one end of which was stuck an almost incongruously slender cigarette. He was inhaling the smoke in long, deep drags and exhaling it through his nose in a rush.

Perhaps feeling the weight of Amrita's stare, the Inspector turned. And looked. Marble-hard. Marble-cold. Lifting his free hand, he fumbled in his breast pocket for his cigarette box and tapped it against his side as though to shake out a fresh Red and White. Changing his mind, he next twirled both ends of his mustache to a point. Then he brought his fingers forward, placing them in the middle of his mouth and spread them outward to brush back the fur spilling onto his lips.

Amrita looked back.

As he blew furiously into his funnel, the tip of his cigarette blazed in a ring of red.

Life is what happens to you when you are busy doing something else, and sometimes—in a moment of close proximity—it may reveal a face that will horrify you. Violating the very core of your being. Mocking the integrity of your beliefs. Standing them outside your body like a group of gawking strangers gathered for a mourning.

Don't dwell on it, they say. It can make you mad.

"I wish it would," now thought Amrita. For if sanity meant being like *them,* she wanted no part of it. She was through with the sanity of bipeds.

Make me mad. Make me mad. Why do such things happen? To some rather than others? And where is God when they occur?

But the night was still. The moon shone outside serenely, same as ever, and the breeze continued to blow its shadow wavily upon the bare stone floor.

"Mummy, Amar is not giving me a chance," Amrita wailed to her mother.

The brother and sister were playing shopkeepershopkeeper in the back courtyard. They had dragged together two cots and placed them at an angle in the corner, leaving just a little room at the junction for an opening. This was their door. Their business venture was shoes. Amardeep had made himself the shopkeeper because, he said, he was older. And in any case girls did not run businesses. She could be the customer, he said quite graciously. But Amrita had grown tired of playing the customer. She too wanted to be the owner.

"Amar," Kundan called from inside, "give Amrita a chance."

"Girls! You are no fun. I wish Girish was here."

"I wish Meenu was here."

"Mummy, canwe go tosee *Mera Naam Joker?*" asked Amardeep, changing the subject.

"Yes, Mummy, canwe go tosee *Mera Naam Joker?*" repeated Amrita.

"We'll see. But you have to be good. Now play together without fighting."

"We have tobe good. Good. Better. Best," said Amardeep.

"We have tobe good. Good. Gooder. Good-e-rest," said Amrita.

For a few moments all was quiet. Then, Amrita wailed again, "Mummy, Amar is still not giving me a chance." Now Kundan came out. Ganga was rushing madly down Amrita's back. The rubber band around her hair was like a chokehold allowing mere spits of water through so that large strands of hair lay disordered across her face. Amardeep's *joori* had lost its handkerchief and was tilted precariously to the right, while the oiled-up hair had given in to gravity. His legs sported long red lanes of highways. Pitiful links from south to north.

"Clean up immediately," she ordered. Then, calming down a bit, Kundan continued, "Either take turns at being the shopkeeper and the customer or play separately."

They played separately.

Because Kundan wouldn't let them drag more cots around, they had to share the space and the materials. At first, each tried to place their cot horizontally side by side in front like a screen. Trying to gain as much space as possible. This just looked drab, however. When Amardeep lifted his cot lengthways and leaned it against the wall like a tent, Amrita did the same.

"Copycat."

"Copycatt-er."

"Copycattesst."

"Copycatt-e-rest."

Determined to outdo each other they designated one open side the door, but the other side remained without cover. The vertical strings of jute that held together the jute matting to the base of the cot served as a window with long bars. To look through it they had to crouch on the brick floor and then raise their heads upward at an awkward angle. The wares were also divided. Both of them were now shopkeepers with their very own walls and meagerly supplied stores.

"Chupp-pals, san-dals, shoes."

"Chupp-pals, san-dals, shoes."

Sitting cramped inside their tents, loudly they hawked their wares, but no one came. There was no customer.

And that night she had written a letter. Just the way Miss Gibson had taught the class.

A letter to God

(The title was centered like the heading of a class assignment.)

My god (was scratched out).

dear god (was changed to)

Dear GOD,

my name is Amrita Chaddha. I live in number 333, the yellow house with the wite border on the long road that goes around. In Bengali market. Near Conni Place. and Nath Sweets if you forget. And a little guava tree in the front garden. My mother's name is Kundan and fathers name si Gurmehar. I have a brother also. Amardeep. he fights with me. All The Time. Pleeeese God, make him not fight. Also, pleeeese make Rinku talk to me. She is not talking to me. she says I took her book but I didn't. Rohit did but I didn't tell. She told everyone. No one is talking to me. Pleeeese God make everyone talk. to me. Also, shall I tell tomorrow? About Rohit?

Amrita

Three quarters of the letter was written in thick, black lead with a double line curving around the letters like a shadow where the lead was split, before it wound down to an abrupt smudge. The next couple of letters stood shakily where it seemed Amrita had tried to fix the broken point by placing it back in its socket and continuing to write gingerly. However, under too much pressure the edges of the socket had splintered onto the paper. And the pencil had to be sharpened. The rest of the letter was written in a thin, reedy point that almost tore through the paper at times.

The letter was full of dark eraser marks where Amrita had rubbed hard on the paper and even used her spit to make the corrections. It was obvious that she had tried very hard to write correctly and without spelling mistakes. ("Students, write correctly and without spelling mistakes," Miss Gibson reminded her class daily.) Even her name had been canceled and rewritten.

LOVE,

AMRITA

Amrita had given the letter to her mother to post. The next day Rinku had told her that Rohit had confessed his crime and so all was well. They were all friends again.

Amrita now wondered whatever happened to that letter. *Did it ever reach God?* She wondered if she should write another letter to God now... How would she begin? And can things be healed between adults quite so easily?

21 *Of Monsters and No God*

WHEN AMARDEEP FIRST suggested going out for a walk in the neighborhood, Amrita refused. She had so much to do. And so little time. Every night, she put her hammer to the task. Thud thud thud, it went. Pounding a beat parallel to her heart. Only harder. Could her family hear her? And the neighborhood? Did they keep awake as she did? Night after night. Everything looked so different. Who was that old young woman in the mirror? And the one by that window, peering dully between the quivering slender branches of the *motia* vine? What were they looking for? Do severed limbs and separated cells have memory? Do they, *did* they, long for union as she did? The well was so close. The fall would be steep and long. Promise of oblivion with a money-back guarantee. Her wild eyes had peeped over its edge already; what strange sights it had shown her. The bottom shaped like a giant pair of undulating lips. Mesmerizing in sway. Blood galloped to her head. Thunderously. Blanching the heart. Making it stumble and miss. A beat. Vision swam from pupil to iris and away. Air emptied her lungs only to trap itself in her vocal cords. *BOO,* she shouted. Weakly. *OOB* came back. *OOBOOBOOBOOBOO.* She felt herself teeter dizzily.

But Amardeep would not take no for an answer. So she agreed to go out with him. Now, her heart was beating fast. In anticipation. And fear.

The moon was a crescent swing in the sky, too flimsy and delicate for a ride. It was late in the evening the next day, after dinner. Around nine thirty or so. Several people were already outside to pick up where they had left off before they had gone in for dinner and the news hour.

Gurmehar and Kundan were also standing outside with a group of neighbors. Kundan waved to Mrs. Mahindra standing all alone on her second-floor balcony. Mrs. Mahindra waved back. Then looked aside. She did not want to appear as though she was peeping. Kundan turned back to the group.

"Aunty, I had gone to the ration store this evening...to get sugar," Suchitra began.

"Was it open?" Kundan asked. "I had looked in at around four thirty and then it was closed."

"It was open but I couldn't even reach the counter."

"Crowds, hmm?" Kundan nodded knowingly.

"I needed some kerosene also. Our gas finished yesterday. I had ordered it a few days ago. I mean I shook the tank. I knew there was very little. I thought it better to order ahead of time."

"You really need to get a second cylinder," Kundan advised.

"Ganesh is trying. He is getting a letter from—"

"Did you tell Aunty, Uncle about the line at the petrol pumps?" Ganesh joined the conversation.

"I was just telling them about the ration store."

"My God, I stood at the pump for two-and-a-half hours to wait my turn."

"At least you got the petrol, Ganesh. I was telling Aunty we have no cooking fuel."

"Thank God, I picked up something on the way."

"Uncle *ji*," Suchitra now turned to Gurmehar, "did you hear the latest about whether they are going to televise *Ramayana* or not?"

"No, I don't know anything about it. Ask your Aunty. Kundan, what about you? Do you know anything?"

"Just that the project is in its production stage. It has just been endorsed by the Prime Minister. But they don't expect to launch it for a few years." Kundan had obviously been following the proceedings in the paper.

"It should be interesting," Suchitra reflected loudly.

"Just a forum for trouble I assure you," Ganesh shook his head. "What do you think Uncle *ji?*"

"Don't get me into this. We'll just wait and see."

Just then Mrs. and Mr. Nanda who were also out on a stroll joined them. Ganesh and Suchitra rolled their eyes and pointedly started a conversation with Gurmehar. As Gurmehar moved slightly, almost turning his back to Mrs. Nanda, Mr. Nanda came and took his place next to him. This left Kundan next to Mrs. Nanda.

"How nice to see you outside Kundan."

"It's a beautiful night."

"I went to the temple today," Kiki Nanda began.

"That's nice," Kundan tried to summon interest.

"Yes. I said a little prayer for Amrita, our poorgirl, and I've got a little *parshad* for her as well. I'll send it with Mangru later."

Mangru was the twelve-year-old boy she had imported from some village in Bihar. "Drought and poverty, poverty and drought, you know. We had to do something. We have a moral conscience, you know. Nanda *ji* and I decided to deliver him from almost-certain death by starvation," she claimed. A year ago, a broker had delivered Mangru to the Nandas, taking his commission and leaving behind a sickly, crying boy. Soon the child had stopped crying. Now, he worked for the Nandas; in exchange, they fed him and clothed him and sent a small sum of money to his family.

"That's very kind of you," Kundan murmured.

"But I've been thinking I tell you," she lowered her voice and leaned forward confidentially.

Oh no, she's been thinking, Kundan thought. She did not want to know about what, but it would have been rude not to ask. "About what?" she asked loudly.

Kiki Nanda looked pleased like she had come up with a great plan. "Remember that day when we discussed Amrita's future? A week or so ago?"

Kundan remembered that day well. And the monologue. She nodded. It was enough for Kiki Nanda.

"Well, *pundit ji*—he was busy preparing for a *puja* over a new

Maruti but he still talked to me—he said that if Amrita keeps a fast every Monday, you know, for Shiv *ji*, there is a good chance she can gain a husband."

"I see." Kundan's lips were tight from keeping her temper. She tapped Gurmehar on the shoulder and asked if he wanted to continue the walk. He saw her face and immediately agreed.

The sound of TV sets was very loud in the street. *Buniyaad* had just finished, and the commercials of companies that had sponsored the episode could be heard loud and clear all down the street. Other commercials took over. Halls promised the relief of menthol vapor action to itchy throats and stuffy noses. Clearasil and Pond's encouraged girls and women to enhance their complexions, subliminally promising great dividends. A prominent male actor spoke huskily from the gently curved TV screens urging women to breastfeed their babies; he spoke with conviction. Boys and men audibly ran in from work or play to soap themselves with aah—the lemon-scented freshness soap (there were so many); other boys and men loudly licked their chops to show appreciation for the basmati rice *pulao* they were served.

Across the street, they nodded at Mrs. Rastogi who was out with her children. Almost automatically, the grown-ups looked at the Bhallas' home. That is, what used to be the Bhallas' home. Eight months after the incident it was just an empty house with black, broken windows that winked blindly in the moonlight. Above, charred shutters leaned forward like a hairline that meets the brow in deep consternation. Occasionally dropping a loosening brick. All around, grass and weeds mingled and creepers ran amok, leaning sickly around the house in a heavy embrace. "Hello Chaddha Uncle," the four-year-old Nitish could always be trusted to say, as he leaned dangerously out of the front window. "Good...good...goodnight," he would say.

The Bhallas had left the neighborhood after the fire. The arsonists had not been apprehended. Walking down the street, Kundan could see in the brief glance of Mrs. Rastogi the memory of that night. Somehow that night, the Bhallas had run out into the street in their nightclothes, bedraggled from sleep and fear. Who would take them in? Would not that be tantamount to inviting danger into their own homes? The Rastogis had taken them in. As Kundan watched, Mrs. Rastogi pulled her young children a little closer to her side.

All around there were separate groups of children and grown-ups and even the hired help who had probably finally gotten a moment to themselves. Edward Collins was out on his solitary walk, aloof and uninviting. Gurmehar and Kundan saw some young men who had obviously been cruising on motorbikes huddled outside a still-open small store in the Chawlas' garage. They seemed from a different neighborhood and had just stopped by to buy cigarettes and *paan* here.

"I don't know how the Association allowed the store to be opened in a residence," Kundan commented.

"No one wants to stand out. Not till something happens."

"What will it take? It attracts all kinds of people." When Gurmehar just nodded his head, Kundan continued, "And it's open so late."

"Business has been poor lately," Gurmehar murmured. They continued to stroll.

Meanwhile, Amrita and Amardeep had set out with the intention of taking a short stroll. Though Amrita had her crutches, Amardeep had casually weaved his arm around hers—just in case. Everything was fine for the first few minutes. The neighbors saw the brother and sister together. They smiled and waved, recognizing this was not the right time to approach and chat. Kundan and Gurmehar too watched them anxiously from their side of the street.

As Amrita and Amardeep passed the group around the store, Amrita could feel their eyes on them. They were focused on their linked arms rather than her crutches. *"Lovyers. Sala, hero samajhta hai apne aap ko,"* whispered one of them loud enough for them to hear. Cheap, slurping kissing sounds accompanied these remarks. Amardeep heard them the same as Amrita, but he did not loosen his grip on her. It took every ounce of self-control for him to not lash out. But as anger overwhelmed Amrita, she shook off Amardeep's arm. And they returned home.

That night Amrita remembered one particular evening she had been out with Franz. It had been soon after they had started seeing each other. They had been wandering around when Amrita stopped to look at a window display outside a state emporium.

"My God, look at those colors," he pointed at the eye-popping red and green and gold of the saris.

"They are very beautiful. Shall we go in?"

"Let us."

Inside, Franz felt his senses overcome by the amazing bursts of color and texture of fabrics. "It's hard to resist the stuff here," he smiled at Amrita.

"Tell me about it. Do you like anything in particular?"

"You are kidding, right? I couldn't possibly name one thing." He looked so comical in his amazement that Amrita couldn't help laughing.

Sensing a sale, a clerk immediately sidled up to them. "Can I help you select anything, sir?"

"Oh no, we are just looking. Thanks."

"Just let me know if you need any assistance." Amrita was relieved to see the clerk discreetly disappear. For a while they weaved in and out of various divisions till they came to the section with large and small wall hangings. They were just piled one on top of another. The wall hangings were available in combinations of every color imaginable. Franz picked up several to examine closely the beautiful embroidery that held together different shapes and sizes of plain and colored pieces of glass.

"What do you think of this one?" he asked Amrita, lifting up a diamond-shaped hanging, about four feet all around.

"It's just lovely."

"Where would one put it?"

"Just about anywhere. You can put it on the floor of course. But I wouldn't advise it, unless it is an area that doesn't take a lot of wear and tear. Mostly people put it up on walls or over sofas. It adds a splash of color."

"It sure does that." Franz lifted it again. Looking at it from different angles. "Come on, let's go."

"Aren't you going to buy it?"

"No, I don't think so."

"Just a minute ago, you felt differently. What happened? As prices go, I can tell you, it's not expensive."

"It's not the price."

"Then?"

"Come on, let's go."

"No. I think you should tell me what's wrong."

Franz hesitated momentarily, "I don't really have a settled place. It would just be baggage."

"I see." Now Amrita was quiet for a moment. Then again, "I see," she said. "Yes, let's go."

"Now you are upset with me. I didn't mean to make you upset. It's just that..."

"It's just that you don't have a settled place. I understand that." Amrita stepped out of the store. But as she stepped out of the muted lighting of the interior into the bright light, she stumbled over the raised wooden threshold. As she began to lurch forward, Franz quickly reached out and broke her fall.

"Thanks," she turned into him.

A group of hangers-on outside the cinema across the street who had witnessed the incident let out piercing whistles accompanied by catcalls.

Seeing Amrita's face screw up in distaste, Franz quickly took his hands off her. "I didn't mean to offend you."

"Not you, them," and she pointed at the Romeos across the street.

"Someone should tell them to shove off," and he moved as though he was going to be the one to do that. But Amrita pulled him back. "Let it go," she said. "They are four...and they'll only come back later."

The day after the walk, around seven in the evening, the Chaddhas had two unexpected visitors. Out of a Jonga stepped Makhan Singh and Mahinder Gupta. The owners of the two buses dressed in uniform. Like twins. Or fresh recruits. Of a common cause.

When Mr. Makhan Singh had received a phone call from jail on May 3, he was having a leisurely dinner. In the chandelier-lit dining room of his big, white house. Big, like an elephant. A white elephant that squatted unhappily in a disproportionately small-sized, back courtyard and a front lawn that was dryly unkempt and increasingly overrun by weeds in the absence of a regular gardener. Very ornate, large, white-painted, wrought iron gates locked it in or else it might have escaped long ago. Constructed like (half) a mini castle complete with turrets on the two front sides (the back-side was unimportant), a discreetly placed staircase led to the servants' quarters in the back. While darkness cloaked that area, some lights in the main part of the house were on. They showed Kamala, his wife, cooking in the kitchen down the corridor and his daughter carrying hot *chappatis* to the table.

Since their regular and trusted Sikh servant family had returned to Punjab in a panic, they had had a hard time replacing them. Now, trying to forget Kamala's irritation about having to cope after yet another daily domestic had left without warning, Makhan Singh was trying to concentrate on the news. The situation was very unstable in Amritsar, and he had sustained heavy losses in his venture with Kamala's brother. The fire had gutted an entire section of the factory. At home, one of his drivers had been involved in a serious accident. But...he shook his head...he did not usually bring home such worries to his wife. She had already mentioned wanting to visit her family a couple of times. That would, however, not be convenient at this time.

"*Mayi baap, Singh saab.*"

"*Kaun?*"

"*Aap ka khadim....*"

When Makhan Singh realized who was on the other side, he was not pleased at first. In fact, he put the phone down after only a brief exchange, deaf to the continuing cries on the other end. After all, the fellow had been procrastinating over his offer of a live-in domestic position for months now. These morons never understood when you were doing them a favor. No wonder they did not prosper. And all those unions cropping up in the city. Demanding higher wages and better work conditions. What was that all about? The driver was lucky to have been in his hire as long as he had. Some others Makhan Singh knew (and here he mentally patted himself on the back for his own tolerance) would have fired him long ago.

"Who was it?" Kamala asked as she entered the room, pausing briefly to automatically pick up a few toys strewn on the marble floor and to rearrange the cover around their son sleeping on the velvet sofa.

"Come, sit down for a bit," he patted his wife around her bare midriff dividing his attention between her and the TV.

"Ai ji, bare wo ho. Bitti is around. Babbu may wake up. I got him to sleep with such difficulty. Anyway, who'll do the cooking?" Sliding out of his loose, absentminded embrace, again she asked, "Who was it?"

"Oh just the driver...you know, from the accident... He thought I would drop everything and bail him out."

"The one we...?"

"Yes, that's the one. Any more mutton?" Makhan Singh asked Kamala who seemed to be lost in thought.

"What? Oh yesyes." She returned to the kitchen. But later that night she came up with a plan.

Makhan Singh was not so sure about the plan, but Kamala cozying up to him was convinced, "It will end our troubles forever. We won't have this daily *khhichkhhich* either."

At that Makhan Singh brightened. He was a self-made man in his late forties, and his initial excitement at marrying a woman considerably younger than himself and starting a family had only increased with time. These days he found himself trying to please her in different ways. Now he thought, if he could take care of this issue, maybe his wife would have more time for him. And he would also have more time for his work. He couldn't help thinking that he was indeed tired of the daily wrangling about domestic issues. Time was when one could get a domestic at a sneeze. But now... Anyway, if he wanted to be convincing, he would need Mahinder Gupta to stand by him.

The next day Makhan Singh contacted Mahinder Gupta. One white elephant owner to another. Both of them ran private buses on the same route between Old Delhi and New Delhi. Over the years, they had worked out a successful system whereby they almost possessed a monopoly over this route. Their policy of turning a blind eye to how the drivers and conductors did their job had earned them more goodwill with their staff and more money in their pockets. Now, Makhan Singh dangled long-term financial gain as his bait.

Mahinder Gupta was similar in age to Makhan Singh but without any family responsibilities. Though he too had not married in his younger years, he saw no reason to change his mind when he had accumulated his wealth. His early encounters with sexual experimentation had left him singed, and he had never quite recovered from them. From his teen years, he had known himself to be different from other boys. When they had giggled over the burgeoning breasts of young girls, he had wrinkled his nose distastefully. Ragged for being prudish, he began to believe himself to be so. It was not until a few years later, when he found himself alone with one of the servant's children, that he was faced with a different kind of truth.

That day, Kanti, the maidservant, had been cleaning the room where he was drinking tea and reading the newspaper, when her two-year-old son walked in from the corridor. She usually never brought him to work, but her young daughter who took care of the child had just found employment, and the boy was fractious at being left with a stranger. Kanti immediately got up to take him out. She did not want to lose her job. But the young Mahinder had been understanding. He told her to leave the child alone. As Kanti continued to sweep and dust, however, Mahinder could not take his eyes off the little boy. Dressed in a little jumper, the little boy was naked on the bottom. Mahinder found his eyes returning repeatedly to the innocent, hanging, small balls of the child. He could not help noticing how small they were. *How would they feel?* he wondered. He felt the urge to touch and find out. So under the cover of petting the child, he called him over, sat him down on his knee, and began stroking his behind. Even as Kanti turned her back to the young master who was so generously giving his time to her son, Mahinder's hands moved to the boy's front and over his balls. At first, slowly, tentatively, then more surely. At that touch, Mahinder felt a kind of release that made him stretch his leg out in satisfaction. Over and over he caressed the small, round, wrinkled pouches. Over and over he stretched his leg. A few minutes later when Kanti got ready to leave the room, she found the empty teacup atop a slightly damp, folded newspaper across Mahinder's lap and her son sitting on the ground between his legs quietly playing with his pant cuffs. Thanking the young master for the attention he had given her son, she left the room.

That day, however, had scared Mahinder. He saw what he liked and he saw how easy it was for him to have it. It was all the mother's fault, he rationalized. If Kanti had not brought in her child and then turned her back to him, this would never have happened. *Women are so irresponsible,* he thought.

Striving to forget, he got into a group of friends with too much money and time on their hands. He also started to drink. Egged on to experiment by his newfound friends and not wanting to arouse his family's suspicion, he lurched through life and into the arms of a woman. Seeing her naked in front of him, however, he did not know what to do. He did not feel any curiosity or desire whatsoever. Not like he had felt at the sight of the little naked boy. Since leaving would arouse suspicion, he sat with her till dawn. It was a very long night. After paying off the woman, Mahinder vowed never to put himself through this kind of humiliation again. Women were just not worth it.

Disengaging himself from the party crowd, he now threw himself into work. The result was magnificent. In a short time, he took his company to the top.

Now, when he saw his friend and business competitor struggling with the responsibilities of work and home he congratulated himself on his wise decision. His family had long ago given up on him. All their pleas about inheritance and family name had fallen on deaf ears. They were used to his bachelor ways and his infrequent presence in their life. If he ever felt lonely, no one knew because that was not the sort of weakness he allowed himself to indulge in.

Outwardly, he seemed content with his money and all the recreation it could buy. But as he grew older, for some unknown reason, he seemed to want more and more money. The more challenging the enterprise, the more he liked it. In a strange kind of way, it gave him the same stretched-leg satisfaction that stroking the small boy's balls had given him all those years ago. So Makhan Singh's proposal was a welcome opportunity.

Together, Makhan Singh and Mahinder Gupta made the short trip to the jailhouse. Now perhaps they could get on with their normal routines. And after winning the case, for a while, they did.

But now suddenly a flying rumor revealed something else was brewing. Really, would these people never learn? Still, it would be better to nip it in the bud. So this time, determined in their quest, they decided to surprise Gurmehar at his home. They timed their visit to just before dinnertime; they found the entire family present.

"What do you want?" Gurmehar's voice was raised and his face was beginning to turn red.

"Let us sit down and have a calm conversation."

"We have nothing to talk about."

"We just think that we can end everything amicably. We have something for you," and Mahinder Gupta placed some money on the table. "It is five thousand rupees. You can count it."

"Five thousand. Is that the price you put on what happened to my daughter?"

"We are not putting a price on your daughter. We couldn't. Of course, we couldn't. This is just a small contribution—"

"For what?" this time Kundan intervened. "We are not yet collecting a donation. Anyway, what do you want in return?"

"Nothing much, *Behan ji*. It is just a matter between us men. You don't need to worry yourself at all," Makhan Singh tried to propitiate her.

Kundan looked up at Makhan Singh. He was wearing a loosely coiled turban in royal blue held together on top by a silver pin.

His neatly glued-back beard seemed to be balanced on the arms of a pencil-thin, stretched mustache. She ran her eyes up and down his dated Safari suit made of some sky-blue, flimsy material (almost certainly from Dubai) and decorated with garish, large gold-gilt buttons on the two breast pockets. The top two buttons of his shirt were undone with the lapels pulled back. Round his neck was wrapped a short, chunky, gold chain with a gold brick pendant nestling on curly chest hair. Oversized goggles bulged like a displaced breast in the middle of the shirt, one arm hanging drunkenly over the third button. On his hairy right wrist he wore a heavy gold watch with a chained design over a folded handkerchief—to prevent catching his arm hair in the links. And in his right hand, he held a large, imported mobile phone—his cellular attachment. His feet were shod in gray-colored, patent-leather shoes in a snakeskin pattern and a two-inch heel. For height. They had a pointy steel tip.

From Makhan Singh, Kundan turned to give the same treatment to Mahinder Gupta. Gupta was a clean-shaven, shorter, squatter version of Singh. A twin soul in maroon-and-magenta-*paan* lips over which hung a mustache—thick and bushy in the middle but tapering at the ends to upward-twisting semicircles. A few stray strands, like vertical bars, curved over his upper lip and into his mouth.

Did they shop together for a discount?

Shaking off that hysterical thought, Kundan turned back to Makhan Singh. *"Behan ji* is not a fool. *Behan ji* understands everything. And right now you need to get out of my house. Or you will have something to worry yourself about," she said.

"Nahin, nahin, Behan ji, you misunderstood. We did not mean to insult you. It is just that we don't want to bother you."

"What do you want?" Amardeep asked.

"We just thought that we could end matters once and for all if you would just sign here." They offered Gurmehar a piece of paper.

Gurmehar took it. It was a brief statement that absolved the owners of all responsibility, now or in the future, for the accident. In exchange for five thousand rupees.

"Leave my house."

"We thought we could talk amicably. We don't want to have to use other means..."

"What other means, Mahinder Gupta?" Gurmehar was now angry. "Are you threatening me and my family? Who do you think you are dealing with?"

"No, no, Chaddha *ji,* Singh sahib, Gupta didn't mean anything like that. Is it the money? We can increase it a bit—five hundred, a thousand... Nothing is too much for your daughter of course. We can settle this here and now forever if you just sign this paper. It's just a formality."

"Leave my house. Right now. I am only being polite because you are standing in my house, otherwise I would tell you what I really think of you."

Outside, some passersby and neighbors had begun to gather attracted by the loud voices coming from the house. Mahinder Gupta and Makhan Singh retreated to their Jonga. As Mahinder Gupta quickly tried to maneuver his girth behind the wheel, his elbow struck against the horn making it sound like an alarm. Angered, he curled his fingers in a tight fist and landed it with even greater emphasis on the horn. Makhan Singh went around to get into the passenger seat. But as he raised his foot to get into his seat, he chanced to look down. There, on the ground, was a small army of ants laboring to their destination. They seemed to be following behind their leader, a slightly bigger ant. Slate-eyed, Makhan Singh brought down his foot—steel tip to high heel—on them. Grinding into dust the leader and as many of the others as possible. Then he got into the Jonga, and they drove away.

The incident with the strangers in the street together with the episode with the two bus owners had made Amrita furious. Then reflective. Were these men born with an inclination toward blind cruelty? Are they all? The alphabet they speak is the same. They avail the same language. How is it then that the words they utter fragment all sense and meaning? Of what are they afraid? What is the landscape of their mind? Of what do the voices in their head speak? Or have they silenced every sound? Now that they had left, how quiet the night was. This is a land where no larks trill. No nightingales quiver. No clouds trail glory. Hot, hot, the west wind blows. Hot with the thrumming, melting beat of nomadic Thar desert sands. Pulsing heat, pulsing longing. Where do you go when the body betrays the soul? When the country betrays its promise? And what do you do when the heart turns against itself? When what you feel extends far beyond the five senses but you remain limited even in its expression by the language of the senses?

Amrita had heard the exchange, staring unseeingly at her wheelchair. Curiously moved and unmoved. By a world gone mad. She only asked for the TV to be moved back to her parents' room. Now, even the background sounds of the TV were not there to break the silence.

A little later that evening everybody was gathered around Amrita's bed, having dinner.

"Nitin called today," Gurmehar said to Kundan.

"What did he say?"

"Nothing much. Just the usual hellohello. Plans are going ahead for Girish's wedding." Kundan did not reply. Everyone ate quietly for a while.

"Oh, I almost forgot. I got a letter from Mira today." Mira was Kundan's friend who was married and settled in Chandigarh. In the flurry of the day she had almost forgotten about it.

"How is she? Is she still trying to make Ved diet? She's been doing that for what, twenty years now?" Gurmehar asked.

Kundan smiled, "Well, she says things are still unstable in Chandigarh. In many areas, vehicles driven by Hindus and cut-Sikhs are being targeted; women cannot leave their houses without their heads covered. But listen to this, a couple of months ago, some friends of theirs witnessed an attack on some fireworks factory in Amritsar. Its proprietor is a Sindhi Hindu. So we know what that means. The people, seeing a sudden fireworks display, ran out with raised hopes to look at the display—thinking there was something to celebrate. But...one part of it was totally gutted... The night watchman suffered second-degree burns... People lost jobs...

She hopes to be able to come to Delhi to visit her family around Diwali. Nimmi and Om are visiting her currently. Om had to make an office trip but Nimmi refused to let him make it alone."

"This cauliflower is really good, Mama," Amardeep now said. Soon, Kundan, Gurmehar, and Amardeep were discussing passionately the merits of cauliflower over cabbage.

"Do you believe there is any justice in the world?" Amrita suddenly broke in. There was silence. Everybody's voice sounded vacuous and loud in the face of this question.

Your Honor, the question before the House is, what has the maximum merit: A dose of cauliflower? A dose of cabbage? Or a dose of justice? And what indeed is this thing called justice? Is it green and leafy and full of vitamins, or is it without color and taste?

The Prosecution had spoken and the Defense must respond.

"There are different types of justice," Gurmehar began.

"NO! I am not talking of a justice that is of different kinds. I am talking of a justice that is supposed to be universal. The justice of God, not of human beings," Amrita was brimming with emotion.

"God's justice is something we often don't understand till long after the fact," Kundan offered.

"The fact of what?"

"The fact of life."

"Well, that's no good then, is it?"

"It may seem so at the time."

" 'If you abide in my word you shall know the truth, and the truth shall make you free,' says the *Bible*. 'Believe in me as the one refuge, cast aside all doubt and fear. I shall save you from all sins. This is truth,' says the *Gita*. Isn't this what God promises in all religions?"

Everyone in the room was silent. Mrs. Joshi next door chose that moment to burst into a throbbing number. *"A-a aaja. A-a aaja. A-a-aaja aa."*

"No, I don't understand," Amrita shook her head, "Look at all that's been happening, and tell me how you can sit there and discuss the merits of cauliflower and cabbage."

"God does not love us less because we face challenges though you may think so living in a world of rewards and punishments,"

Kundan had tapped into Amrita's fear. "The experiences we encounter are not a judgement upon us, our response to those experiences is. Here," Kundan calmly offered Amrita a little more vegetables.

That night, the white shape was on the run again. Once again, Amrita chased after it following its trail of blood, and its taunt, "I defy you. Catch me, if you can."

22   *In the Shadow of the Moon*

FIVE DAYS HAD passed since the encounter with the cruisers in the street. Amrita had blocked all of Amardeep's attempts to draw her out again. This morning he entered her room determined to get his way.

"Amrita, I have to show you something in the garden."

"What is it?"

"I can't tell you. It's a surprise. You have to come out." Amrita knew there was no surprise, but something made her want to go outside. For some reason she wanted to look at the guava tree. Inspect the branches to see how they were doing under the heat of the midday sun at the end of June. If there were going to be any buds this year. The atmosphere had been getting oppressive lately. Also, she was restless.

"Okay." Amardeep had come prepared to do battle but found himself easily victorious. He did not waste time in gloating. Just hustled her outside. In a moment, Amrita felt the warmth of the sun on her body. Rejuvenating and wilting. Wilting and rejuvenating. The heat was like a physical presence, a pressure that fell on the pores of her skin and was not to be denied. The pores welcomed this longtime absentee in watery joy, like the holy waters of baptism.

Amrita did not mind that it was hot and sweaty. Even before moving to her tree, she rushed to lean in comfort against the low, white, metal-grilled gate in the boundary wall. The gate that had grown shorter and shorter with each passing year they had lived there. What barred sights it had shown her as a child and later... those that were free.

Like any other morning, today, too, the street was busy with vendors selling their wares. Fruit sellers selling fruit. *"Kele le-lo."* Vegetable sellers selling vegetables. *"Go-bi, ti-n-da, pya-az, ta-maa-tarr...,"* he repeated his list over and over again, attracting housewives to rush out and buy his fresh crop. Over their voices, an errant cobbler could be heard announcing his entry into the street, *"Mo-chi-i-i-i-e."*

Under their breath, both Amrita and Amardeep repeated, almost unconsciously in childhood unison, *"Mo-chi-i-i-i-e."* Then they dissolved into helpless laughter.

Their laughter attracted a young child, hardly two years old, who was helping her mother pick vegetables from the seller's basket. *"Lang-ra,"* she pulled at her mother's side, pointing at Amrita. *"Lang-ra. Dekho Mummy, lang-ra,"* she announced with the wonder of discovery. Of sound and meaning.

Responding mechanically to the child's tug, to the words rather than their implication, the mother cursorily looked up to see her pointing to a woman. Before she knew it, the gender-specific correction spilled from her lips, *"Lang-ra nahin, lang-ri."* "Not lame man, lame woman." Amrita heard these words. And so did Amardeep. The vegetable seller stood quiet. The mother realized her mistake a split second after the words left her mouth. She put down her vegetables immediately in a rush of embarrassment and mortification. Holding her child, she brought her over to Amrita to apologize. "Sorry *ji*, so very sorry."

"Sorry." So foreign-made, that word. So imported. As ill-fitting as the copies of Levi's jeans made in local markets.

Amrita had learned that at six.

Gurmehar had come home at night and been told the tale of the children's mischief. A mischief that could have led to their being hurt.

When Kundan related the incident, she cried. Out of fear of what might have happened had she not returned in time. Gurmehar too was angry with fear. Calling the children to his side, he scolded, "I am not a lovesick teenager, and I don't speak the way they do. But when you make your mummy cry, you cross the limit. And I will not tolerate that. Do you hear me? I will not tolerate that."

When Amrita and Amardeep stared at him, wide-eyed and quiet, he continued, "You are not babies anymore. You are old enough to understand these things."

The children still remained silent. Then he asked the dreaded question, "Whose idea was it to play with fire?"

Not wanting to be the one who had hurt Mummy, Amrita bent the truth, "It was all Amar's idea. I did not do anything at all. I just stood on the side." Amardeep looked at the traitor. But he still did not tell on her. He was punished for it of course.

Kundan, however, had caught that look and was disturbed by it. On her insistence, when Amardeep later reluctantly told her the truth, she confronted Amrita.

"Mummy, I'm sorry, very, very sorry," Amrita pleaded with Kundan. She would never, never tell lies again. She had not meant to hurt anyone. It had just kind of come out of her mouth. She would never do it again. Never, never.

But Kundan did not accept that sorry. "Have I not told you that every time you tell a lie it hurts the world? It becomes a little less. *We* become a little less. *Haven'tI?Haven'tI?* Is this what they teach you at that fancyshmancy English school of yours? *Isit?Isit?*"

Amrita looked at her mother's face. It was not twisted in anger. *That* would have been easier to deal with. No, it seemed the glitter in her eyes had gone away—somewhere. Leaving little Amu behind. Alone. Disappointment makes one look like that. And hurt. They are far more formidable adversaries than anger.

In a tired voice, without expression, Kundan told her, "Sorry is the easiest word in the English language. It is a cop-out. You can't just say sorry and expect everything to be okay again. You have to be very, very careful with words. Because words, once uttered, are there forever, they can never be taken back totally. They become your permanent record."

Kundan's words squeezed Amrita's heart. Squeeze squeeze squeeze, it went. Like a lemon in a pitcher of water with no sugar in it.

Amrita cried bitterly at the thought of her permanent record that would now show her a liar forever and ever. The moon was a little less bright because she, little Amu, had lied. Fear, that little monster with two legs, came and sat close to her heart. For a moment she wondered if it meant that she would come back to this earth in her next life as a lizard. She shivered at that thought, unable to pursue it. So she looked for ways to do something to balance that record, if not erase it.

"Swear upon God by Jesus Christ, Mummy. Cross my hea-rt and hope to d-i-e."

Her persistence finally won. Kundan told her that sorry is as sorry does, it is more than a word, that she must *show* she was sorry by always being truthful. She must not hurt others. "Now go tell Papa what you did. And be nice to Amar. You have hurt him." Fear was dislodged immediately by Happiness. Amrita smiled through her tears, relieved both at the possibility of regaining her mother's favor and because she would not now have to come back as a lizard.

◗ ● ◖

That night, Gurmehar returned home from work to find Kundan in the street. A dust storm had been brewing all afternoon. The sun, like a rotten orange, seemed to have fallen from the sky. Splashing pulp and juice upon canvas flowing in a downward gradient. So that the sky had been getting darker and heavier with dirty, reddish-brown streaks. The birds, confused by the sudden onset of darkness, had briefly protested their displeasure but finally flown away home in a flurry. All day long humidity had sat like an abrasive, wet blanket, uncomfortably close to the skin. Now the wind was beginning to pick up. Buffeting the blooms, unthreading their twines. From time to time the wind would blow with full force, carrying in its invisible folds blinding grit and lifting the litter lying in the street only to throw it down again a little farther—twisted a little out of shape. The softer, more quiet whimper of the wind that had infiltrated the day with unease was beginning to be replaced by the periodic gut-wrenching howl of an animal in anguish.

Holding her *chunni* in place over her head by bunching it under her chin in a tight fist and shielding her eyes under a hat-rimmed hand, Kundan waited for Gurmehar. The wind ballooned her *chunni* behind her in a cape making her look like a nun about to fly away. Amardeep had told Kundan what had happened in the morning outside their gate. She knew that Amrita had smilingly accepted the mother and child's apology and then withdrawn into her room, where she had been lying ever since. Even her favorite old radio, with the faint impression of the sticker of the angelic Murphy baby with one finger on the chin in question, was quiet.

"Good student, but...very talkative. Does not keep silent. Talks even with finger on her lips."

Every unit test brought home another report card with remarks written in red ink. This time the red ink was deeper, more permanent.

But Kundan understood well that quiet. It was the same quiet that had entered her heart when she was a child. And still later. Not slowly nor slyly. But swiftly, suddenly, like a shadow that leaps into the body. *When memories jet and suddenly plummet. When emotions stir to quickly blur. When boundaries overrun and past, present, and future merge into an inchoate glob. When the earth splits and takes back into its womb that which it had borne. When the heart develops a puncture that seeps blood constantly.* A quiet born not because you had nothing to express. But because you had so much to say that the words collected inside your mouth. In a rush. Letters, tall and short, round and thin, that strained the tongue, the teeth, the hollows of the cheek, appalled by the reality they had seen. Appalled. A. Palled. Letters with a pall over their heads. Dead letters. Letters, that stumbling, tumbling, upon each other fell out of the lips and lay momentarily stunned on the ground as gibberish. Letters that finally left, turned their backs and fled, without so much as a see you soon.

They must be coaxed back.

So Kundan waited to talk to Gurmehar about the incident out of earshot of Amrita.

Afterward, Kundan turned to go back in, but Gurmehar was too restless. "I'll be back soon," he allayed her concern. "I know the streets. It's not as though I can get lost." Circling around the neighborhood, unmindful of the rushing people around him, Gurmehar felt his blood boiling. Something was not right with Vikas Khanna. His own tentative attempts had been stonewalled by Khanna's colleagues. And what of Makhan Singh and Mahinder Gupta? In the beginning, after he had ignored their attempts to establish contact with him, had they then approached Khanna? Is that why Khanna had called him to talk of an out-of-court settlement? Had he rushed the case? Turned a blind eye? How did Singh and Gupta have the nerve, the nerve, to come here? They have become too bold. Or, are they desperate? Who were those witnesses? Maybe Daruwalla can suggest something. He must find out if he is done with his Bombay case.

Only yesterday, when Amrita had come to him with hurts and challenges, he had been able to fix them. Gurmehar automatically bent to ease a faint pain in his right leg, just below the knee. He had had it for some weeks now. Without telling Kundan, he had had it checked by the doctor. But the doctor couldn't find any physical reason for the pain. He had just prescribed some mild pain killers and told Gurmehar to come back if the pain persisted for more than a few weeks. Not for the first time Gurmehar wished he could change places with Amrita. He recognized her quiet. A quiet that settles like sleep upon your heart and mind and leaves your shell of a body to wander aimlessly, seeking a refuge that does not exist. Not on the outside. *"Sache paadshah, mere bache te mehar karo,"* Gurmehar raised his head to invoke God's grace on his child. But the raging wind blew grit into his eyes, blinding him momentarily, so that he stepped on a tin can startling a stray dog scurrying for shelter. Nearby, hearing the dog's yelp uncomfortably close, a cat hissed from its temporary refuge behind the milk booth. Oblivious to all, with a wry smile, Gurmehar remembered how, as a child, Amrita was always running to him with questions.

"Chandok sir looked angry. No one was listening Papa. Papa, Papa," Amrita tugged at his hand.

"Hunh, what? Come on hurry up, I want to listen to Lala *ji*. It's an important election coming up."

But Amrita stayed her ground. Hands folded tightly across her chest, wearing a scowl on her face. The ponytail behind her head bobbed up and down like a repeated mark of exclamation. Gurmehar couldn't help it. He smiled. His little shadow took her place again.

"Papa, where does the moon go when it is not full?" Before he could think of an answer, her mind had already moved on to the next question. "And how do hear-ts break? Aren't they ins-i-de our body? Un-der the skin? Do they bleed and turn colorless when they break? And where do they go?" Gurmehar was a little taken aback by this sudden onslaught of questions. "It's all in *Daag*." The TV screen had been littered with broken hearts. *Daag*, a mark of shame, a mark of identification. Such as the moon seems to carry. She had been almost nine then. And with the mind of an almost nine-year-old she provided her own answers. "I sup-pose broken hear-ts must go to live on the broken moon," she had said. Gurmehar was relieved that his answer was not needed.

Even then Amrita had been fascinated by the marble that —seemingly—hung stringless in the sky, by the fact that people were always making attempts to land there. First the robot, then the dog, then the human. On July 20, 1969, she had watched the direct telecast of one small step for man—one giant leap for mankind. Playing in the courtyard that night, the moon did not seem so remote. Loudly, she elocuted into the not-so-distant-afterall mouth of the silvery microphone, "Ask not what the coun-try can do for you, ask what you can do for the coun-try." And skipping a step, she laughed, "One small step for Amu—one gi-ant leap for the world."

That mission of Apollo 11, how it had changed the world. And how it had not.

So many years later when India sent its very own astronaut in space, the Prime Minister's conversation with him was telecast to the entire nation. How everyone had followed with common joy and a sense of achievement this curiously personal yet national moment. "How does India look from space?" he was asked. Quick as lightning he had replied, *"Saare jehan se achha."* "Better than all the world."

The Hindi film industry, like the proverbial nightingale, continued to sing. The old and new crop of heroes and heroines still bayed to the moon in happiness and in sadness. And the moon continued to be the friend and fellow companion of the lonely and the forgotten.

Gurmehar now asked himself the same question, "Where do broken hearts go?" But the angry, dark night sky above offered him no answer, no way to take upon himself at least some of his child's pain. *"Amritya,"* he called out in his head in agony. Gurmehar realized he could not fix everything for Amrita. She had been categorized and relegated to a new word, with its own nuances. *"Quatil, quatil,"* he murmured under his breath, scaring away a few of the passing neighborhood children hurrying on their way home. "Murderer, murderer."

Amrita was trapped in her grief and memories. Her grief-stricken memories. Memories, that, ever since her accident, came alive in the crevices of her brain night after night—like fragments of tunes heard on the radio—as she traversed the perimeter of the lengthening and shortening shadow of the barred moon on her bedroom floor. Pacing it up and down and sideways, like a crazed, caged animal. Winding around a jumble of letters that lay stunned on the ground. Confounded. Dismayed. By their circumstance. Their legs broken, unable to stand up straight, they had folded upon themselves. Withdrawn. From the page of life. Leaving her unhinged, untwined, undone. A shouting silence her haunting companion. A lunatic in the dark, lonely, eclipse of her heart.

This is the Yuva Vani station of All India Radio. The time now is 8:05 p.m. In the Groove. Tonight, presented by Amrita Chaddha.

"Brain Damage"

◗ ● ◖

Kundan, too, was lost in her memories. As she prepared tea in the kitchen, she remembered the many stories she had told Amrita and Amardeep when they were little and used to lie on both sides of her on the *charpai* in the back courtyard. It was quite uncomfortable, that cot. Jute matting held together on four arms and legs of wood. She always held both her children to her side as she told her stories under the summer nighttime sky. The sky that late at night, lit by a smiling moon and large luminous stars hanging low like lanterns, breathed a breeze that was warm and inviting with the promise of a lover's embrace. Those were the long-suffering days when Gurmehar was facing the challenges of his changing profession. When he would come home very late from work to find Kundan waiting up for him. From time to time, as Kundan told her stories, she noticed that Amrita would slip a little distance away from her, on to the edge of the cot and on to its wooden arm with her legs almost falling over the side. Kundan always noticed, but she never said a word. She just raised her arm and pulled Amrita back into her side.

This evening Kundan remembered a particular story she used to tell her children. It was a story from her repertoire about Akbar and Birbal. Akbar was the strong Mughal king who had unified India under his rule. He was known for the *nava ratan,* nine gems, in his court. Each gem was a person who represented an exceptional art or skill. Birbal was one of the gems at his court and known for his exceptional intelligence. And the King was always trying to best him.

One day, Akbar asked his court, "Who is the most beautiful child in the world?" Everyone was ready with an answer. And it was the same. His grandson of course. Akbar was pleased, but he also knew that Birbal had not spoken. So he turned to Birbal and repeated his question. Birbal said, "I heard you King, but I am thinking."

"And does it take you so long to think?"

Birbal, too, knew of Akbar's new grandson and he certainly did not want to face the wrath of the King. He knew therefore he had to be subtle yet truthful. He invited the King for a drive through the city.

"Now?"

"It is urgent," Birbal insisted. The entire court was aghast at Birbal's temerity, but they also knew him to be wise. The King agreed. The carriage was brought around, and the company set out with an army of soldiers behind.

"Where are you taking me?" asked Akbar of Birbal.

"I'm going to show you the most beautiful child in the world," replied Birbal with great calm.

"And does the child live away from the palace?" questioned the King.

"Just wait and see," Birbal wisely said. Meanwhile, the horses were flying away through the city limits and had now reached the outskirts of a colony of poor people.

"Why have you brought me here?" the King asked. "This place is full of poor people and filth. No beauty could flourish here." Their carriage had now come to stop by a hut. While many locals gathered around the carriage to see why the King had graced their province with a visit, Birbal was looking around keenly through the window. Seeing what he was looking for, he turned to the King.

"There, King, look, there lies the most beautiful child in the world." But the King could not see that. All the King saw was a young woman playing with a filthy child covered with mud and flies. "Where, Birbal, where?" Again Birbal pointed out of the window and asked the King to look more closely. This time the King saw a mother with her child. Each time she raised the child a little, he would burst into gurgles of joy. This made the mother laugh too and so they continued to play over and over again. They were not aware of their surroundings—of the King or his court.

Akbar admitted defeat. He understood that to any mother, her own child is the most beautiful in the world. Whether the child is filthy, poor, or ugly.

Or lame.

That night, Kundan entered Amrita's room with a purpose. Her love was fierce. It made her unafraid. She was ready to battle *Yama,* if she had to. To snatch her child back from the very jaws of Death. She would claim her blood. For it was with blood, not water, that she had nurtured her seed, the blood that had flowed from her heart to her child's. Making it beat. Heart of her heart. The child she had carried for nine months in her womb, the child she would carry forever if need be.

Pulling the little chair by the window, she therefore sat down to keep her vigil.

At once, the shadow of the moon altered to rearrange itself on her person and arrested in mid-step the lope of the lunatic. "Amritu, *beta* Amritu." Thrice she called, before Amrita looked at her. Like honey wrapping itself in folds around the dipper. Little Amu heard that call faraway reminding her it was getting dark and telling her to stop her play and come home. Kundan placed her hand on Amrita's forehead, caressingly. Her eyes were filled with a gentle fire. Kundan was ready to answer the question that Amrita had goaded her with so many weeks ago: "So how do you know, Mama?" Without further ado, she began to talk.

Book II

23   *Lover's Lane*

LOOKING ALL AROUND at the milling crowds at the Red Fort grounds, Gurmehar knew there was no way he would be able to find Nadi Singh here. *"Was I supposed to meet him at the Ramlila grounds?"* he wondered. *"I'll give him a few more minutes."* He looked up and straight ahead at the majestic battlements.

Once the Mughal emperor Shah Jahan held court here. From his peacock throne. Now, every Independence Day, the Prime Minister addresses the nation from this historic site. Human animals reenacting their story. All kinds of rallies are held here. Politicians and the animals of the Apollo and Gemini Circus have all performed in this place. Facing the grounds, across the road, are several thousand shanties. Their inhabitants swell the crowds that are routinely "encouraged" to make the numbers at any government rally.

Close by, one end of the Old Fort houses the zoo with its varieties of animals ranging from exotic birds to swinging and bobbing red, fat-bottomed monkeys. Strange birds from strange lands that laugh raucously at the strangeness they see. Foolish people caged in their complacence. Grinning monkeys. Monkeys that grin. Like humans without a conscience. Having bartered it away for a cheap shot at someone else. For a while, inside the recesses of the ruins of the Old Fort, prostitutes held their own type of court till they were disbanded by public morality and the police ring.

Nowadays, like the Red Fort, the Old Fort is an attractive stop for tourism. Tourist guides, the new custodians of national memory, ingratiate themselves (according to the size of their commission) with rich and well-dressed Indians and not-so-rich and not-so-well-dressed foreigners, with the magic of Sound and Light shows held at dusk. A quick and easy history lesson or a somersault for a buck and a clap, rolling India along on a bullock cart and beautifully captured through the advanced technology of a high-speed exotic lens.

Tired of waiting, Gurmehar decided to go to the Ramlila grounds. This, too, is a popular spot for all kinds of rallies. For a moment he felt overwhelmed by the teeming crowds. Then, remembering a spot at which they had previously met, he decided to give it one last try. Sure enough, Nadi was standing there. He was not angry at all; he had been enjoying watching the revelers. Gurmehar joined the scene.

The crowds at the Ramlila grounds are veterans of the annual programming. Every year, during Dussehra, nineteen days before Diwali, Delhi is dressed in lights and gold and silver streamers to celebrate the victory of good over evil. The victorious return of Rama with his wife Sita and brother Laxman to Ayodhya after their fourteen-year banishment. A time filled with adventure and challenge toward the end of which Sita was abducted by Ravana, the king of Lanka, and culminating in Ravana's defeat by Rama's army led by the monkey god Hanuman.

The story is old and well known. Every child growing up in India, despite education and family background, is impacted by its moral. The fun lies not in finding out the ending but in being able to sing along and shout along and participate in the telling. It's a powerful communal experience.

The Ramlila goes on for several days. Every day the same story is told to thousands of avid viewers who return over and over again. With male actors still acting women's roles in this local theater, the drama is obvious and often hilarious. The year when Laxman, played by a woman, lost his wig on stage, became just as much a part of the experience as the actual story itself. When the gawdy, large, sun-colored ball collapsed under its own weight during a night scene, it sat on the floor in awkward obeisance to the paper moon. Even laughter did not take away from the intensity of the experience somehow. When Rama agreed to uphold his stepmother's edict with respect, the people cheered. They also cheered at Laxman's show of brotherly love and Sita's show of purity when she refused to give in to Ravana's attentions. They almost booed the poor actor playing Ravana off the stage, even before he could say a single line.

Every year there is a fight over this role. No one really wants this role because they know how hated it is. (Though the new wave of character acting in Indian cinema is changing this view.) Ravana—with his ten heads and many arms—is the enemy, the powerful and undefeated opponent of the gods and the underworld, and it is not uncommon for people to pick up their metal folding seats and throw them onto the stage in anger and judgement at his actions. This role has especially become notorious (and faintly, hysterically romantic) since the time an actor playing Ravana actually abducted the woman playing Sita. The real-life drama just increased the fervor of belief in the hearts of the people. They also wait to see what new thing will happen each year. The end is especially dramatic.

After losing all his commanders in battle, swollen with pride, overconfident of his prowess and the boons that he had been granted (protecting him from all except men), and disregarding ill omens such as the unscheduled eclipse of the sun, Ravana set out to the battlefield on his own divine chariot. In his overweening pride, he thought he had conquered death. There followed a massive battle between Rama and Ravana. But no matter how many times Ravana's body was struck, it re-created itself.

As the battle became more fierce, Matali brought his master Indra's chariot for Rama's use. This time Ravana was wounded, but his charioteer carried him off the battlefield. Ravana was furious when he recovered consciousness. He insisted on returning to do battle. Once again, on the battlefield, there followed a grim battle between him and Rama.

Matali, Rama's charioteer, reminded him that Ravana's end was approaching and that this was the right time to use the *Brahma-astra,* the weapon of Brahma. Rama uttered the appropriate spell and sent forth the *Brahma-astra.* The weapon pierced Ravana's chest, enshrined within which lay the secret of his invincibility. The secret was shattered, and Ravana lay dead upon the battle-field. Gods blew their trumpets and heaped upon Rama a shower of flowers.

As Gurmehar and Nadi watched, the key players prepared for the end. Dussehra culminates with the burning of the effigies of the evil king Ravana and his two brothers Meghnath and Kum-bhkarana. It was dusk, when day meets night, so the actor play-ing Rama drove up on his chariot toward the giant effigies of the enemy and shot at them with a ball of fire from his bow and arrow. There have been times when during smaller, local shows, Rama has not been successful at making his mark. In order to avoid this public embarrassment, and in order to keep the moment of glory and drama intact, there was a lot of help on hand. The effigies, filled with crackers, went up in spectacular flames against the backdrop of the city and a dusky sky.

❯ ● ❮

The atmosphere in the canteen was noisy as usual during the lunch hour. A giggling batch of young women in their early twen-ties stood on the side waiting their turn to be served. They were dressed in starched, printed, cotton saris, with carefully formed knife pleats. These young women stood out in stark contrast to the older matrons who sat decorously in groups around tables covered with oddly shaped streaks and ring-shaped stains formed by wet teacups. No one complained about the streaks or stains anymore. At one time they had, quite loudly. Now, if anyone com-plained, the rest usually smiled before turning away—they knew the complainant must be a newcomer. It was simply a question of economics. With jobs and salaries being such a touchy issue, no one wanted to get into what might begin as a minor complaint but would most definitely end as a threat of strike. So the tables remained, at best, summarily wiped. And if the customers felt strongly enough, they could clean them themselves. The canteen was patronized mostly by the clerical staff, many of whom recognized that a little bit of wet or dry dirt was yet another shot by fate against their lives. They were resigned.

Sambar-dosa was on the menu that day, so the line was longer than usual. Living in the North, there were not many places where one could get good, tasty, authentic, South Indian food. Not without going to a fancy restaurant. The recent addition of Ranganathan, the new cook, who had grown up and trained in Mangalore, had changed all this for the daily rush of employees of the Secretariat. Soon after his first customer had gulped down his dosa, washing it down with big swallows of hot coffee in a short, stubby steel glass with a slightly folding rim, news of his arrival had spread among the regulars. In fact, Ranganathan was so good that news of his prowess had even reached the officers' mess. While enjoying their gastronomic delights more privately, the officers had seriously discussed its impact on the workers who needed no more reasons to slack off. They feared his cooking might increase the frequency of the staff's breaks. But the workers feared something entirely different: if Ranganathan was so good, he would not last too long here. So they might as well enjoy his cooking and thereby their own work, while he was there. Therefore the need to relieve themselves from the daily monotony by taking a drag or catching up on the score of the latest cricket match began now to be accomplished in the accompanying aroma of garlicky hot spices and oil smells that stung the eyes and clung to clothes.

"I hope there are some dosas left for us." Nimmi voiced what all her friends were thinking.

"Look at those men in front. They have two to three dosas piled on each plate. Gosh, someone should tell them there is a limit to how much their paunches can continue to grow," giggled Mira. "Look Kundan, look at that man, I'm convinced his pant button is about to burst. One, two, come on, come on."

"You are so wicked, Mira," scolded Kundan. "Wait and see, your husband is going to be a fat man and then you'll wish you had not been so cruel." Kundan and Nimmi were laughing at Mira, but Mira was not amused. She tossed her head and said with great conviction that she would not tolerate that kind of indiscipline in any man. While her two friends hooted with laughter, Mira continued to glower at them till suddenly she gave up the pose and joined in the laughter.

The laughing young women attracted the attention of two men who were just entering the room. They were wearing turbans tied in the latest fashion and seemed to be in their late twenties. Gurmehar was visiting his friend Nadi Singh in the building. He worked nearby in an agricultural office. Since it was lunchtime, they could grab a bite to eat in the canteen. The two men had been friends for a long time, in fact, ever since Gurmehar had come down from Shimla.

At first he had found it difficult to even breathe in the thick city air. It seemed to him there was no space for anything here; new buildings were cropping up everywhere. Side by side with the architecture in pink stone with which the British had crowned their administrative achievements, there was coming up a new culture of modern Indian buildings. These new buildings at first bore a striking resemblance to their older counterparts, the architects perhaps not yet ready to cut the umbilical cord that though finally strangling had yet connected them with the only source of life they had known for so long.

Raghubirpur had been a source of life for Gurmehar once. Though he had chafed against the lofty goals set for him by Pyaara Singh, he did not seriously act upon these feelings till his mother's death propelled him to leave. A much-loved and longed-for son and brother, he had been spoiled beyond belief by all around him, especially the women in his life. Given every material comfort before the desire had been articulated, he had grown to expect that that was how life was meant to be. His mother's death changed all that. Night after night, *Darji* rocked his memories outside his wife's room. The loving sisters, now increasingly busy with their own families, turned their focus to other matters. As Gurmehar realized that he was no longer the focus of his family's universe, he floundered. For a while he wandered around till he finally escaped to Shimla.

"Akela hi chal diya, is umeed mein
Kahin to milegi meri zameen, mera asman."

But the poet's hope and horizon have a curious relationship. And while the large picture windows through which he peered showed him images of a *kala angrez,* a brown sahib, he failed to see the incongruency of the term, or that these windows also reflected a faint image of himself, always on the outside.

It took him four years to finally see how far he had traveled from Raghubirpur, and what he had become. Returning to Raghubirpur was not an option. His father was dead. His inheritance appropriated by his two younger brothers-in-law. Gurmehar had received news of all this months after his father's funeral when a letter from a well-wisher in Raghubirpur had caught up with him. Gurmehar remembered his last words with his father. So final they had been. After those words, the funeral seemed a mere formality.

And so he never found out how Pyaara Singh would have responded to his return. If he ever doubted his decision, he consoled himself by remembering that his father would never apologize: he was of the old school, a time in which it was unthinkable for a parent, especially a father, to bow down before his son. If his mother had been alive, he felt sure that his father would have come around, but then if his mother had been alive, he would not have left home in the first place. He would have been married to one of the many eligible young girls whose parents had been courting his parents almost from the day of his birth. But his mother was dead. And *that* was not to be.

None of these thoughts could be discerned from the faintly aloof, half smile on Gurmehar's face as he walked into the busy canteen that afternoon. He was meeting with Nadi Singh to talk more about the plan the two of them had been discussing for some time now, of starting their independent business. Both were working as Junior Assistants in different ministries at the time. Since their two offices were fairly close to each other, it allowed them to meet during their lunchbreaks. The very thought of launching a venture of his own added a sparkle to Gurmehar's eyes. His own excitement caused him to overlook Nadi Singh's more cautious response.

"We should look into possible office space," suggested Gurmehar.

"It's a little soon for that," Nadi murmured in response.

"It's never too soon. Nadi, *yaar*, we don't have to make an immediate decision, you know. Just look at it."

"It sounds like you have something specific in mind."

"Well, I heard of this terrific spot...."

"It sounds like that property dealer, that Bhatia, has been talking to you again." Nadi's voice was wry.

"Bhatia is good. He has sold several plots in the Lajpat Nagar area."

"Oh, so we are talking of Lajpat Nagar. Isn't that too far? From Connaught Place, I mean."

"Half an hour or so."

"Also, there is really not much there. Small government houses, small wooden shops..."

"Hey, it's not CP, but it isn't as if we could afford to buy a place there at this time. Sure, we would have richer customers and a richer market in general over here, but Lajpat Nagar is not so bad, it's up-and-coming. In ten years, you wait and see how it will have developed. And it's right by more prosperous and up-and-coming neighborhoods. It's bound to help."

"Yeah, well, we have to wait and see."

"Let's not wait too long. People are buying the shopping spaces very fast. Bhatia was telling me last night—"

"You saw Bhatia last night?"

"Yeah."

"What did he say?"

"Well, he was telling me of this prime location. No, don't sneer. He's very dependable."

"No property dealer is dependable," mocked Nadi.

"You are too suspicious," Gurmehar laughed at his friend. "I don't think you trust anyone. Not even your father."

"Don't start that," warned Nadi.

"All right. So, what do you say? Are you at least ready to meet him? You know, just to discuss things and see what he has to offer. We don't have to sign on anything."

"Yeah, let's talk about it some more. Right now I have to run."

"I thought we were going to have lunch together." Gurmehar was a little irritated.

"I thought so too, but K. Nangia wants me to work on this ten-page report and have it before him by two thirty this afternoon." Since lunchtime was from one to two, Nadi was clearly skating on thin ice. He had never been on more than nodding terms with his immediate boss.

K. Nangia, as he was unpopularly known by his immediate staff, was not an easy man to deal with. At fifty-three, he felt himself too old to adapt to the new species of employees that rather preened themselves on the concept of India for Indians. It was not that he had anything against that sentiment; after all, had he not fought for independence himself. It was just that he felt that these puling young dogs did not understand anything about hard work and fighting for a cause. No, they had made standing around at corners and gossiping into an art form, and they could invent amazing reasons for not missing any part of a cricket match. And what about the violence at the Ramlila grounds last night? The newspapers had covered it fully and with gusto. How embarrassing. It is 1958, for God's sake. When will they learn the meaning of dignity? He shook his head—*never*—as though in answer to his own question. Though Nangia had protested against British rule, time had dulled his memory, transforming large problems into minor irritations, and so now he remembered working in that "more professional" atmosphere with fondness. (He wouldn't admit that openly to anyone of course.) An atmosphere where time was important, and its waste was unthinkable leave alone punishable. The only memory of that time was left in the buildings of Lutyens and Baker. All else was already changed or in the process of changing. He had been lucky enough to find use for his skills in this new government. He knew he was not well liked among his staff, and he felt no special concern about that. Indeed, he felt a strange sense of power at that response because he felt it to be appropriate to his station. He was not here to be liked. He had higher things to accomplish, work to do. He had been given a task to accomplish and he was going to do it beyond the best of his ability. Others in his department, who clearly did not share his goals, felt he needed to relax a little more, be a little more like them. In other words, they wanted him to follow their motto: don't do today what you can leave till tomorrow. With two such different worldviews a clash was inevitable.

Nadi did not want to be the one to provoke a clash, however. He had found this job with great difficulty, and he was not about to give it up. Though he had been discussing the possibility of starting a new business with Gurmehar, he was as yet nowhere as convinced about the workability of that project as Gurmehar seemed to think. So although Nangia had thrown this job at him at the last minute just before lunchtime, not giving Nadi any chance to cancel his meeting with Gurmehar, he knew he would not protest. After talking to Gurmehar briefly, therefore, Nadi got up to go back and do what needed to be done.

Abruptly abandoned by his friend, for a moment Gurmehar was at a loss. He considered going back to his office but then realized that eating lunch in his canteen would be no different than eating lunch here. He decided to stay. As he stood in line for his dosa and sambar, he allowed his eyes to roam around the room till they lit on the group of young women he had noticed earlier. They seemed to be engrossed in each other and having a good time. *"I wonder what they are talking about?"* he puzzled briefly till he was reminded to move forward in the queue. *"It is so silly the way the men and women are sitting separately in the room; it was so different in Shimla."* He could feel his frustration at such attitudes rising within him like an unwanted attack of bile.

"Move along, mister," the person behind reminded him a little mockingly. He had seen the way Gurmehar's eyes had lingered over the young women in the room. Startled, and a little embarrassed, Gurmehar moved along. Soon he was at the counter and with his order returned to the main section to look for a seat. There was an empty seat at the three women's table. And it seemed to him that they even looked at him briefly as he passed their table on the way to another at which a couple of men sat eating.

"May I sit here?"

"No problem."

Gurmehar sat and ate his food quietly with the men, all the while glancing at the group of women. If anyone had asked him of his feelings at that time, he could not have explained them precisely. He just knew that he was feeling something, and whatever it was, it felt good. But it was not until one of the young women leaned forward and exclaimed, "Kundan, you can't really mean that...," that he realized it was this woman called Kundan whom he had been focusing on. The woman with long hair in a thick braid down her back and gentle doe eyes. She was somehow the cause of his strange new feelings. He wondered how he could talk to her.

◗ ● ◖

Two weeks later, Gurmehar made another trip to Nadi's office for lunch. This time it was to see Kundan. It had been a long two weeks, but, on the advice of his friend, Gurmehar had decided to wait.

"There is no way that you can directly approach her. No, that would be too dangerous a move, it might scare her away," Nadi had reminded him two weeks ago when Gurmehar had phoned him from his office to announce his feelings.

"That's ridiculous," Gurmehar frowned in response.

"Ridiculous or not, it's the truth."

"I suppose so."

"And I, my friend, know so."

Gurmehar did not bother to answer. He was too annoyed. Moreover, he really needed Nadi's help if he was to succeed in any way with this woman.

"So what do you suggest?" he finally asked.

"Lie low."

"Lie low?"

"Yes—for a few weeks," Nadi added slowly.

"Honestly, Nadi, you sound like something out of a Raj Kapoor film."

"Raj Kapoor, Pradeep Kumar, Dilip Kumar, what does it matter. That's the only way."

"You need to stop seeing so many movies. *Anarkali,* wasn't it, that you saw—what—seventeen times?" Gurmehar ribbed Nadi.

"Bina Rai is worth it. *Zindagi usi ki hai, jo kisi ka ho gaya-a-a-a/ pyaar hi me kho gaya...*" He sang with zest about the equation between life and love.

"Yes, yes, but this is real life," Gurmehar interrupted. "I can't take that chance with my Anarkali."

"Then let her take a chance with you." Nadi was now at his most difficult. He was lost in the splendor of Mughal times and the lyrical romance of Anarkali who had taken her love for the emperor Jahangir (then Prince Salim) to her grave though she was walled alive. Despite being irritated by Nadi's digression, Gurmehar could not really deny its good sense. After all, Kundan deserved his consideration. Also, this would give him a little time to put together some kind of plan.

"You will marry her of course," Nadi half stated, half questioned.

"Of course," Gurmehar was vehement. "What do you take me for, or her for that matter?"

"Hey, I was just checking."

"Don't bother. As though I would consider anything else with her. She looks—" But here Nadi interrupted Gurmehar, pleading a ton of work and errands to run before they could meet again.

❯ ● ❮

The canteen was full as usual during the lunch hour. Full and loud and humid. The ceiling fans spinning madly above made little difference. Entering into the room Gurmehar felt briefly overwhelmed by the whirl of fans, the chatter of people, the buzz of flies, and the clammer of steel and aluminum dishes on hard surfaces.

This was his third meeting with Kundan. It was never alone of course. After all, social and cultural etiquette must be maintained, the scriptures must be followed.

As Kundan and Gurmehar saw more of each other, Kundan felt

the frustration of the group meetings. Almost every day, during the lunch hour, everyone would stroll around the vast lawns or toward CP. In order to avoid unnecessary attention, Kundan would often walk a step ahead with Swaran while Gurmehar followed with Nadi Singh. Private conversation was impossible. Gurmehar too wanted to share things he had not told anyone, things he had not even allowed himself to think about in years. Between breaks and telephone calls, they managed somehow. For Gurmehar, it was like revisiting Raghubirpur. Bittersweet.

24   *God's Plan*

THE *PRABHAT PHERI* passing through the streets of Raghubir-pur was a discreet and dignified affair. Their peaceful faces be-lied the turmoil in the country. The small, local brass band that usually accompanied the various *pheris* was conspicuous by its absence. Though it charged only an *anna* for its services at this time of year, it had not been invited this time. Only momentarily taken aback by this break in tradition, the small band of women, men, and children, well-dressed and alert, gave no sign of it being anything but normal to be singing devotional songs loudly in the street at four o'clock in the morning. They expected, and got, no grief from the neighbors. It was an annual affair, so people were used to it. Even the stray dogs, curled tightly into themselves in alleys and behind local stores, cocked no more than half an eye open as the procession passed close to them.

In the chill air of the late November pre-dawn, when the moon still hung in the sky with the stars in companion fiery brilliance and the thin, white, winter mist yet hung over the mud road mix-ing briefly in spaces with the thicker gray fumes of a dying coal fire beside a huddled human form under a thin blanket, to the accompaniment of trembling cymbals, through chattering teeth and stiff tongues, the devotees undauntedly sang their message of faith. They were on their way from Sardar Pyaara Singh Chad-dha's house, where everyone had congregated to refresh and fortify themselves with hot *elaichi* chai in *kulhars* and *mathis* and *shakar paras* so fragrant and *khasta* that they came away in their hands—layer after layer. After exchanging conversation, performing brief *kirtan* and *ardas,* they had let themselves out into the street. The procession followed the regular route, passing through the winding streets for half an hour before winding down at the *gurdwara* on *Bhai* Nahal Singh Road.

The flag with the bold Sikh insignia was blowing proudly in the breeze. The insignia that symbolizes physical and spiritual bravery. It consists of two curved swords as a reminder to the Sikhs to serve the Ultimate Reality by teaching the truth and by fighting to defend what is right. The swords contain a *chakkar* or circle, which reminds the Sikhs that there is one Reality. And in the middle lies the *khanda*, the double-edged sword that is used to prepare *amrit* or nectar.

Bhai ji took over in the *gurdwara*. After the usual reading from *Guru Granth Sahib*, the local group of *ragis* sang *kirtan*. Toward the end of the *kirtan*, another priest carried in on his head a large dish of *karah parshad* that had been prepared in the kitchen on the premises. As the service came to a close and everyone rose for the conclusion of the *Diwan, Bhai ji* moved forward and passed the holy *kirpan* through the *parshad*. Six verses of the *Anand Sahib* of Guru Amar Das were read. The *Mul Mantra*, the first inaugural hymn of the *Guru Granth Sahib,* was recited:

> *Ikk oan kaar*
> *sat nam*
> *karta purakh*
> *nir bhau*
> *nir vair*
> *akal murat*
> *ajuni saibhang*
> *gur parsad.*

Then a section of *Sukhmani Sahib* of Guru Arjan was sung. A special prayer was made for Pyaara Singh's family who had hosted the *pheri. Ardas* was led by Pyaara Singh. Finally, the *Guru Granth Sahib* was randomly opened. The passage read became the lesson for the day. *"Wahe guru ji ka khalsa, wahe guru ji ki fateh ho. Bolo satnam, satnam, satnam ji, wahe guru, wahe guru, wahe guru ji."* Mesmerized by the message of peace and hope and the steadily waving long white hairs of the *chaur,* everyone in the congregation quietly waited their turn to receive the *parshad.* Then they were ready to go.

At first, slowly filtering into the compound, the small group of people around the *jooti sewa* soon began to dissipate like the mist in the light of day. Sardar Pyaara Singh too sent his wife home with the children while he stayed back to help with the cleanup. He was worried.

In 1929, the picture in India was not at all clear. The prospect of further constitutional reforms was spreading a wave of agitation throughout the country. Gandhi's letter to Lord Irwin urged the British to take responsibility and respond to the unrest; he announced a plan for nonviolent noncooperation.

From a distance, Pyaara Singh's bent form gave no indication of his identity as a man of substance.

25 *Measuring for Success*

SARDAR PYAARA SINGH of Raghubirpur was a god-fearing man. He never failed to stop by the *gurdwara* every day on the way to his General Merchant store. Not allowing himself—till he had propitiated the Higher Being—to feel that very natural pride that surged within him every time he looked up and beheld that big bold sign on top of his fair-sized shop: PYAARA SINGH. GENERAL MERCHANT. Bold, black letters painted upon a pristine white background. Made of tin, the sign hung fairly low on the store wall, requiring the taller customers to duck each time they entered the store to buy goods. During the monsoon, the wild winds sometimes made the tin rattle and shake. The wind beat upon the metal, lifting it and bringing it down on the wall with force. The rain added its own pressure, almost holding it to the wall to reveal something stark, something mysterious, something that no one really knew or understood. Over the years, the constant movement of the sign against the wall—up and down, up and down, a frenzy of shaking with the wind and the rain—had taken its toll on the sole nail that was plastered into the wall and had held the sign up for so long. The nail now hung drunkenly at an angle, seemingly straining and chafing against its burden. It seemed ready to give in.

For a long time the inhabitants of Raghubirpur had waited for this to happen. But in vain. And now this nonevent had ceased to be of any significance in their daily lives. It was so long ago since the sign had been nailed into its position that no one really questioned it anymore. Moreover, they had grown accustomed to its inconvenience just as they had grown accustomed to the rise of Bijlani in their town and the British in their country. So far as they were concerned it was this last change that had been the easiest to accept.

Living away from the Center had helped. The politics of Delhi, the politics of Nehru, Patel, and others, could be overlooked if not forgotten over here. Peripheral vision had softened many blows which may have felt harder otherwise. They knew from daily experiences that it was better to forget. That at times it was better to imagine. And so what could not be acted upon they had learned simply to push to the back of their minds. It could be said that the hearts of poets beat within their bodies, or perhaps it was simply ignorance that helped them plod through a life that would scare many an educated response.

In any case, the sign occupied its current position because the man who had put it up had misjudged a scuffmark on the wall to be the mark for the nail. And so he had nailed it in and sealed it with plaster for good. Pyaara Singh had originally been displeased, especially as this was a new shop, but he did not want to waste any more time or money. He also knew with the acumen of a businessman that if he verbally expressed his own dissatisfaction, that is, if he was weak, then he might have to give in to the others. And so, with folded hands, downcast eyes, and hesitant tone, he fielded anyone who may have dared to suggest that he either replace the sign or put up another, smaller one. And so the sign remained. Young kids, especially boys, used the sign to perfect their slingshots with pebbles. To a lesser man this may have been reason enough to drive them away with threats, abuse, or reports to their parents. But Pyaara Singh did not have the heart to do so. He even gave them sweets sometimes.

26   *A Humble Beginning*

PYAARA SINGH WAS a farseeing man. But he had not always been like this. Married at the age of eighteen to a beautiful, young girl from the village of Tohra eighty miles from Raghubirpur, he had been ready to begin his life as a householder. It was not to be. The young bride, twelve years of age, died before the henna on her hands had a chance to fade. There was no known cause for her sudden death. To the young Pyaara Singh, finding a dead woman in his bed one morning when he woke up was a trauma that took eight years to overcome.

Seeing their only son's pain, Pyaara Singh's father, the respected Kartar Singh, in consultation with his wife, Kulwant Kaur, shed his hesitation and approached the palmist and then the *pundit* at the local *mandir* for help. He was beginning to understand the wisdom of his forefathers: the day you have a child, you become a hostage to fortune. The palmist twisted and turned Pyaara Singh's hand, plumping it and stretching it alternately, to read the lines; he saw the present as just a challenging phase. *Pundit ji* asked a few questions about Pyaara Singh's time and date of birth, explaining the scientific basis of *his* system. Kulwant Kaur had to be called in. After all the formalities were over, *pundit ji* informed the anxious parents that the lines of the stars showed their son to be a *manglik*; he must marry only another *manglik*. Since his first wife had not been a *manglik,* she had died.

"A marriage with a woman who does not share the same astrological configuration as your son will lead to the death of the woman each time," explained *pundit* Hari Ram. Had they killed their son's young bride, the anxious parents wanted to know. *Pundit* Hari Ram was not a *pundit* for no reason. He assured this sincere and God-fearing couple that no, what had happened was meant to be. Next time, however, would be a different story.

Next time was a different story. After years of convincing their son, when he agreed to marriage a second time, they took great precautions to either get the birth chart of the prospective bride or ask for her time and date of birth so that they themselves could get it made. By a process of elimination they arrived at the decision that Rupinder Kaur's horoscope best matched their son's. She was even a *Khukhrain Khatri,* just a little young. Twelve to his twenty-six. Being a modern young man with a moral conscience, Pyaara Singh tried to express his concern about the age difference to his parents; he did not get very far. Insistence would have been disrespectful of their years and their wisdom. So he gave in.

Pyaara Singh and his wife Rupinder Kaur were blessed with three children, all girls and separated from each other by one year. But he knew that even today, though he was fifty-one years old, there was life in him yet. And his wife, fourteen years his junior, was pregnant again. He hoped it would be a boy. Who knew, if he was kind to the neighborhood boys, God may be kind to him. *"Wahe Guru, mere sache Paadshah, mehar karo,"* he prayed for grace every morning and evening. He even traveled two hundred and thirty miles northwest to make a pilgrimage to the Golden Temple in Amritsar.

There, Pyaara Singh bathed in the pool, looking in wonder at the surrounding marble walkway enclosed by a marble-covered porch several stories high. Walking through one of the four entrances into the temple, he spent a long time reading the verses carved on the wall.

He walked with great zeal toward the center where the *Guru Granth Sahib* rests on silk and brocade under a jewel-studded canopy. From a second floor balcony, *granthis* took turns to read from the holy book—overlapping each turn to avoid a break. Lost in the beauty of the verse he felt himself invincible. In that moment he believed anything was possible. After *karah parshad,* he looked around.

Facing the Golden Temple was the *Akal Takht* or "Throne of the Formless." Guru Hargobind held a court of justice here.

Pyaara Singh returned home reinvigorated. But he need not have feared; he had few enemies. In fact, there wasn't a child in his gully who did not know of him and his generosity. If it had been in their hands, Pyaara Singh would have fathered many sons by now.

The adults were a different matter. It was not that they were particularly antagonistic toward him, just not so easily won over as the children. So, though no one had any particular reason to wish him ill, they observed more critically the man who was never seen in anything less than his immaculate long, white, cotton shirt and *pajama* and *jootis.* Locally made, polished leather *jootis* for everyday wear and *tilledar jootis* from Lahore with their elaborately pointy and upwardly curving front for special occasions. Crowned with his well-starched, white, *turredar pugri,* he was a sight to behold. Though of medium height, in fact no more than five feet six inches, he carried himself with a pride that made him seem taller. He furthered this impression by making a great pretense of ducking at the entrance of his store though the bottom of the sign missed him clearly by several inches. That he or his store servants bought all household goods, including fresh vegetables daily—obviating the need for his wife to come out and mingle unnecessarily in the market place—also increased his standing in the community. A pious lady and a good housewife, she appeared mostly at ceremonial gatherings. At these times she was well dressed and bejeweled as befitted the wife of a man of his status.

Pyaara Singh prided himself on being a modern man. He smiled in a superior fashion as he remembered that he was not like his friend Kareem Raza, whose mother, wife, and sisters lived in the *zenana,* the women's section of their house, and maintained *purdah* from the men. No, his wife merely had to cover her head with her *dupatta* or stand with eyes downcast in the company of men. A little more so in front of complete strangers than in front of male relatives, of course.

In keeping with his modernity, his daughters had all been enrolled in a small neighborhood school. That the eldest girl, Pyaari, at the age of thirteen, had had a rude awakening on her return home from school one day when she was told to quickly change into red wedding garments, was something he did not allow himself to dwell on. *She has to be married, she is almost a woman,* he told himself. Moreover, it was a prize match, not to be missed; Roop Singh was a *zamindar* no less. Such matches did not come by very easily or often. "Pyaari will soon forget. Once she is married, especially once she holds a child in her arms, she will know that *Darji* was right. She will forgive me and be embarrassed about the fuss she made." Pyaari, however, even after twelve years of marriage and two children, had not forgiven him. The rift between daughter and father that had begun that fateful afternoon had only widened—first with tears and then with bitter silence.

With his second daughter, Swaran, he once again took action for her future by arranging a match. This time, three years after Pyaari's marriage, in his eagerness to settle her future he married his fifteen-year-old daughter to a widower, Gurmukh Singh, twice her age who had children from his previous marriage.

Gurmukh Singh had not finished mourning the loss of his ex-wife, the ashes had not been cold yet when marriage proposals had begun to arrive. What were his parents to do? What was he to do? The parents could not keep refusing the various possible *samdhis;* the son could not keep mourning forever. They all knew that they would finally give in. After all, Gurmukh could not remain a widower all his life. Also, there were the infant children to think of. They needed a mother. So it was decided. Why not marry when they were in a strong position to pick and choose? They chose and picked Swaran, who was a little better prepared for this harvest gathering than her older sister had been. That she was neither excited nor sad was neither here nor there. She would adjust and learn to be comfortable. In her effort to adjust, she had produced four daughters, one every year, and, after a slump of four years, was now pregnant again.

Pyaara Singh felt he had won his greatest victory in the match he found for his youngest daughter, Ramanjit Kaur. For Harbans Singh was a hotelier. Moreover, his family were landowners in Rawalpindi and Lahore. They were moneyed people, and their family could be traced back several generations. It was these latter reasons really that had tipped the balance in favor of this alliance. Even after years of being in business himself, he still found it a little difficult to shake the conventional shame attached to the trading professions. The winds of change however were blowing strong, and he knew that they would successfully bury old opinion.

On being told of her impending nuptials Ramanjit was happy. She looked forward to being married and going away to Lahore. She had heard that it was the fashion center of this part of India, and *mems* walked around there openly arm in arm with men. Even Punjabi women living in Lahore were said to dress more boldly and express themselves in a manner that would shock Raghubir-pur. She was particularly curious to see who was the *gori mem* who had married a Sikh man. Everyone said she was more *Sikhni* than the *Sikhnis* and always arrived at the *gurdwara* with her husband and in-laws in an impeccable *salwar kameez* and a glittering *dupatta* that never slipped her head. With bent head and folded hands when she wished everybody *Sat-Sri-Akal* in her pretty accented Punjabi, she won them over as no British army ever had. At sixteen, the thought of getting away from her father and doing something shocking like the *other* white *mems* (not this one married to the Sikh), seemed vaguely exciting and adventurous.

But now that she had three children of her own as well as a hotel to look after and when drives or walks on the mall were a rare rather than a frequent part of her daily life, a visit home to help her mother through her pregnancy seemed like a godsend vacation.

27 *Riding the Rails*

PYAARA SINGH KNEW he had a lot to be grateful for even though the British had come and stuck like leeches to India, and years of servitude had taken its toll on the country and on the national character. Being a somewhat educated man, and priding himself on his loving consideration of his daughters' futures, he believed that much good had also been achieved. The construction of railway lines twenty miles from Raghubirpur had brought in new job opportunities and increased mercantile and social links—sadly, already forgotten by the people who gathered in corners, under trees, on the terrace and on the verandas noisily gulping hot tea and gossiping about what they would do differently given half a chance. But they would never be given the chance to serve their country because they had never understood that it was their choice to make. Meanwhile, they continued to find fault with the war efforts of the freedom fighters. They knew with perfect hindsight how the revolt of 1857 should have been fought. If they had been in charge, no one could have broken their ranks. They also criticized the current politics. *Sardar* and *Chacha* were at loggerheads. Gandhi was being ignored. It shocked them to hear him referred to in this way; it was sacrilegious. While they spent their time quibbling over his name—Gandhi *ji* or *Mahatma* Gandhi or the more popular *Bapu*—India had come a long way in the last seventy years without any contribution from them. Fueled by the

RSS, they continued, however, to be led by the here and now. The rumblings for a separate Muslim state with its independent government threatened their peace, especially as their town bordered many towns with a high concentration of Muslims; the protection of women and children was their main concern, they claimed.

But as the British had spread their wings over all of India, they had introduced their native companies and thus successfully weeded out growth opportunities for many indigenous entrepreneurs. One by one, many great houses of business had fallen. Pyaara Singh witnessed this through his growing years. Not wanting to suffer the same fate as so many young men of his generation, he decided upon a plan. The first was to do a business that did not invite the competition of Britishers. The second was to cultivate some amount of acquaintanceship with the British in the right places, just enough to help him in his business and not enough to antagonize his own people.

By opening a General Merchant store Pyaara Singh knew that he was doing the right thing. While it marked a break from his ancestral tradition of agriculture and was not particularly prestigious or especially financially rewarding, he yet knew it to be right for him. With confidence Pyaara Singh set about establishing himself. He had only a little money of his own. Most of the earnest money for the store came from the marriage settlement with which his wife had graced his home. Her entrance in his life was therefore propitious. She had literally brought *Lakshmi* with her. Living in a primarily Hindu neighborhood, Pyaara Singh had not been unaffected by this belief. With money in hand, Pyaara Singh ran to the owner of the vacant store, Lala Sita Ram. It was a short exchange.

"*Namaste,* Lala *ji.*"

"*Sat Sri Akal,* Pyaara Singh."

It was an auspicious beginning. Each had won over the other by appropriating the other's manner of greeting.

Lala Sita Ram sat regally in the front porch of his compound on a *diwan,* a flat wooden bed raised on four legs, covered with a thick mattress and white sheet and two round, long pillows against which he leaned back in cushioned comfort. By his side, there was a wooden chessboard with fancily carved ivory pieces. The files and ranks were beautifully defined in colored lacquer. Lala *ji* seemed to be in the middle of a game. With himself. In front of him lay a wooden desk that opened upward. It was a little inconvenient to use as he had to lift all his papers each time he had to take anything out of the desk. Still, he had liked the look of it and decided to put up with the inconvenience. By his side, on the floor, lay some ledgers and an ink pot with some quills. And a half-full glass of *shardayayi* with some crushed dried fruit still clinging to its milk-rimmed mouth.

A little to the left and in the back corner of the compound was a well. A measure of the Lala's personal standing. A young female servant stood next to it with legs crossed for better balance, holding her sari neatly tucked in between. When the young child by her side insisted on drawing water from the well, to stop his tantrum she allowed him to hold on to the rope close to the pail while she herself held on to it where it left the wheel above. This way she could control the rope and protect the child.

Lala Sita Ram's means were also evident in the fact that he employed a personal servant to daily oil and massage his body. The little boy, whom he called *mundu,* worked hard on polishing his master's big protruding multi-layered belly and bald pate—that he usually kept hidden under a white turban. Now, the boy put down the straw fan that he was waving behind his master's back and ran to freshen the hookah with the long, curved inhaling pipe and copper tips that the Lala had had specially made for himself. As the boy came forward to place the hookah by the Lala, Pyaara Singh couldn't help wondering if the rumors about the Lala smoking a special concoction of opium in his tobacco were true. But he was careful not to show more than respectful thoughts on his face.

Lala *ji* pointed to the chess set. "Do you play?"

"A little." Pyaara Singh was being modest.

"Shall we have a game?"

Pyaara Singh understood this was some kind of test. He took his seat across the board and started setting his side.

In those days the face of a man was often enough reason to make a deal, and Lala *ji* saw Pyaara Singh had come with money. Moreover, it was Diwali. A time of joy and celebration among the Hindus and Sikhs. For the Sikhs, Diwali is a reminder of the imprisonment and release of Guru Hargobind. The Emperor Jahangir had had the Guru imprisoned because of nonpayment of taxes by his father and for raising an army. He was held at the fort in Gwalior together with fifty-two Hindu Princes. At Diwali, the Emperor decided to release the Guru, who, however, refused to leave without the Hindu Princes. The Emperor commanded that only those who could pass through a narrow passage holding on to the Guru's clothes would be released. It seemed like an insurmountable task, but the Guru had a plan. He had a cloak brought to him with long tassels at the end of it. Holding on to these tassels, everyone walked out to freedom.

As a Hindu, Lala Sita Ram knew, on this day more than on others, it would be inauspicious to turn down this offer; it would be tantamount to turning away Lakshmi on her lotus throne from his door. And who knew if she would ever return again. In any case, if the Lala had any second thoughts about this matter he was not encouraged to pursue them by his wife who had watched Pyaara Singh's entry and followed the entire conversation from behind the sitting room door.

"*Suno ji,*" she called.

"What Bhagwanti?"

"One minute, *ji.*"

"Oh, all right," shrugged Lala *ji* and got up to answer her reluctantly. "Now, what is it? Be quick. I'm in the middle of a business deal."

"Today is Diwali," she stated quietly.

"Yes, yes, I know."

"I'm glad. Here are some *laddoos.* We must not forget what day it is," she reminded him once again.

Lala Sita Ram quietly took the sweets. He knew there was no way out now. Not that he had been looking for one particularly. Still, it wouldn't have hurt to keep Pyaara Singh waiting till he conducted some further market research. After all, the store had been put up for sale only recently, and it wasn't as though he was desperate for money. Normally, Lala Sita Ram did not allow his wife any control over his business life. But today was Diwali and, moreover, he knew Pyaara Singh's family by sight. They were known to be decent people. He also prided himself in giving young people a chance, especially when there was nothing wrong with the offer in the first place. And so telling himself that this was his chance to do good for the people and build some goodwill with God at the same time, he agreed to sell the store to Pyaara Singh.

If Bhagwanti had suspected the reasons that motivated the conclusion of the sale, she might have been shocked and tried to appease the wrath of God by making everyone in the family fast and pray the appropriate number of days as told by her *pundit*. But Lala Sita Ram had been married for years and had learned to avoid unnecessary pitfalls by sharing only that information that would be noncontroversial and not disrupt the peace and harmony he liked to enjoy in his house.

So Pyaara Singh became a proprietor at the age of twenty-six. Pyaara Singh had spent many years building his business to where it was today. He spent many long hours in his store. He went personally to the wholesalers to pick up the orders. Depending upon the sale, sometimes this was once a month or once a week or more often. He never wanted to turn a customer away from his store. He knew that a satisfied customer is a customer who will return and one who will possibly recommend his business to others. Courtesy became the key to his service. And efficiency. But all this did not happen in one day. He had studied the general market. Moreover, he had studied his competition. His was not the only general merchant's store in the area.

Bijlani had had his little store, or *khoka* as it was popularly called, for a very long time. He had established a monopoly and was used to having his own way. Customers at his store often had to wait for their orders to be filled. They also had to put up with abrupt speech. He was especially cruel to the poor. Seeing them stand in line outside his store in the heat seemed to give him some kind of pleasure. Putting the shutter of his store down just when a skeletal field worker reached his turn gave him even more satisfaction.

"It's not yet lunchtime, Bijlani *ji*," some poor mite may muster up a whisper.

"What? What did you say?" Bijlani fumed through his flaring nostrils.

"Nothing, nothing at all."

Bijlani's code was that what people were not willing to wait for, they need not buy. The same went for his prices. Though he did offer a credit service, it was at so exploitative a rate that the general public was openly appalled. But it made no difference to Bijlani. He knew his was the only general goods store and if the people wanted his wares, they must come to him.

Pyaara Singh changed all that. And quite naturally this started a rivalry between the two merchants. Bijlani came of trader stock. His family had been in some kind of trade or another for generations. He knew how to fight dirty. But Pyaara Singh had the determination to succeed. He also had public sentiment on his side. The public was sick of Bijlani's rudeness and wanted him pulled down a rung or two.

Over a period of two years Bijlani tried by many a foul means to drive the rookie out of town. Pyaara Singh suffered many losses. Consignment of goods disappeared, carts of grain were found overturned in the fields, the merchandise unredeemable. Once, some of the spokes of a cart's wheel suddenly gave in, and the goods it was carrying came tumbling down into the dust. Another time, a perfectly docile pair of oxen suddenly began running wildly as they tried to escape some strategically placed burrs under their yoke, thus overturning goods yet again. As Bijlani grew more desperate, so did his schemes. The next time a consignment didn't arrive, Pyaara Singh and his friends found that the drivers had been accosted and roughed up, bags of grain slashed, and the grain left to trickle to a finish.

Pyaara Singh was a peace-loving man, not a foolish one. He knew something had to be done once and for all to put a stop to the mean-spiritedness of Bijlani. He realized that despite his scruples, in order to do this, he must out-Bijlani Bijlani.

How to do this and not compromise his own integrity? After discussion with his elders, he came up with a simple plan. He would place one of his own men to work for Bijlani. He had to be careful in choosing a man both low in profile and yet intelligent enough to carry out his task. Gopal, the grain cleaner, was just such a man. He was quiet but friendly and an even better listener. For weeks nothing happened, till one night. When Gopal reported a plan to start a fire in Pyaara Singh's store, he took the news seriously. Along with five other men, Pyaara Singh lay in wait inside the store. It was dangerous because they now knew exactly what Bijlani was capable of. It was a long wait. Not knowing the exact day Bijlani meant to execute his plan, they hid behind great bags of grain for five nights in a row before Bijlani struck on the sixth night. Grown proud with his past successes, he had also grown a little careless. That is what Pyaara Singh was counting on. He was not disappointed. There wasn't much of a fight after all. The criminals were caught red-handed and turned in to the police. Pyaara Singh had established his credibility.

After the battle with Bijlani, Pyaara Singh became more savvy of the world. It was not that he was distrustful of others, but his experience and success in overcoming Bijlani had taught him and others around him that he was not a man to be messed around with. It was also around that time that he stopped wearing colored *pugris* and smoothing his beard with oil. Though white turbans were generally worn by older men of his community, especially with the *turra* or fan on top, they became his personal hallmark. He also began leaving his beard down. Over the last two years of his fight for survival, his jet-black hair had turned completely white. Some saw this as a pity. Others saw this as a mark of his wisdom. Though still a young man with one daughter and a wife barely fourteen years of age and pregnant again, he had come to be accepted in the community as a man of substance.

He now took care of a lot of the business himself. Initially, he also did the paperwork for the store. Often the only time to do this task was at night. He never shirked his task nor left it till the next day. He knew he really couldn't afford to do that because it would increase his burden even more for the next day.

Those were the changing years when the British were contemplating the shift of their Empire from Calcutta to Delhi. By 1903, Bengal had become a huge conglomerate of provinces that included Assam, Bihar, and Orissa. Delhi was also close to the summer capital, Shimla. As Britain mourned the death of Edward VII in May 1910, the Union Jack flew at half-mast, and the Empire in India was thrown into gloom. Not for long, however. George V was declared the successor, and the British got ready one more time to celebrate a coronation with pomp and ceremony in Delhi in 1911.

With the defeat of Bijlani, Pyaara Singh, too, heralded a new order of things to come in Raghubirpur. Through all of this Rupinder Kaur stood by his side. It could even be said that she played by his side for she was but a child yet, and hopscotch and jump rope in the backyard of their house with her neighborhood friends was much more appealing to her than the serious duties of a wife. If someone had tried to explain these to her, she would have been embarrassed and run away and hid herself. Yet, without really understanding, she instinctively did what was expected of her. She was a good wife and had already given her husband one child. God willing, more would follow. She must try to give him a son next time though. This much she had gathered even as she tried to throw the smooth piece of slate into the correct square and then negotiate her little body over it. Pyaara Singh never said anything to her. So she went about her business and Pyaara Singh went about his. And somewhere along the line the two established an understanding that was often seen as enviable by others of their age-group even if the elders thought it inappropriate and a challenge to the old established order.

28   *Fighting Fate*

GURMEHAR SINGH ANNOUNCED his entry into the world at eight fifteen in the night with a loud, piercing cry, clearing his breathing passages of mucus at the same time. In the courtyard, a band of *hijras* danced in celebration to the rhythm of *dhols* and loud claps. These eunuchs knew their takings would be large that day. Pyaara Singh, who had longed to hear those infant notes for years, was not there.

◗ ● ◖

Pyaara Singh was a religious man, even a superstitious one, and he had not missed a moment when he had not bent his head in front of the *gurdwara* everytime he had passed it. The local *gurdwara* faced the west, but he had taken to heart Guru Nanak's message that God does not dwell in any particular direction. He is present everywhere. If this was true—and he believed it was—then his quick obeisance in the general direction of where he knew the holy book, *Guru Granth Sahib,* was placed inside the *gurdwara,* would be more than enough. Just in case it wasn't, he paid his respects in person several times a day. He had paid for *langars* for the people, he had paid for special *kirtans* and prayers to be performed for God's blessing, he had done *jooti sewa*—standing outside the *gurdwara* in rain and sunshine. This last service, performed by a man who could command others to do almost anything at his bidding, made a greater impression on the people than all else he had done; it touched their hearts. Understanding the need for a man to father a male child they hoped his humility would be rewarded.

Pyaara Singh, however, was determined to have more than hope on his side. This time, on the very eve of his child's birth, even as his wife lay in labor surrounded by the local midwife, older ladies from the neighborhood, and the three grown-up daughters who hovered anxiously outside their mother's door and tried to keep their children from making too much noise as they played hide-and-seek in oblivion of the impending birth of their aunt or uncle, Pyaara Singh was leaving nothing to chance. He was not pacing. As befitted a man of his standing, he was sitting in the next room with his head buried in the local paper while he anxiously awaited the news. But he was not really reading. He was thinking about a conversation he had had earlier that morning. Just that morning he had heard about the old Hindu lady in the neighboring village of Fikran who performed miracles and promised sons and heirs where there were none. There was a slight problem, however.

The changing times were hard on people of different religions, especially Hindus and Sikhs. Hindus and Sikhs, who had once lived side by side with each other and had eaten from the same plates, were now suspicious of each other. The British had fairly mastered the principle of divide and rule, successfully dividing what was once a more harmonious state. Or so people liked to think, preferring to forget the repeated success of this policy during the long period of Muslim invasions. It was more romantic to think of India as *Ramrajya,* the perfect state of Rama during the golden age, that had been split asunder by a corroding enemy than to look at themselves and see where they had played right into the hands of the enemy.

"Buffoons. It is twenty-five years since I tried this last, but I can show them how to do it right."

Pumped with pride and national thoughts, in the early noon hours before his wife gave birth, he decided to drive out to meet Chand Bibi. Though he fancied himself a progressive man and generally denounced voodoo practices, still, things took on a different complexion when the matter concerned him. Moreover, he felt this was his last chance. God had given him another chance in his *pukka* years and he did not want to foul it this time. He wanted to make sure that he did what was expected of him and had a son. After all, as a respected member of the community, a proprietor, and a man of standing, it was his duty to provide a male heir. His wife, too, came from a family of some standing in her village. Many sons graced both their families and it was not to be tolerated without a fight or a prayer that there would be no male heir to carry on the family name and tradition now. His name would not die with him.

To live through his son would be to cheat death. Almost. He was prepared to be almost victorious. As almost victorious as other men of his *khatri biradari* in front of whom he did not want to be shamed by appearing less than a man. Parminder Singh Khanna, his much younger cousin from Rawalpindi, had spoken fondly of his son on his last visit. On the way back to the railway station, where Pyaara Singh had personally dropped him in his carriage, Parminder Singh had confided his dream of having more sons.

"Two at least, though I'll take what God gives me."

"You are a lucky man," Pyaara Singh spoke quietly.

"It is all God's grace."

"Ahh, you are so right, so right." Listening to him, Pyaara Singh felt a twinge of envy. To have a son, to build a bridge to the future. To walk with head held high, his starched turban intact on top of his head and not sullied and limp with the sweat of fear and shame was his life's goal.

He first knew that his prayers would be answered and that his life would not have been lived in vain when, on his arrival, Chand Bibi told him she had been expecting him. At these words he almost relaxed and permitted himself a smile of hope before withdrawing once again into dignity and the stance of humility much like that of a beggar at a rich man's door.

Chand Bibi's fame and the near accuracy of her predictions had spread far and wide. Farther and wider than any place she, herself, had traveled to. But when anyone told her of how they had heard of her performing miracles in one part of the land and another person told another story of her performance at the same time in another part of the land, she never contradicted either. She just smiled quietly and graciously accepted all that people gave her to express their gratiude for her good work. She was not known to talk much. She encouraged her subjects—as she liked to call the many people who flocked from far and near to ask for help or just to see her—to talk. Wherever she was known to be, there was talk.

talk talk talk

Plenty of talk. Noise, sound, vibration, a universe at work. Yet very little ever originated in her.

Chand Bibi had always attracted crowds. At one time, more than two decades ago, those crowds were different. They consisted of young lords and the Princes of States, even a local maharaja or two. Her art had captured the imaginations of many a young man. When she put on her *ghungroos* and twirled her long, frock-like Anarkali dress made of the finest materials over a *churidar pajama*, they were ready to sign their wealth and estates over to her. The heart of many a young man had beaten furiously to the rhythm of *"ta thai, thai ta"* as she moved to the throb of the drums. Kathak had once been the dance of religious devotion. Popularized during the Muslim rule of India, kings and ordinary citizens alike kept alive this tradition inside and outside their courts. Chand Bibi's perfect demonstration of this princely dance form re-created for scores the ambiance of a lost world.

Her beauty was the icing on the cake. Even now people talked of her round face with its creamy complexion, luminous like the moon when full. She had perfectly arched dark brows; long, faintly wavy nut-brown hair; and a medium-sized mole just above the left side of her mouth that only served to draw further attention to her lips. Her perfect, bow-shaped lips were naturally red. The hint of *paan* with its betel juice made them look ripe like a piece of fruit luscious and ready to bite into. Which one of her features was more spectacular was impossible to determine even by a connoisseur of beauty.

But no one really knew anything much about Chand Bibi. Some people speculated that she had belonged to a courtesan house, a *kotha,* and now in old age had retired after a distinguished career. Others said that she had given up dancing a long time ago because of a broken heart, a young man who had promised to marry her and take her away from her lifestyle. They believed that his family had intervened and put a stop to what would have amounted to a very shameful union. Others challenged this story. They believed that Chand Bibi was so beautiful and talented that she could have any man. It was pain in her joints that had forced her to lead a more quiet life. This latter reason seemed so prosaic that a lot of people rejected it purely on the basis of their inability to imagine her suffering anything so mundane as joint pains. But what did Chand Bibi think of all these rumors? No one had ever had the guts to ask her something that personal. It was enough that she allowed them in her presence. And so the rumors about her past were never put to rest.

The rumors were fueled again at the sudden reappearance of Chand Bibi some ten years later. This time the Chand Bibi people saw was even more intense than the one they had known before. This time she was a woman who was covered from head to toe in a simple, white cotton sari. This Chand Bibi, too, was a sorceress. She, too, gave an audience, but it was of a different nature than before. This time she drew her following from her power over the unknown. She foretold the future; she had also been known to reverse bad acts. The hapless people, mostly farmers and laborers, but also zamindars and small rajas came to her for knowledge. No one was turned away. She saw them all, she helped them all. Her radiant face seemed ageless though they knew her to be an aging woman. And the people, washed and renewed by her radiance, came away with a sense of exhaustion and the impression of having been in the presence of something larger than their own reality. Yet if they were asked to repeat her words after their visit, they could never really pinpoint anything. Was she a *dhhongi,* a pretender, or was she a woman in touch with her soul and hence closer to the absolute soul of the universe? Even as the more progressive of her audience asked themselves these questions, they were forced to submit to the unknown as—unexplained to all— her predictions continued to bear fruit.

In the case of Pyaara Singh things happened no differently. In fact, his visit with her lasted no more than a few minutes though it felt like hours to him. She immediately told him, "I have been expecting you." Those were the only words that left her mouth during the entire encounter. In preparation for his visit, she had everything ready. She took him into an inside room where she pointed to a makeshift child's hammock. It was made of an old piece of sari, folded many times and pulled at each end into a knot around the posts of two high, wooden cots. There was no child inside the hammock, so it hung limply, waiting, like a yearning, young girl's womb. Chand Bibi first placed a girl doll in the hammock. For a moment, Pyaara Singh was disconcerted. It was a little toy, the kind one could buy from any store for a few paise. Pyaara Singh himself stocked his store with them in response to the great demand by the rising crop of new parents who had begun to spoil their children with ready-made toys in place of more traditional homemade rag dolls and puppets. He hastily returned his attention to her as she took out the doll and turned the hammock upside down. This was a little tricky considering it was made of cloth and its corners were tied to bedposts, but the message was clear. She had turned the tide around. It was as though she had loudly said, "Enough. There have been enough girls in this house. It is time for a boy." With this she gently pressed her hands against her eyes. Pyaara Singh knew his visit was over. He still had a million questions to ask, a million assurances he would have liked to have. But he knew he had been dismissed. Chand Bibi had spoken. Chand Bibi had done, and now he must leave.

Quiet and hesitant in front of no man, Pyaara Singh yet knew when he must give in gracefully. He left his gifts and offerings by the side of the door. To offer them to her personally would have meant too much of an insult. These were expressions of gratitude, not payment. Every person who came to her door knew that. Bowing his head in acknowledgement of her knowledge and ability, he withdrew from the room.

The drive back to Raghubirpur was very long. Yet Pyaara Singh now hurried back, anxious to be home at the moment his great miracle took place. He had done what any decent man worth his salt was supposed to do to ensure his manhood and the future of his family name. He felt satisfied. If he had any niggling doubts, he swept them away for the present under the dust raised by his horse carriage, not to be acknowledged until fate decreed them necessary. He even permitted himself to hum a little.

Tu mera pita, tu hai mera mata
Tu mera bandhap, tu mera bhrata.
You are my father, you are my mother
You are my friend, you are my brother.

Though the horses were tired from their long journey, made not once but twice that day in a short space of time without any rest, it seemed as though for once they, too, were willing to overlook their fatigue. It was as though they understood their master's destination; they were going home to something that held the promise of the future. And they were proud to participate in the moment. So they raced along, under the cooling rays of the moon, the bells around their necks swinging in harmony to the rhythm of the song.

On arrival, Pyaara Singh was greeted by his three daughters and the housemaids. "*Darji*, it is a son, we have a brother." No jealousy marked their voices at the sudden appearance after all these years of a male heir who was bound to change all their lives and fortunes. They were not even embarrassed to have a brother younger than their own children. It was a miracle. It was a gift. It was fitting that their father should have a male heir. Moreover, such confusions caused by mothers and daughters giving birth at the same time were quite common.

In his absence, Pyaara Singh's son had been born. After waiting for Pyaara Singh for a long time, the *hijras* had left with partial gifts and promises and threats to return the next day. "Gurmehar," burst from Pyaara Singh's mouth and he broke into a frenzy of weeping. "Gurmehar," he shouted again as the rest of the household took a back seat in the face of his just excitement. The guru had shown his *mehar,* his beneficence, and so Pyaara Singh named his son on the driveway of his house, his one leg yet inside the carriage. Surrounded by raised voices and increasing pandemonium, the horses neighed and had to be held back by the reins as Pyaara Singh alighted. He was jubilant. He was humbled. He was a changed man. His thoughts immediately rushed to Chand Bibi, and he almost got right back into the carriage in his excitement to retrace his steps, get down on his knees, and thank her for her miracle. Somehow, he was contained from doing so. Refusing, however, to be contained from expressing his gratitude in some way, he immediately ordered a fresh carriage to be drawn and sweets carried to her village.

Leaving his daughters to carry out his orders, Pyaara Singh hastened toward the room where his wife was now resting. Since it was a couple of hours since the baby was born and the laboring mother had had time to overcome her initial bout of pain, he was now welcome in her room. Anytime before this and he would merely have been a hindrance, getting in the way of women who best knew how to function at this great moment of mystery that could crumble even those men who had faced bullets and bayonets in war. To fight the British was one thing, to undergo personally or face the agony of a woman in labor was another.

It is a moot point that had the women inside the birthing rooms been allowed to marshal armies, the war with Britain may have ended a lot earlier.

Pyaara Singh did not think of any of these things at this time, however. It was not war, national justice, or amity among the Indians that occupied his thoughts as he rushed into the room his wife was in. For a moment he was blinded as he moved from the bright light into the darkened room. His foot struck against a basket protruding from underneath a table. As he bent to see what it was, the smell of guavas that Rupinder Kaur had craved during her pregnancy filled his senses. The curtains were drawn, an old woman was sitting by his wife's bedside, swinging a hand fan made of cane, slowly, desultorily. As he moved toward his wife's bed, he stopped again as he encountered the old woman. The old woman, too, saw him and immediately rose to walk out and give the master of the house a moment alone with his wife. Pyaara Singh was not heartless. He first made sure that his wife was all right, then he moved toward his son. His son.

"Gurmehar," he whispered and made to brush his hand gently over the child's almost bald head. "Gurmehar," he whispered again but the child continued to sleep peacefully, oblivious to the world of national and family politics, of cultural traditions and superstitions.

"Rupinder Kaur *ji*, how are you? Are you all right? You look tired." Having feasted on his son with his own eyes, he now turned his attention to his wife. Rupinder Kaur was not a particularly shy woman. She was a woman of her time, but she was a woman with four older brothers, who, together with their father, had spoiled her and given her confidence. In Kauntrila, her family was well known and well respected. Everyone had seen the Kohlis' daughter grow in the shadow of her older brothers as she followed them around, more often than not in their way. But they had put up with it with good cheer. Especially her youngest older brother, Rupinder Singh. His protective love for her had been evident from day one when he had taken one look at her and taken her under his wing. It began with a desire to have someone younger to take care of and order around at the same time. It soon grew to be a strong bond. A bond that the parents celebrated by naming the sister with the same name as her brother. Now no one could harm her. If anyone tried, there would be her brothers to answer to.

She also knew a husband's love. So when Pyaara Singh greeted his son before he greeted her, she did not mind it. She understood how much it meant to him to have a son. She understood and appreciated especially the fact that though he had desperately wanted a son from the time they had been married, he had yet never blamed her for her inability to have sons as did the husbands of many of her friends. She also knew of all the efforts he had made this time to propitiate any outside intelligence that might have influence on the gender of their child. His visit to Chand Bibi had been made suddenly, but even of that she had been informed inside the birthing room. So, no, she did not blame her husband for first expressing his happiness to see his son. And she did not remind him that he could not name his son till the naming ceremony. His son. Her son. Their son.

"*Sardar ji*, our son is beautiful," she said, looking down at the yet-wrinkled child with only a faint lining of hair on his head. It was not really an answer to his question. Yet Pyaara Singh understood. She had called him *"Sardar ji."* He knew she did that only in moments of deep emotion. Seeing her drooping eyelids and right arm gently draped around the child curled into her side as though yet not aware that he had changed mediums, Pyaara Singh felt a surge of love he had never felt before. That minute he decided his son would be a great man. Greater than him. Greater than this small town of Raghubirpur allowed him to be. Greater than the British had allowed many Indians from respected families like his to be. He knew the sign on his shop would not read "Pyaara Singh and Son."

And that was all right.

1930 was a very good year.

29 *Reaping the Crop*

IN THE YEARS following the birth of his son, Pyaara Singh's business grew like a note becomes a tune. The depression that had hurt so many did not hurt him as he traveled far and wide and made careful investments, buying goods from wholesalers at low prices as they tried to get rid of their stock in a frenzy of fear of the impending unknown and selling them at high rates in the open market—often back to the same people he had initially purchased them from—as they now scrambled to regain their stock in hopes of reestablishing themselves. Pyaara Singh was a good man, a fair man, and also a very astute man. Moreover, he was not in this game for charity. As many businesses, especially small ones, collapsed, Pyaara Singh's stature loomed larger than anybody's in the horizon.

As Gurmehar left his mother's lap to crawl and then toddle around the *jamun* tree in the back courtyard, Pyaara Singh carried on his business as usual. Around the time of his son's birth, he had a rough, round, wooden table built that was placed prominently under the tree. As the *jamuns* fell to the ground or over the table, some were eaten and others were pressed to a pulp under feet. In time, the dried pulp left a dark purple stain. Under the sun, wind, and rain, the planks expanded then contracted then settled into a comfortable groove, and the wood darkened in hue to become smooth around the edges. Here, in the evenings, Pyaara Singh sometimes exchanged pipes and conversation with his friends.

"*Kunwar* Jodha Mal squealed loudly last week. The papers reeked of it all week long," Hari Ram said with some joy. Everyone knew there was no love lost between him and the local lord.

"He sure did. Once again, the fat prince must curb his spending. But Nigel-what's-his-name has a battle on his hands. A people's man, that's how he styles himself." Kareem Raza inhaled deeply from his pipe, held it in for a moment, then exhaled into the sky in a long breath.

"People's man indeed. Which people? Goodluck. That's like asking the King to consult the janitor," Hari Ram's retort was quick.

Pyaara Singh heard of the rejection of Jinnah's safeguards for Muslim interests that marked the downward trend in Hindu-Muslim relations over a glass of *shardayayi* with his friend Kareem Raza. The two were alone, the night was young, and the breeze blew liftingly through the leaves, making them brush against each other and sigh in release.

"What do you think of Muhammad Iqbal's address to the Muslim League in Allahabad?" Pyaara Singh began quietly.

"Well, he certainly seems to be fanning flames by describing the inconceivability of India's existence under a single government. He has said that not territory but religious community defines and divides the people. And so he is asking for a confederated India with a Muslim state that would include Punjab, North West Frontier Province, Sindh, and Baluchistan."

"Don't forget though that it is these young pups at Cambridge, in fact, who, opposing federation, are demanding partition into Pakistan, the land of the *Paks,* the spiritually pure and clean," Pyaara Singh mildly raised his voice. Nearby, the young Gurmehar stopped momentarily in mid-play at this change of tone.

"Jinnah's encouragement of the two-nation theory has been no help. It did come to the Lahore resolution, did it not?" There was sadness in Kareem Raza's voice.

"And now the war."

"Remember Colonel Hawthorne?"

"Who?" Pyaara Singh was distracted.

"He stayed at my house...about...three years ago...."

"Oh yes, the one who came and stuck. I remember, you had to finally ask him to leave. But what does that have to do with this situation? This is not our concern."

"If our children fight in it, then it is."

What Kareem Raza said made sense. What was new? As Indian soldiers prepared to fight for their step-country, Pyaara Singh thanked God that he was too old and his son far too young to enlist.

Everyone knew that in times of war goods were often rationed and inflation was rampant. Pyaara Singh traveled far and wide by rail to add to his stores, often paying a high price for them. But what was considered a high price in remote, small villages from where he stocked his store was not so high by Raghubirpur standards. So his returns in his hometown were higher. Thus, he soon established himself as a major proprietor no less than the likes of Lala Sita Ram in whose drawing room he had once quivered as he sat waiting to know if he was going to be able to begin business at all. He had gone into business expecting no more than a modest financial gain, but years of hard work and good fortune had brought him more than he had hoped for.

To mark his change in status he got constructed a tall double-story house with an open terrace where he could escape during the cruel heat of the summer. He also got constructed for his wife a room, all in marble, where the holy book was placed on silk-covered marble under a canopy of brocade. All in all, he had gained victory without having to fight for or against the British at all.

On the day of Gurmehar's naming ceremony the holy book had miraculously opened on the letter *G;* other than that, nothing remarkable happened to him in the first sixteen years of his life. He grew up like any other young boy of his family status. He went to school, played in the street with other little boys, and even threw pebbles with the rest of them at the sign hanging more precariously than ever above his father's store. Pyaara Singh and Rupinder Kaur spoiled the boy. So did the three sisters. Every time they visited home, they showered their little brother with love and gifts. At other times, they sent him things that their own sons had outgrown. Playing in the street with his best friend since the age of four, Mehmood Raza, the grandson of Kareem Raza, his father's friend, Gurmehar soon grew to be a young man.

In fairness to Gurmehar, it must be admitted that being a child of older parents, he was often sickly. Combine this with the fact that he had been gained by fouling fate by the turn of the cradle and you have a recipe for heartache. What could his parents do? Indeed, what would any parents do? Pyaara Singh and Rupinder Kaur did what anyone else would have done in their place. They mollycoddled him. But instead of shaking him out of his frequent fits of moodiness, this had the effect of driving him deeper into himself. It broke the mother's heart. It roused the father's impatience and eventually his anger. And finally it undid Gurmehar. At sixteen, his fate seemed set in a mold. Sixteen was a very difficult year for Gurmehar. It was the year his mother died. So along with adolescence, he also had to cope with her death. The scent of adolescence though strong at the time, passes, but the smell of death often lingers and can contaminate a lifetime.

His mother's death was the deciding factor. With her death it seemed he had no one to run to in his need. He had long ago learned not to run to his father. This man of sixty-seven bore no semblance to the man who had fought and won many a battle in the field of life, who had blazed a trail through his revolutionary relationship with his wife, who had driven to the gates of fate to bring home a son. Gurmehar had heard many stories of the way in which his father had married off his sisters. The man who had occasioned these disasters did not seem as though he might understand the crisis of a young heart. And so it seemed almost unfair that it was his mother, who was so much younger than his father, who was the one who died.

But death has no respect for age. It strikes anywhere at any time, and it had chosen his mother for its next sacrifice. Suffering of no known cause Rupinder Kaur had died quietly in her bed one night. No one was given the chance to pray on her behalf. No one had the chance to visit any seer. In any case, Chand Bibi now was long dead. Everyone had to bow in front of the fact of death, including Pyaara Singh.

On the day of his wife's *uthala*, Pyaara Singh went into the room he had visited many times day and night. His wife's room had never looked more empty. He put down his *pugri* on her bed and wept. He knew he was now alone. His daughters had long been gone from his life. Though he met them from time to time, they truly belonged to their husbands' families. With his oldest daughter he had a rift that time had never mended. Her infrequent presence in his house was more a thorn in his side than any comfort. His much-prayed-for son had been drifting away from him for a long time. This knowledge made him kneel against his wife's bed and sob and pray: "Rupinder Kaur *ji*, why have you left me? Why have you gone at a time I needed you most? What happened to all our children? I do not recognize them at all. When you were here you took care of things. You made sure that there was peace among us all. You knew what to say to each of them and to me, with never a furrow on your brow. Who is going to do that now?"

If Rupinder Kaur could have answered, she would have said what she had been saying to him all these years: *"Sardar ji,* what are you talking about? Everything will be all right. Your children love you. You have done well by them. You did the best you knew how, and you did it for their good. They will recognize that if not today then tomorrow when their own children get older. Don't worry. Be patient."

But Pyaara Singh had never been a patient man. That was an aspect of his wife's character that had brought him balance in their union of more than four decades. He was to recognize the value of his loss in the years to come. And never more so than in the ensuing days after his wife's death in his interaction with the son for whom he had tricked fate.

◗ ● ◖

Bit by bit, Gurmehar pieced his life for Kundan. It was now her turn. She took him with her to Karnal. There, to visit her headmaster father and his wife, her mother.

30 *The Birth of Poetry*

Aisa bhog lagao mere mohan sab amrit ho jai
Aisa bhog lagao mere mohan sab amrit ho jai
Sab amrit ho jai mere mohan, sab amrit ho jai
Aisa bhog lagao mere mohan sab amrit ho jai.

SINCE THE *POOJA* was at Manmit Sharma's house, she was holding the white silk cloth with silver tassels on one end. The other end was in the hands of Gurmit, her sister. Both of them were very well dressed in beautiful, printed silk saris with their *palloos* over their heads, one end of which was neatly tucked between their teeth—lest it slip. Behind them pictures of gods and goddesses covered in garlands of marigold were set up on the makeshift dais which was covered with a pretty, pink silk cloth with a narrow silver brocade border. There were pictures of Rama and Sita in various poses. There was one of Rama standing respectfully with bowed head in front of his father, King Dashratha, and his three mothers—his birth mother, Kaushalya, and his stepmothers, Kaikeyi and Sumitra. There was one of Rama turning to leave the palace life with his wife and brother. They were all dressed in simple clothes. There was one of Laxman drawing the *rekha*, the boundary line, around Sita's hut that she must not cross while he went to investigate the sound he had heard in the forest. There was one of Sita sitting pitifully below the tree in solitary confinement in the Ashoka grove in Lanka just before Hanuman flew in to bring her news of hope. She had indeed crossed the line. The place of honor was given to two oversized pictures. One picture showed Rama's meeting with Bharata at the end of the banishment; in the background was the throne at Ayodhya on which had sat Rama's slippers for fourteen years. The other picture showed Rama and Sita sitting on their rightful thrones after their return to Ayodhya. Behind them stood Laxman, with bowed head, the very image of dutifulness and brotherhood. In front of them kneeled the monkey god, Hanuman, with his hands folded and head bowed in veneration. Behind him, his long tail curled upward and round in two perfect concentric circles.

In front of the pictures was placed a bowl of *charnamat* and boxes of *motichoor laddoos.* Silver foil or *virk* was clinging to them.

Manmit and Gurmit's heads were turned away from the dais during *Bhog,* the sacred moment when their offerings were infused with the spirit of God. The *pundit ji* had read from the *Ramayana* in Sanskrit, explaining passages in Hindi to his audience in great detail. While he read, his body and voice swayed back and forth in rhythm to the singsong quality of the verse. The congregation listened keenly, unconsciously mimicking his rhythm.

One day Narada *muni* visited the ashrama of Valmiki. Valmiki asked him, "Who of all heroes in the world possesses the most virtue and wisdom?"

Narada had anticipated the question. "Rama," he said, "the ruler of Ayodhya." He then told Valmiki the story of Rama.

After Narada left, Valmiki went to the river Tamasa for his morning routine. There, in a nearby tree, he saw two *krauncha* birds singing their song of joy and love. Till a sudden hunter's arrow abruptly killed the male bird. Watching the agony of her mate, the brokenhearted female bird lamented piteously.

Valmiki could not bear it. He immediately broke out in anger, cursing the hunter to a homeless wanderer's life. Recovering himself though, Valmiki was distressed at his servitude to emotion. But he also marveled at the anger and pity that had resulted in poetry. This is all part of God's creation plan, his *leela,* he thought.

In meditation, Brahma appeared to Valmiki. "Do not be afraid," he admonished. He told the sage that he had experienced these things so that he could write the story of Rama. "From sorrow *(soka)* sprang verse *(sloka),* and you must tell the story in this rhythm and meter." Brahma would give him the vision to see all that had happened, and Valmiki would sing it to benefit the world.

Then, Valmiki wrote the *Ramayana* and taught it to his disciples.

All during the recitation from the *Ramayana,* the attendant ladies had sat quietly on white cotton sheets over a red-and-black-striped *dhurrie*—only fidgeting from time to time when one or the other of their legs went to sleep—with their covered heads bowed and hands folded in their laps. Now, they were all standing. Some were even clapping their hands lightly in rhythm with the song. Others seemed in trance with their eyes rolled half into their sockets, almost lost in ecstatic beauty and awe of the moment when their offerings turned into nectar.

The men usually left the women alone during these moments. They were there, some on the side and back, others outside; but everyone acknowledged the women's greater mastery over these rituals. So they quietly waited their turn to receive in cupped hands —one below the other—the holy offering of sweetened watery milk and slightly bitter *tulsi* leaves.

As the *pundit ji* blew on the conch and tinkled the bell, one little girl, about seven years old, dressed in a parrot-green *lehnga choli* and *chunni* with silver edging detached herself from the adults and began performing a little dance in front of the congregation. At first, the adults were startled by her act, and several of them moved to rebuke her. But even as they moved to do so, they discovered that the child Kundan was not joking or being disrespectful in any way; she was truly acting out her religious ecstasy.

❯ ● ❮

In 1945, Professor Hardayal Sharma became the Headmaster of the Government Boys Higher Secondary School in Karnal. He had got this position on the basis of his BA in History from Punjab University. That, and the fact that his wife's uncle knew the Superintendent of the school district who was responsible for choosing the right candidate. The position had fallen vacant after the sudden departure of Manik Ram, MA.

When Hardayal Sharma heard of this position, he longed for it as a pregnant woman longs for some bizarre delicacy to satisfy her raging tastebuds. Though it involved a move from Delhi soon after they had arrived there, he knew that if he got this position he would be set for life. With the help of the local politician and the school Superintendent, the reservations of the school Principal were bulldozed, and the job was advertized in the local paper. The interviews were rigged from the start, and no one really had a shot at the job except Hardayal Sharma. The day he was offered the job formally marked the rivalry between him and the Principal. If it had been Sharma's choice he would rather not have excited the wrath or even the attention of his superior. But it was not his choice. Those were hard days, and he had to do what he could to secure an income for his family.

His was a young family. Though they had been married for eleven years, it was only in the last seven years that they had started having children. His wife, Manmit, had quickly borne five children: three girls—Kundan, Kangan, and Kanchan—and two boys —Ram and Ratan. The second and last children were boys. Manmit felt she had done her duty by having two sons, but Hardayal Sharma felt differently. He wanted another son. Also, they were young yet: she, twenty-four, and he, twenty-eight. Or, perhaps a little old, but not too much. Looking at her body, however, he was not certain that she would be able to carry any more children. Or nurture them. Unlike a lot of village women, her body was not big built and strong. Already, feeding five children at her breast had left her with bits of tissue hanging loosely from her chest and a few pebbles of flesh that were a mere memory of what her full breasts used to be.

These days Manmit was not surprised that her husband did not find her attractive anymore. She herself did not think she had any attractions left. Still, she felt comfort in the fact that she was a mother, and a mother of sons at that. Even if she never had another child she knew that she had proved her womanhood. Nowadays, she concentrated on pleasing her husband in other ways. By supporting his ambitions, for instance. To propitiate the gods, she held a *pooja*. To propitiate the humans, she had to think of a plan. That is why when Hardayal mentioned the position of school Headmaster and murmured something about her uncle knowing the Superintendent of schools, she immediately went to see her parents to ask them to ask her uncle to speak for her husband.

The prominence of the role his wife had played in this achievement (as in all others) in his life, Hardayal soon dismissed and turned his focus on consolidating his image at school. To have secured this fairly prestigious position at this young age was a remarkable accomplishment; no one knew that more than him. From his first day at school his students and colleagues began to recognize that too. In the classroom and staff room (though he was the Headmaster, he had not been assigned any separate office space; only the Principal enjoyed that privilege) he introduced himself as "Sir", not "Masterji" or "Teacher." It somehow made him feel more in control. He disciplined the children with a rod of bamboo, or what the children called his rod of wrath. He had been brought up to believe that if you spare the rod, you spoil the child. He was full of cliches that he had picked up from reading too many books in English. So he was very surprised that the beauty he knew of only second-hand and in borrowed context was something that Manmit was privy to.

That is why catching Manmit with a book in her hands one day, he spoke almost accusingly, "I did not know you liked to read."

"It's just something Gurmit gave me," Manmit was a little defensive.

"What is it? *Soz-e Watan*. What kind of a title is that I ask you?"

"It was confiscated and burned by the British government. But Premchand, despite the ill treatment of the British Government, continued to write under this name."

"Confiscated and burned? I don't think you should be reading these kinds of books. Here, give it to me."

"Just listen to this introduction. He said, that thing which cannot provide joy and happiness, cannot be beautiful. And that which cannot be beautiful, cannot be the Truth. Where there is joy and happiness, there lies Truth."

But Hardayal did not want to listen. "Give it to me," he repeated as though talking to one of his students.

Rather than argue, Manmit handed him the book.

Hardayal preferred to speak in English every chance he got rather than speak in the more widely spoken Punjabi, Hindi, or Urdu in his area. Even if someone talked to him in these languages, he replied in English. *The dolts,* he often thought. *They'll never amount to anything. Not if they don't learn English.*

Even if by some miracle the British were to leave, he knew that the English language was here to stay. Accordingly, his taste ran more to the English Romantic poets like Wordsworth whose romantic ideas about a child trailing clouds of glory or whose lingering in a field of daffodils could wring tears from a man who considered self-restraint a virtue above all else. He had a selection of Wordsworth's poetry that he often took out and reread slowly, clearly, and with great passion. It was as though in that moment he was one with the great poet talking about flowers that he might never see or even recognize were they right under his nose. Still, it gave him great joy, great peace, a sense of the wonder of the beauty of the world outside of the little town of Karnal where he lived and would die. It was his means of escape.

Manmit was subjected to this means of escape often. She had devised a way of protecting her children from too much talk of what seemed to her a way of life that was all too easily available in India. After all, one couldn't travel very far without being run down by some agricultural landscape or other. She saw no romance in the idea of fields run over with flowers. Being a farmer's daughter her focus was on crops. She did not therefore really understand her husband's passion for what was staring him in the face every day so close to home. Also, she found a contradiction between her husband's love for a natural landscape within poetry and his preference for a more urban life for himself. But being a pious and dutiful housewife she usually suppressed these thoughts. She told herself they were unworthy of a wife, of his wife. Indeed, the only reason she understood any of Wordsworth was because her husband, not satisfied with reading in English to a woman who did not understand it, would painstakingly translate the poet's ideas to her. Not wanting to hurt her husband with her lack of understanding, enthusiasm, or any real feeling for ideas that so obviously moved him, she put on a look of interest and pretended to listen. For a while she genuinely tried. She asked him countless questions about the artist and his art. But Hardayal did not really want to be bothered with answering questions that for him disrupted his pleasure of art and culture. Either that or he did not really know the answers. He had read this poetry in an introductory class on English literature in his college days. It had been a time for general impressions enhanced by stories of the romance of the Raj. Why must Manmit drag in the mundane? In an effort to quell her mundaneness he would look at her with impatience, screw up his eyes and press his lips, even glare at her.

Unable to control his irritation he once shouted in frustration, "Gosh, you idiot, why can't you understand such a simple thing?" His hand holding the book was raised as though he might hit her, but he never did. Not then nor at any other time, and Manmit was grateful for that. She knew he could have done so, with impunity.

Afraid of any such treatment at the hands of a man, Manmit had voiced her fears to her mother, *"Biji,* I don't think I should get married." That was a bold statement for a thirteen-year-old girl to make, but Bishen Dei was a loving woman and her husband a reasonable man. She did not scold her daughter into silence therefore. She just asked, "Why, Mito?" Manmit knew she had her mother's ear. She would not have called her Mito otherwise.

"Pammi just got back from her in-laws' place. She told me that her husband had slapped her."

"Did she tell you why?"

"For no reason at all."

"Hmm, you can't clap with one hand," she said gently. But seeing her daughter was not really satisfied, she continued, "I will talk to *Baoji*."

Two days later she talked to her daughter again. It was to give her news of her marriage to an educated young man from Lahore. He had his BA degree. There would be no question of any violence. An educated son-in-law was the parents' way of ensuring their daughter's future. *Baoji* had listened to his wife, then told her to tell their daughter not to be worried. All had been taken care of. It being a delicate matter, a matter regarding marriage, father and daughter were separated by a wall of shame and tradition that was too solid for them to break to really be able to talk. They must depend upon the mother to act as a go-between and dispel her fears.

That had been several years ago. And now, when Hardayal Sharma's BA became the very cause for his impatience with his wife, she consoled herself by reasoning that her parents were really too old to be burdened by such details, especially as nothing had happened finally—not really. But though Hardayal had not hit her, Manmit had been scared. People can have more than one face. After that incident she perfected the art of listening with a blank face. So the time with her husband became a time to let her imagination run loose. A time when she figured out the household budget or what she might cook for dinner. A time when she marveled at the chaste women and chastity-imposing men who listened complacently to the *Ramayana* and the return of the rightful heirs. Manmit could not help thinking that the story did not end with the return of the exiles. Only after she had survived the test by fire, was Sita considered pure again. However, soon after their return, on the basis of a chance remark—questioning the chastity of a woman who had lived away from her husband's house—made by one of his subjects, Rama banished his faithful and pregnant Queen from the palace. It was finally during the great sacrifice establishing Rama's undisputed rule that they came face to face again. But Sita had had enough. It was then that the earth split and took back into its womb that which it had borne.

If Hardayal Sharma suspected any of these rebellious thoughts, he never let Manmit know. He needed a silent listener too badly to jeopardize his position with her.

As Hardayal and his wife drifted away from each other, over the next few years she turned inward more and more for comfort. If she had turned to her children, she might have saved both herself and them, but she did not, and it was her loss and theirs. Each time she quietly accepted what Hardayal said, he was emboldened to further rudeness and lack of sensitivity. His disposal of his oldest daughter was a case in point.

"I met Gurdayal today," he opened his conversation with his wife one day. Manmit did not reply. Normally, Hardayal would not have cared, needing no encouragement to continue talking. But today he was feeling good. Having been in the friendly company of his younger brother and his wife, who was Manmit's younger sister, he was willing to be coaxed and gentled by his own wife. So he was a little annoyed when she did not immediately comply. He decided to try again.

"Gurdayal was asking after you. So was Gurmit."

"What did they say?" This time Manmit joined the conversation.

"They want to speak to both of us this evening," he said rather mysteriously.

"This evening? What's up? I hope everything is all right with them." Manmit was worried about her sister.

At the time Manmit had got married to Hardayal, her sister had been married to Gurdayal. It seemed the decision had been made by their respective parents long before the birth of their children. In the initial scheme of things—when Manmit had been an only child for several years—she was supposed to marry the younger brother, but when time came for them to marry, the parents decided that that did not make any sense anymore when there were two boys and two girls. So they sat all four round the holy fire and married them all together. At thirteen Manmit had been just old enough to understand what was going on, but her younger sister who was only nine did not. Since then Manmit had taken charge.

Gurmit was also lucky in that the sisters' mother-in-law was progressive, willing to allow her time to grow up. She was therefore not required to come and sit among the women of the town when they came to see the new brides. She was tucked in bed and fast asleep in a room across from the parents-in-law's bedroom. Hira Devi had made it clear her younger daughter-in-law was too young to fulfill any of the functions of marriage. She must first grow up. There followed several years of fun and frolic during which Gurmit and Gurdayal became great friends. They played *gulli-danda, gite, stapu,* and even fought like brother and sister. And though Gurmit had discontinued school after a while, Gurdayal kept her up with all that he learned at school. Pigeon *Kabutar. Uran* Fly. Look *Dekho. Asman* Sky. By the time she was fifteen and he twenty-one, they had settled into a comfortable rhythm.

Their happiness was marred in the years to come, however, by the fact that they had no children. They had visited doctors and quacks, *pundits* and promise-makers, but no one had been able to provide them with the one thing they felt would make their happiness complete.

Manmit, of course, was privy to all this but even she could not help her sister. She knew that her sister lacked for nothing material. That even though her husband was BA fail, he was a good man and a hardworking one. With these qualities he had built himself a formidable business in New Delhi and was presently negotiating to extend it to Britain. He had already visited London to meet his backers. He had not excelled at school, academics simply not being his thing. It was true that he had joined BA simply on the insistence of his older brother and had tried three times to clear the first-year exams. It was also true that his English was not the pristine prose or poetry of the great English writers. It was more functional, a language he had learned from movies, papers, the men he met for business in clubs. But what he lacked in academic knowledge, he more than compensated through his uncanny intuition and understanding of people. To talk to him was to gain a friend, a confidant. And so, despite his apparent shortcomings, his ability to communicate with people of all ages and backgrounds was such that it had inevitably led to his success.

"They must want to tell us about the London trip," Manmit hazarded returning once again to the conversation with her husband.

"No."

"No? Then what?" she asked. "Is everything okay?" she asked again but this time with a shade of worry in her voice. "If you know, why don't you tell me?"

"Wait and see."

"This is extremely cruel of you," she asserted. Anxiety was making her bold. "It is several hours before we will see them, you should tell me the news. I am your wife."

But Hardayal could not be shaken. He had seemingly made up his mind. In reality, after having built up the conversation he was not willing to back down now and admit that he really did not know much himself. That Gurdayal had refused to say anything to him alone without the presence of the two women. It had mortified Hardayal to be superseded in family loyalty by someone else—and that women.

31   *The Burning of Memory*

THAT EVENING WAS to be a landmark in all their lives. It was a typical summer day. Warm, humid, with the smoke rolling in from the nearby factories. It was not an evening to sit outdoors. Tea on the lawns sounded very cultured and English, but it was really a very uncomfortable affair in the summertime in Karnal. Not only did the sun not relent and reduce its heat till late at night, but also all attempts to bring down the temperature by watering the garden or the brick courtyard were counterproductive. On touching the hot surface the water sizzled and evaporated, immediately creating the atmosphere of a sauna. Moreover, the mosquitoes, grown fat on the blood of their human prey and abundant filth in side streets, formed a formidable enemy. If Hardayal had had his way, everyone would have been subjected to the traditional English tea complete with white-cloth-covered table and delicate Royal Doulton service in a rose pattern that he had managed to procure in the black market and that he insisted on displaying from time to time—especially in front of his younger brother with the London connection.

But his younger brother and sister-in-law had minds of their own. They strolled in with a small basket of fresh guavas they had brought along as a memento of their short incursion into Allahabad following their trip to London.

"Thought you'd prefer some really good guavas. These are authentic. Not like those little ones we usually get in the market. Here, try one. Better than anything you can get in London," Gurdayal said to his brother.

Hardayal was having a hard time disguising his chagrin. He had set his heart on receiving a shiny new Ekco A22 radio in brown Bakelite and chrome finish; he had told Gurdayal about it being introduced at the Britain Can Make It exhibition a few years ago. Now he was holding a basket of guavas that he could easily procure in the local market. No British radio. But loudly he said, "Most certainly, better than anything you can get in London."

Seeing the table for tea set outside, Gurdayal and Gurmit both immediately protested. "You surely don't mean to subject us to the heat and mosquitoes outside," ribbed Gurdayal.

"No, of course not." Hardayal backed off almost instantly. He knew when he was beat, especially by his London-returned brother. "It must have been the servant. You know how it is. You tell them one thing, they do another."

Manmit witnessed with a blank face how quickly and successfully Gurdayal was able to get what he wanted without really getting into an argument with her husband. She ordered the servant to reset the table inside.

"But *memsahib*, sahib told—"

"Be quiet, you insolent idiot," immediately interjected Hardayal. "First you make a mistake, then you compound it by telling lies. Where will it end? I ask you, where will it end? This country can never amount to anything so long as there are people such as you."

Hardayal's temper was well known. The servants were always getting the brunt of it and had learned that in order to retain their jobs in this household they must often accept the burden of their master's actions. The indifference and lethargy of their mistress more than made up for it. They could fool her with no difficulty at all and so managed to even the scales in their favor. If they noticed that their mistress often had to suffer for their actions, they chose not to think about it. They had to take care of themselves.

Inside, everyone soon settled down. Enjoying the hot samosas and *jalebis* from the corner sweets store they exchanged memories of their beloved Lahore.

Those were bittersweet memories. They had a lot of land then. Their grandfather had been a *Rai Bahadur,* given a title by the British in recognition of his loyalty to them and donations of money into an already overflowing royal coffer. They also had a younger brother then. But Krishandayal had become a martyr to the cause of independence. The fires of Partition and enmity among people who had once lived together peacefully were beginning to make way to suspicion and wariness. Krishandayal did not belong to any political group. If anything he was a God-fearing man, a man of deep emotions and sentiments. With his young bride and their newborn child, he could often be seen going to the temple.

That afternoon in 1942 was no different when they had set out to visit the temple. They never made it there. The Indian National Congress's resolution demanding complete independence from the British with the threat of civil disobedience had split the party. Sentiments were running high. A procession of supporters of young Hindu college students protesting against the inclusion of Indian soldiers fighting for a foreign cause on foreign land stopped them on their way. For a little while they did not do anything, just waited for the people to pass. After all, it was meant to be a peaceful demonstration. But a small faction within the large crowd suddenly changed the nature of the demonstration. It all began with one stone thrown on public property. It was meant to be symbolic of things to come if the government persisted in its course. The symbol was soon lost in the thoughtless repetition of this act by countless others. Before the police could arrive there was a lot of damage done to public property. Stones were the major weapons. But knives and sticks had also been used.

The police were quick to respond. In the absence of the Police Commissioner, the Superintendent decided to teach the young hoodlums a well-deserved lesson. Soon, thin young men in shorts that showed their knobby knees to disadvantage, carrying wooden sticks and holding cane shields, appeared on the scene and began beating people at random. There was pandemonium everywhere. Krishandayal and his family, who had been watching the demonstrators along with some others, suddenly found themselves in the thick of things; Krishandayal knew he had to try to find safety for his family. The mob was out of control and would not care to discriminate between a grown-up and a child or a male and a female. With beating heart, he tried to do the only thing he could. He told Kunti to run. Somehow that was the wrong thing to do. An overconscientious young man, seeing through eyes blinded by the mob's passionate call for duty to the country, saw Krishandayal run and thought he saw a deserter. He turned to his companions and shouted, "Catch that coward. Don't let him escape." What would have happened if Krishandayal had been alone no one would ever know. Maybe he could have saved himself. He was a fast runner and a very fit young man. But he was not alone. He was slowed by his responsibility and love for his family. The crowd soon cornered him and began raining sticks on his head. "This is why India is not free. Because of people like you. Deserter. Shame on you," shouted the student who had initially mistaken him for part of the demonstrating crowd. "Shame, shame," the crowd took up the chant. Krishandayal didn't really have a chance. He was long dead before the crowd stopped raining sticks on him.

Kunti, who had witnessed the horrifying attack, shouted and pleaded in vain for her husband's life to be spared. Shielding her infant with one arm, she tried to hold back anybody she could. No one cared. The crowd had found a victim even if it was not the one they had been looking for. Jostled, kicked, beaten, dragged, Kunti finally made her way to the front of the ranks where she threw herself on her husband's body to try to protect him. Little did she know he was already a corpse and she had merely sealed the fate of her child and herself. The crowd had realized she was a woman and though it did not particularly want to kill her, it needed more self-control than it possessed to rein itself in. A random *lathi* landed squarely on her head, felling her and smothering the infant between the bodies of its mother and father.

Barely had the mob begun to realize what had happened when police reinforcements had arrived, and though the crowd tried to scatter, the police formed a circle around them barricading their exit. It drove the students wild. They turned to their leaders for new direction only to find that the leaders had long since split. Seeing the turn their demonstration was beginning to take with the pursuit of Krishandayal, the student leaders realized they had lost control. That the crowd had a mind of its own. It wouldn't be long before the police would be there with tear gas and rifles. This was not the time for being in the front line. As a result, those who had been merely at the periphery of the march found themselves in the dead center. Unprepared, and without a leader, they did not stand a chance.

It was all over pretty quickly. The crowd was herded into police vans where they were pushed and thrown on top of each other just like the carcasses that lay in the street behind them. Some tried to make one last desperate stand, pelting the general public and the police with sticks and stones they had managed to hide on their persons. *"Inquilab zindabad"* and *"Hamari mangein poori karo"* were slogans that deafened the quiet of the evening, almost in harmony with the sounds of the police *lathis* raining on their backs.

By this time family members of Krishandayal and Kunti had been informed of the massacre in the street. Tumer Chand, Krishandayal's father, and Hardayal and Gurdayal raced out into the street even before the messenger had finished telling his tale. Bhiku, the neighborhood janitor, had been a passerby who had witnessed the entire gruesome mishap. He had tried to rush back to inform the family but had been delayed by the crowd that—minutes before the arrival of the police—had sighted him and tried to hunt him down just as they had hunted down Krishandayal moments before. Unencumbered and energized by the fear of his own possible outcome, he had run as fast as his thin legs would carry him. Running through a maze of streets with a small band of people behind him, he shouted aloud, begging someone, anyone, to open their door and let him in.

"For God's sake, let me in. I beg of you. For God's sake, open your door. Have mercy. Let me in."

Though tired and panting, he was not ready to give in. Never had he felt so keenly his caste and class as he ran through the rich neighborhood of shut doors and windows. He knew without having to look up that there would be people peeping from behind those shut and curtained apertures—unwilling or simply too afraid to help. But he did not give up asking for help. This was not a time for suffering silently, not if he wanted to live.

Hamida Begum was one of those peering from behind the curtain in her drawing room. She had been called to her present post by her young daughter who had been playing in the courtyard when she had heard the tumult outside. Chhoti had immediately gone to her mother to ask her what it was. Pulling the child to herself, Hamida Begum told her: "Nothing, child. It is nothing."

"Why are you crying then, *Ammi jaan?*"

"I am not crying," Hamida Begum reassured her daughter through shaky laughter. "You've become very naughty. And ask too many questions. Little girls shouldn't ask so many questions."

"Can littlebo-ys ask toomany, somany, questions, *Ammi jaan?* Canthey *Ammi jaan,* canthey?" was Chhoti's immediate response. And not waiting to see what her mother had to say about any of this, she continued almost to herself, "I'm going tobecome a man whenIgrowup."

Hamida Begum did not pay much attention to her five-year-old's prattle. Or ask her what made her say such a thing. Time enough for her to grow up and find out that you were born and died a woman just as you were born and died a Muslim or a Hindu. Memories of another demonstration, another chance victim, another chase clouded her eyes, but her vision remained clear. *Kafir.*

So when she heard, as did all her neighbors, the shouts of Bhiku out in the street, her heart did not melt. Let him die. Yes, let him die crying, begging for mercy. It was time for her to collect. The Hindus who lived in the neighborhood through which Raza Murad had run for his life had turned deaf ears to his pleas. No one had come out to his aid, and she had been left alone to raise their daughter who was still growing in her womb at the time. Back again with her parents, living in their house, a woman and yet less than that, a woman who had not been able to hold on to her man. Or so some of the older relatives made her feel. Well, today, she would make sure and hold on to her child. Practically alone in the house for once while her parents visited some relatives in Rawalpindi, having left her in the care of an old female relative who did not really matter and servants who were out running some errands, she was in charge of her fate and that of the man outside. It was a heady feeling.

"*Ammi, Ammi,* look." But as mother and daughter looked, Hamida Begum suddenly saw not Bhiku but the image of her own dead husband, running through the streets crying for help. Startled, she tried to shake that fancy. But the harder she tried, the closer and more vivid her image became. Before she could think too much, she ran to the wooden door that kept the world of the street outside. From the window she had seen him turning into her street and she knew that it would only be in a matter of seconds that he would pass by her door. Speed was of the essence, so was cunning. A split second before he passed by, she opened her door and stuck out her hand. It was really just a part of her *dupatta* that could be seen from outside but it was all that was needed. Bhiku was running so fast that he almost ran past the waving bit of fabric. The deafening roar of the crowd was behind him. The quiet street trapped their noise and magnified it manifold. But he saw that fabric and slipped through the door before the owner could change her mind.

The door was shut immediately. It seemed that within seconds, long before Bhiku was able to catch his breath, the drama was over. The crowd, still in pursuit of their prey, had passed this street and turned the corner. Bhiku, not her husband, lay spent, "Water, water please." After only a slight hesitation, Hamida Begum collected herself and gave him a glass of water. He drank thirstily, tiredly touching his lips to the rim, not pouring the water into his cupped hand. They both knew it was another first. But neither commented on it. Only after he had finished that glass and the next, he looked up to his savior and thanked her. He couldn't really see her face that was covered with her *dupatta* and angled away from him. It did not really matter. Like an angel, she had appeared from nowhere and saved him. She had taken a great risk. If the crowd had seen her action there would have been hell to pay. The relationship between Hindus and Muslims was increasingly strained. This may have broken the bow. But it was not to be. Not then.

"You must rest a little. Take that *charpai* under the tree."

"No, *Bibi,* I'm fine here."

"Why are you breathing sofunny?" piped in the child from behind her mother.

"Don't disturb him. He needs to rest."

"It's all right, *Bibi.*"

Bhiku lay there under the shade of the tree for a little while. Soon, however, though exhausted and heartsick from what he had witnessed, he left—knowing that he mustn't jeopardize the lives of those who had saved him, that he had a mission to accomplish, and that if he did not leave now he might be trapped there for a long time. There was bound to be a curfew. This time when he stepped into the street, all was quiet. Within minutes therefore he was able to reach his destination.

His appearance at Tumer Chand's house caused a stir. Everyone collected to find out what had happened.

"Krishandayal...sahib," was all he was able to say before he collapsed into tears.

"What happened to my Krishan? What happened to him?" interrupted Hira Devi. In her panic for her youngest child, Krishan-dayal, she dropped the plate in which she was making *chaat.* The sweet potatoes and potatoes and bananas and guavas fell stunned to the ground.

"Be quiet," a harried Tumer Chand interrupted his wife. "Let him speak. What happened to Krishan, Bhiku?"

"Sahib, there was a student demonstration in the mall..."

"Yes, yes, we know about the student demonstration today. But what does that have to do with Krishan?"

"He was there."

"But he's not a student. So no one would...he's okay...isn't he?"

"He's okay, isn't he?" repeated Gurdayal and then Hardayal after their father. Bhiku's silence was as deafening now as the roar of the manic crowd that had gone berserk in the streets around the mall. There was nothing to it; they must all go there. As Hira Bai let out a cry of anguish and made to follow, barefoot and without her *dupatta,* Tumer Chand turned to her in appeal and unknowingly crushed a firm, young guava on the floor to a pulp. His voice was now very calm, "Arrangements will have to be made." Though his wife was beating her breasts with her fists and asking God where she had gone wrong, and even his sons were openly crying, Tumer Chand was dry-eyed. He knew there would be a lifetime for tears. Those were the words that his friend Humayun Khan had uttered when Tumer Chand had gone to offer condolences for *his* son's disappearance in a Hindu district one night five months ago. The body had later been found mutilated almost beyond recognition. The murderer was never apprehended.

Now on the way to the scene of the crime he wondered how many more sons would die, how many sisters lose their brothers, how many wives their husbands, how many daughters be raped, how many aging parents carry their sons out of this world on their tired and bent shoulders, before the Muslims and the Hindus and the Sikhs realized that they were in a common war against the British? That they belonged to the same mother country.

A strange wind had been blowing for a long time; it carried the smell of dead human flesh and tears that had run rancid, and no good could come of it. No good ever came of anything if man and man were at war with each other; if man and woman did not see eye to eye; if Hindus, Muslims, Sikhs, and Christians did not learn to live together in amity. Tumer Chand had suspected this all along to be true, but never was it truer than on the evening of his own son's death.

A subdued Tumer Chand and his fired-up two sons arrived at the Police Station only to find out that they had a long wait ahead of them. Though they were taken in to identify the bodies, they could not be given custody of them before the Police Commissioner arrived and signed the release papers. The sons, wanting to spare their father, had offered to be the ones to identify the bodies. But Tumer Chand did not want to be protected. *Protected from what?* he wondered. When a father has lived beyond his son, to shoulder his corpse, what more is left for him to fear? No, he would go in. He wanted to go in and see what they had done to his child, his little Krishan. He would go in and see him one last time.

The bodies were being kept on ice, but in this heat they would decompose fast. The Superintendent had told the Subedar to make arrangements for more ice but had been informed that the local ice maker had closed his shop for the day after having sold his entire stock to a wedding party. Everyone could only hope that the Commissioner would arrive before the stench from the bodies began to make staying inside the Station impossible. Meanwhile, the family continued to wait.

All over the city, funeral fires were raging; flames that were red and blue with a very dark center leaped higher and higher in a dance of demonic delight.

Hira Devi took charge of arranging the mourning. Though she had also lost her daughter-in-law and grandson, in the first flush of grief her focus was on her son. Her youngest, the core of her heart. She sent for the professional crier. She sent messages to relatives and friends. A *syapa* was arranged and the house was prepared for mourning for thirteen days. There was darkness everywhere.

Outside, the men sat armed, ready to face an enemy attack; they knew that these were not times to indulge in sorrow. Inside, the women took over. In death, as at birth, they were the custodians of life. Within hours, the women started arriving. Dressed in white clothes, hair undone, they embraced Hira Devi in a full-bodied embrace. They howled like animals in the grip of agony. The closer their relation to Hira Devi, the louder they howled. It was a show of sisterhood. That a mother who had suffered the pangs of childbirth now had to suffer the pangs of separation at death was the worst curse imaginable. The pain felt at the cut severing the umbilical cord—decades ago—was at its keenest today.

For thirteen days and thirteen nights, they howled. Beating their chests with fists and slaps, pulling their hair at fate, asking God for forgiveness for their sins. A son had been lost and he would be missed.

During this time no fires were lit, no food was prepared. The hearth was cold. At first, the women refused all offers of food and drink. But soon it became difficult to keep up the crying without sustenance. Their tear ducts were empty, but the mourning was not complete. So when good neighbors and friends began trickling in with gifts of food, it was a secret relief to many.

For the children it was a frightening experience. Bad enough during the day, but especially terrifying during the night when the women sat in the courtyard and lamented at the moon. So they clung in the shadows of the men.

Thirteen days later, after the long-winded passionate offerings to the dead, the mourners returned to their homes and their families. For the Sharmas, it was only the beginning of grief. Death, especially of your child, scars the heart. Creating a vacuum that nothing can fill.

The move from Lahore was just a matter of time after that. While the Quit India motion was made against the British, ironically it was the Sharmas who were the first to have to quit their land. Gurdayal was the first to leave. He moved to Delhi. Hardayal followed with his family. At the time, Kundan was visiting her grandparents, so Hardayal decided to bring her with him on his next trip when he came to collect his parents. Arriving in Delhi, however, he heard reports of increasing violence in Lahore. Jinnah's cooperation with the British was leading to the Muslim League obtaining greater power in the imperial province. Hardayal immediately turned around and went back. It took him a while to persuade his parents of the wisdom of leaving. They did not want to leave the land where they had made so many memories. But even they had to accept that the memories in recent years had been more bad than good. So with a heavy heart they agreed to go.

Within days, conditions had changed for the worse. When the contact with whom Hardayal had arranged passage fell through, he scrambled to find an alternative. When Sikander Khan, an old Pathan friend of his to whom he went for advice, offered to take him and his family as far as the border, he felt relieved yet concerned.

"Sikander Khan, this may hurt you." Hardayal was afraid for his friend.

"Not as much as it has hurt you."

It was settled. They would meet the next day; it was supposed to be a dark night. With the moon behind clouds. As Sikander Khan was known for transporting his produce across the country, he would pretend to be making a business trip in his truck. And his friends could hide in the back with the vegetables under the hay and the tarpaulin. Hardayal agreed. They slipped into the night to meet Sikander Khan.

For the rest of their lives, they regretted looking back. At the turn of the street, not able to resist the urge, they had turned to see some people—their faces sheltered by the tails of their turbans—throwing a piece of burning cloth wrapped around a stick into the animal barn. As it quickly caught fire, they had broken into the house. There was no time for emotion. It was even more imperative they run.

The truck hurtled over uneven terrain at high speed in the middle of the night, knocking around its passengers like unsteady heads of cabbage. Hardayal wondered if life would ever be normal again. By his side, Hira Devi was determined to not let anyone steal any more of her children. So she clutched little Kundan to her breasts and told her they were playing hide-and-seek. Almost afraid to breathe, Kundan remained silent. The rules were deadly this time. She must not get caught. Only Tumer Chand did not worry. He sat quietly with his beads, having given his life up to God. The only word anyone heard him utter again was "Om." "Om."

Four hours into the journey, when the truck came to an abrupt halt, desperately they all tried to hang on to each other and the side rails. From beneath the hay and the tarpaulin they could hear muffled sounds of argument. It seemed some Muslim gang had heard rumors about a truck carrying Hindus going toward the border. Death seeemed to have followed them and was now knocking on their door. They could do nothing but wait.

"What a preposterous idea!" Sikander Khan exclaimed.

"We know of your friendship with Hindus."

"But this is different. Do you dare to doubt me?"

He lifted the edge of the tarpaulin and began exposing pieces of produce. "Does this look like a Hindu?" he asked contemptuously. "Or this, or this, or this? Would you like me to show you the entire contents of my truck piece by piece?"

It was a bluff; it worked. Sikander Khan's reputation as a man of integrity was well known. It could calm even the smoldering fires of these young men. Seeing his anger and indignation, the young men felt ashamed for doubting him and even a little afraid; they knew how powerful he was. With many apologies he was let go.

At the border, Sikander Khan embraced his friend. They both knew they would never see each other again.

"Hurry, hurry, before someone gets you," were the last words Hardayal heard before he turned away with his family into a truck full of refugees going to Delhi.

32 Human Flesh for Sale

HARDAYAL AND GURDAYAL did not focus too long on the memories of their brother and his young family's murder, their entire family's grief, or the horrific journey from Lahore to Delhi. All their lives had changed and so had their fortunes. No, Gurdayal had initiated this meeting for another purpose. After discussing the matter with his wife for a long time, they had decided to relieve their older brother of the burden of one of his daughters. Even though Hardayal was a Headmaster, still, it would be one less dowry for him to worry about. And *they* would have a child to bring up.

Hardayal and Manmit were taken aback. They had not suspected this to be the purpose of the visit. Still, once mentioned, the subject could not be swept underneath the carpet.

"Who did you have in mind?" asked Hardayal.

"*Ai ji,* what are you saying?" interrupted Manmit. "There is no question of us giving up one of our children, *Dewar ji,*" she said to Gurdayal. "Gurmit, you should have known better." The normally peace-loving Manmit had been forced into making a stand.

"This house is our house. You have always made that clear. Our house is yours, *Bhabhi ji,*" said Gurdayal before his elder brother could give in to his ready temper. "Whether the child plays in this house or that one, what does it matter?"

"If it doesn't matter, why do you need to take our child to Delhi? Let her play here."

"*Didi,* you have the joy of many children. I don't. We don't. This would give us the chance to have a child of our own who would be loved by two sets of parents," contributed Gurmit to her husband's statements.

"No, it is really out of the question. You can adopt a child from any children's home. You know there are so many children who have been orphaned by the Partition, others who were lost during the exodus from Pakistan to India. Adopt one of them, and give them a home. My children already have a home." Manmit's heart was beating fast and for once she was very angry. Angry with all of them, but most especially with her husband who had remained silent during the entire exchange. Using the pretext of seeing what the servant was up to and why he was so late in clearing away the table, she left the room.

It seemed to be the end of the discussion. But unknown to Manmit, Hardayal had other ideas. Over the next couple of days by studiously avoiding the subject, he first allayed his wife's suspicions. Then, one day he arrived home early from work. Manmit was immediately alarmed and rushed out to see if all was okay. All was more than okay, and today Hardayal had picked up a special treat of *gulab jamuns* on the way home for all his children. He had also brought home with him a book that Kundan had been asking for for a long time. Manmit found him in the hall with the children hanging around him, enjoying the company that was measured out to them in small doses. Standing by the side of the door, she felt a twinge of sadness for Gurdayal and Gurmit who would never experience a similar joy. But she really couldn't be held responsible for that, she quickly told herself and moved forward to join the scene.

Such interactions were not common in their household. More often than not, the children, warned of their father's approach— he had a habit of clearing his throat loudly before entering the gate of his house—would all sidle away into the background. It was not that he was an unkind man or had ever been known to hit them, but the threat of both was always felt under the surface. In any case, the children did not behave like their natural selves around him. It was both their loss: the father never got to know his children and the children never got to experience the joy of having a father.

With Manmit's appearance, Hardayal jerked up as though caught doing something wrong. Looking at his red face, she wondered momentarily at it but soon dismissed it as her imagination. But it was not her imagination. That night Hardayal turned to her. It was a long time since he had touched her in any way.

"I've been thinking about Gurdayal and Gurmit's visit." Manmit's heart began to beat erratically at these words. She also felt a strange ache in her stomach that she could not explain to herself. She remained quiet under his touch however and let him speak.

"Manmit, I think we should think about their offer seriously," began Hardayal softly hoping to influence his wife through gentleness where waywardness would not work.

"What is there to think about? We cannot give away one of our children. It is not a piece of cattle we are talking about, we are talking of our flesh and blood."

"Yes, but will we love any of them less for being away?" reasoned Hardayal.

"And how would we decide which one to give away?"

"You are too emotional. First of all, we are not giving away—"

"Really, and what would you call it?" interrupted Manmit, careless now of the consequences. This was not an argument over Wordsworth but of her children, and she was not going to remain quiet.

"I would call it being generous. What kind of a woman are you? How can you stand there and witness your sister's pain?"

"That is not fair. And what of my pain, or yours for that matter, if we lose one of our children? Or doesn't your own blood matter to you? Well, even if it doesn't, to me it does. I carried each of these children for nine months. For nine months I guarded them with my life, and I'm not about to stop doing that."

Hardayal withdrew his caress. He realized that this time it was not going to be an easy victory. This time Manmit was fighting back. Being a thinking man, he let the matter rest for that day, but he hadn't given up. The more he thought about it, the more sense it made to him. If thoughts of saving some money crossed his mind, he told himself that that was just incidental; he justified it all in his head by thinking that they would really be doing their brother and sister a good turn. And so he did not give up. In fact, he had already communicated his decision to Gurdayal and Gurmit. Manmit saw this for the betrayal it was. She felt sold out by her husband but determined to make her stand till the last.

In the years to come she told herself that if she had had her husband by her side, no one could have taken Kundan away from her. That it was impossible to stay strong against three. After all, what more could she have done? She had done all she could. In the end, the decision that it should be Kundan who should be given away was also a simple one. The boys could not be parted with —that was understood by Gurdayal and Gurmit, and so they had not asked for them. Kangan and Kanchan could not be separated because they were twins. That left Kundan. It was understood that there would be no formal adoption; after all, nothing could go wrong between blood brothers and sisters. The holocaust was over, the British were gone, Gandhi was dead, and—with the adoption of the Constitution—Indians were masters of their own fate. Time would teach them all the cost they would have to pay.

And so the twelve-year-old Kundan came away to live in her rich aunt and uncle's big house on Prithviraj Road in New Delhi. At first she did not understand the implications of what had happened to her. But when she was taken to be enrolled in school, she knew that things were not all right. The new school uniform, the new school bag, and the permission to redecorate her room any way she wanted made her heart beat so fast that even a visit to Kwality restaurant in Connaught Place could not keep it still; all in all, it was too late, and she was there to stay.

▶ ● ◀

Once Gurmehar and Kundan started to talk, nothing could stop them. They found every opportunity to be together. Nadi Singh and Swaran and Nimmi and Mira. They would all walk around in Connaught Place for a little while, trying to give as much privacy to the young lovers as possible.

From there the next step was inevitable. But they had not counted upon any serious opposition from anyone to their marriage. Hindu-Sikh unions were not unknown. And so they were taken unawares. Despite Gurmehar's advice, Kundan had insisted that it would be easier if she first faced her family alone. It would give her time to prepare them.

When Kundan told her parents about Gurmehar, they were not pleased by what they saw as nothing more than the squalor of good intentions. His religion, his job, his family, all were objectionable. These objections came from two sets of parents. One, her biological parents who had given her away like a parcel to their less fortunate siblings. Two, from her aunt and uncle, who had passed her back a year and six months later (the same, except for the almost invisible puncture in her heart that seeped blood constantly) after they found a more acceptable, male candidate for adoption from a suddenly widowed poor relative. But they had felt guilty, so they took Kundan back for short visits from time to time.

There was no future in Karnal. So, after finishing her BA, Kundan had come to New Delhi to work in a government office. There was no question of her living with strangers. What would people say? So, despite reservations and knowing this was the only way for her to achieve her goals, she found herself living once again with her aunt and uncle.

Now both families were outraged. For a young woman of good family to be in love and bring her own proposal of marriage was uncommon.

"Preposterous! Unthinkable! A Sikh? A Sikh clerk? And no family to stand by him? What will people say? They will *thoothoo* upon us. All my hard-earned life is undone. My professional reputation is bound to suffer. We are lost, ruined. You have not left us to belong anywhere. You have blotted the honor of generations. Our heads are forever bowed in shame." Beside himself with anger, Hardayal now turned to Manmit, "Do you see what your laxness has resulted in? You wanted to give your daughter more freedom. See for yourself what results it has borne."

Seeing the veins throbbing on Hardayal's forehead, nervously

Manmit stepped in, "Is this why we fed you and clothed you? So that you could grow up and shame us? It would have been better if we had wrung your neck the day you were born. It would have been better if we had broken your legs before you learned to walk. It would have been better if you had pulled your own tongue out before speaking this evil. Oh to have lived to hear this, to see this inauspicious moment.

"*Kulta, kulachhani,* that is what people will say. And they will blame us. The Sharmas have no control over their daughter. Look at how they let her come to Delhi. And what about me? Is this why I gave you so much freedom? So that you could fritter it away. I allowed you to go and work. Not go for walks with men and fall in love with them. Where is your self-control? Have you forgotten your family name? Have you forgotten your family values, your *dharma?* Are we dead that you forgot that marriage is something parents think about and take care of? You might as well have arranged for our funeral. Oh that you should ever have been born."

"*Bhabhi ji.*"

"*Didi.*" Gurdayal and Gurmit tried to intervene.

"Leave me alone. I have lived long enough. Let me die." Manmit's heart was beating fast.

"All is still not lost. Perhaps we can salvage the situation. Let us have a family meeting. We must inform the elders. Perhaps, in their wisdom, they can help us come up with a plan. Of course, we must be humble," Gurdayal suggested.

"Ofcourseofcourse, we must be ready to do anything," advised Gurmit.

But Manmit had seen the devil of fury in her husband's eye. And his repeatedly clenching and unclenching fist. It was the same look that so many years ago had made him raise his hand at her. Then, he had been able to restrain himself. She was not so sure now. So she turned to her sister and continued, "To have lived to see this day. My milk gone sour. Better to have received news of her death. Bring me some iron needles hot from the fire. Let me gouge my eyes out." Weeping hysterically and beating her breasts, Manmit next addressed the rest of her children, "Let this be a warning to you. Watch and learn what happens when you break a mother's heart." The grown children, strangely estranged from their sister who was family and yet not family, stood silent and mesmerized as their mother broke away from their aunt's attempts to restrain her and rushed forward to slap Kundan across the face. Once, twice, three times. "Yes, yes, it was an evil hour at which you were born. It must have been. How else could this have happened? Where did we go wrong? Oh, where did we go wrong?"

Where *did* they go wrong? Their generosity in letting her go out and work with those common people was supposed to bend her with gratitude. They were wrong. Kundan heard them. Their faces disfigured, their voices distorted by emotion. Though her head snapped back and forth from the slaps, she did not raise her hands to retaliate or even protect herself. In any case, the sting of the words was far worse than the sting of her mother's palm. Also, she had seen the sidelong glance her mother gave her father and the look of terror in her face before she unleashed herself. Seeing Kundan turn toward the door, Manmit raised her voice even more. Hoarsely, she screamed, "If you leave now, you can never come back. Never. These doors will be shut to you forever. I am telling you, forever." Kundan kept walking. "Come back," screamed Manmit as she slid to the floor in a fit of weeping. "Look at me. Do you hear me? Come back."

But Kundan did not look at her or come back. Kundan and Gurmehar were married in a private ceremony. No family member was present, but there were many friends.

The hot, blustery winds of change were blowing over the vast, dry plains of the land raising dust and uncovering old attitudes. Exposing old wounds that were yet raw and screaming with pain. And if the people did not change with these changing times, it was clear they would be left behind.

Both families were indeed left behind by the fissure created by their actions. A fissure that untended grew to be a chasm where old voices echoed hollowly as they bounced back and forth hitting against each other, in vain, to escape the maze of their own creation.

33   *Dancing Inside the Box*

LIFE WAS NOT easy for the newlyweds. In fact, Gurmehar found life to be quite different from the way he had imagined it to be. He now had to think of his wife and the children they both wanted to have.

So Gurmehar took a fresh stock of his plans for the future. He had long felt that he was in a dead-end job and that he needed to get out of there if he ever wanted to amount to anything. His plans with Nadi Singh were an option, but on pressing Nadi he had discovered that Nadi was not really interested. That he was too scared to take a risk. Also, things were beginning to go sour between him and Swaran. Gurmehar knew that he could not take the capital risk on his own.

While Gurmehar tried to master the business world, Kundan took charge of things at home. She taught herself to fry the vegetables so that they were never under- or overdone. She trained her ear to recognize the exact number of whistles it took a pressure cooker to cook different types of pulses and curries. She learned to roll a *chapatti* so round and thin that it puffed pridefully like a football. Like the air, she wrapped herself in every available space in Gurmehar's life.

It was at this time that Mehmood Raza, Gurmehar's childhood friend from Raghubirpur with whom he had gone to Shimla, arrived in Delhi. Mehmood Raza came with big plans. Raza was still single so they met at Gurmehar's home, where Raza would come everyday for dinner and praise Kundan's cooking lavishly.

"*Parjaiji ji,* this *daal,* oh *subhaan allah.* And this mutton. What can I say? Words are not enough to describe how good it is." He smacked his lips in appreciation.

Gurmehar looked pleased, but Kundan was not comfortable. "He sounds a little insincere," she later said to Gurmehar.

"No no, you don't know him. That's just his way. Once you get to know him you'll realize how sincere he is. Very genuine." Kundan kept quiet. After all, Gurmehar had known him for several years.

Now Gurmehar decided to start a business venture with Mehmood Raza. Gurmehar would put up most of the money. "What will Raza contribute?" Kundan asked.

"His business acumen. He has a lot of contacts, wholesalers and the like. We'll need that to get the business off the ground."

Once again Kundan was uneasy, but before long the partnership papers were drawn up and everything was signed and sealed. When she read that each was to be liable for the other, she had to bite her tongue in order not to put a damper on the enterprise. They had leased a very small shop in Lajpat Nagar. They would sell cloth. Without realizing how, Gurmehar had run full circle into the very fate he had feared and had been trying to escape since the age of sixteen. If he ever thought so, he quieted his mind by telling himself that this was different. Quite how, he could not have explained.

Neither of them wanted their name on the business, so they decided to call it "Beauty Cloth Center." Raza was to be in charge of all the travel to procure the materials from Chandni Chowk wholesale dealers. Once they were more established, he would make trips to Bangalore and Benaras and purchase directly from the manufacturers who supplied the Chandni Chowk wholesalers. Meanwhile, Gurmehar would sit at the store. At first, Gurmehar had resisted that plan, but Raza convinced him that it would only be for a while till they could afford to hire a salesman, and then Gurmehar could sit in an inner office.

Though the business got off to a rickety start, in a few months things seemed as though they might improve after all. Kundan told herself she must have been mistaken about her misgivings about Raza, and she was extra nice to him, telling him to come for dinner whenever he liked. He did.

Appearances are important; Gurmehar knew that they can make or break a business. So he began preparing for each day the night before. Before going to bed he would polish his shoes and bring them to such a shine that he could see his face in them. He started by setting out all the materials he might need: Cherry polish, two Bata brushes, a blunt knife, and a soft rag. First, he gave his shoes a quick wipe. If there was any dried mud or any unnecessary material on them, he scraped it off with the knife. Then, he took just the right amount of polish on a brush and began to rub it in circular strokes on the shoe. He did this slowly, stopping frequently to view his handiwork. Then he gave the other shoe the same attention. Satisfied, he picked up the dry brush. Rubbing his fingers quickly through it to dislodge any lint, he now brushed it in sweeping strokes across the surface of both shoes. Next, he carefully folded the rag in long, flat folds. Repeating the movement across, he made a thick pad out of his rag. This thick pad he now rubbed gently over the entire shoe, giving special attention to the toe. Most nights he stopped at this point, placing the shoes in a safe place and covering them with a rag. At other times, he gave his shoes extra attention. "What are you doing?" the newly-wed Kundan asked amidst giggles, seeing Gurmehar bent over the kitchen stove with a shoe. "Holding the shoe over a low flame distributes the polish that may be thickening unevenly on its surface," he explained with a grin.

Every morning, Kundan helped Gurmehar get ready for work. Tying the turban was a ritual. It had to be done just right. Combing out the hair on his head with a short, wide-toothed comb, Gurmehar first rolled it into a secure yet comfortable knot on top. Next, he applied a light coating of Fixo, a glue-like substance, to his flowing beard and combed through it to straighten any tangles. Combing out his mustache, he now secured the comb in the back of his head just under his topknot. Dividing the beard in the middle, he twisted each half into a thin roll at the end, which he secured backward along his cheeks. Sometimes with a net, sometimes not. To give the glue time to set, he held his beard together with a narrow piece of cloth tied in a top knot. Any hairs straying from beneath the cloth were set back in their place with a small, slender hook-like needle made of steel. The *thatha* around his beard made his face plump up unnaturally and allowed him to only mumble for a while. *"Weh motian walyeo, tussi kithe ho?"* he mumbled out to Kundan to help him with the next step. *"Hunne aayi,"* she shouted back. While Kundan held one end of his freshly starched turban, he held the other on the opposite side. Pretending competition, they both laughingly tugged at their sides to take out any kinks in the material. Then both rolled their sides inward in a thin but not very tight roll after which they moved forward to meet in the middle where Kundan handed over her side to Gurmehar. From there, while Kundan prepared breakfast, Gurmehar laid the five yards of rolls on the back of a chair and slowly wound them around his head in a point at the middle and top. Now he was almost ready to leave for work.

Ten months passed this way. Till one day, Gurmehar discovered for the first time a discrepancy in the accounts. It was the day on which he received a notice at home for nonpayment of some bills. He knew that Raza had promised to take care of those bills personally when he met with the wholesalers. The next day, Gurmehar confronted Raza. Raza laughed lightly and explained that he must have forgotten and that he would take care of it.

With hindsight Gurmehar later realized he should have dumped Raza right then, but he had given him a chance. And another and another. It was really not a surprise when seven months later Gurmehar received a registered letter from the lawyers of several of their wholesalers that informed him of the magnitude of his debt. Since Raza was supposed to be away on business, Gurmehar had not seen him for several days. Now, Gurmehar frantically tried to contact Raza at his flat. The landlady informed him that Raza had resigned his lease. A further search revealed that Raza had left the country.

At such short notice, Gurmehar had no choice but to declare bankruptcy and sell off his supplies at considerable loss to liquify his assets. The creditors were ruthless. By the time they were done, all Gurmehar had left of the store was the sign on top, and that was not worth even its weight in metal.

At this time, a chance acquaintance introduced Gurmehar to the insurance industry. Though life insurance had been taken over by the government of India in 1952, private companies were still in control of general insurance. He knew that he could go far. Gurmehar worked day and night to increase his business. And for a while all was well. It seemed that life would be okay after all.

In 1971, however, began the second phase of deprivatization of the insurance business. The government took over the management. In 1973, the nationalization was complete. The private companies were reduced from 106 to four. All these companies were now under a single, controlling body known as the General Insurance Corporation of India, or GIC.

As a Development Officer under this system, working for the New India Assurance Company Limited (the only company that used the term "Assurance"), Gurmehar had to procure business, the cost of which could not exceed the limit stipulated by the company. As his salary was equal to 7 percent of his business, he had to be extra careful to maintain his limit. Gurmehar worked hard and long to do so. He knew that the company would forgive, for one year or two, if the business limit was low, but in the long run it would stop your allowances.

Deprivatization was a terrible blow to the business. It dulled the competitive edge and put a cap on the salaries of the officers. In the years to come, there were many struggles, many challenges as Gurmehar learned to play this new game.

Kundan and Gurmehar had met at a time when they had just begun forging hard hats for their hearts. So they understood well that repeated disappointments can sear the soul, trapping one like a clay figurine inside a musical box; a dancer whose feet do not move, a dancer who must dance in stilted and measured moves at every turn of the screw.

Book III

34   *July 1985:*
A Fresh Morning

IT HAD RAINED the previous night. Though the parched tarmac of endless roads had greedily quenched its thirst without evidence, the soil was less able to hide its nighttime exploits. There was a faint scent in the air, the scent of moist earth. To the Delhite, it is a good scent; a scent that most closely resembles satisfaction.

The trees and other roadside shrubberies were beginning to look up. The delicate stalks seemed ready to shrug off the limpness and droop that had come over them in the last few months. Tender leaves had carefully unfurled and stretched themselves, like cupped palms beneath a stream, for a drink in the rain. The big flowers and the little flowers were all chest out in petal satisfaction. The cosmos and periwinkles were huddled together as though unable to resist this moment to hug and celebrate. The long, hot summer was coming to a close, and the greens were as jubilant as the people. They were green with pride.

Even tiny weeds had arrowed upward breaking the earth in pinpricks. Bleeding it. Intermittently. Appearing suddenly in the most unexpected of places. Lounging casually by the wayside to bid squatter's rights. Refusing to be denied the pleasure of the rains as much as anyone else. As the poor children darted into the streets, rushing back and forth, kick-splashing in the puddles, singing and screaming in uninhibited joy, they were like little weeds themselves that grow and flourish everywhere. The frogs and toads croaking waterily under the rapidly thickening green in the shallow puddles leaped away at their approach, narrowly missing princedoms.

Under a hip-swinging breeze mildly bumping clouds and making them frolic, sullen stray dogs shook themselves free of moisture to reclaim their territory. And barked. Because they could. A wandering cat, mindful of her jungle-royal ancestry, jumped on the front wall and randomly stopped to stretch her front and hind-legs as far apart as she could to purr the question, *"Main aaun?"* Her tail was raised and curled behind her in a semicircle, like a question mark. No one invited her in. The freshly bathed crows sat around on treetops and telephone poles cawing idly at the droplets of water clinging to leaves and wires and carrying miniature rainbows within them. The tiny sparrows, oblivious of the convex-eyed stare of the garden geckos, chirped madly amidst thick foliage drowning each other's song.

During the peak of the summer, the rains dissipate the smog for a while. Then, when the sun comes out again, the sky and the earth function as lids to successfully trap the moisture in the atmosphere to increase the humidity. But the July rains are different. They fall incessantly, cooling the temperatures in the plains. Releasing fragrance and longing.

It was two days since Kundan's long night vigil. Sitting in the chair by the drawing room window, Amrita looked at the morning scene outside with amusement. The dancing street children always amazed her. It took so little to make them happy. Oblivious of the national and international games, they were intent on their own little games of catch and kick-splash. Their joy was to be envied.

She remembered when she had been like them. Had she ever been like them? She seemed to have been eavesdropping on other peoples' lives forever. First, in her mother's womb and later, growing up. Perhaps those are life's best lessons. As she gazed out blindly, Amrita noticed with a start the guava tree that had witnessed her childhood triumphs and travails, her trusted companion by day and bugbear by night. It did not look as big as it used to. It was not so long since she had last looked at it, but already the tree seemed to have grown more gnarled. With knobby joints bending its slight trunk crookedly a little closer to the ground. And bits of bark, like fine parchment, curling on themselves. Recoiling perhaps from the starkness of the world. Or just withdrawing in distaste. Slender stems of leaves crisscrossed each other like intricate roadwork or connective tissue. Between them, daylight threw its dappled mark upon the ground. Amrita thought of all the times she had been afraid of looking at the tree in the dark. Was the fear real or a habit? She did not know.

A day later, Amrita was rummaging through her German books, frantically looking for Franz's phone number, but she couldn't find it. *Is it a sign? Have I succeeded in pushing him away?* For weeks now she had maintained an outer reserve so that no one could discern the battle raging within her. The battle between her innermost desire and what seemed appropriate. She had tried to do what she thought was right. But secretly, she both feared and longed for the former's victory. *Has my armor been too tough? Have I left it too long?*

"Mama, did Franz leave a contact number when he called?" she casually asked as her mother entered her room. When Kundan immediately fished out his number from the back of her daily accounts notebook, Amrita was suspicious of her mother's quick response but elected to remain silent. Dialing the number was agony.

Hearing Franz's voice was worse. She was sorry for avoiding him. He was more sorry about her accident. He had been in a small village near Kanpur when it happened. He wanted to see her. Now. Could he come over? Yes.

Waiting for him to come over that afternoon, she realized how truly afraid she had been. Of his "NO."

As Kundan let the polite and impatient Franz in, she kept her pleasantries brief. "Go right in. She's in her room. That one in the corner. Can I get you tea or *nimbu pani?* I mean lemonade."

"*Nimbu pani* will be fine. Thanks." He stepped forward, then turned back to offer help.

"No," Kundan smilingly shook her head and went to get the lemonade.

Impatient to see Franz, Amrita was now amazed at her own past stubbornness. His presence first made her speechless, and the wheelchair seemed to pivot and wheel itself between them both. But Franz did not notice. He was busy looking at Amrita.

Amrita's eyes, whirlpools of dark honey centers with edges that were beginning to soften in thaw, swirled with the turmoil of every conflicting emotion she had felt since long before the accident. As Franz moved forward to hold Amrita, Kundan in the drawing room felt her stomach clench in response. Only the memory of the gentle touch of little Amu's tiny fingers caressing her nape could ease the tenderness in the wall of Kundan's stomach and keep her legs from collapsing into a puddle. She went back into the kitchen with the glasses of lemonade.

In Amrita's room, the wheelchair sat brashly naked. Provoking response.

Franz understood well that life can change in so little time.

35   *The Solitary Reaper*

"I HATE THURSDAY."

Amrita shuddered. Shuddered at its proximity to Wednesday. She knew for a fact that Wednesday could be pretty awful too.

When Franz did not immediately continue, Amrita gently touched his arm. He did not respond to her touch, as though his body had traveled with him in his thoughts. Amrita remained quiet.

"It was unnaturally sunny. The bells were ringing. Church bells... not particularly loud... I remember that." For a moment, Franz raised his hands as though to cover his ears from that softly overwhelming sound, but then becoming aware of Amrita's presence he quickly pulled them down. Then, apologetically, self-consciously, he laughed.

Amrita did not laugh back. "Was it very early?" she merely asked.

"No, middle of the day, actually. Noisy as usual all around, but I remember those bells."

"So...?"

"Oh, I don't know. A wedding, a funeral, unnatural sunshine perhaps?" Amrita hadn't quite meant that, but hearing the edge in his voice, she let it go. Franz was quiet again. Amrita placed her hand on his arm again. This time Franz covered her hand with his.

"I was the first to find her."

"Who?" Then, quickly, "Your mother?"

Franz nodded, inhaling deeply as though he had been running. He had run that day, oh how he had run. First, he had hurried back from school through the bright streets to eat and go out with the other boys. They were to go to the neighborhood fair. He had been excited about that. To hang about with his friends, go on a few rides, perhaps even speak to that girl...Louisa? And then he had hurried back out into the streets again. Those narrow streets that seemed to grow narrower and blinding with every step that led him into Wellington Street and into his father's office and away from the mother who had slipped away from them a very long time ago.

He could still see her. Slumped over the rocking chair to which she had grown partial in recent years. Staring unseeingly at her trailing left arm while her neck hung at an awkward angle over her right arm, he had run toward her, "Mother, mother, oh mother." Unable to make her unnaturally heavy body sit up, he had then run outside to get help. Stonehenge had followed him out through the open door. It was all over quite quickly.

Seeing that Franz was lost in a maze again, Amrita prompted him, "Your father...?"

"Oh he was angry."

"Angry?"

"Angry. Angry at the woman who had left him alone. Angry at me, at himself, at the neighbors, just anyone really, who had survived when she hadn't."

"That must have been hard. I mean, it wasn't your fault..."

Franz laughed a little cynically, "Fault..." He wondered whose fault it was for the events that had shaped her life. A young girl whose bloom had faded and whose eyes looked withered and weary well before her time. She had been through a changing decade, like others of her generation. A decade when age moved in leaps, not crept slowly nor shyly. A decade when the earth and the sky darkened and swelled ominously then burst, splintering the edges of human belief. But before that, it always seemed to be summer and it always seemed to be hot and the air strummed in tuneful melody.

She never talked about that other time in her life, but Jusuf had known. He knew from those times when she would gasp for air even on a bright and clear day that her eyes were seeing things they should not have seen. The love and family that had been forced away. Then decimated. The legacy of grief and guilt left behind. Despite that knowledge, even in her death he raged in pain to his son, "I was never enough. Never enough for her. Take heed, my boy. Pick a woman for whom you are enough."

Jusuf Gorani, the refugee who had staked his claim on his love while working the second shift on the shipping dock at Bermondsey one cold and wet winter evening. Searching for a happier landscape, they had moved to Tollington. He had gone to work. She had stayed at home. He had insisted on it. After all, they were still learning the language of this new landscape to which they had escaped. Also, ten years older, he was in a hurry to start a family.

"Joshua," that was what Jusuf wanted to name their son. But Marie was adamant. She had set her heart on calling him Franz. That was their first argument.

Wanting to do well by his family, Jusuf worked harder and longer shifts. Studying at night school, attending union meetings about the health hazards at the collieries, were all steps toward his dream of getting a decent job at a newspaper in Leeds. Meanwhile, Marie, never having mastered the language, grew lonely and tired, and despaired of it all coming to pass. There were more arguments.

"I don't remember the details," Franz looked past Amrita. He had been too young, but he remembered waking up during one argument and finding himself on the bay window seat where he had fallen asleep and remained undiscovered behind the curtain.

"Did your father become a reporter?" Amrita gently prodded Franz from behind the curtain into the present.

"Yes, and we moved to Leeds." Franz remembered Leeds. What had his mother thought about all these changes? He really did not know. He just recalled her becoming increasingly silent. By that time she could summon little enthusiasm for Jusuf's first byline or even his attempts at rejuvenating their family life.

"He did try, you know, especially toward the end."

"And your mother? Did she try?" Amrita wanted to ask, but now was not the time.

When Amrita remained silent, Franz repeated, "He did try, I

know that." But, initially, in his own struggle to establish himself, Jusuf had failed to focus on Marie, on them. By the time he realized that, it was too late. And so, Jusuf, who had appeared solid all these years, suddenly found himself rudderless without his wife. After walking about like a madman for a while, the bitterness took hold of him; there seemed no point in going on.

"What did you do?" Amrita felt a strange disquiet, looking at this man who had lived a whole life she knew nothing about.

"Drank till I could drink no more. And there were women of course."

"And did that help?"

"Momentarily. Then it all came back."

"So then?"

"Back to the grind," Franz laughed mildly at himself. He had wandered around the halls of academia for a decade searching for answers in dusty tomes, till he stumbled into India.

They talked long that day. Talked with their mouths and eyes. Taking turns. Talking and listening. In tandem. Finding their rhythm. Long into the evening when the shadows began to lengthen and stretch to indicate the end of day.

"Life must have been really hard for your mother. She was so young when it all happened." Amrita felt the inadequacy of her sympathy, her words.

"It was very difficult. She did not talk about her initial escape from Berlin to Amsterdam or later her journey to England. She just shut us out. I think she had some idea of wanting to protect me from even its memory."

"That is not possible." Amrita repeated herself passionately, "That is not possible."

"I don't think she felt that way. She wanted to forget and I think, maybe, not talking about the past was her way of forgetting." Franz had a faraway look in his eyes as he spoke. As though he was in another land with another woman.

"It must have been very lonely, and devastating," Amrita broke in loudly. Then, "Keeping it to yourself just makes it all worse," she said more quietly. It was a confession.

What happened? Amrita wondered silently. For a moment the memory lay there between them, a mocking reminder of a life purloined.

"She did not try. She gave up. Betrayed us. She could have believed in me. She should have believed in me." Time had only added to his doubt.

"Did she not believe in...my father...and me?"

As Franz looked at Amrita, she had a flash of him as a child, small and vulnerable. About his mother she thought, *Did she believe in herself?* But aloud she asked, "Did she know her...value?"

"It was understood."

"Not by her, perhaps." Amrita recognized the familiar cloud cover of unanswered questions, incomplete sentences, looking for a punctuation mark.

"It is the worst thing you can do," he continued as though there had been no break. "No man, woman, nation—no one can claim life apart." Franz shifted the discussion slightly.

"Nation?"

"Well, nations do this too. In the spirit of competitiveness with which they pursue their policies." Amrita was taken aback to hear the echo of her memories. Now she was quiet for a moment.

"I guess you are right. And they harness whatever they can to succeed."

As Amrita talked with Franz, she felt something inside of her that had become constricted begin to loosen. The magician's cup floated through her mind, pouring its never-ending stream, "And this is the water of India." She felt the strong arm of memory reach out to her. Again. But this time to remind her about the difference between *kal* and *kaal*. *Kal* as part of *kaal*.

Time can be cruel. Time can be kind. But always, always, it repeats itself in different ways. The universe does not dance a single dance. The life-creating dance of Brahma is balanced by the death dance of Shiva which is in turn balanced by the life-regenerating dance of Vishnu. Giving us many, many chances. Which we take or do not take according to our actions or inactions.

Franz left that evening only to return the next day, and the next, and the next.

36   *Across the Water*

THE DAY AMRITA called Franz, Minnie called Amardeep. They decided to meet outside DePaul's as usual. Good cold coffee and patties so close to the Jantar Mantar bus stop made it a convenient place for a rendezvous. Also, they were always sure to meet a lot of the university crowd on their way back home from college. Today, Menaka and Chand were also with them. They were very excited because they had both been accepted into the MBA program at the London School of Economics.

"Congratulations, *yaa*," Minnie bubbled.

"Congratscongrats," Amardeep joined in.

"Thanks, you guys," Menaka was beside herself with joy and could barely understand what anyone was saying. Though there were still two months to get through before their departure, it seemed to Minnie that Menaka, at least, had already left.

After finishing their drinks and snacks, Menaka and Chand left. Amardeep noticed that Minnie's initial enthusiasm had given way to quiet. "Hey, Minnie Mouse, Sylvester got your tongue?"

"Ve-e-rr-y funny. You seem to have mixed up your comic strips."

"What's biting you?"

"I was thinking how hard could it be—this MBA entrance exam and the admission process?"

"Well, you should have asked them. You didn't say much earlier."

"I know, I was thinking."

"About what?" Amardeep knew this had to be serious.

"Well, what if I took these exams?"

"Why would you want to do that?"

"To get out." Minnie was a little irritated.

"To get out of what?"

"This mess. This mess we are in. We all are in."

"We are not in any mess."

For a moment Minnie looked at Amardeep skeptically. She even considered a harsh comeback but finally decided against it. "We are, we all are," she quietly repeated. "You have to know that Amar, you have to know that," she again repeated herself. But Amardeep remained quiet. For sometime now he had known himself that he was in a mess, that they were all in a mess, but he did not know how to get out or he thought he could not get out. That was why he had been drifting for the last couple of years.

Loudly, he said, "We can clean it up." But his voice lacked conviction. And Minnie could hear that. She continued, this time more forcefully, "Don't you see Amar, we can't clean it up. Also, really, do you want to clean it up? What would you get after that? Another mess under that and under that and under that."

"Yes, but it is our mess."

"Oh, don't be such a wedge." Now Minnie was angry. "For what? I ask you. For what? Who cares? I ask you, does anyone even care where things are going? Anyone who is anybody or will be anybody in the future has either already left the country or is waiting to buy a ticket."

"That is just escape."

"It is salvation. Or...or...necessity."

"No, it is escape Minnie. At least call a spade what it is."

Amardeep too was getting angry. By this time they had reached the bus stop and were standing in line waiting for their bus. This bus stop was a little more organized; people stood here in lines. Though it was universally acknowledged that desperation could make people break through them at any time. Amardeep's motorcycle was out of commission, and he wanted to visit a friend in Taran apartments, so he decided to take the same bus as Minnie.

He would only have a short walk from the bus depot. The line was very long and curved twice. In order not to fall into the next line for another bus, the people had pushed themselves as far back as possible. This had made the line lean uncomfortably close to the toilets. This is where Amardeep and Minnie found a place for themselves.

The fruit juice stall was only a few feet from the toilets. The ambrosial smells of the luscious mangoes and oranges mixed and mingled with the strong stench of hot, fresh urine. The small puddle nearby with tributaries leading in both directions was of uncertain origin. Flies moved freely and lingeringly between the urine and the fruit like the attentions of an indiscriminate lover. Amardeep and Minnie knew that they had to stand wherever there was space without making any fuss or they would lose their place.

For a while talking was suspended. In fifteen minutes, with the arrival of a bus, their line moved forward. Minnie didn't realize till then that she had been holding her breath. She now released it in relief. Amardeep smiled at her. She smiled back.

"Why do you think the toilets and juice stalls are so close together? It makes no sense," she wondered aloud.

"To make the trip from the juice stall after drinking the juice easier for the people, I think. It's a conspiracy and the juice seller must have paid the municipality for this arrangement," Amardeep ventured not entirely unseriously.

"I think we should both apply to go abroad," Minnie suddenly changed the topic.

Amardeep, though taken aback by her comment, was in truth not really surprised by what she was saying. He had suspected in the back of his mind that this was where this whole conversation was headed. If he thought back to their conversation on the phone even last night when they had both first heard of Menaka and Chand's scholarships, he could admit to himself that it was only a matter of time before their discussion took this turn. He had known of course that Minnie had gone through some tough times in the last few months. Who hadn't? For a moment he allowed himself to be resentful. What made her think that her times were tougher than those of others? Had she forgotten what had happened to him on the way back from the university that day? And the other times of which he had not told anyone. Anyone, that is, except Amrita. And yes, what of Amrita? Where would she go?

"Amrita was mentioning this article to me that she had read in the Sunday newspaper magazine about brain drain," Minnie interrupted his thoughts. Amardeep felt a guilty start at Amrita's name.

"Poor Amrita," this time he said it loudly.

"*Poor* Amrita!" Minnie exclaimed.

"So you don't think her life is in a mess, as it were?"

"What are you talking about?"

"Move on, mister, the bus will not wait for you," someone rudely reminded Amardeep from behind. He and Minnie had been so engrossed in their conversation that they had failed to notice that another bus had arrived. The people were really relieved. They had been waiting for over an hour in the heat. Two previous trips had been missed because the buses had broken down. This was a regular occurrence. In the next few minutes they boarded the bus, finding themselves seats together at the back. The conductor kept filling the bus, asking passengers to move on. Helping them along with his own rough hand if need be. When a woman protested at his manhandling, he merely reminded her this was not her private car. She immediately kept quiet. The press of passengers was immense. The noise of several muted and not-so-muted conversations, the blaring radio of the driver and the transistor radios of a couple of other people who insisted on listening to their own kind of music and were obviously well prepared, all vied with each other. Minnie had a headache. She and Amardeep remained silent for the forty-five minutes it took till her bus stop arrived; he carried on.

37 *A Cup of Tea*

THE NEXT DAY Mandakini sounded excited on the telephone. She had been very occupied with Aslam recently. The incident with her arranged marriage had catapulted their relationship to a more serious level. They met each other every day and talked to each other in between. Amrita got daily reports from her friend. Now, Mandakini could barely talk.

"Last night I had the strangest dream."

"What was it?"

Mandakini was known for her vivid dreams. Ignoring the grin in Amrita's voice, Mandakini continued, "I saw a wild elephant grazing in the bush and an ant crawling up its trunk."

"Oh lord, poor ant, what a way to die!" Amrita gently ribbed.

"No, it was—"

"What, with the ant still inside?" asked Amrita. When Mandakini did not reply, "Now tell me what's been happening, everything exactly," Amrita laughed into the phone.

"Well, Amrita, you really should listen more carefully," began Mandakini indignantly. But she quickly gave up her mock affront and dissolved into breathless talk. "As you know, though Aslam's parents were not opposed to our being together, they were not enthusiastic about approaching my parents. Aslam has been trying to work on them, but they have maintained their stubborn position just as much as my father has his. They disagree with my father and feel they shouldn't have to coax anyone to marry their son."

"Hmm," Amrita encouraged.

"But Aslam has managed to convince them that though they are absolutely right—and Amrita they are right, I can see that—anyways, though they are right, they must be bigger in this situation. If doing this will help achieve their son's happiness, both our happiness, then it is worth it."

"So have they agreed?"

"Yes. They are not ecstatic about it. I don't want to give you the wrong impression. But they are willing to do it. Especially as they have met me and they both like me. Oh Amrita, I'm so happy."

"This is wonderful. I hope your father will agree now."

"He will. He told me his condition and now he has no reason to refuse. Aslam's parents are coming over this evening for tea."

Later that night there was another phone call from Mandakini. Her parents had met Aslam's parents. It was a start.

38   *Shopping for Life*

THAT NIGHT REGULAR TV programming was interrupted to bring an emergency news flash. There had been another Sikh terrorist attack in support of an independent Sikh nation. Five bodies had been found in Chitranjan Park, two on the Okhla Industrial Estate Road near Taran apartments. Before the newsreader had finished her story, Amardeep leaped off his chair and toward the phone. Everyone had the same thought in mind: Minnie.

"Damn, the phone is engaged."

"She may be trying to reach you," Kundan offered. But Amardeep kept his trembling finger on the dial. He wanted to take his motorcycle out and drive down to her place immediately, but Gurmehar and Kundan wouldn't let him do that. Just as he left the room to pace the veranda, the phone rang. It was Minnie.

"I've been trying your phone for so long," he almost shouted.

"The phone has been occupied nonstop. Everyone had the same idea as you. So..."

"So you could have called me first."

"You are the first person I have called, Amar. My parents have been on the phone till now," she appeased him. Listening to her voice, Amardeep was beginning to feel better. After a few minutes they put their phones down.

The next day it was in all the papers. In Chitto Park, around seven thirty in the evening, on a busy, well-lit street in front of the vegetable and fish markets, two gunmen suddenly appeared from nowhere on a motorcycle. The one riding pillion had an automatic weapon. He opened fire, aiming nowhere, hitting everywhere. Turning the air heavy with the smell of sweat and fear, rancid with the smell of dead fish and dead humans.

Three men, two women. There was pandemonium. People began running. In all directions. Stray dogs that normally roamed these streets with as great freedom as their human counterparts also looked for cover. Shopkeepers began downing their shutters, with some customers in and some out. The ones who managed to get in were the lucky ones. The others found shelter as best they could. They really didn't have a choice.

In the open street, behind an electricity pole, under an overturned dumpster, even among the wicker baskets filled with straw that contained fruits and vegetables, their bodies lay riddled with bullets like sieves through which Hindu women look at the moon on *karva chauth* night before ending their daylong fast for their husbands' lives. Blood seeped through open wounds like a secret inviting interpretation and intermingled with the juice of the tomatoes that were on sale for ten rupees a kilo. Two secrets, two tributaries in a single puddle. Origin unknown.

The gunmen then proceeded toward the Haryana border thinking to escape through Suraj Kund. The Okhla Industrial Estate Road offered a shortcut. There was some new construction there, but it was well known that there was still not adequate lighting in the area.

Consequently, their next two victims were two male factory workers who were returning from work after a late shift. Since the bus service was extremely undependable in that area, they had been forced to walk to the bus stop near Taran apartments. It was more than a two-mile walk. They had done it before. This time, however, they did not make it. At the police station, the police discovered a small plastic tag stuffed deep in one of the victim's jeans pocket. It had slipped through the torn pocket lining. Only the exposed, sharp edge of the safety pin on its back had some-how kept it hanging on a thread in the fabric weave. It said, "Mo-han Krishen. Administrative Staff, Production."

They were bipeds. Human beings with two legs. One and two.

Left, left, left right left. Left, left, left right left.

The police, egged on by hysterical public opinion, tried to dis-pense this case as quickly as possible. The murder of the two factory workers could have been a real problem for them. After all, the turnaround time for serving the poorer dead is no different from that of serving the poorer living. It is like waiting to be served in the ration lines that extend long and deep under the cruel heat of the midday sun, and then just when a hungry soul reaches the window, the *punsari*, dispenser, may—on a whim—shut the doors in his face to take a well-deserved break for lunch, or tea, or *biri*, or snooze, or something. But the identification on body number seven's person was a lucky break for the police. It led them to the identity of his companion as well. It made them look good. It brought closure to their case.

But not for the common people. For them, there was no way to understand these senseless massacres. All seven had been in-nocent, unarmed people whose only fault had been being in the wrong place at the wrong time. Fear was sweeping the city, and it knew no barriers. The streets were empty. The local businesses were suffering. And the summer heat just drove the people madder. They wanted some blood to be spilled. Eye for an eye.

▶ ● ◀

For Madhumati, initially, the news of Mohan Krishen's murder sounded like the death knell for herself. Locking herself in her tiny room, she wept till her family came and took her back home. But three days later, she returned. The funeral was over. A couple of neighbors bathed him and set him on a rough platform of wood. When the time came, they prized the old mother away and hoisted the body on their shoulders to the cremation ground. *Ram Naam, satya hai. Satya bolo, satya hai.* Luckily, a neighbor had been able to use a contact to arrange a spot and a *pundit*. Under the heat of the leaping flames, the old mother sank slowly to the ground. With no official status, Madhumati remained in the shadows throughout the proceedings. Now there were affairs to be settled. She had already set aside the jewelry and trousseau she had been collecting.

"It's too early," Mrs. Munjal protested mildly at her return. "You should spend some time at home with your family, your cousins."

"It is best this way," Madhumati gently shook her head.

"But you need the time..."

"For what?" Madhumati was almost belligerent.

"To heal..."

"To think of what might have been? No, it is no friend."

For a moment Mrs. Munjal remained awkwardly silent. Then seeing Madhumati determined, she spoke again. This time carefully picking her words, "Perhaps this may be best. Your place is also here. And if you should want to consider extending it to...domestic duties?"

Madhumati merely shrugged. "Why not?" Her eyes were dull and dry; she barely noticed when Mrs. Munjal left the room.

The next day, Mrs. Munjal was surprised to see Madhumati dressed to go out. She was not kept in suspense for very long.

"I need to go to the Khanna factory for a little while. To pick up some of his things," she said.

"Yes, yes. His parents?"

"His father is dead, and mother is too old. I want to do this...."

Mrs. Munjal nodded.

Madhumati arrived at the factory in time for her appointment. When the Assistant to the Floor Manager was informed of her arrival, he was in the factory area. He had just finished making inspection rounds of the women's section. Now he scratched the side of his nose and fiddled with the pencil stub behind his ear. Then he fumbled in his shirt pocket for his yellow, plastic measuring tape. Idly he looked at the faded measurement, shook his head, then marched to one end of a row and sat down at his desk. Here he took out a book over which he pored for about five minutes, then hastily glanced at the clock overhead and hurried out to the lobby.

Anxiously waiting for the Assistant, Madhumati for the first time looked around the area where Mohan Krishen must have come to work every day. It was a smallish room, with a red cement floor. The curtainless windows were dark brown in color. Their metal grille covered with bird droppings, fresh and caked. As a bird flew into the room and alighted on a frame, Madhumati saw it was a picture of an old couple. It was covered with a garland of dried flowers. She moved closer to look at it. The bright morning light that bathed the room with an air of cheer also created a blinding glare upon the picture. Suddenly restless, she left the room to go up front and ask for the missing Assistant.

Seeing no one at the front desk, she was just wondering what to do next when a woman of about forty-five walked in. She seemed to be walking toward the door behind the receptionist's desk.

"Excuse me…" When the woman did not turn, Madhumati tried again. This time louder, "Excuse me…."

"Did you say something to me?" the woman stopped. Just then, a young woman in a *salwar kameez* came rushing into the area, "I had just stepped into the bathroom…." Turning to Madhumati, she said a little irritatedly, "He has been informed."

"I have been waiting…"

"See that this young woman is taken care of," and the older woman disappeared through the door.

Outside, just as the Receptionist turned to talk to Madhumati, the Assistant arrived. Relieved, the Receptionist was just turning to her work when the intercom buzzed her into the inner room. Pen and pad in hand, she rushed into the room.

"Who is that young woman?" She had been struck by something in her demeanor.

"What?" Pad in hand, ready to take notes, the Receptionist was a little taken aback by this line of questioning.

"I am talking of the young woman outside."

The Receptionist told her what she knew.

"Hmm."

"Will that be all?"

"Ask her to come in."

"Who?"

"That young woman."

"Here?"

"Yes. Don't let her leave. Hurry."

Puzzled, the Receptioninst rushed out to catch Madhumati. She caught her just as she was leaving the building.

"What is it?"

"Mrs. Khanna wants to talk to you."

"I thought Mrs. Khanna is dead."

"The woman you met in the front is Mrs. Khanna, Mrs. Harjinder Khanna. Old Mr. Parminder Singh and Mrs. Taran Kaur Khanna's middle daughter-in-law. She took over after...the tragedy. You know about it?"

Madhumati nodded sympathetically. She knew about the tragedy. Mohan Krishen had told her about it. "I wonder what she wants from me?" she thought aloud.

The Receptionist shrugged, "Don't keep her waiting."

Bemused, Madhumati followed the Receptionist back into the building she had just left, thinking she was severing her final tie with her past. But it seemed the past was not yet done.

When Madhumati stepped into the inner office, she was greeted by not one but two women called Mrs. Khanna. They were the two older daughters-in-law, who had stepped into the breach left by the loss of their husbands. A little strategic questioning of the Assistant on the telephone had revealed Madhumati's relation to their employee.

"Thank you, that will be all." Mrs. Harjinder Khanna turned to her sister-in-law, "What do you think?"

"Why not?" Mrs. Harminder Khanna respected her hunch.

So it was that when Madhumati walked into the office, she was met with a blunt question from Mrs. Harjinder Khanna, "Would you like to come work for us?"

"I already have a job," she stammered.

"Doing what?"

"I look after children, a home."

"And you are no doubt good at it. Excellent. But have you thought of doing something different?"

"What? I can't sew."

"We are not asking you to sew. Administrative Staff for Production is what we are looking for."

"But I...?" Madhumati was dazed. Only a few hours earlier, she had set out on a different mission. And now, here she was being offered a job. Mohan Krishen's job.

"Can you do it?"

Could she do it? As the room faded, Madhumati focused on the two women with gray-streaked hair pulled into buns. One in a *salwar kameez,* the other in a sari. Together, they looked invincible, yet she knew that that was not true. She looked from one to the other. They looked back. Neither coaxed from her any kind of answer. They just waited.

"I will do it," the words burst from Madhumati almost without her volition.

"We will be in touch. Leave your address with the Receptionist." She had been dismissed.

"Yes." Still in a daze, Madhumati left the room. In the bus, on the way back to the Munjals', she realized the enormity of what had happened. As the trees and the electricity poles got left behind, she wondered what she would say to everyone. But one thing was suddenly clear. Before leaving, she knew she must visit the Chaddhas.

39   *Cold Drinks and Hot Air*

THREE DAYS AFTER the Chitto Park disaster, Minnie asked Amardeep to meet her outside the university canteen at one o'clock. There was quite a huge crowd there at all times. Everyone was milling around ordering samosas, *breadpakoras,* cold drinks, and tea. Cold drinks were the most expensive here because the canteen management realized they had a ready market of students who would pay the asking price. After all, the cooler water could not be depended on. Not only did the students have to wait in line at the cooler, but it was also sometimes hard to find a cooler with no chewing gum sticking to its side or scum or snot floating in its tilted leaking trough. Also, because of frequent power cuts, generators that operated the coolers were often down. So it was a miracle if the water was actually cool.

Amardeep had been a little surprised by the size of this meeting, considering it was still the holidays. For a while, he couldn't see Minnie in the crowd. So he decided to wait for her on the side. Meanwhile, he listened to the speaker. The speaker was a young man in his twenties, very earnest and very idealistic in his manner. He had on a Nehru cap and *khadi kurta pajama.* "Isn't he the same guy I heard a few weeks ago?" Amardeep idly wondered.

"Brothers and sisters, we have to do something. We cannot let this wave of violence go on. We are no longer under the British. This is our country and we have a right to decide who shall rule us and how. I ask you, are you satisfied with the government's efforts to control the crisis?"

Several students shouted, "No."

"Well then," he continued, "we have to do something. To salvage the dream. We have that power."

"But what can we do?" someone asked.

"We can do many things. To begin with, we can hold a peace march at the Boat Club," the speaker suggested.

"Peace marches are no use. We must do something else Mohan *ji*," another voice heckled.

"Yes, yes, *pyaare* Mohan," mocked the group around the voice.

The speaker raised his voice over them, "No. Don't listen to them. We need to be heard."

"What about the police?" Someone reminded the speaker of violence and arrests.

"Not if we do it peacefully," the speaker insisted. "We are brothers and sisters, and we are in this together. As I told you, I know what I'm talking about. I have seen this violence personally...."

The speaker was still speaking when Amardeep felt a hand on his shoulder. It was Minnie.

"Let's get out of here," she said. "I didn't realize they were having this meeting here today or else I would have suggested another place."

"That's all right. It's hard these days to find any place where there isn't something or other political going on. Are you okay?" Amardeep asked.

"I have decided to apply abroad," Minnie abruptly replied.

"What?" In the canteen crush and the loud noise he thought he might have misheard. He shouldn't have been surprised, but he was. Minnie had never spoken of her plans this decisively.

"It's no use your saying anything, Amar. My mind is made up. I will be taking my entrance exams in a few months." When Amar looked back blankly, she continued, "I think you too should take the exams."

"I have to think about it. This is so sudden." Amardeep was feeling a littled dazed.

"Come on, Amar, it is not sudden at all. This is what we have been talking about for so long now. Even on the day we met Menaka and Chand." Amardeep knew that. He now had to think what it would mean to him if she left and he did not.

"What does this mean for us?" he asked.

"Us? We are so young. I want to study, work, that sort of thing before I make up my mind about anything else. I thought you felt the same."

"I do," Amardeep quickly asserted. He was beginning to accept what she had said. And really, he, too, had thought of it several times. Amrita's accident had been the final straw. Watching her had made him want to go out and wring someone's neck. But never had he felt so helpless. So this time, he repeated more strongly, "I do."

A pact was made. They would both apply to go abroad. And they would try to get into the same university. But having made this decision, Amardeep needed to tell his family. He knew he would have a hard time with his father.

That night Gurmehar stopped Amardeep to have a serious talk with him. *"If only he would talk to me, try a little,"* Gurmehar wished. Father and son did not have these talks frequently, so both were uncomfortable to begin with.

"Oh, good, I wanted to tell you and Mama something as well," Amardeep spoke rapidly.

"What is it? You go ahead"

"No, no, you do," Amardeep was in no hurry.

"I'm a little concerned for your future," Gurmehar began. Amardeep listened silently.

"Look at Titu, he's nicely settled in his career. Now don't say anything. Hear me out first. I know you are currently in college and doing quite well, but I think your heart seems elsewhere. And since the happenings in the city, I feel as though you are living a life about which we do not know everything."

"There is nothing to know."

"You know what I mean. Something's on your mind."

Amardeep shrugged, so Gurmehar continued, "I have these insurance books here for you to look at."

"Why would I want to do that?" The talk had not even got underway and Amardeep was already irritated.

"It's something for you to look through in case you are interested," Gurmehar tried again.

"I'm not interested," Amardeep flatly refused.

"At least look through them. You might be interested. The entrance exam is really quite simple. By taking that you can start at the position that I struggled to get to for twenty years. Now look at Girish, he took—"

It was the wrong example. "I am not Girish. I don't want to get to that position. Now or ever." Amardeep was adamant.

"You wouldn't have to struggle. Like I did. I already have an established clientele. You could just take it over. I would introduce you to everyone."

But Amardeep wanted no part of his father's life. It was not that he did not respect his father's work. It was more that for years he had watched his father struggle in a profession that he considered people were far too ignorant to comprehend leave alone appreciate. Also, he knew that he did not have the commitment that made his father finally so successful. But he did not share these thoughts with his father. He blurted out, "I've decided to apply to go abroad."

For a moment Gurmehar didn't think he had heard right. "What?" he said. Amardeep repeated his statement.

"Don't you think you should give this a try first?" Gurmehar persisted. But Amardeep did not answer.

Gurmehar mistook his son's silence for shame—on his account. It became one more nail in the coffin of the relationship between father and son.

40   *A Difficult Decision*

"WHAT ARE YOU doing here...in India?" Amrita suddenly asked Franz. It was a week since his first visit. Franz was a little taken aback by the suddenness of the question but not entirely unprepared. He understood the question behind the question. Amrita already knew why he was in India. What she wanted to know was why he continued to stay.

"Getting to know the country, the people?" he now said.

"Why India?"

"Why not India?"

"I mean is there any particular reason?" Amrita was a little irritated at not getting a straight answer.

"Did you read about the attempt to close down the Cortonwood colliery in Yorkshire last March?"

It sounded like a change of subject but she went along with it. "Yes, isn't it resolved now?"

"Technically, but the returning miners continue to be ill-treated by the managers and those in control."

"But you were living in London at the time, weren't you?"

"Yes, but as I told you my father worked in a colliery for a time. After his death, I found several articles he had written in his early days at the *Yorkshire Post*. They were stuffed in a box in the attic."

"How could Britain afford to shut down this colliery?"

"Over the years, there had been an increase in import of coal.

Many stations were operating on oil. Most of all, the law on industrial relations, especially the one on secondary picketing, had been altered to the disadvantage of trade unions."

"You were curious?"

"More than that. Much more than that. The miners were blocked from joining the picket lines. It was horrible. Never have I seen such terror and disillusionment in the faces of people."

"With?"

"Some leaders of the Labor party, even fellow trade unionists—all sold them out. As necessity forced the end of the strike, people became increasingly divided against each other."

"But still...why India?" Amrita returned to her original question.

"My readings brought me here, as I told you earlier. It is one of the oldest civilizations and has undergone so much change, so much challenge, from within and without. Yet, it endures."

"Ah, the old stereotype. You mean, *we* endure," Amrita interrupted with a cynical laugh.

"Yes, the people. And because of that, the country as well." Franz paused and then continued, "I wonder what's the secret."

"It's no secret. Individuals and groups harness separatist and factional forces to their own purpose. And the rest must respond to that. Just like the British did to bring India under their rule. If you look back at our history during that time, you will see that there were Hindustanis, Bengalis, Marathas, and Sikhs, but no Indians. In fact, India was divided into more than six hundred princely states even in 1858 when the British government assumed direct control. They were able to buy the services of one community against another."

"Yet Hindus are synonymous with India."

"Don't be misled by that. Don't forget there are Hindus from Punjab, Bengal, Maharashtra, the South—Tamils, Andhrites, et cetera."

"Basically, the different states."

"Right, conversely, there are Punjabis who may be Sikhs or Hindus or Muslims."

"Yet, with all these differences, Hinduism has survived for centuries before and after many such attacks by Muslims and Christians."

"Yes, this resiliency does seem like a miracle, when you put it like that. With independence, the Indians tried to follow the Western model. But I wonder if we have been so focused on borrowing from the West that we have not taken into account our own rich and varied traditions. What have we created here? Is it some new kind of monster? Is it a unified India or have we merely envisaged a Western nation in our land? So that it is an effort to look at ourselves today because the only beauty and glory we see lie far, far behind in our past. Meanwhile, the present is ugly, unruly, and out of sync with the rhythm of the universe." Amrita had thought long and hard about the concept of nationhood in the last few years. Like many other Indians, she had been compelled to do so. Now she turned to Franz with a question, "Do you believe the concept of nation does or can exist anymore?"

It was a frightening question. Not just in India, but also all over the world, factionalism and ethnic violence was breaking out. But before Franz could reply, Amrita continued.

"The British challenged the concept of a single, unified India. They called it 'a mere geographical expression like Europe or Africa.' Since then Indians and foreigners alike have questioned this notion of nation. Calling India an 'amorphous, anonymous, unruly mob' and 'a muddled state of mind.'"

"The British should speak. They have had to grapple with the notion of nation themselves in this decade. Look at what Thatcher inherited. Externally, Wales, Scotland, and Northern Ireland have been questioning the authority of the Parliament. Internally, there are problems of law and order, welfare is misused, and education is at its lowest ebb. The only way out for Thatcher has been a return to national pride."

"How do you accomplish that?"

"Well, some events just happen by chance. Breakdown of the opposition led to a clear parliamentary mandate. The Labor Party gave rise to the Council for Social Democracy, which became the Social Democratic Party. Thatcherism advertises that social inequality is inevitable and even desirable. After all, success is based on personal effort and is therefore deserved."

"Isn't that a bit simplistic? After all, doesn't society function on the basis of interdependence?"

"Yes, but the Labor opposition was unable to adequately voice its vision. Also, the people wanted a strong government, economic growth, tax cuts, and an improved standard of living. They wanted a strong British identity. Still others wanted the nationalism of the Scots, Welsh, and Irish."

"No wonder there has been such tremendous opposition to Britain joining the EEC."

"That was a blow to many nationalists. But the government has tried to turn it around and show this move will propel the British economy. Falklands was also about that."

"It was quite funny, the portrayal of a fight over this small piece of land superimposed by images of the grandeur of World War II."

"It was, but it got the desired results. The 1983 elections brought back to power the Tories and Thatcher. It's another story that it costs Britain billions to now defend their miniscule war trophy. The media circus around the royal weddings is a continuation of that."

"But what about the person on the street?"

"Ah, that's a different question. Ask the person who is unemployed what he or she thinks about nationality and you will get some interesting answers. The royal wedding was covered extensively. It was a sight—white skinheads walking down the streets of London draped in the Union Jack. Some covered in red, white, and blue grease paint. In Brixton, however, the people clearly did not want the reporters. Young Blacks hanging around a wire enclosure, under cover of marijuana smoke—these images showed their reality as prisoners. On a wall, Haile Selassie spoke: 'The world is dead and everyone in it a corpse. Blessed is the man who stand and shout it out.'"

"You remember—every detail—of what was written," Amrita whispered, partly in question but partly in understanding.

"You remember every detail of what was written," Franz replied with conviction. Like much else in life, Franz had found that our thoughts, too, don't belong to us. We are always responding to external stimuli. "You interact with the headlines till memory becomes a series of reports and reactions to pieces of news, blurring the boundaries between your own and someone else's reality."

"Is there a boundary?" Amrita wondered silently. Franz continued.

"I read an account of an interview of some unemployed men in Wolverhampton. Many of these men had decided that the breakup of their country is due to Indians. Unflinchingly, and without expression, the interviewee spat that he would send 'all them darkies back home.' No, he did not want them starved and beaten like Hitler. But he declared that his thoughts were the same as that of many other people. Only he was saying them out loud."

"And is this nationalism?"

"I suppose, for the masses. I think you have to decide what you mean by nation and nationalism," Franz asserted with emphasis. Amrita was passionate about her concern and she was looking for some answers. Now she looked at Franz more closely.

"I think you are right. The old boundaries do not work anymore. Not in this atmosphere of displacement and travel. Yes, I think you are right. I think we have to alter our thinking. The concept of nation as we know it is a Western notion and India needs to lose that concept." Then more boldly, she said, "Perhaps the world needs to lose that concept."

"How?" This time Franz looked at Amrita.

Amrita was still thinking aloud about the past. "Nationalism was a good and useful tool to get the British out of India. Like Vishnu who reincarnates himself to save the world, nationalism served as the energy that came down to earth to accomplish its task. But now, like that energy, it must return to its source." Amrita was fired. Her face was red with excitement as she leaned forward into Franz as though trying to infuse him with some of her energy.

"You must be careful though when you use your Hindu symbolisms. It sounds like a Hindu takeover and where would that lead anyone? Back to the beginning."

"No, it is not a Hindu takeover. Hinduism calls for a strict adherence to set action and behavior, to *dharma*. The ancient texts, the *Shrutis,* set these down. Hinduism even believes in Untouchability. But I am not setting up a return to *Ramrajya,* though *that* was considered the seat of justice."

"But isn't its existence moot. I mean if the pregnant Sita was exiled after her return from the forest. Then returned to the earth, rather than to Rama."

"Others dispute that. However, we must all be very careful considering what a stronghold religion has on the hearts and imaginations of the people. We all need to work with the knowledge that *that* idea in the hands of the masses can and *will* lead to disaster. Knowing that many of these rules are unforgivable, we need to get out of the mire of individual institutions—religious and secular."

"So how do you view nationalism?"

Amrita was deep in thought. She knew this was an important answer for herself more than for anyone else. "I think it is being bound by more than geographical boundaries. A geographical nationalism is limiting. It is a slave-inducing mechanism, leaving the individual out of count. In the final analysis, it is petty and dehumanizes the individual."

"And the individual needs to recover his spirit. Because nationalism is spiritual, it is all encompassing," Franz ended Amrita's thought.

"Yes, yes, that's what it is. That's what it should be," Amrita was sure.

"But how do we implement it practically?"

"Details would have to be worked out... but...by restructuring education, thinking about...a global family, perhaps?"

"Hmm, a citizen of the world. Is that feasible? I mean, isn't that very idealistic?"

"So what's wrong with that?"

▶ ● ◀

The next day when Franz arrived, Amrita found herself thinking that the human race has to be put above the private selfish interests of various individuals and groups and institutions. And the only way to do this is for both men and women to unite.

"But how do human beings unite?" Amrita felt overwhelmed by the greatness of that task. "Not only is the world split by ethnic differences, there are serious rifts between men and women."

"They must simply overcome their differences," Franz said. This time Franz was idealistic.

"I don't think it's that simple," Amrita almost smiled.

"Don't you think the future of the human race is big enough of a cause to patch those differences?" Franz was a little impatient.

"One would think so. But you have to understand there is a long history of male oppression that women have faced. It makes them suspicious of joining ranks with the men quite so readily. Race, class, and sexuality further split each gender and each from each. But, I agree, women have to take their rightful place to fight for the future of *our* human race. This does not mean the end of their other battles. It just announces the beginning of a new goal. And, who knows, it might even bring together the men and the women—this fight for a common goal."

"But Amrita, seriously, do you think all this is possible?" Franz was looking straight into Amrita's eyes. She could not look away. She did not want to look away. She knew it would require framing men and women beyond binary biology and cultural expectations; it would require nurturing individual psychological experiences of the masculine and feminine within each one of us with the possibility of a union between those traits.

"I do." There was conviction in her answer. Franz was serious too.

"I do too," he answered. "It is a scary task ahead of everyone." It was a statement. No answer was required but Amrita gave one anyway.

"But if we try, we can do it," she said.

"Tall order, that," Franz commented.

"Undeniably, but you will notice that when you have high expectations from people they usually deliver. There is no option. Especially when we all have everything to gain. Do you know where Ramesh is today?"

"Who?" Franz was a little startled by this question.

"My helper."

"No, where is she?"

"She is at a rally for more rights for domestic workers—many of whom are Dalits—at the Boat Club."

"Aah. To return to our original point, where is all this supposed to take place?" Franz asked.

"Right here, everywhere," Amrita was fired again.

"What about the masses of people who believe that what happens happens because it has been preordained?"

"They will have to rethink that notion," Amrita said.

"It will be difficult."

"It will be very difficult."

◗ ● ◖

The next day, Amrita and Franz picked up their conversation from where they had left off. Amrita had had a little time to think about what she had said and now had some fresh doubts.

"Have you ever thought of revenge?" Amrita asked Franz.

"Yes. Many times." Franz's answer was unhesitating. "Especially when I was growing up, I would have done almost anything to make my mother present in my life. I wanted to personally bring to justice the bigots from her past."

"Justice, that's another interesting concept. In the interest of justice so much more ill takes place. I want to know why Justice wears a blindfold. It doesn't feel like it does so to be impartial. More because it truly cannot see."

"That's very cynical."

"That's reality. Go back to history. Right here. Anywhere. With your parents. Or mine." Amrita was not entirely convinced of this concept of justice.

"But there is always something larger. Behind. Spinning the wheels of government. It is the—"

"...The call to nationalism. Then and always."

"Undoubtedly," Franz agreed.

"It is so tempting though, an eye for an eye. Anything less, in fact, seems nothing at all. Doesn't it allow the perpetrator to go scot-free?" Amrita asked.

"Isn't it Gandhi who said something like, 'If we all take an eye for an eye the whole world will go blind'?"

"Gandhi is dead. And, in any case, you should read the accounts of the people who were close to him. They talk of how difficult, and expensive, it was to follow the Gandhian lifestyle," Amrita said with a slight smile.

"The details perhaps. But, what about the principle? That's where it all begins."

"We live the details. That's what constitutes life," loudly Amrita replied.

But later that night, Amrita thought about the principle.

❯ ● ❮

"The principle of love is not as easy as you make it sound," she began the next time Franz visited her.

"I never claimed it was easy."

"And for it to work, men and women have to be willing to get to know each other.... Do you think it possible for men and women to ever really know each other?" Amrita had remembered that question from their stumped conversation months ago. Unlike that time, however, now Franz looked at her. He knew it was important, that question. And even more important was the answer to that question. He couldn't help knowing that this time Amrita wouldn't be getting up and going anywhere in a rush. In any case, he knew also that he would always follow.

He had begun to feel that way soon after he met Amrita, but it was too new an emotion and so he had resisted. Also, he was a little afraid. With every day they met, the feeling had grown stronger, however. He had a deep desire to know her, the way he had learned to know himself. To reach behind her face.

The news of her accident had left him angry. Besting the *sardar* of Hariganj through sheer persistence and sincerity seemed paltry now. He couldn't wait to be with her. So when she refused to meet him, he was surprised. At first he thought he understood; he could wait. But when days turned into weeks and she still refused to see him, he began to grow angry. Contact with Mandakini and

Kundan was not enough. Memory, like Tantalus, bore its eternal burden. Circling daily around Connaught Place, he revisited all their haunts, even bought a wall hanging they had both admired.

In a measure, to make bearable the unbearable, he drove around the pockmarked city streets in a light-headed daze one rainy, black, desolate night in June. As the rain pelted down, the roads in Connaught Place glistened wetly under the florescent light of the streetlamps blurring the boundaries between heaven and earth. Skies do fall. The streets were like a sauna, but the litter and the homeless, having blown themselves into other nooks, continued to sleep. A little limp, but basically undisturbed. Unwinding his window, he shouted into the black night, "I am Joshua come back from the dead. Come to take my own. Do you hear me? Come to take my own." But all around, the downed shutters shouted Amrita's missive, mockingly. The imperceptibly shivering concrete and steel and plateglass jungle, the billboards, and the garish neon lights winked in unsubtle invitation, threatening to lose him in their whorls. No palm reader slunk in any doorway to unravel the skeins of his fortune. Only the restless spirits of the dead or doomed walk the streets on such a night. He kept driving.

Circling around the streets he found himself in Amrita's neighborhood, where he finally parked outside her house. The windshield wipers moved in synchronous rhythm to his lashes, periodically blotting the streetlight and bringing it back, but still the rain and the tears continued to fall. The dark clouds clapped their thunder. Flashing white in wrath. Distantly, a dog barked, testing his lungs for power. Then gave up, reassured. For a while, Franz sat there in the street, resentful of the stoic silence of the boundary wall, of the shadowy mystery of the guava tree, even of the moonlight that must—on other nights—pour itself liquidly inside her bedroom window. And of her. What right had she to unilaterally make this decision for both of them? To pinch an artery here, to open another there, to redirect the flow of their lives? And having made this decision, was she now sleeping peacefully inside? There were events that had taken place in the city that she had hinted at, events that had touched her and her family's lives, but she had refused to elaborate. Saying the time was not right. She would tell him when the time was right. Well, he was here. Where was she? *Oh Amrita, have you forgotten? Let me in, please let me in.* The curtains at her window remained firmly closed, only slightly parted in the middle. She used not to be so cruel. She was more his mother's daughter than he was his mother's son. *Was it some caulk that women were born with that made them naturally pain resistant? Or has she grown deaf as well as lame?* he thought cruelly to himself. The repeated whistles of the night watchman, however, urged all homeless wanderers to another direction. In order to avoid suspicion, he left. But only to exchange one scene for another.

"Forget me," she said. She asked for too much. As always. Where should he go? Where was the land where the breeze did not blow? The stars never shone? Perhaps he should move to another dimension. Where sight and vision walked separate paths, where breath and life were not synonymous, where the heart could unlearn its beat. Walking daily with their fingers and gaze loosely twined, no more than hinting at the language of their hearts and spirit, the noise of the crowds and the city always fell away to be replaced by a joyful sound. Sometimes silence. It must have been love. Now his fingers stretched achingly outward before knotting on each other or falling hopelessly apart. Even his gaze seemed to deflect off of objects in a glassy daze. Had he once honestly believed that he could separate himself from love, extract its essence and filter it into his life? A formulaic kind of loving. Inoculated against pain. And how foolish in retrospect. Laughable, really. And frightening the possibilities. He promised himself that, given another chance, he would not keep his feelings a secret.

So now when Amrita asked him the same question she had asked him months ago, he said, "I would like to believe that." Looking into Amrita's eyes, he repeated, "I need to believe that. I do believe that." Then, "As much as they are willing to let each other in," he answered the question in her eyes.

"It is an individual decision?"

"It would have to be," he said. "No one can make that kind of choice for anyone or take that kind of responsibility."

"To love one another. It was so easy to do that as a child."

"So was hate."

"Yes."

"We are not children anymore."

"No, we are not."

For a while both were quiet, till suddenly Franz leaned toward Amrita, "I believe in love," he said. Despite the wait and the planning, the words that came out were neither poetic nor even clear.

"Yes, I know. So do I."

"No, I am talking of love between a man and a woman. Me and you." Amrita looked up at the earnestness in his voice. "Do you?" he asked tentatively.

"Yes." Amrita's answer was firm. "It almost surprises me to say that," she half smiled.

Franz noticed the lurking sadness in her eyes. "Love is like justice...," he began.

"I don't think so, I don't care for that comparison."

"Just think, commitment to fairness without any prejudice."

"I don't think so."

"Then what?"

"It is like beauty."

"Beauty?"

"Yes, that which is true and brings us joy and happiness."

"Justice does that."

"No, beauty does that."

41 An Intruder in the Backyard

"HAVEN'T HEARD YOU practicing lately, *Bhabhi ji*," Gurmehar prodded Mrs. Joshi lightly as he and Kundan stopped to talk to their neighbors that evening. The moon hung large and had a reddish glow.

"What *Bhai* sahib, it's difficult to sing these days." Mrs. Joshi's reply was a little sad.

"No, no," Kundan interrupted, "don't let anything stop your singing."

"That's what I've been telling her but she refuses to listen to me. After all, I'm just the husband," Mr. Joshi joked.

"Come on *ji*, what are you saying? I always listen to you, but," Mrs. Joshi began till she caught the glint in her husband's eyes. She looked at him with a laugh and promise of later retaliation. Suddenly, lowering her voice, she whispered, "There's that strange man again."

"Who? Oh, it's only Mr. Collins," Kundan looked around, then smiled in his direction.

"Still, these days..."

"He's lived here longer than we have."

"Still...I would really like to know what he did to his wife and children."

"How do you know he did anything?"

"I don't...of course."

"Of course," Kundan was a little curt.

"Let's not let our imagination get away," Mr. Joshi suggested.

For a moment Mrs. Joshi remained silent, then she continued, "Kundan *ji*, haven't seen Franz today. Everything is okay, I hope."

"He phoned." Kundan didn't elaborate.

▶ ● ◀

Gurmehar had come back home several days ago from meeting Mr. Daruwalla to hear Amrita's animated voice. He looked in question toward Kundan. "Franz," she mouthed. Gurmehar immediately walked toward the voices.

"Papa this is..."

"Hello, I am..."

"Franz. I know." Gurmehar stood in the doorway looking at his daughter sitting up in bed and at the young man who quickly stood up from the wheelchair by her side on seeing him. For a moment, Gurmehar felt a twinge. Shrugging it off, he moved forward, hand outstretched.

"I hear you have been traveling all over the country. Any sights that we have not read about?" Gurmehar asked.

"I was in the area around Kanpur recently. In Hariganj, life was the same as usual. I didn't hear anything. But when I came into the city, I heard of violence in the bazaars. I had been advised that I would be okay so long as I pretty much kept to myself. I met this guy, a colleague, who had earlier been working on a matter in Sri Nagar; they are turning hostile to foreigners there."

Fillers of holes, go back! We can fill our own holes.

The villagers had appeared fascinated by Franz's interest in them. Overwhelming him with their hospitality. Gratified, moreover, thinking it good strategy, he was eager to accept their friendliness. When the *sardar* of the village personally stopped by with his invitation, Franz arrived punctually to find that preparations for his visit were still in progress.

"Four thirty? Is it that already?" the *sardar* shouted to no one in particular. Then, "Oy Shamu, come here." When the shivering

Shamu came up, he continued to shout as though talking to a deaf person, "Where did you go and die? All should have been arranged long ago."

"But *Sardar* sahib..."

But the *sardar* had already turned away to someone else, "Basanti, see if *chaishai* is ready...or..." Here he turned to his guest and briefly consulted him, "Or will it be milk? Very fresh. Straight from the cows..."

"That won't be necessary," Franz hastily refused, having seen a woman lean into one of the aluminum pails filled with frothy white milk to scoop out a floating piece of straw with her bare hand.

"Did you hear that?" *Sardar* sahib shouted. "That won't be necessary." From somewhere inside could be heard some brave woman's voice, "I think the whole village heard that." The *sardar* kept giving orders. Since, by now, the seating area had been set up, he began to move his guest toward it. "Come, let's sit. So now, where were we?"

"I was talking about the survey...."

"Survey? Ah yes, but first let's relax. Sit down, sit down."

Watching the *sardar* fold himself with ease onto the *charpai*, Franz too tried to do the same. But the material of his pants did not give as easily as the *sardar's dhoti*.

"Take a chair, take a chair," the *sardar* offered kindly, quieting the surrounding titter. Soon, some of his cronies came and joined them, and the talk remained general for a while.

Many villagers had collected close by under a tree to openly eavesdrop on their talks. Nobody stopped them; it was customary. The *sardar* reclined comfortably on the *charpai*, fingering his *janau* with one hand and guiding his hookah with the other. He had offered Franz a hookah, but when Franz had politely refused, he had ordered it away. A few of the men coughed self-consciously at what they saw as youthful immaturity, but the *sardar* silenced them with a look. The company held steaming glasses of tea and had settled in for an evening of discussion.

"So you want to talk to the men?" the *sardar* signaled the change in subject.

"Women too, if possible," Franz was courteous. He had been wondering if they would ever get to the point.

The *sardar* drew a deep breath from his hookah. The rest of the men waited to release their own. "That would be more tricky," he enunciated slowly. "Not for me personally," he hastened to added pridefully. "My daughter and daughter-in-law have gone to primary school. But for the others."

"Of course," Franz consented. "What about talking to the women in the presence of the men in their family? So that—"

"Ahh, hmm, will have to think about that. Why, Chandu, what do you think?"

Chandu, taken by surprise by the *sardar's* query, could merely stutter, "Revolutionary, new-fangled, whatever you think *Sardar* sahib."

"Bah," the *sardar* roared. "And you call yourselves men. Good for only smoking a hookah." Some men sitting farther away around the tree on their haunches sucked deeply on their *biris,* looked at each other, and laughed. The women behind them hid their mouths in their *palloos* and giggled helplessly at Chandu's plight. Chandu went red at this public reprimand, especially in front of the women, but did not say or do anything to contradict the *sardar.*

"Wonderful idea as I said to you earlier, to make our very own list of things we'd like to change in our area...local movement," the *sardar* announced. "Of course, we have done similar things ourselves," he turned to Franz. When Franz inclined his head respectfully, he continued, "Must talk more about it later. Now it is time for dinner. Let us relax and be entertained for a little while. Basanti, some more tea here."

Franz tried to be as comfortable as possible with a horde of people staring at him as he swallowed and breathed. Each time he spoke, he could feel all eyes glued to his face and hear a giggle or two in the background. It was already several days since his arrival, and the *sardar* had been nothing but polite to him. Yet, if all their meetings ended as this one, he feared he would never be done.

As the sun dipped slowly into the horizon, it seemed to set the whole landscape on fire. The faded board advertising the movie

Safar, the small sign advertising the barber's services, even the evenly spread *bajri* in front of the *sardar's* yard glowed shyly. Looking at the fire on the people, for a moment Franz wondered at his temerity in taking on this task. Is this why Rajiv Sehgal had sent him? Because he knew he must fail! What did he know that they didn't? Like the crushed weeds beneath their feet, they had come out of this ground and seemed to know this air more intimately than he ever would. But as he looked, the sun made a quick bow to beat a hasty exit, and dusk began falling on broken ground and vast, empty fields. Nearby, a small, skeletal boy dragged a reluctant and even more skeletal dog on a rough jute string. *"Haddi,"* someone aimed a sharp-edged stone at the two; both yelped, almost tripping into the gouged street, then scurried away into the evening. As Franz looked up, a sickle moon arose to drape the slender, naked branches of trees with pale moonlight. Even the narrow gutters that overflowed with liquid and solid waste seemed to guise themselves and drift away. Their smells taken over by the pungent odor of dung cakes as housewives began lighting their hearths and the poor and the homeless sat around at corners to boil their concoctions of grass and water in bent, crooked vessels.

Franz wondered about Amrita. If her eyes were laughing at some other poor bugger right now. They had been there even that day in his office at King's College. Side by side with his mother's eyes. Mocking him, taunting him into action. He must finish this task as soon as possible and get back to her. There was so much to say.

Listening to Franz, Gurmehar quietly shook his head, then looked at Kundan as she entered the room.

"Did you go down to the Ganga?" Amrita turned the conversation.

"Actually, yes. Carter, the other person I mentioned, he and I went down to one of the ghats...Ganga ghat? We wanted to see for ourselves what so many people talk about."

"And?" Amrita asked with a smile.

Franz's lips curved upward a little, and with only a very slightly raised eyebrow he said, "The water level was very low, so the steps that normally lay covered under water were exposed. We went down to the water, but there was really nothing more than a dirty stream to look at with garbage and some soggy garlands floating on top."

▶●◀

Since Franz's first visit, the whole neighborhood had been abuzz with curiosity. Mrs. Nanda (she came personally, "so that Mangru can have some free time") and some others had taken to dropping in suddenly to ask for a bit of curd to set milk. Kundan usually shut the door to Amrita's room when the neighbors came calling, hoping to divert their attention.

"What's going on? Is this a meeting?" It was Ganesh Raghunathan.

"Where's Raghunathan junior?" Gurmehar joked. The Raghunathans had a small son who was not with them now. Gurmehar was very popular with kids. It was a mystery to Amardeep.

"Junior is with his grandparents," Suchitra Raghunathan told them.

"Aren't your parents in Bombay?"

"No, he's with Ganesh's parents. Here, in Delhi. In Punjabi Bagh."

"Why? Everything's okay, isn't it? It has to be if you both are here."

"Well..." While Suchitra hesitated, Ganesha jumped in.

"We hadn't meant to talk about it but there was an attack at our house," he quietly said.

"What?" almost everyone shouted. Mrs. Mahindra and the Munjals had also joined them by now. The atmosphere suddenly changed from lightheartedness to serious concern.

"Are you all right?"

"Your son?"

"How come we have not heard about it?"

"We were just too shaken by the whole incident. We came home day before yesterday after picking up our son from the crèche to find an attempt had been made to break into our house. We immediately reported it of course."

"Crèche? Where is Malti, the *aya*?"

"Well, that's another story. We want to think it's separate. But she ran away last week."

"Sounds fishy."

"Hmm...day before yesterday...that was the night there was no electricity for several hours in the evening," Mohit Munjal interrupted.

"Yes," Ganesh agreed. He continued, "We were very scared for our son so we took him that night itself to my parents' house."

"What about you? Your safety?"

"The police said that it just looked like an opportunist taking advantage of the situation."

"What do you think about the accord with the Moderates?" Gurmehar did not realize he had spoken loudly till he found all eyes focused on him.

"Well, it does promise to restore elections. Also offers greater economic and political power," Mr. Joshi spoke tentatively.

"Don't forget it offers to officially recognize the Sikh religion," Ganesh quickly intervened.

"Ah, yes, but does everyone see it that way? To the extremists it is just a betrayal of their goals," Suchitra was impatient.

"So what happens next?" Mrs. Joshi sounded a little nervous.

"Uff, uff, uff. Uff, uff, uff," muttered Gurmehar almost despite himself.

"Perhaps you shouldn't stay at home for a few days?" Kundan wondered aloud to Suchitra and Ganesh. "You can sleep at our place. It will be a tight fit but if you don't mind, we can do it."

Strike two. Everyone looked uncomfortably toward what used to be the Bhallas' home. It had to be scary, everyone felt. Should they call a Residents Association meeting? Should they arrange for a gunman to watch the streets? To have an intruder in one's own backyard is very different from when he is still across the fence. Their neighborhood was not so impervious then.

42 *Striking Out*

TWO DAYS LATER, Minnie and Amardeep entered Amrita's room to find her talking to Franz. Gurmehar had not discussed Amardeep's announcement with anyone, thinking and hoping it was something his son had said out of anger. Now Amardeep had come to tell Amrita of his decision to apply to go abroad with Minnie. As they entered the room, they could hear Albinoni's Adagio in G minor. Franz had brought over some of his favorite tapes, and Amrita listened to them day and night. The smell of hot samosas and *jalebis* hung in the room. And Amrita was coaching Franz.

"Sa-mo-sa, *ja-le-bee*," she sounded.

"Sha-mau-sha, *jaa-lebi?*" he tried.

"No," she laughed. "Try again. Sa-Sa-mo-sa. *Ja-le-bee.*"

"Are there any for us?" Amardeep interrupted laughingly.

"Plenty. We were expecting you," and Amrita shoved the plates toward her brother and Minnie. "I was expecting you a little earlier," Amrita continued.

"Yeah, well, we had some things to work out." Amardeep was a little cagey.

"Sounds serious."

"It is."

"We have both decided to apply to go abroad next year," Amardeep said.

"Where?"

"America or England. Whichever works out."

"Why now?" Amrita was curious. As the tape ended, she leaned forward to change the side. The sounds of Dvorak's symphony no. 9, Opus 95, began to fill the room.

"Lots of reasons," Amardeep began to say calmly. "Lots of reasons," he repeated with emphasis.

"Give one," Franz joined the discussion.

"Opportunity...look at this mess. What's around us. Amrita's accident, the court case."

"And have you seen what's out there?" Franz asked.

"Not this at least."

"But something similar."

"People are more civilized there."

"Civilized?"

"Actually, more...rational, I think is the word."

"Rational? Surely, you have been reading of the outbreaks of ethnic violence in Europe, America...everywhere...they are getting worse. Even look at religion. Someone said quite correctly that we have sacrificed God at the cross of denominationalism."

"What are you doing here?" Amardeep turned the focus of the conversation. The gloves were off. The two men really didn't know each other. Every time Franz came over, Amardeep was out with Minnie or on his way to or back from meeting her.

"I was looking for some meaning to my life. It just led me here," Franz replied calmly.

"And do you intend to stay? Or has the poverty and the filth rubbed off some of the meaning? Is this just an ethnic diversion for you, like Amrita."

"*Amardeeeeeep,*" Amrita was angry with her brother yet curious to know Franz's answer.

"It's not a diversion at all." Quiet. Sincere. And sure.

"Are you not concerned what it will mean for you to stay here?"

"Mean? In what way?" Franz looked puzzled.

"I mean what will it mean in terms of you or any children you may decide to have."

"I am not concerned."

"Well, you should be. After all, what are you? *Who* are you? How do you define yourself? British? Ethnic Albanian-German Jew? Or future Naturalized Indian? Who *are* you?"

"*Amar,*" interjected Amrita again. The conversation had taken a dangerous turn. "You don't have to answer that Franz." But Franz was calm.

"No, let me answer that. I would like to answer that. I am all these and more."

"Ha, we have a man who would call himself a human being," Amardeep was contemptuous. "That's a cop-out. It's not so simple."

"It really is," insisted Franz. "I am so much more. You tell me, Amar, you are so proud of being Indian, your pure Indian heritage. If you decide to stay wherever you go, in England or America, what will that make you?"

"That won't happen," Amardeep murmured.

"But it might," Minnie intervened. Amardeep looked at her.

"I can't talk of something that may or may not happen in the distant future," he compromised.

"Not so distant. The future is now, Amar. The future is now," Franz was emphatic. "If you really look carefully at your life and mine and take away the names, could you tell the difference between our experiences—excepting the details?" When Amardeep did not answer, he continued, "Tell me then where would you draw the boundaries? Who draws the boundaries? Who names these names? And who tells us what to think? Do atoms only move in a certain formation? And if so, does that mean all movement is fixed?"

"I had forgotten about the behavior of particles," Amrita ventured.

"But what would we be without those boundaries?" Minnie now stepped in. "We need those boundaries for definition of others, of ourselves. We can't just go around calling ourselves human beings."

"Yes, we do need those boundaries initially. But don't you think we limit ourselves when we continue to stay within them?"

"How?" Even Amardeep was curious.

"How? Because life is so much more. Human beings are so much more. They *can* be so much more. Living within boundaries is like living without imagination, without dreams, without possibilities." Franz was leaning forward in earnestness.

"Or getting lost in all of those things. Most people can barely get through a single day even with those boundaries showing them the path to follow," Amardeep said with skepticism.

"But don't you see Amar," Amrita jumped in, "there *is* no single path. And the tragedy lies in the fact that what you say is an undeniable possibility. Which is why what happens, happens. The boundaries that people live within are the ones they have placed around themselves, around their hearts. But it doesn't have to be like that. Life doesn't have to be so small. Not if we live in engagement with our consciousness."

Amardeep looked at Amrita as though confronted by a traitor. Even Amrita was startled by the strength of her statement. Slowly, over the last few weeks, Amrita had begun to change her thinking, coming out of the lassitude she seemed to have been lost in for so long. She looked at Franz for a long time.

The arrival of Gurmehar and Kundan from their evening walk broke up the group. In any case, Amardeep wanted to take Minnie home before it got too late.

After Franz left, Amrita lay thinking about him. He had looked quiet, reflective, she thought, after Amardeep and Minnie left the room. His eyes a deep, wet gray. When she asked him what he was thinking about, he had at first just shrugged. Then said he was thinking about home. Home. Not Britain. "Do you think about it often?" she wanted to ask. But she bit her tongue. What must it be like to be away from the place you were born in? Played and fought in? Grew up in? Did he miss the smell of the grass? Did he miss the smell of the earth? The sky? The air? The creak of a stair? Did his heart skip a beat, then run rapidly, his eyes and ears open wide, at the subtle nuance of a voice? The gentle curve of a cheek? The imperceptible tilt of a neck? Did the voices from his past shriek and shout? Did the architecture of the buildings, the streets of Delhi remind him in every line and curve that he was an outsider? Was home a place that, over time, would become enshrined in his heart—idealized and forever frozen like the memory of people who die young? And would he then resent her? Or would he be able to make another home for himself? Is home a place or a feeling?

And what about Amardeep?

That night Amrita couldn't get Amardeep out of her mind. Her brother, her friend, her partner in chess and many a crime that went unwitnessed except by the moon. How far along had they come? And how far apart? Would they move even farther? Do new interests erase old memories? Does the moon shine differently in different places? She understood that things don't remain the same; we don't remain the same. Still, to let loose those bonds that had been forged playing around the guava tree was not going to be easy. The thought of the guava tree brought a smile to Amrita's eyes. She remembered the times they had hidden under its sparse foliage rocking to the rhythm of a nonsense rhyme.

Akar bakar bambe bo...

The project was to catch the escaped convict, and they tried to do just that as they sat with arms outstretched, fingers spread-eagled on the ground. The person singing the rhyme punched down on one finger at a time with every syllable. Wherever the rhyme ended, that finger was withdrawn into the secret of the cup of the hand. Since both of them had to put out the same number of fingers—to avoid unfairness—the person singing the rhyme would often have a foot spread out with a hand. This only increased the hilarity of the play as they tried to fold an unfoldable toe. The one who was able to lose all digits at stake first was the winner.

That it was hot and muddy did not bother them. That they were fully visible to the grown-ups they were trying to escape did not cross their minds. Perhaps that was a blessing. And so they had grown up. In heat, in dust, with limbs contorted in skirmish and much laughter they had forged a bond. *Langoors. Angoors.* Like laburnums.

Those bonds that were reinforced daily in countless confidences and even more fights, and by formal displays of affection at least two times a year. How they both had squirmed and giggled, alternately, on those days. To get up early, bathe, put on good clothes, and tie the thread of unity and promise had seemed funny then. Even primitive.

"Behan ne rakhri banni, vira teri lummi umri hove." Both she and Amardeep doubled up with laughter then and were routinely scolded for lack of respect to national and family tradition. Ah, the good old days when national and family tradition could be followed by tying a knot and singing a song. But would the knot hold once Amardeep had left? Or would new interests replace old ties? "That's ridiculous, of course it will be the same," she quickly told herself. "And there is Franz." The thought of Franz made her smile and think of him in anticipation.

43   *Diving into the Center*

IN THE LAST few days, Gurmehar had met with Mr. Daruwalla and gone over the case. Mr. Daruwalla listened to everything quietly. Till the Prosecutor was mentioned.

"*Vikas* Khanna. I see, I see. Hmm."

"Why? Is there something I should know? I did try to find out about him, but no one would say anything."

"Well...there are some stories...he is here on transfer. There have been rumblings about two of his cases in Delhi already. But no one lodged a complaint."

"I never heard that." Gurmehar was agitated.

"No, you wouldn't. It's one of those closely guarded secrets...."

"But..." Gurmehar stopped.

"If you bring me all the papers that have been filed, I could give you a better answer," he said.

The next day, having studied the papers, he called Gurmehar and asked him to bring Amrita in. "For all those times I have kept you talking to me," Mr. Daruwalla finished abruptly and sheepishly.

At first, Amrita was not enthusiastic about the idea. She just wanted to forget about the case. They had already been over it, and nothing had come of it. That night, however, for the first time since the accident she allowed her mind to travel more than to the periphery of the wreck. She traveled into its center.

The ferryman was at the shore with his boat of sorrow; he had

been expecting her. She got in. Where was the garland of marigold? She narrowed her eyes into the horizonless gloom. It was
a moonless night. Darkness lay like a thick coat over the water,
making it look more murky and mysterious than usual. When the
heavy stillness of the night was broken by a sudden breeze. As the
wind blew over the water, its surface shook and shivered, rising in
tiny waves to embrace the elusive wind. The thrust of the paddles
knifed the water bleeding secrets of the deep that it had carried
for centuries in its womb.

It began as an ordinary day. With no indication that by mid-after-
noon it would rend the connective tissue between the past, present, and future. Split time. Into two. One part, thrown away. The
other, a stump, some ugly scar tissue. A well full of memories. With
hope a word that dangled from its mouth. And raging longing.

   That, of course, came later. What came first was the heat...

   On Wednesday, May 1, the heat was excruciating. It was so hot
that the heat prickled the skin, making it rise in bumps that swelled
with red anger at every scratch. The hot wind vibrated and exhaled
sharp-edged dust particles from time to time, as though seized
by fire. Breathing heavily on guavas and melons and mangoes
and cantalopes, it made the greens darken, turn into yellows and
soft browns. Under wet muslin and portable fans, the tiny cells
swelled with sweetness to split and spill their fragrant juice in
overriding joy. The heat rose from the polished, dark metallic surface of the brittle, parched road in a thick haze. Bleeding tar. It
lingered around curbs, grew turgid on food smells, then hung listlessly over filthy puddles of water and urine. Sporting giant flies
spritzing feces in a wet buzz, dead mosquitoes swimming side by
side with larvae. Even ants lay limply in their mud hills while, at
their doorstep, wilting dog flowers mildly barked their protest. The
heat pierced, nailed, then skidded off shiny surfaces. Like a blitz-
krieg. Swiftly. Suddenly. Concertedly. Making the people cower
in protection.

   Amrita could feel beads of sweat running down her legs. Her sari
was clinging to her back; her petticoat kept getting in between her

legs wrapping the sari into it tightly—like a funnel. To walk even a single step she had to hold her sari, surreptitiously, away from her body with one hand. She stood under the bus shelter for a moment. But that was almost worse because the roof merely trapped in the heat making the atmosphere humid. On one end of the shelter, a listless cow surveyed the crowd negotiating around her and occasionally swished its tail to brush off an itinerant fly and glare half-heartedly at it from a half-open eye. Posters, big and small, were pasted on every available concrete surface. Around pillars and on the ceiling. One poster urged people to plan their families, have fewer children. "One or two. Stp!" The painter had misspelled or missed the *o* in the word "stop"; in any case, he had decided to leave it as it is. Another poster hinted at mysterious (yet proven) ways to overcome infertility. Yet another carried information about some demonstration at the Boat Club. Several advertised old and new films. *Mera Naam Joker. The Killing Fields. Star Trek III: The Search for Spock.* Revivals and piracies. On one side, a large banner had the words *"Garibi Hatao"* printed across. Poverty Remove. Re. Move. To someplace else. Out of sight of helmeted hearts behind tinted glass windows. Or simply erase. Vaporize. Into nonexistence. It was not clear. Underneath, a sickly beggar woman sat wrapped in her poverty with an aluminum plate holding a few coins in front of her to provoke people's generosity or guilt. Periodically swaying back and forth and muttering to herself, she was oblivious of the stares she drew. Beside her, two infants with unnaturally protruding bellies—pregnant with desires that would almost certainly never become reality—played silently, their nakedness covered by an uneven coating of wet snot, dust, and flies. Amrita turned restlessly. Big, bold, red letters painted across the boundary wall, next to the public toilets, invited people to consult with Chowdhary Yogendra Singh, Sexologist. There was even a picture of a man in an intricately twisted turban and he was sporting a big, bushy mustache with spread-eagled ends. The picture no doubt was to encourage confidence. Someone had freshly urinated over the Chowdhary's mustache, giving his mouth a dribbling look. Amrita quickly looked away. For a few moments, she amused herself looking at the sparse crowd. Nearby, a little boy was pulling at his mother's sari. The harassed woman, balancing a baby and a bag, met Amrita's eyes in brief sympathy. Then darted toward another shelter. Amrita, herself tired of waiting, and with no bus in sight, looked around for a scooter. She saw two standing on the side, next to the *chaat* wallah.

"*Bhaiya,* will you go to Bengali Market?" Amrita asked one of them.

"I'm on break," the driver said irritatedly.

"I can give you a few bucks over the fare," Amrita offered.

"Can't you see I'm resting?" The scooter wallah sounded angry. He was lounging on his seat talking to the *chaat* wallah like other drivers did as they passed through the stop. That, and busy peeking and sniggering at the beggar woman whose random movements had slipped the bit of rag *palloo*—no blouse—covering her chest so that one drooping curve of her shriveled breast lay partially exposed. A lost soul. Lost forever. Amrita let it go. There was no point in arguing with him.

Amrita approached the second one. He had heard her conversation. He let her repeat herself.

"*Bhaiya,* will you go to Bengali Market?"

"It's too close," he said.

She offered him a few bucks over as well.

"Fare plus ten," he said with a wicked smile. He knew his demand was outrageous.

"Double? Forget it."

A few minutes later, seeing a scooter approach on the front level of the road, she hastened to move in his line of vision, but he sailed right past her waving hand even though he had no passenger.

Amrita opened her purse to look at her watch. It was too hot to wear it; the leather strap just left an itchy red rash on her skin in the heat. The time was three thirty. She had been standing at the stop for thirty-five minutes. "God, they really need to speed up the bus service during this time. Do they think everyone gets to sit at home with nothing to do in the heat?"

Looking toward Delhi Gate, she was relieved to see some buses coming down the road. "I hope one of them is mine." Pushing down her slipping sunglasses, she got ready to move forward. But as the two buses drove into the curve of the inner stops, she backed away. The buses were packed with people. There were people inside and outside. There were so many people at the front and back entrances that some people seemed to be standing not on any surface but held together by the sheer press of human bodies. Some were even standing on the back bumper with their backs sticking out in a curve, their behinds bobbing up and down, as they precariously held on to the rail that runs around the bus on top. *Langoors. Angoors.* Like laburnums. On the top of one bus there were some strapped baskets. They seemed to have chickens in them. Amrita couldn't tell if they were alive. The squawking of birds could so easily have been a sound of protest or a sound of mourning for death in lockup.

Amrita was beginning to feel frustrated. It seemed to be getting hotter by the minute. She wondered if she should start walking. Maybe, on the way, she would get a scooter. But no, there was a DTC bus coming down the road, and it looked fairly empty. It was even the right number. Amrita moved toward the bus entrance as the bus seemed to slow to a stop. Only, it did not stop. The driver was just playing. He kept the bus moving, laughing with his buddies in the front. It was their chance to mock the general public who, they felt, kept them down. "Not so much in control now, are you?" his moving tires seemed to say. From behind, Amrita heard a few men around the scooter wallah snigger at her plight as they saw her make several attempts to reach the entrance. Amrita held back. Throwing one last look at the beggar woman who was now alternately chuckling and crying, she decided to start walking.

Hardly had she moved when she saw two buses, a private and a mini, coming down the road. Perhaps this time she would be lucky. The private bus got in a split-second first. Luckily it was the right number. It was packed but less packed than the others before, and Amrita didn't have far to go. Just a few stops. She could put up with ten minutes of discomfort. But everyone else around her also seemed to have the same idea because even before the bus stopped everyone leaped toward it. The conductor got off at the stop and started hustling everyone in, packing in as many as possible. All the while telling other passengers inside the bus, through the window, "Mishter, madum, moveaanmoveaan, planty of shpaesh. Add-jusht pleaj."

Amrita's moment of hesitation meant she was one of the last people to get in. However, she got in and was even able to push her way to the top step of the footboard. Within seconds she regretted her decision. Not only because the bus was more packed than she had realized but also because next to her were standing a group of men for whom the situation was perfect for a little game playing. As Amrita looked to make a spot for herself, her eyes collided with theirs. Their expressions were ugly. Not threatening physical violence, but lecherous. She looked away. At the other people. At an older woman sitting in the back next to the window on the long seat. At the conductor who quickly looked away from her glance —he had obviously been watching her discomfort with the men. There was a lot of noise in the bus. She looked out at the minibus that moments earlier had screeched to a halt right by the private bus. She could hear the drivers screaming at each other. From the front, she heard muffled sounds of several people egging the driver to drive faster, *"Chal yaar, aurtez aurtez."* Though she could not hear them clearly, similar loud sounds were emanating from the other bus as well. She made out that the driver of her bus was in a race with the driver of the minibus; it seemed that that had been going on for some time.

For a few moments Amrita distracted herself with thoughts of Franz. She could remember his touch, his breath, his voice...even the tone of his voice. Its imperceptible hint of a grin or mischief or wryness in argument. Did he think of her? Miss her? What would he say now? "Amrita, really, we've got to do something about this behavior. It's out of hand...."

Amrita's attention returned to her physical reality as one of the men next to her moved a little closer. Just a little, but enough to make her notice him. She looked at him and at the others. They looked back. Their eyes were gleaming with excitement. Amrita's discomfort only made them bolder. Like a challenge. The men never spoke to each other once, but in a strange way they seemed bonded over a common goal.

One of them started humming under his breath, *"Mere sapnon ki rani kab aye gi tu,"* staring at Amrita suggestively with his eyes. Another man distorted his lips in kissing shapes, pouting them and running his tongue over them. Rounding his lips and hollowing his cheeks in a sucking motion. Amrita looked down and tried to lean away, but as she did that, the man behind tried to lean into her ever so slightly. Pressing himself forward, then backward. Again and again. There was no talk.

Amrita once again looked appealingly at the people who were sitting around. From their eyes she could see that they had been following what was happening but were afraid to get involved. Their eyes kept returning to the scene in voyeuristic fascination to slide right off it when they thought some kind of a demand may be made of them. Feeling alone, Amrita knew her best bet was to just try and get away from these men. As the bus jerked forward, trying to lean away from the third man's rhythmic touch, she still managed to keep a strained grip on the overhead steel rod covered in black vinyl. But—a few yards later—when the bus jolted to a sudden stop, the force of the jolt jerked her body so hard that she lost her hold and slipped.

As people below her all turned sideways and braced themselves against both sides, a narrow path mysteriously opened in the center. Through it, Amrita just hurtled down the gap. Her head fell backward and the jarred, pumping muscle in her chest cavity thundered erratically outside it. Making her ears burn and sing. Her nostrils flared as hot air rushed in scraping painfully against the mucus membrane. Her pupils swam from left to right and back again looking for a port. As her back struck on the footboard, a tiny, protruding nail caught in her blouse and tore down its length, scoring her back. Long lanes of red from south to north. Split, torn, potholed. Her *palloo* rushed behind her like a servant follows its master. Her hands, unable to find purchase on the steps or the backs of people, made contact with the hot surface of the road.

Grazing against the rough, hot surface, the exposed skin seared on contact. And ripped open. Unfurling rudely, suddenly, unprepared. Gushing froth. Thick and red. Separating flesh from bone. Strength from sinew. Meaning from action. Meanwhile, her legs had landed awkwardly on the road. Her left leg tucked under her body and her right leg spread out in front of her. Like a mother in the pangs of breach birth with but half a fetus exposed. Before she could gather her right leg in as well, she saw in the periphery of her eye the black bumper of the square-faced, squat, light-blue minibus approaching her. Every minute cell tried to dissolve into nothingness in a bid to escape, "Help! Help!" But, mercilessly, the right tire rolled and rolled. Crunching her right leg. While the heat, like a giant killer shark, opened its red cavernous mouth to assimilate everything.

) ● (

The next morning, Amrita agreed to meet Mr. Daruwalla. For the principle. Of. It. At Mr. Daruwalla's office, Amrita was at first skittish, but he was a skilled tactician.

"Why don't you tell me in your own words exactly what happened?"

"It's there in the FIR and—"

"I would like to hear it from your own mouth," Mr. Daruwalla insisted.

"I got on to a crowded bus at ITO. I was standing on the top step of the footboard. When the bus jolted, I slipped on to the road. The bus overtaking from behind ran over my leg."

"That's okay for the short version. But what really happened? And this time don't leave anything out." When Amrita was still quiet, Mr. Daruwalla looked keenly at the young woman sitting in front of him in contained dignity for a moment and then leaned forward. He was not a top-notch lawyer for nothing. He understood education is no match for experience. So he said, "These gray hairs of mine did not just get gray in the heat of the midday sun. They grew gray in the heat of life, and they have seen a thing or two that you have yet to see. You must tailor your response to your audience. Most people interpret silence as weakness and even guilt.

Often thinking that the one who speaks first and the loudest is the one truly aggrieved." He wanted her to understand that they were not dealing here with the men who ran away. If they were, *they* would almost certainly try to establish that she had somehow invited their attention. No, they were dealing with more than human behavior; they were dealing with its pathology. Most of all, they were dealing with lack of imagination and moral turpitude. Mr. Daruwalla leaned back.

Gurmehar had never heard Mr. Daruwalla talk like this. Amrita was looking at the short, slender, dark man in an even darker suit. The suit was a strange color, not quite black not quite brown, and Amrita was fixed on it as though her life depended on it. Suddenly she looked up and began to speak.

"It was three thirty in the afternoon..."

"Chea-ter-cock."

"You chea-ter-cock."

Rematch.

44 *A Game of Chess*

THE ROOM WAS abuzz with conversation when Amrita entered with Franz. Her family and friends behind them. Mr. Rabindranath Chattopadhyaya walked a step ahead consulting with his Assistant on some last-minute detail. The case was not that big, but the fact that it was a retrial—which was in itself a rare occurrence—added substance to it. The presence of Mr. Chattopadhyaya had also drawn attention to the case.

At forty-six, he was of medium height, warm-hued, and lean, and his slicked-back hair was full and jet-black. Known for his Chowringhee roots, he clearly treated his body as a temple. For his impeccably tailored, stylish black suit teamed with a crisp white shirt and white neck band, for his gleaming black pointy-toed, lace-up shoes with just a hint of a white sock showing above, he intrigued both men and women. For his brilliant strategy, for his stage presence, he was both admired and feared, depending on whose side he stood. His dark robe trumpeted him in line with other caped crusaders. So all the clerks and small-time workers at the court who could get away from work were inside the room that day. Also present was the press. The cameras had not been allowed inside so they were all parked on the driveway and in the corridors. They said they had received a tip from the DUTA office, but they could not or would not reveal their precise source. A few members of the DUTA, wearing their badges, sat conspicuously together in the back. Mrs. Rita Chandrawarkar had called Amrita the day before as a matter of routine. When she heard of the trial, she made a few calls to other members. A few members of the bus drivers' and conductors' union were also gathered in the back. Earlier, they had been chanting slogans, but now they sat subdued after a warning from the Court Attendant that they would be put out with the rest of their group if they did not maintain order.

Amrita had shunned the use of her wheelchair. Now, feeling the collective gaze of the crowd as she came through the doors on her crutches, she felt a phantom sensation. And felt both knees buckle just a bit.

Judge Vrinda Kishen was presiding. Barely five feet tall and slightly built, white-streaked hair combed back into the usual neat bun, her serene face was graced by a simple red dot on the forehead that did not proclaim the determined woman who had pursued her own legal education while supporting her husband's career. Mother to two grown children, she was known to be a formidable personage who did not suffer any kind of foolery in her court. All arose as she entered the room and took her seat. The opening arguments began.

After briefing the court on the lacunae in the previous trial, Mr. Chattopadhyaya painted the scene of the accident.

"Your Honor, who has not seen these private buses?" It was a rhetorical question. Especially as it was really doubtful if the dapper Mr. Chattopadhyaya had ever actually traveled in one. Yet Mr. Chattopadhyaya stopped and looked around the room as though inviting anyone to dare to contradict him. No one dared. He continued in his deep-well voice, "We all know how packed to capacity they are. That they shouldn't be or that we need to have a better transportation system or even motorway system are all questions that I am willing to take up with the court on any day, but today, today I ask you to consider just the fact that these buses are always overcrowded. Packed to far more than capacity. We need not get into them, I am sure my esteemed colleagues will point out. But how can we not, when we have waited minute after minute for a way to get to wherever we are going? We are dependent on these buses. So we take them. But what happens once we, no let me correct myself, when a woman, a young woman gets into one of these buses? Must she now put up with more than the crowds?" Once again Mr. Chattopadhyaya paused. "Yes, she must. She has to. The Romeos who lurk in these buses take up more than space. They impose themselves, verbally and physically, upon these women. The others know, but it still happens."

The court was silent. Before continuing, Mr. Chattopadhyaya turned to his desk to sip some water. He sipped it so leisurely that some people sitting toward the front swore later that with each swallow they felt the water go down their own throats and swallowed right along with him. "What also happens are the foolish races that bus drivers get into with each other. Egged on by others, we may say. Perhaps, but it cannot be denied that when they are driving, they are the ones in control. As such, they owe it to their passengers to be responsible. By not doing so, they take their own and other people's lives in their hands."

As Mr. Chattopadhyaya described the time of day, the 44.1 degrees Celsius heat with steam rising from the hot, tar surface, he modestly handed the record keeper the meteorological data. All eyes turned to Amrita, picturing her on that hot road. Then, at the twins in blue and maroon who looked at each other and then at their steel tips.

Despite strategizing all last night in the lawyer's office, back home they had gone over the events of the last two months.

On May 4, after a leisurely breakfast, Makhan Singh had approached Mahinder Gupta. Contrary to his expectations, he did not have to persuade him very long or hard. Since it was Saturday, they had two days to plan their strategy. Also, it would do no harm for the drivers to rot in jail for a few more days. Give them time to appreciate the favor being done to them.

The next step was a visit to the jailhouse. Outside, relatives of poor prisoners sat around. Hopelessly. Others were waived through after a little palm oiling. Inside, in a narrow ward with high barred windows housing fifteen other men, the two drivers were leaning listlessly against a wall waiting to be acknowledged. They had not seen anyone from their families in two days. Now that they were face-to-face and could exchange their ideas freely, they were silent.

There had been some question about the burden of responsibility between the private bus driver and the minibus driver, for Amrita had slipped from the footboard of one bus and under the wheels of another. But the drivers in consultation with the owners and lawyers had all agreed that it would be better for them to come together to present a solid defense.

After sorting out the drivers, Makhan Singh and Mahinder Gupta tried several times to see Gurmehar, but they were blocked each time. Others had been more approachable. Johnnie Walker had helped make many friends in the past. The Inspector turned out to be a friendly fellow.

"Mahipal Singh, how about a glass tomorrow around five o'clock?" Mahinder Gupta murmured before leaving the police station. Together with Makhan Singh, he was visiting the SHO to "just check on things."

"You'll have to excuse me...," Mahipal Singh began, but it was evident he was clearly flattered.

"Comecome, excuse you for what. A glass is not much to ask for, is it?" Makhan Singh interrupted. "You take a glass don't you? It's good for health. Even the doctors say that nowadays."

"A glass will be nice. But still..."

"It's settled then. Tomorrow at five o'clock. No need to worry. We'll pick you up. It is quite pleasant to sit around the pool at Chelmsford Club and share a quiet glass with a friend at the end of a hectic day."

The next day, Makhan Singh and Mahinder Gupta arrived at Mahipal Singh's house in their Jonga. Nervous but flattered at the implications of friendship in their offer, Mahipal Singh had informed his family about his visit to the club. In preparation for the event, he had advised his wife to dress appropriately.

"Wear that new silk sari I got you," he told her.

"But I was planning to wear it for Diwali," she protested.

"This is no less than Diwali," he scolded her. "Make sure you straighten your face and prepare Pappi as well."

Pammi was a little irritated. She had been saving that sari for later that year. And now she would have to worry about what to wear for Diwali. "Who are these men? What does it matter what I am wearing? After all, it is not as if I'm going with you to the club," she nudged.

"Creating the right impression is important. How many times have I told you that? You never know when an opportunity may present itself. One must always be prepared."

So when the Jonga-driving twins arrived and blew their horn imperiously, Mahipal Singh did not go outside immediately. Walking up to the door, they were greeted by Pammi in her powdered face and printed silk sari. "Come in, *he* will just be here," she said, offering them a plate of sweets. Declining the sweets, they impatiently stood around the drawing room entrance.

From behind the curtain of another door, Mahipal Singh listened to his wife's efforts to engage them in conversation. Listening to her refer to him as "vo" in Hindi when he had expressly told her to use his name today, he felt a little impatient. But there was not much he could do about it at this time.

"Where is Mahipal Singh? Could you ask him to hurry up? We have a table reserved," Mahinder Gupta prodded the now uncomfortably silent Pammi.

Glad to escape, Pammi left the room to fetch her husband.

It was no use procrastinating any longer. Mahipal Singh now entered the room with his young son in tow. "Say *Namaste* to Uncle, *beta*," he prompted.

"*Namaste*Uncle, *Namaste*Uncle," the child parroted one by one to the two men and then stood stiffly in his starched cotton shirt and shorts. His freshly washed face topped by oil-slicked, back-combed hair in thickly separated strands waited obediently to be told what next to do.

"What class are you in?" Makhan Singh asked, pandering to the unspoken paternal pride.

"Fifth, Uncle."

"So how is cricket this season? What position do you play?" Makhan Singh tried to engage the boy in an absentminded conversation.

"I'm an all-rounder. I bowl and bat. Like Kapil Dev," Pappi returned proudly.

"How about Sunil Gavaskar?"

"Oh yes, he's good too," Pappi spoke with confidence.

"Show Uncle your trophy Pappi *beta*," Mahipal Singh prompted. "He won it at school," he told the men. "Very intelligent in studies too. Shining. You should see his report cards. Stood first last year. Out of two hundred and fifty students. Next year I shall enroll him into a public school. Child must be convented these days. I have plans...he'll go far." Mahipal Singh turned to look fondly at his son, only to catch him—oblivious of the grown-ups—with a finger drilling deep in his nose trying to pry lose some dried snot.

As Mahipal Singh turned red in the face, Makhan Singh politely murmured something in praise to the boy. But Mahinder Gupta cut short the conversation, "We really should be leaving."

"Just a moment Gupta *ji*, Pammi will just be here with some tea," Mahipal Singh tried to take control of the situation. He wanted to be able to say that he had entertained these two men for tea. "Go tell Mummy to hurry," he told Pappi, relieved to have a reason to excuse him.

"We are getting late. This way we'll be stuck in traffic. We'll wet our whistles at the club. Come on," Mahinder Gupta insisted. Mahipal Singh gave up. Raising his voice to inform his wife not to bother with tea, he left the house with the two men.

Outside, Golakh Ram was just untying the string from around his rolled pant cuffs after parking his bicycle. In compliance to Mahipal Singh's suggestion, he had tried to hurry over as soon as he could after work. Barely acknowledged by the three men, he worriedly turned toward the house to get a glass of water before beginning his long ride home; he was just in time to see Pammi shutting the front door. Resentfully, he bent down once again to tie the string around his pant cuffs.

At the club, one glass led to two and then three. Pappi's future came up; public school fees are so high. Soon all their tongues were loosened, and they were talking like old friends.

The Public Prosecutor was the next point of focus for the two owners. He made no coy excuses not to meet them. In fact, from the very start, he had been prepared to be friendly. *"Matters must be discussed, maturely, you see. Man to man."* He was partial to stuffed white envelopes, hand-delivered to his house and nicely sealed. Flap down with no open sides.

The second time around, things had looked more serious. Following their brief evening stop at the Chaddhas' to settle the case, deciding that firing the bus drivers and conductors at this late stage would seem too much like an admission of guilt, the owners had retained their staff; they planned—as before—to lay the burden of responsibility on Amrita.

Pooling their fortune, they had next shopped around for a top-notch lawyer.

Mr. Iyengar came from a family of long-eared lawyers. Though his father had moved north and settled in Delhi after the Partition, their roots still lay in Tamil Nadu. Thanks to a long-dead ancestor, Mr. Iyengar was extraordinarily fair, six feet tall, and reed thin. No matter what he ate, he remained thin and perpetually cold. Perhaps for this reason, he favored wearing layers under loose-fitting, dark suits that looked even bulkier under a robe. Over his sharp, thin nose and in the halo of his bald head, his intelligence shone brightly from his broad forehead. At forty-eight, his voice was seasoned with life.

Mr. Iyengar and his team had read the case files and the dismissal report from the District Court. So now he adjusted his collar and began mildly, "No one can deny the pain that has been inflicted upon this young woman." It was a good beginning; it dissipated somewhat the tension that had divided the room into two. "But the question in front of us today is, who is responsible for that pain? It is my belief, and I say this with the greatest respect, that the victim, Miss Amrita Chaddha, needs to take responsibility for her own imprudence. On May 1, at three thirty in the afternoon, she was standing at ITO waiting for a bus. She had been standing here for a while, but not that long—as her own FIR at the hospital shows. Dated, May 5." Here, he turned his feet, encased in special-ordered, patent leather, sturdy size thirteens, to present the FIR as evidence to the court.

"So what made Miss Chaddha take that crowded bus? I think it would be fair to surmise that she had been wont to do this before. Nothing had happened to her in the past, and she did not expect anything to happen this time as well. But the fact of the matter is, and anyone—I mean anyone, woman or man—knows, that they get into these buses at their own risk. Not just private buses and minibuses, but DTC buses as well are often packed. However, I, too, am willing to keep that debate for a future occasion." Here, Mr. Iyengar bowed slightly in the direction of Mr. Chattopadhyaya.

"Everyone also knows that Romeos abound in these buses. And accordingly, they must make up their minds to use or not use this mode of transport. Did anyone force Miss Chaddha to get into the private bus that day? No. She did it on her own. Did anyone push her off the bus? No, she slipped because she was standing precariously on the footboard. Did anyone deliberately run their wheels over her? No, it just happened."

With every word Mr. Iyengar uttered, Amrita's heart sank lower and lower in the pit of her stomach. She felt nauseated like she felt on the first downward curve of the giant wheel. ("Ai-lae-faint r-i-i-de." "Kaa-mul r-i-i-de.")

But the battle had just begun. Mr. Chattopadhyaya called Amrita to the stand. All eyes focused on the hair in a single braid, tiny hearts of gold in ears, smudges of kohl around the eyes, and the crutches arranged around the sari. It was an ivory-based cotton, with mint-green-colored vines printed all across its middle. Its border and *palloo* had a block print of a train of elephants with their trunks up. At the base of the pleats, the raised trunks stood aligned like trumpets.

The windows shut out the sounds outside. Inside, the one air conditioner hiccupped periodically. The fans above moved languidly, almost against their will, pushing air from wing to wing. The thin, long arms of a large, ugly, round clock moved in exaggerated jerks. On a wall, there was a plain photograph of Gandhi in his customary *dhoti* mounted on a brown-painted, wooden frame. The caption underneath read: *Satyameva Jayate.*

The initial dance was predictable. Prompted by Mr. Chattopadhyaya, Amrita described the sequence of events. Mr. Iyengar in his cross-examination asked his stock questions: whether she was forced to get into the bus, if she was pushed off of it, and if she thought the minibus driver deliberately drove over her. When Amrita replied in the negative to all three, he lifted his shoulders slightly with palms raised and turned upward, as if to say, "What else?" and "What are we doing here?"

The Defense now began bringing out their witnesses. The bus conductors made it sound as though Amrita virtually jumped off the footboard of the private bus and threw herself in front of the minibus. Mr. Chattopadhyaya nodded quietly and let them go. The twins grinned.

Next, both the bus drivers, Balwinder Singh and Gopal Das, were sworn in; they made the usual assertions of careful driving and red lights determining speed and denials of even knowing each other. Mr. Chattopadhyaya listened quietly, finally asked if they could read, begged pardon for any insult, and then simply produced the work order that was filed with the Municipal Corporation over the community tap incident. Mr. Chattopadhyaya had pursued Madhumati's report from her cousin Prasad a few months ago to reconstruct the incident over the use of the tap.

Mr. Chattopadhyaya bowed slightly toward the bench and submitted the work order. Mr. Iyengar pulled his left earlobe and looked uncomfortably at the twins. The twins looked at each other, having lost their grins.

Despite what had just happened, both bus owners thought it best to stick to their plan and so testified on the impeccable work record of their staff. They denied offering money in exchange for exemption from responsibility. They denied having used any scare tactics at all. They did not deny having gone to the Chaddhas' home (the neighbors had testified on seeing their Jonga and hearing their loud voices), but they maintained that they had approached the Chaddhas only as a courtesy and a measure of their goodwill. Mr. Makhan Singh claimed his refusal to take Gopal Das' call from jail was just a misunderstanding, and he went to see him later. He also claimed that his problem in finding a live-in domestic had nothing to do with the case.

Looking impatiently at some dust motes in the air, Mr. Chattopadhyaya abruptly thanked the bus owners, "No further questions."

"No further questions?" Judge Kishen leaned forward with raised eyebrows. "Counselor, are you saying you have finished your cross-examination?" she asked.

"Not quite. I would like permission to recall the two main witnesses of the Defense," Mr. Chattopadhyaya announced to the court.

Prithipal Singh and Gurvinder Singh were brought in one at a time. They had previously testified that they had been standing at the ITO stop and had seen Amrita talking with some friends. Being engrossed in them, they claimed, she had not paid attention to her own safety when she got on to the bus.

Momentarily Mr. Chattopadhyaya seemed to engage them in a casual conversation. They were visiting from Amritsar, they had said.

"How do you like Delhi so far?"

"Quite violent...lot of traffic...rude people." They didn't quite know what to make of this question.

Mr. Chattopadhyaya nodded his head as though in commiseration. "Yes, yes, Delhi is a big city," he said. "And you come from a small locality...where everyone knows everyone else, right?"

"Yes sir."

"Refresh my memory, I read this but I would just like you to tell it to me yourself...now, what is it you do there?"

"Work in a firecrackers factory."

"You mean firecrackers for Diwali and such?"

"Yes sir."

"I see, I see. And the name of this factory is?"

"Nihalani Fireworks."

"Who is Nihalani?"

"He is the owner."

"Very generous I hear, is that right?"

"He is a good employer." They were cautious.

"He must be. You recently received a bonus, did you not?"

"Yes sir. He gives that to everyone from time to time."

"Good, good." Then, gaze fixed on his trim fingernails, almost absentmindedly, "There was a recent terrorist attack on his factory was there not?"

"Yes sir."

"Quite a lot of damage. Some workers were laid off. Some Sikh workers. Am I right?"

"Yes sir."

"Many of them in your department... Just let me know when I am not right," he offered mildly.

"Yes sir."

"And not only did you get to keep your jobs, you also got a bonus.... He must be very generous." Mr. Chattopadhyaya looked and sounded like a benign uncle.

"Yes sir."

"I see, I see. Is he not the brother-in-law of Mr. Makhan Singh? But of course you must know that as Mr. Makhan Singh has an interest in the factory and often visits there." So quietly did Mr. Chattopadhyaya ask his question, that it took them completely unawares. They were silent.

Rocking gently on to the tip of his shoes, Mr. Chattopadhyaya asked, "Am I right?"

"We don't know anything about family—" they began, but Mr. Chattopadhyaya interrupted them, this time his voice dripping ice.

"I thought everyone in the local community knows everything about everybody? Do you or do you not know that Mr. Nihalani is the brother of Mr. Makhan Singh's wife? Now this time, think before answering. And remember the penalty of lying under oath."

"I think so sir." They seemed to have recovered their memory.

There was silence in the court.

"But that is not all," Mr. Chattopadhyaya continued speaking in a Kashmir winter tone. "Think again, you have a register at the factory where you have to enter the times you come in and leave. Do you not?"

"Yes sir."

"Your salary is based on the hours you put in, is it not?"

"Yes sir."

"I ask you again, where were you on the afternoon of May 1?"

There was silence.

"Do you have any memory of signing a register on May 1?"

There was silence.

"You were, in fact, not in Delhi at all, were you?"

When there was still silence, Mr. Chattopadhyaya turned to his assistant and picked up a photocopy of a page filled with signatures. One by one, firmly he asked each of them, "Do you recognize this signature? Is it yours?"

"It looks like it," was the weak response.

"I didn't hear you. Can you say that again?" Mr. Chattopadhyaya held his left index finger lightly behind his left ear to angle his head forward dramatically.

"It looks like it." A little more loudly.

Ignoring the gasps from the gallery, his manner urbane, Mr. Chattopadhyaya turned to address Judge Kishen.

"Your Honor, handwriting experts have matched the writing; I now submit this page as evidence that Mr. Prithipal Singh and Mr. Gurvinder Singh were not even in Delhi on May 1. The first time they saw Miss Chaddha at all was on the day of the last trial. The first time they saw Mr. Balwinder Singh and Mr. Gopal Das was also on the day of the trial. The next day they all celebrated their victory in the shanty colony in Chandni Chowk."

When Gurmehar told Mr. Daruwalla about what Madhumati had told Kundan, Mr. Daruwalla immediately knew they were on to something. Overconfident, the Defense had not covered their trail entirely. Researching a little bit had meant making a trip to Amritsar.

After meeting Amrita, Mr. Daruwalla decided to call in a favor.

He made a phone call to the Deputy Police Commissioner. Mr. Vinod Kothari listened to Mr. Daruwalla. Promising to help him fully, Kothari put down the phone. A few minutes later, Kothari was on the phone again. This time to the Police Commissioner. Though this was a relatively small case, the political situation in Delhi at this time was far too delicate to treat it lightly. All measures must be taken to secure the integrity of the Center.

Mr. Raunaq Singh received the Deputy Commissioner's call in his office. He had been working under great controversy for some time. Many Sikh extremists claimed he was a mere puppet, the Center's attempt to throw dust in their eyes. Mr. Raunaq Singh heard out Kothari quietly. He agreed that all efforts must be made to get to the bottom of the case.

"Take care. Leave no stone unturned," he said. "And report back to me."

The Deputy Commissioner now made a few discreet calls to various police staff members, old and new recruits. Then he called the area police station to speak to the SHO.

"Put me on to Mahipal Singh."

"He's busy."

"Tell him it's urgent."

"He can't come to the phone right now."

"Tell him it is the Deputy Police Commissioner. He will come to the phone."

Mahipal Singh picked up the phone. "What can I do for you, Deputy Commissioner sahib?"

"Oh just a small favor, if you have the time...?"

"Oh yes, yes, anything." Mahipal Singh was flustered to have the Deputy Commissioner on the line.

"It's about the accident at ITO on May 1..."

"Oh...yes. Small thing sir, nothing for you to worry about. All taken care of."

"I'm interested in the records...."

"I would like to help you. Really, I would. Unfortunately, the records were lost in a fire. In fact, I was just outside overseeing the renovation of that wing."

"That's too bad. It's just that someone has reported...during the renovation cleanup...finding a partially burnt, empty cigarette packet in the office near the fire...it has red and white stripes on it. Do you know anyone who smokes that brand...?"

The rest had been almost too easy. The Deputy Commissioner explained to the Inspector in no uncertain terms the serious consequences of such involvement. He could either cooperate or... But the talk had successfully jolted the Inspector's memory. There was in fact a sketchy list of witnesses. Which they hadn't been able to work with. You know, no addresses, so many people in the city with the same name. Mr. Kothari said he understood, but...Mahipal Singh could have the list on his desk by the end of the week. How about this evening. It was not a question. Yes, sir. Mr. Vinod Kothari made a call to Mr. Daruwalla.

From there, Mr. Daruwalla set his assistants to work. They placed ads in leading newspapers for witnesses to this case to come forward. Day and night they went through the lists and through the anonymous streets of Delhi sifting for possible leads.

In less than a week they had a thick file of new information that showed the lacunae in the first trial. Not only had the Prosecution not used the relevant evidence, but also fresh and independent evidence threw new light upon the case.

Without delay a writ was filed against the Delhi Administration in the High Court. Under other circumstances, the investigation and trial could have dragged on for a long time. But considering the sensitive political atmosphere in the capital, the response was immediate. The Delhi Administration was summoned. A separate investigation into the SHO's and the Public Prosecutor's handling of the case was instituted. Abuse of power would not be tolerated. Meanwhile, the Prosecution branch was asked to reconstruct the case.

Mr. Chattopadhyaya was assigned to the case. The new witnesses were called in and fresh FIRs were taken. With pressure from above, the retrial was set for ten days later.

Mr. Iyengar now stood up, his voluminous coat flapping outward.

His single-cuffed wide pants also flared to sweep his shoes. A very serious charge had been made against his clients. The twins looked a little sick. He requested a brief recess; it was granted. After the Defense returned to their seats, Mr. Chattopadhyaya began once again.

When Mr. Chattopadhyaya called his expert witness Dr. Rita Thakur to the witness box, a murmur of anticipation went around the members of press in the room. A prominent Sociologist at the University of Delhi and a women's rights activist, she had served as an expert witness in several cases and was known for her outspokenness.

Professor Thakur explained the realness and gravity of the issue. That it's not a question of coy or meek modesty but an issue of safety and human rights. And despite the Administration's various attempts to address the issue, it remains unresolved. "It is not Eve teasing that takes place, but sexual assault."

"Don't you think sexual assault is too harsh a term for such instances?" Mr. Iyengar hastened to ask in his turn.

Professor Thakur looked calmly at Mr. Iyengar before asking a series of questions of her own. "Have you ever feared for your physical safety, Counsel? Has anyone pressed against you, closer and closer, against your will, till you could smell their breath and see ugly intention in their eyes? What if there was more than one? And what if they did not stop at looking? Till you have felt this way, you may well call it teasing. We belittle the issue and we belittle the intelligence of women when we call it teasing."

Not having felt that way, Mr. Iyengar withdrew, looking sullenly chastised. Moving toward the Judge, he asked, "Even if we believe all this to be correct, Your Honor, where is all this leading? We have no proof that there were any men troubling Ms. Chaddha in the first place."

Judge Kishen looked at Mr. Chattopadhyaya questioningly.

"Your Honor, I would like to introduce some new witnesses who will throw new light on the testimony of the Defense."

Mrs. Juneja, sixty-three years old, was a retired schoolteacher. On May 1, she had been on her way back from her daughter's house in Chandni Chowk, in the private bus. She was sitting next to the window on the long seat that runs behind the back width of the bus, just behind the footboard. She testified that though she was sitting in the last row in a packed bus and the details were muffled, the loud angry voices of the slogan sounders and erratic driving made it clear that some kind of fight was going on in the front. She also detailed how the men had misbehaved with Amrita.

Turning to the judge, Mr. Iyengar couldn't resist a dig at Mr. Chattopadhyaya, "Counsel seems to be lost in the maze of his own argument. If there were men misbehaving with Ms. Chaddha, what then does any of this have to do with the drivers?"

Judge Kishen once again looked at Mr. Chattopadhyaya.

Mr. Chattopadhyaya's response was incisive. "The case is not so simple. It is imperative that we understand what all passengers, but especially female passengers, have to put up with in these buses. The diverse components of this incident do not take away from the culpability of the drivers. They underscore it. The men at the back of the bus ran away; the Defense is trying to do the same. Make no mistake, the reckless driving of both the drivers is what caused the accident. I therefore call to the stand my final witness."

Lalit Mohan, a graduate student, who had got on to the minibus, was dressed in a Nehru cap and *khadi kurta pajama*. That day, when he had seen the minibus, he had been standing at another bus stop. So he started running to try to catch it. He leaped toward its single entrance and exit. The bus conductor stood sideways with one arm stretched outward encouraging him to make a running jump on to the footboard. Finding a foothold, Lalit Mohan had slowly inched his way on to the front, by the bonnet.

"The music was blaring. The driver was talking to a bunch of people around him on the bonnet. They were all egging him to a race with the private bus driver."

"And was there a race?"

"Yes."

"How do you know it was a race?"

"A lot of people sitting in the front, on and around the bonnet, were talking to the driver. Both buses had originated at the Chandni Chowk stop and were carrying many supporters of opposing factions." Lalit Mohan testified that many passengers in the bus he was in, the minibus, were going to a Hindu demonstration at the Boat Club. They were talking loudly of people in the other bus, many of whom were going to another demonstration, a Sikh one, to be held at the same time. They were all anxious to report to their stands in time to receive their incentives. He had also heard murmurs of an altercation between the two bus drivers about some personal matter relating to a water tap at Chandni Chowk, and that the two bus drivers, following the same route, had been going head-to-head on the road from the starting point. As both buses were running almost parallel to each other, even Lalit Mohan had heard each driver accusing the other's community for causing all the troubles in the country.

The private bus slipped forward with the sound of the driver shouting, *"Raj Karega Khalsa."* But as the minibus driver was going to move, a stray cow that had been languidly resting under the bus shed next to it got up to cross the road just in front of his bus. Hip-heavy waddle on rickety spindles. The minibus driver, already engulfed by communal memory and sentiment, was further enraged by the unfairness of losing face because of a crossing cow. He angrily blew his horn. *Moo.* Giving a piece of his mind to his startled bovine obstruction and braying, *"Har Har Mahadeva,"* he accelerated. He raced to overtake the private bus, illegally, from the left so that he could park parallel to it and shout his piece of mind to the other driver. At the crossing, unable to stop immediately in front of Amrita, the wheels of the bus kept on turning.

As the young man described the scene, the crash diagram chalk marks and the splashes of dark red blood arose from the tar face of that hot, pockmarked road to enter the room.

"Do you believe the minibus driver sped forward carelessly because of the race?" asked Mr. Chattopadhyaya.

"Objection." This time Mr. Iyengar's objection was weak like his limply hanging suit. It was overruled.

"Undoubtedly."

Wrapping up the case did not take long, after which the Judge took a thirty-minute recess.

Judge Kishen denounced as cowardly the bus owners, drivers, and conductors as well as the public who had watched and in many ways participated in this drama. It is only a matter of time before the long arm of justice ferrets out the criminals and holds them accountable for their actions, she said.

"The court is not the moral custodian of its citizens. However, we all need to realize the importance of awakening our moral conscience, our sense of responsibility, if we want to run smoothly the mechanism of society. This responsibility is our foundation stone, and we all need to remember that the foundation stone must be very strong so that the structure on top of it may rest securely, so that another stone may shine in all its brilliance atop the dome."

As Mr. Chattopadhyaya put his arms around a solemn Amrita in an avuncular manner, and Gurmehar and Kundan and everyone else rushed forward, pandemonium broke out in the room. While the DUTA members congratulated each other on their victory, the *karamcharis* were dissatisfied with all this talk of foundation stones. Rigor and lack of recognition was how they saw it. It was fine to praise foundation stones when you were not one of them. Some reporters rushed out to phone in their stories in time for the evening news. Others rushed forward, microphones and recorders in hand, toward Amrita.

As Amrita walked out of the courthouse, she was surrounded by reporters.

"Can you tell us exactly what transpired with the owners at your house?"

"No comment."

"What are your thoughts at this time, Ms. Chaddha?"

"Relief."

"Anything else?"

"Do you hate the bus drivers and all else connected with the incident?"

"Yes, how much do you hate these people?"

"It is not hatred I feel."

"What? What did she say?"

"She said, it is not hatred she feels."

"How can that be?"

"Then what exactly do you feel Ms. Chaddha?"

Amrita shrugged quietly.

For a moment, the faces of the hungry reporters seemed to fall, as though cheated out of a headline.

Then a persistent young reporter shouted from the back, "Have you forgotten Ms. Chaddha that you are now lame? How can you not hate the men who have collectively contributed to...that?" The young man had used the forbidden word that others had tried to avoid. Though he too had cringed at using it, he had touched a raw nerve. Amrita turned to answer him.

"That is a question that would take me far too long to answer here," she said.

Amrita turned away from the reporters and toward the DUTA members who had come on her behalf and without her solicitation. Looking around at her family and friends, she stood there on the lawns, a lonely figure on two crutches, staring at the statue of Justice in front of the square, modern structure of the courthouse. As a mild breeze struck, it blew her *palloo,* making the trunks of the elephants wave like flags in the wind. She looked up into the sky, but the silver microphone had not yet been set up. So she turned and stepped toward Franz. Amid the rumblings of the bus *karamchari* union, Franz drove her away from the courthouse in his car.

45   Mehndi

EVERYONE HAD GONE to a wedding on Roshanara road, and they would be very late getting back home. Pyaari had dropped in suddenly. To see her deargirl, her Amarta, and to share some news of her own. Maithili, her grandchild, was getting married; the proposal had been unexpected but too good to be passed. This time, no one protested too much at Amrita's refusal to go. Initially, she was a little peeved at not being pressed. But then she was glad. Franz, too, had called to cancel his visit. Something had come up suddenly, and he had to take care of it. With the hired help gone at the end of the day, she would have some time to herself.

It was a beautiful evening, just perfect for a wedding. In the neighborhood there was another wedding. Ruby, the Walias' daughter, was also getting married. When the wandering band of *hijras* appeared outside their home, they had quickly paid them off telling them there was no need to perform. For the last two days the family had been singing almost nonstop. Every night after dinner they gathered in the drawing room with a *dholki*. While one person beat the rhythm with their hands making hard and quick contact on the two sides of the horizontal drum, another person beat the same rhythm with a spoon on top of the drum's casing. Red hands, hoarse throats, torn drums, were not enough to stop the revelers. Punjabi *tappe, boliyan,* and *jugni* could be heard all around the block.

O jugni ja wari Kulkutte
Jithe ikkon roti pakke
Janan khae, janani takke
Vir merya o jugni
O Vir merya o jugni kehndi hai
O naan guran da lehndi hai.

The accelerated beat, incisive observations, and the sheer joy and flirtatiousness of the words accompanied by uninhibited sounds of *bhangra* and *giddha* had been making Amrita's blood run wild with longing.

From her chair, she could partially see the wedding arrangements the Walias had made. The beautifully decorated *shamiana*, a tented canopy, in the park; long, beaded strands of marigolds covering the walls of the bride's home; and the poles and canopy along the path the wedding procession would take from the end of the street to their gate. The groom was a Hindu-Punjabi living in San Diego, California. Had his own computer business. And income in six figures. Dollars, not rupees.

Every neighbor in the street had been invited and distributed a plate of *laddoos*. For some, like the old film songs blaring on the public address system, a chance to share their memories; for others, an insurance against complaints about noise.

"Doingwell, yes?" Suddenly the overpainted face of Mrs. Kiki Nanda in wedding guest finery and chunky gold jewelry appeared over the boundary wall. For the last two months, she had bothered Kundan to let her come and just talk to her "poorgirl." It had taken all of Kundan's self-control to not tell Kiki Nanda what to do with her pity.

"Doing well, thanks."

"Goodgirl. And that young man of yours, that foreign man… what's his name, I forget?" she probed. Amrita did not satisfy her.

"Let me not keep you from the wedding," Amrita offered.

"Oh no no, notatall. You poorthing, all alone. Your mother should not have left you. Where is she? At the wedding already? A little early, isn't it?"

"No, they had to go to a family wedding...."Amrita was finding it very difficult to be civil.

"Chchchch. And they left you alone? Even that foreign man? You have to be extra careful with them, you know?" She gave Amrita a knowing look that was not returned. "Chchchch, poorthing...." Luckily, Mr. Nanda looked back and found his wife missing; he returned and coaxed her away.

Outside, the street children had already started gathering around the tent kitchen. Though they were shooed away with the same consistency as were the stray dogs, they both kept coming back.

It was growing dusk. The sun, reluctant to set, reached out in crimson-fingered streaks across the sky as though it would hold on to day a little longer. But night clouds were fast encroaching from the other side, carrying in their folds a waning moon. Courage and Destiny took their places. Two leaders ready to faceoff.

"Courage is a dead thing. There are no heroes anymore," Amrita commented to Gurmehar as he came into her room. "Somehow they exist only within the pages of books or in the past or somewhere remote." Makhan Singh and Mahinder Gupta had just left their house, and in the kitchen Amardeep was helping Kundan put everything on the trolley in readiness for dinner.

"Don't forget those pages were once alive," Gurmehar reminded her, picking up a newspaper from the floor.

"Yes, perhaps, but it's still a rare commodity. Now mediocrity, that's a whole other story," she added a little cynically. Though the memory of Makhan Singh and Mahinder Gupta was fresh in his mind as well, Gurmehar did not rise to her challenge. He folded the paper and placed it to the side.

"Are you sure you have been looking in the right places?"

"Why, is there a special place I should look?" Amrita was spoiling for an argument.

"Don't look for an announcement," Gurmehar began seriously. Then, "Pain must not be allowed to become a way of life."

Only a few weeks ago, Amrita had almost dismissed that conversation. Chasing footsteps in the sand after the main event was over. Forgetting that another wave would just as easily sweep those footsteps away.

Now Amrita considered how easily we forget in times of peace the lessons we learned in times of war. Consumed by the trajectory of fear, hate, and hurt, we forget that love too has a trajectory of its own. We forget that by opening ourselves to another human being, by taking a chance upon life, life just may take a chance upon us. Creating the space and the possibility for us to be saved.

We forget that our mind is a biological phenomenon with its own behavior. That between desire and determinism there is a gap that can be filled only by human action. But we have to act on the presupposition of freedom. We can't just wait to find out what someone has determined for us. And that human act often translates itself into courage. Courage indeed does not lie under banners. It arrives unannounced. It is more often a call to necessity, to challenge. It means to live life with passion, loving deeply and truly and responsibly every single moment—no matter what it brings—so that it may be an opportunity for us to learn and grow and preserve for posterity with pride a legacy as bright or brighter than the one we ourselves inherited.

Amrita pictured Ruby waiting in crimson and gold, surrounded by friends and female relatives. Her hands and feet would be covered with *mehndi*. Lines of henna, separate but meeting each other in complicated ancient patterns. Individual yet intertwined. They carry within them the Truth of life. Trying to figure them out is like trying to figure out the mystery of life. It can't be done. And, therefore, is better left alone. It is better to live within the mystery itself.

Amrita thought of the long night with her mother. Truth and lies. Promises made and promises broken. In the chess game of life there are always adversaries. But of all the choices people make, the worst is to wear a hard hat around the heart. When we do that, we may lock trouble out, but we also lock ourselves on the over-crowded edge of life. Living in occasional peeks and the reflected glory of the bright side.

Sitting in a corner of the lawn, Amrita looked up from her van-tage position behind the delicate branches of the guava tree, at a flock of sparrows in the sky. Every evening, they flew in undulat-ing waves into the horizon. But the next day found them chirping on the branches of the guava tree, making it tremble and stir in response. She looked at the tree now. Tiny, tight buds were begin-ning to appear on its branches; she had to restrain herself from giving in to her childlike desire to sink her nails into their thick juice. Leaning into a cluster of leaves, she breathed in their sub-tle, distinct, slightly bitter flavor. Satisfied, she leaned back. By her side, the magenta blooms of the bouganvillea seemed to overtake the boundary wall in a riot of color.

On the ground lay a couple of copies of recent daily as well as evening editions of newspapers from the day of the court hear-ing and the day following. She had read them all. In some issues of the evening news her story had made it to the bottom cor-ner of the front page, next to news of Anatoly Karpov fighting to retain the title of World Champion. He had held it for ten years. But Gary Kasparov was determined to challenge the established power. The national dailies carried a shorter article, lumping her story with all the other news of local interest, on the third page. Almost all the papers had captured the picture of her standing on crutches outside the courthouse. In the picture there was no one by her side. The captions varied from "After Midnight" to "Step-ping Out." Underneath was a brief article that clinically listed the chain of events from the criminal suit to the civil action suit. In the first, the bus drivers were given two years in jail and had to pay a fine of one thousand rupees. A separate investigation was to be conducted into the bus owners' attempts to obstruct justice. Later, in front of the Motor Accident Claim Tribunal, the Defense crumbled again and this time was held liable for damages. The insurance companies had to pay fifty thousand in damages. Further, under supervision of the court, they had to pay for all hospital bills related to the injury.

One article in particular had caught Amrita's eye. "Modern Saint or Modern Fool" brought critical and theoretical reasoning to bear upon Amrita's responses to the reporters. The staff writer wondered if such a response was realistic and conducive to survival. Was it not in fact a recipe for disaster? An invitation for history to repeat itself? The writer also dismissed Judge Kishen's last words. "In this day of prefabricated public housing, with hollow walls and little to no foundation, Judge Kishen's reference to the foundation stone is like a reference to the glory of Delhi—a thing of the past," the writer deconstructed.

Amrita took careful note of her surroundings. The birds chirped every day, but their voices carried a note of freedom in the garden. The flowers bloomed here in full glory, delicate spines twined securely around wooden stakes or sturdily erect with the arrogance and surety of youth and beauty. The grass here seemed greener, more healthy and content. Thick, short, pointy spikes that almost burst with pride at their own selves. Underneath, short and long earthworms, nature's seasonal laborers, punctured the earth in a lazy slither. So that the many-mouthed earth, eternal beggar for moisture, grinned toothlessly. And over it all lay the thick, heavy fragrance of the *motia* vine that grew in the neighbor's yard and, in an overflow of abundance and beauty, draped itself over the ledge of her bedroom window.

The July rains also heralded the end of the summer holidays. She thought again of Amardeep applying to go abroad. Yes, he would go.

Lost in the narcotic beauty of the garden, Amrita was startled to find Franz standing a few steps from her. He was looking at her fixedly. She looked fixedly back. She did not say that she had not been expecting him. It was enough that it was so and that he had come. As her heart began to race, she did not try to rein her thoughts.

For a while, Amrita and Franz sat in the lawn drinking *nimbu pani.* (Just fill a pitcher with water and put sugar and stir and stir and then squeeze some lemons into it.) Amrita looked radiant, emanating some of the fire of the sun. Yet her long brown hair flowing loose and free formed a halo around her face, hinting at the softness and mystery of the moon's shadows. There was something unnatural and wonderful about her tonight. And she knew it. Like a witch in power, she settled herself more comfortably. Almost without thought, Franz leaned forward to caress a stray strand of her hair. She smiled.

"These mosquitoes are killing me," he said, slapping at his arms for emphasis. Amrita smiled again. This time knowingly. Then, for no reason at all, she laughed. As her eyes glittered and her lips curved into a bow, Franz couldn't help himself. He laughed back.

The fragrance of the *motia* now permeated the dusk and bathed it in an ethereal beauty. The newly risen moon covered the vine with a silvery light. Without any conscious decision, both Amrita and Franz moved to go in. Franz walked along. Inside, the light from the streetlamps led them to her room. Already, the rising moon had begun to lay its soft sheet across the floor. The softness would lengthen with time before beginning its journey back home.

For a moment they both stood by the window drinking in the heady smells and sounds of the night carried in on the wings of a gentle breeze. Till suddenly the rhythmic beat of the *dhols* pierced through the night to announce the arrival of the bridegroom's party. From a distance, the *bhangra* dancers looked like a series of unfolded letters holding each other up as they moved down the colorfully lit street toward the Walias' gate. Amrita and Franz felt the beat of their hearts echo the beat of the drums.

Automatically, Franz leaned forward and took the crutches from Amrita's hands and placed them on the side. As he did so, his long, lean body hunched over her at an angle—one shoulder higher than the other; she automatically leaned away from the moon's shadow and into the curve of his embrace. The horizontal bars quickly lifted themselves from the soft cotton sheet on the floor to now fall over the reflected figure of the man whose head seemed to have fallen into his neck. Almost in slow motion, Franz's lips moved from the tangle of Amrita's hair to every feature on her face to her long neck and around it to slowly begin a journey down her back. Skin against skin. Up and down and sideways he rubbed. At first slowly, tentatively, then more surely.

As one shadow mingled with the other, Amrita looked down and mouthed silently, *"I defy you."*

* 9 7 8 1 9 3 7 4 8 4 8 0 4 *